R

ENDLESS MERCY

ENDLESS MERCY

TRACIE PETERSON
AND KIMBERLEY WOODHOUSE

BETHANYHOUSE
a division of Baker Publishing Group
Minneapolis, Minnesota

Published by Bethany House Publishers
11400 Hampshire Avenue South
Bloomington, Minnesota 55438
www.bethanyhouse.com

Bethany House Publishers is a division of
Baker Publishing Group, Grand Rapids, Michigan

Printed in the United States of America

Library of Congress Cataloging-in-Publication Data
Names: Peterson, Tracie, author. | Woodhouse, Kimberley, author.
Title: Endless mercy / Tracie Peterson and Kimberley Woodhouse.
Description: Minneapolis, Minnesota : Bethany House, a division of Baker
    Publishing Group, [2021] | Series: The treasures of nome ; 2
Identifiers: LCCN 2020035712 | ISBN 9780764232503 (trade paperback) | ISBN
    9780764232510 (cloth) | ISBN 9781493430024 (ebook)
Subjects: GSAFD: Love stories.
Classification: LCC PS3566.E7717 E49 2021 | DDC 813/.54—dc23
LC record available at https://lccn.loc.gov/2020035712

Unless otherwise noted, Scripture quotations are from the King James Version of the Bible.

First Corinthians 13:4–8 is from the New King James Version®. Copyright © 1982 by Thomas Nelson. Used by permission. All rights reserved.

Cover design by Jennifer Parker

Kimberley Woodhouse is represented by The Steve Laube Agency.

21 22 23 24 25 26 27   7 6 5 4 3 2 1

To our Shepherd, who not only puts up with Your little sheep but paid the ultimate sacrifice for us.

And to our sheep peeps, Kim Tucker and Amanda Schmitt. This story wouldn't have been the same without you.

And to the real Madysen. Keep singing, beautiful girl.

Dear Reader

Tracie and I are thrilled to have you join us for the second book in our TREASURES OF NOME Series. We've enjoyed getting the reader mail from you about how much you loved *Forever Hidden* and the Powell sisters.

The namesakes for the characters in this series are beloved to us. These three sisters are precious and, oh, so talented. Another big thanks to Merle and Monica for allowing us to name characters after their daughters. Yes, the real Powell girls all have gorgeous red hair. And yes, they are all very musical. But I wouldn't want them to have to go through what we put our characters through!

Many people are puzzled about a dairy and poultry farm surviving in Alaska. Believe me, I understand. When my family moved to Alaska from Louisiana it was quite a shock. First, I thought I'd be going to six months of daylight and six months of darkness. Second, I wondered how anything could survive up there. But some of the stereotypes we put on places are wrong. Just like when I tell people I grew up in Louisiana and they ask if I had a pet alligator or lived on a swamp. Go ahead, you can laugh with me. No, I didn't have an alligator, and no, I didn't live on a swamp. Same thing for our largest state. Alaska doesn't have six months of darkness and six months of daylight. Not even up in Barrow, the northernmost point of the state. It is an absolutely gorgeous wonderland, and while winters there can be quite brutal, farms have been thriving there for a long time. To give you some fun, you can search for the Alaska Dairy Co. and Poultry Yard in Nome, Alaska, to see some historic photos of the real dairy farm that was in Nome during this time.

So let's head back to Nome and the Powell/Bundrant/Roselli family. I know I'm personally wondering what the chickens are up to. . . .

Enjoy the journey,
Kimberley and Tracie

Prologue

"These are ugly." Madysen Powell scrunched up her nose and looked down at the rock in her hand. The warm, yellow glow from the lantern didn't help it look any better. "Let's look somewhere else." With a toss, she chucked the stone against the dirt wall.

"They're *rocks*, Maddy." Jeb leaned his head back and let out a groan. "What'd you expect?"

"To find some special ones." Placing her hands on her hips, she sent him a scowl. "That's what you promised when we came here." Boys. They were so dumb.

"I said we could *try* to find special rocks, but I never promised they wouldn't be ugly. This is a mine, ya know."

"You have no imagination."

"Why ya gotta use those big words all the time? I'm sure I got plenty of . . . magination, or whatever you said." He crossed his scrawny arms over his chest.

With a roll of her eyes and a tap of her foot, she crossed her arms and mimicked his expression. "I'm sure you do." She took a long glance down the dark mine shaft and a great idea struck. "Let's race!"

"In the dark?"

"What? Are you a fraidycat?" She lifted her lantern and shot him a taunting glare. "Or you just don't wanna lose again . . . to a *girl*."

"I ain't afraid of losing to you, because you can't beat me." He lifted his chin and held up his lantern too.

"Catch me if you can!" Madysen giggled as she took off down the narrow corridor of the shaft.

"No fair, Maddy!" Jeb's voice echoed behind her. "You got a head start—that's cheating!" The sound of his steps hinted that he was only a few paces off her heels.

"It's not cheating. You're just slower than me!" Pumping her legs for all she was worth, she held the lamp in front of her as she ran. She was fast. Faster than any boy or girl her age in Cripple Creek. And that included Jeb Morrison, who was a whole year and a half older. He'd been bragging about his ninth birthday coming up. The same day she'd raced him to the mercantile. And won.

This tunnel was perfect. Long and straight, it gradually sloped down into the belly of the mountain. No one ever found any gold or silver here, so it had been abandoned for a while. Which made it the perfect place for them to run. She should have thought of it before.

"I'll catch ya, just watch." Jeb's huffing and puffing sounded like Mama's metronome ticking the beats in *vivace*.

Vivace. The word was fun to say.

V-i-v-a-c-e. A letter with every stride, she repeated it over and over. Mama made her a new spelling list this week, and it was all tempo words. Words like *larghissimo* and *adagietto* weren't as fun as *grave* and *vivace*. Probably because they were harder to spell. But Mama insisted. And Maddy didn't mind. She loved music.

Almost as much as she loved running.

Cripple Creek didn't have a lot of areas that made for good

running. Active mines everywhere, rocks all over the place, and adults always telling them to go play somewhere else.

At least no one would bother them here. She could run as fast and as much as she wanted. Picking up speed down the slope, she leaned back so her momentum wouldn't cause her to tumble. Too many times—when she was little—she'd made that mistake on the side of the mountain.

The air grew cooler with every breath she took. No way Jeb could catch her now.

How she loved the feel of her feet pounding the ground. Faster and faster. At times, she dreamed her feet didn't even touch it. The damp air pressed into her face as she practically flew over the surface of the earth. Just like eagles. Except they never flew in mines.

Running and music. She could do them all day long. Even though Mama told her that ladies shouldn't run.

Better get in all her running now while she had the chance. Probably had three good years of running left in her before she grew up and got old. By then, she'd be ten and almost a full-grown lady. But she wouldn't be serious like Whitney. No. Her older sister didn't know how to have fun anymore. But Maddy did. She let her smile widen.

The path leveled out, which meant she was almost to the end. Slowing down, she made it to the back of the shaft and touched it with her hand. "I win!"

"Ah, shucks! No fair, Maddy!" Jeb slowed to a stop and bent over to set his lantern down. Putting his hands on his knees, he sucked in air with great big gulps.

A deep rumbling beneath her feet made her gasp and turn around.

"Maddy!" Jeb's voice wasn't playful anymore.

She held up her lantern toward him and watched him tumble to the ground. "Jeb!" The rumbling stopped. But for how long?

He jumped back to his feet and wiped off his hands. "I don't think we should be in here." He picked up his lantern and held it high, turning in a slow motion.

Madysen frowned. Pebbles and dirt fell from above.

Several seconds passed while they caught their breath.

Then everything quieted.

Good. She didn't like the rumbling.

"I think you're just sore that I beat you." Throwing him a grin with her taunt, she raised her eyebrows.

"This time . . ." He turned around and ran. "Race you back!"

"Hey!" She took off after him.

"You won't beat me again, Maddy. Just watch!"

Silly Jeb. He *thought* he could beat her. But even with his head start, she was gaining on him.

The rumbling sound started again, but this time it made the ground shudder like God had picked up the mountain and shook it out like a rug. They tumbled to the ground as rocks and dirt rained down on them again from above.

"Run, Maddy!" Her friend looked over his shoulder and jumped back to his feet, his eyes wide.

"Jeb!" She got up and made it a couple of steps before she fell down and hit her knees to the hard earth, gripping the lantern for all she was worth. The tunnel was no longer smooth and straight. Rocks of all sizes littered the path.

Maddy looked up and watched the ceiling open and pour its contents in front of her. "*Help!*" Her scream bounced off the wall of stones and dirt that now blocked her path and separated her from the one way out. "Help! Please, help!"

Several moments later, her voice was hoarse from yelling. Swallowing against the raw scratchiness in her throat, she lifted the lantern higher. The thumping in her chest grew faster. Her ears pounded, and everything in her wanted to scream and cry all at the same time.

She lifted her chin against the urge and bit her lip. Brave. Be brave.

She wasn't a fraidycat.

But as she blinked, hot tears escaped.

The ground stopped shaking, but tiny pebbles and dirt skittered down from the wall in front of her until everything halted and the cool air stilled. A scary silence surrounded her.

As a shiver raced up her back, her legs trembled. So she sat on the ground and tucked her skirt around her legs. Another swallow. Her throat hurt. What would happen? Was Jeb on the other side trying to get her out? Or would he leave her all alone to go and get help?

The thought of being alone in the dark made her shiver again. She wasn't feeling brave at all. Tears choked her. "Jeb . . . *help*!"

Christopher Powell swiped a hand down his face. He should clean himself up before Melly saw him. Maybe he shouldn't have gone back to the saloon so early in the day. Nah, he was fine. Wasn't even drunk. He wouldn't go back tonight. Yeah. That would make his wife happy.

Tripping over something he didn't see, he heard voices coming from his cabin. With a bit of focus, he listened. A low-timbered voice.

Great. His wife's father was here. Just what he needed. To feel insignificant and incompetent again. It wasn't Chris's fault that he couldn't make a fortune at anything he put his hand to like good ol' Chuck Bundrant. Maybe he should go back to the saloon after all. At least he fit in there.

He turned on his heel, but his wife's cries tore at him. Why was she upset? He stepped forward a few paces to listen.

"She's been gone for hours, Papa," Melly sobbed. "No one knows where she is. I wanted to come get you earlier, but I thought we could find her."

"Don't you worry, Melly." Chuck's bossy voice echoed

through the cracks in the thin cabin walls. "I'll go put a search team together. I employ plenty of men. We'll find her. I promise."

Find who? Who was missing? One of his girls? His heart skipped, and he stormed through the door. "What's wrong?"

Melissa ran to him and put her arms around him. "I'm so glad you're home—Maddy is missing. We can't find her anywhere." The grief in her voice made him feel like the lowest of the low. If he'd been here . . . then maybe . . . No. It didn't matter. Chris peered into his other daughters' wide eyes. Whitney and Havyn clung to each other behind their mother. Tears streamed down Havyn's cheeks, while Whitney said soft, comforting words and shot daggers at him with her eyes.

At twelve years old, she was the oldest and mother hen of the group. And she'd become wise to the world's temptations. At least *his*. She had come to the saloon a few times to find him and drag him home. Not something a father wanted his daughter to do. But she was a stubborn one. Just like her dad.

Avoiding eye contact with his wife's father, Chris held Melly close. "I'll go look for her."

"Papa's going to put together a search team. Maybe you could go with them." She pulled back and gazed up into his eyes. A gaze that still held hope and love for him. God only knew why.

"I'm glad he's getting a group together, but I'll do better on my own. I'm her father, I bet I can find her." Lifting his chin, he dared a look at Chuck. "Thank you for helping us search."

The older man didn't flinch. "The only thing that matters now is Madysen. I'll get the word out, and we'll send teams in every direction. We'll comb this mountain if we have to." Chuck headed toward the door. "Melissa, stay here in case she returns. We'll fire two shots in the air when we find her."

"Thank you, Papa." Melly twisted a hankie in her hands and watched him leave.

"I best get out there as well." Chris gazed at his girls. "I'll find her."

Havyn ran to him and sobbed into his coat.

Whitney crossed her arms over her chest. It had been a while since his eldest daughter had trusted him. But the slight glimmer of hope in her eyes pushed him forward. He would find Maddy and gain everyone's respect again. Then maybe, just maybe, he could turn things around.

"I'll find her. I will. Don't worry." Chris patted Havyn's head and gave Melissa a nod. He *had* to do this.

A half hour later, he searched the streets. How sad was it that he had no idea where his little girl would be? Where did she like to play? Where would she go to hide? The girls were constantly playing hide-and-seek. Did she have any friends other than her sisters?

Hadn't she mentioned a friend named Sally? And wasn't there a Jeb? Or was it Jed? Scratching his days-old beard, he went to the school. Maybe the kids from town would be there and he could ask them questions. Not that his girls went to the school, but they would know other children . . . wouldn't they?

Taking long strides, Chris set out for the schoolhouse on the edge of town. But when he reached it, it was locked up tight. Blast! Today was Saturday.

He shoved his hands in his pockets and tried to ignore his overwhelming thirst. But it nagged and pulled at him until he licked his lips. Maybe just one drink. It couldn't hurt. Probably make him think clearer too 'cause then he wouldn't be distracted by it.

He closed his eyes. No wonder he was such a horrible father— his little girl was lost, and he couldn't even keep his focus on her for an hour before he started thinking about liquor.

A new resolve filled his mind. Melly and the girls deserved better. This was his chance. He could be a better man. He could. He balled his fists at his side and took a long, deep breath. He *would* do this. Maddy needed him.

Pushing his legs back into motion, he ran back to town.

Two young girls darted across his path.

"Hey!"

His harsh tone made them stop, and they turned to him with eyes as big as saucers.

"Have you seen Madysen Powell?"

They relaxed a bit. One of the girls shrugged.

The other looked to her friend. Then back at him. "She was playing with Jeb Morrison this morning. Down near the mines." The little girl grabbed her friend's hand, and they took off running again.

The mines? Didn't these kids know it was dangerous to play near any of the mines?

Chris headed for the mercantile. Someone had to know where he could find Jeb Morrison.

As he yanked the door open to the merc, the little bell above the door gave a jangle. Would anyone listen to him? Most people didn't pay attention to town drunks.

Even as he thought it, his stomach plummeted. Everything stopped, and he stood on the threshold unable to breathe. That's how the town saw him . . . as one of the drunks. So why would they even give him the time of day? Was this the life he wanted to live? The reputation he wanted his family to live in the shadow of—that he was a no-good drunk?

He shook off the mounting dread. This was about Maddy. Surely they would help a little girl. He stepped up to the counter.

"How can I help you, Mr. Powell?" At least the man had the decency to know his name and talk to him without condescension.

"I'm looking for Jeb Morrison. He's a friend of my daughter Maddy. She's missing."

A hush fell over the customers in the room.

The man standing at the counter next to him nudged him in the arm. "I saw Jeb and his pa down by the creek just south of here 'afore I came in."

"Thank you." Chris nodded at the man and raced out the door. The thought of finding his daughter and making his wife proud gave him a surge of energy and diminished his thirst. Maybe he could change. If he put his mind to it.

When he reached the creek, a man and his son were washing gold pans.

"You Jeb Morrison?" Chris reached for the kid's arm. Blood pumped through his veins. The kid must know something, and Chris would get it out of him.

"Who's askin'?" The man yanked the boy's arm out of Chris's grasp and narrowed his eyes. When he straightened to his full height, he towered a good foot over Chris. And the breadth of his chest testified to years of hard labor on the mountain.

All the bravado Chris had felt a moment ago vanished. He cleared his throat and forced himself to be congenial. "Name's Chris Powell. I hear that Jeb and my daughter Maddy are friends. She's missing. One of the other kids said she saw Jeb and Maddy playing near the mines this morning, so I thought your boy here might know where she is."

The man looked down at the boy. "You know anything about this? 'Cause if you been playing near the mines, you'll get a beating you'll not soon forget."

The kid shook his head. A little too fast. Something wasn't right in the look of his eyes. Had he turned a touch paler? "Me and Maddy were looking for rocks this morning, but I haven't seen her since." He looked down and kicked the dirt with his shoe.

"Good." The man turned back to Chris. "Seems like we can't help ya. Sorry 'bout that." He crouched back down and picked up the gold pans. "Hope ya find yer girl. We got chores to do."

"Thanks for your help." Chris watched them walk away. What was he supposed to do now? The kid had said they were looking for rocks . . . but where? The look on Jeb's face had said it all. He knew something. Chris just had to get him away from his pa so he would talk.

Staring at the two as they walked farther away, Chris shoved his hands back in his pockets. There had to be some way he could talk to the boy. Maybe if he followed them. And then waited outside their house. It might be the only way.

Decision made, Chris started after them. But only a few steps later, he saw the kid headed back in his direction. Alone.

Chris darted behind a tree. Somehow he had to get Jeb to cough up what he knew without scaring him off. But how?

Light footsteps alerted him to the kid passing. Chris peeked around the tree and watched for several moments. Jeb was headed toward town, his head dipped low.

Following a safe distance behind, Chris worked on what he would say. Calm voice. Don't scare him away. Maddy needed to be found.

When the kid went into the mercantile, Chris followed him. The perfect opportunity.

"I need some tobacco for my pa." The kid plunked down a coin. After several moments, the kid had his purchase tucked under his arm and headed for the door. He looked up, and his eyes widened as he spotted Chris.

Chris held his hands out. "I'm not going to hurt you, and I won't tell your pa. I promise. But I know you know something about where Maddy is. I need you to tell me the truth . . . please."

The kid bit his lip.

"Look, I'm not mad at you, but there must be something wrong. Please. Just tell me."

Jeb's face crumbled and his shoulders slumped. "I'm sorry, mister. I didn't know what to do. My pa will beat me bad if he knows we were playing in the mine." Tears streamed down his face.

Chris grabbed the boy's shoulders and knelt down in front

of him. "There's hundreds of mines, which one? I promise I won't say a word, but I have to find my daughter."

"The Long Shot. But a rumblin' started and the ceiling came down. I don't know where she is." The kid used his sleeve to wipe up his face, but it didn't do any good. The tears came faster. "It was so scary. And so I ran." He gulped and sobbed. "She's probably dead."

A surge of anger roiled inside his chest. He shook the kid. A little hard. "What do you mean? You just left her there?"

"I didn't know what to do!" The kid's sobs turned into wails.

"Is there a problem here?" Some nosy gentleman dressed in a spiffy suit eyed them. Along with other customers.

Chris released Jeb and straightened up. "Nope. No problem." Best to leave before the kid's pa heard about it. Didn't matter anyway. He got what he needed. He turned on his heel and headed out the door toward the Long Shot. He'd need a pick and a lantern if what the kid said was true. Good thing he knew where Chuck kept extra mining supplies. He raced through town and grabbed what he needed. His Maddy couldn't be gone. It couldn't be true. The boy just blew the story up in his mind.

Chris reached the mine, stood for a moment trying to catch his breath. But he couldn't wait any longer. His little girl was in there. As he entered the main shaft, the scent of freshly moved dirt filled his senses. Had there been a collapse? His heart plummeted and then beat even faster. The kid hadn't been exaggerating. The pounding in Chris's ears was deafening. What if Maddy was hurt? Or . . .

No!

He leaned over and put his hands on his knees, shaking his head against the negative thoughts. He drew in several deep breaths.

It was all his fault. He was a failure. At everything.

But he could find his daughter. He *would*.

He straightened. "Maddy! Can you hear me, honey?"

Dirt and rocks littered the shaft floor. This must be what Jeb was talking about. Chris held his lantern, watching every step for debris.

"Maddy!"

The minutes passed as he ventured deeper into the mine. Vast amounts of rubble now covered the shaft floor. Then he saw it. A wall of dirt and rocks in front of him.

"Maddy! Are you in there?" He set the lantern down and felt the wall in front of him. It was loose. That was a good thing. But what if she was buried? What if more came down?

"Maddy! Can you hear me?" He swung the pick at the obstruction in front of him, then pulled down. Maybe he could get it all to move enough so there would be a crack at the top. Or would it just continue to spill out?

He had to take the chance. His gut told him his little girl was behind the wall. "Maddy, I'm coming."

For what seemed like an eternity, he chipped at dirt and rocks, all the while talking as if his daughter could hear him. She had to be there. She had to be.

She was alive. He couldn't fail her. Couldn't fail his family. He'd already done enough damage.

Sweat soaked his clothes even though the air was cool. Every muscle within his body screamed from the repeated motion of swinging and tugging, but he kept pulling at the pick with all he had. Could he even make a dent in the massive mountain of debris in front of him?

"Maddy, I'm coming. It's your dad. I'm here."

More dirt. More rocks. Another swing. Then another.

"Honey, just talk to me. It's going to be okay."

"Daddy?" The sound was muffled and weak, but it was her voice.

Chris climbed up the wall to where he'd made a small hole at the top. He forced his voice through the opening. "Maddy, are you all right?"

"It's cold and I'm scared."

"Don't move, I'm coming. Just keep talking." He lifted the pick and pushed his aching muscles to move as fast as they could. How long had she been there? In the dark and all alone. His heart wrenched and he grimaced. If he had been home rather than at the saloon . . .

Overwhelming thirst took over his mind. His tongue felt like cotton. If only he had a drink.

He closed his eyes against the demons in his mind and swung the pick.

Focus. He could get a drink later. After he rescued Maddy and got her home.

"I wanna go home." His little girl's voice sounded so sad.

"I know, honey. I'm coming. I am." Another swing. The hole widened. If he could just go faster.

"It's so cold." Her voice was shaky now.

He didn't have a lot of time. Swinging the pick for all he was worth, he chipped at the wall of dirt and rock. Over and over and over.

Finally, the hole seemed big enough to get through. He peered into the expanse beyond, but it was all black. "Maddy? Where are you?"

"Over here. The lantern went out."

"Can you see me? Can you climb up to me so I can pull you out?"

"I'll try."

He heard her movements but couldn't see her in the pitch black. Until her hand grabbed onto his. Small and freezing cold, it was still a relief.

"I've got you. Now push with your legs up the wall while I pull, all right?"

"Okay."

As he pulled, he reached down with his other hand to get a better hold. Rumbling began around them.

Maddy screamed.

Dirt rained down.

Chris yanked harder on his daughter. They couldn't be buried alive—

There! She was through the hole. He held her in his arms and grabbed the lantern as the rumbling grew louder. They had to get out fast.

Running over the rough and debris-littered floor, Chris prayed for the first time in years. *God, I know I'm not worthy of You listening to me, but if You help us out of this, I'll turn my life around. I promise.*

Light from the entrance of the tunnel grew in front of him. The ground shook and rolled around them.

Maddy ducked her head into his chest. Protectiveness and love poured through him. He'd have to follow through with his promise to God if they got out of this. And that wasn't such a bad thing, was it?

But he was so thirsty.

Lungs pinching, Chris made it the last few steps out. As soon as he set Maddy down on the ground, a loud crashing made him turn back to the mine. A cloud of dirt and dust roared toward them. He ducked his head and covered Maddy.

His heart pumped. They almost didn't make it.

Madysen started crying. Great big sobs. "Daddy . . . I was so scared." She threw her little arms around his neck. "But I kept praying that God would send somebody to find me."

He clenched his eyes tight. What would he have done if the mine had collapsed on his daughter? The thought was almost too much to bear.

"I love you, sweet girl. And I will always come to find you, no matter where you are. I'll always be there for you."

ONE

The lively tune on the piano couldn't keep up with the smile in Madysen's heart. Too much heartache and grief had enveloped them for too long. But now boisterous laughter, off-key singing from some of the men, and plenty of lively conversation surrounded her as she surveyed the crowd. What a wonderful party. And it was all for her.

Her twenty-first birthday.

The sweet smell of baked goodies filled the air. Tables were packed with cakes, pies, and an array of other treats. How precious that these people cared for her so much.

The Roadhouse was full to the brim, and she would sing with her sisters in a little while to keep all the patrons happy. They were, after all, used to the Powell sisters entertaining them. Herb told them often that the crowds at his Roadhouse were all credit to them. The thought made her smile. Madysen loved every minute of their performances.

For a time they'd entertained every night but Sunday. It had been glorious. Singing and playing for hours.

The performing had gotten her through the toughest times.

Financially, it helped the family during Granddad's bouts with apoplexy . . . but for her? It was life giving. Which made her miss it even more.

But now that their financial worries were lessened, it only made sense to cut back on their performances since there were so many responsibilities at the farm. Granddad needed to recover fully from his illness, and Madysen *had* added an extra burden to everyone when she acquired the sheep. . . . But oh, how she missed performing every night.

She smoothed the skirt of her favorite green dress, smiled, and received more well wishes, but she couldn't quite bring her thoughts into the present. Maybe she longed to perform every night because it reminded her of Mama. Helped her feel connected to her somehow. She missed their mother so much.

A burning sensation started at the back of her eyes. Not now. She couldn't afford tears tonight. Even though grief was still fresh, she and her family desperately needed this bright bit of sunshine. It had been a hard summer.

Forcing her mind to the present, she tapped her toe to Whitney's vivacious piano playing and closed her eyes, letting the glorious sounds of a room full of joyful people fill her senses.

This was how it should be. Everyone getting along. Laughter. Fun. Happiness. If only she could capture it all in a box and pull it out whenever she wanted.

"I can't wait to hear you gals sing tonight." Toothless Jim's voice interrupted her thoughts.

Opening her eyes, she saw his familiar crooked smile. "Why, thank you, kind sir." The old man never missed one of their concerts.

His face flushed pink. "Aww, you always know how to make me feel like a gentleman. Now don't ya go leaving us to tour the world. You got lots of fans right here. And we tip pretty good." He held up a bag and shook it. The clinking of coins accentuated his laugh.

Watching Toothless Jim walk away, Madysen tilted her head. Over the last few months, thoughts of performing beyond Nome had surfaced more often. A comment here or there from one of the newcomers to Nome surprised to find the Powell women's musical talent in such a remote place . . . the memory of Mama encouraging them to use their musical talents because they were gifts from God and should be used for His glory . . . her constant dreaming of beautiful concert halls . . .

It all sent her thoughts in that direction.

Madysen had no problem imagining a life focused on her music, but could she actually think about leaving her family and Alaska? Obviously she couldn't expect to perform full-time here at the Roadhouse. Nome wasn't all that big . . . not like New York, Chicago, or London.

"Madysen?" The voice pulled her out of her thoughts, and she glanced up into her father's hesitant eyes.

Clearing her throat, she blinked several times. Was she ready for this? "Hi, Dad."

Some of the uncertainty left his face, and a slight smile lifted his lips. "I appreciate you inviting me."

She sent him a return smile. But not a full one. Why on earth did she invite him? It didn't feel like a good idea anymore. He hadn't been a part of their lives for over thirteen years, and then he just showed up in Nome. Madysen still couldn't make sense of it.

"I know this hasn't been easy on any of you." His voice cracked, then he looked around the room. Awkward couldn't describe the interaction. "How's Chuck?"

"Granddad is getting stronger every day. Thanks for asking." Eyeing Whitney's fierce glare from across the room as she exited the stage, Madysen gave a little shrug to her eldest sister. Turning back to their dad, she straightened her shoulders. "I'm sorry. Please, if you'll excuse me."

She wiped her hands on her skirt as she took a deep breath

and headed toward her sisters, who were huddled in the corner near the stage.

"What is *he* doing here?" Whit hissed the words.

"I invited him. And don't even ask me why." Madysen let her exasperation with the whole situation tint her words as she waved her hands in front of her sisters.

"You did?" Havyn and Whitney chimed together.

"It was a bad idea, I know. But I guess I felt sorry for him when we didn't invite him to the wedding, and somehow I ended up inviting him here."

Havyn's red hair swung with the shaking of her head. "Oh, no, you don't. Don't blame this on me, or the fact I asked him not to come to the wedding. We all agreed it was for the best."

"I wasn't blaming you. I'm sorry." Madysen put a hand to her forehead. "I just felt guilty. How do I get myself into these things?"

"You have a big heart." Havyn glanced over to their dad. "We should probably take our cue from you, but frankly, it's hard having him around. Without Mama." Her words softened.

Without Mama. No one said a word for several moments.

Losing Mama tore at Madysen's heart every hour of every day. Her world had tilted, and she wasn't sure it would ever be upright again.

"Look, I didn't invite him to be nice or merciful, believe it or not. I'm not really sure *why* I sent the invitation. I feel sorry for him, yes, but in truth I'm also angry. I suppose I thought it might ease both."

Her brother-in-law, John, stepped closer. "I couldn't help but overhear."

Madysen grimaced. "I'm sorry. To all of you." She pressed her hands to her temples. "I shouldn't have invited him."

John patted her shoulder. "No apology necessary."

It soothed her spirit in places she couldn't even explain. Probably because she never had a brother . . . or much of a dad for that matter. Being the youngest in her family was normally a joy, but at times she wrestled with it. Especially when everyone mothered her. With Mama gone, her older sisters wanted to protect her, but they didn't know how to fill the holes. And that was the thing . . . no one could.

He took a moment to look at each of them. "I know how hard this has been on all of you. But it appears your father's not leaving anytime soon. So might I suggest that we deal with it the best we can?"

Several moments passed as they exchanged glances between each other.

Whitney was the first to speak. She lifted her chin. "Yes, as much as I was hoping this would be easier, he does seem to be staying in Nome, so I think we should probably come up with a plan for how we are going to deal with this."

John stepped even closer and motioned the sisters in. "You can't avoid him forever. Whit is right. We need some sort of plan. Do you want me to talk to him?"

Even though everyone always said Madysen was the merciful sister, for some reason she wasn't feeling any toward their father. She watched her sisters for their response. The last few months had changed them all, but they were in this together.

Havyn pursed her lips. "You're right, we can't avoid him, no matter how difficult this is. And as much as I appreciate you offering to speak to him, John, *we* need to figure out how we are going to deal with the situation."

Whitney crossed her arms over her chest. "All right then. Let's make a plan. What do you know about him, John?"

He tilted his head a bit.

The lively party continued around them, which made it difficult for Madysen to stay focused. She'd much rather be distracted by the fun. But John cleared his throat, and she forced herself to listen.

"I've heard that he really is a nice man. So maybe his story of turning his life around is true."

"I highly doubt that." Whit's mama-bear mentality had kicked into high gear. Something Madysen loved about her. "It's going to take a lot more than him showing up in Nome and *telling* us that he's changed to convince me. I'm going to need to see it for myself."

"As much as it hurts to say it, I agree." Havyn ducked her head a bit. "I'm thankful that he's alive and not dead—I am. But this is a lot to swallow. Especially after losing Mama."

Tears sprang to Madysen's eyes. Sometimes she hated the way she became emotional so quickly. "I'm thankful he's alive too. But this is hard. I guess I didn't realize *how* hard. Oh, why did he have to show up this summer?"

"Maddy, I'm sorry, and this is supposed to be your birthday party." Havyn wrapped her arms around her in a big hug. "Do you want us to ask him to leave?"

Her thoughts warred with one another. On one hand, she wished she could avoid it all, while on the other, she had an inkling that Mama would want them to at least show him some respect. She pulled out of Havyn's arms, swiped at her eyes, and straightened her shoulders. "No. I invited him. I should probably go speak with him." She turned on her heel and headed back toward their father.

An arm on her shoulder stopped her. "We're coming with you." The look in Havyn's eyes almost did her in. But they could do this. Together.

With his hands shoved in his pockets, Dad stood right where she'd left him, looking a bit forlorn. How would she feel if someone had invited her to a party and then left her all alone? Especially if she hadn't been in town all that long. Her dad probably didn't know many people. What kind of daughter was she?

Her emotions made everything inside her feel sick. "I'm sorry I left."

"That's understandable, Madysen. I'm sorry I put you in this predicament in the first place." He held out his hands in front of him. "Look, I don't have any idea how to make things right or where to go from here. I've wanted to spend time with you girls . . . get to know you again. But I understand you probably don't want to talk to me." His lips thinned into a straight line.

Was he fighting off tears himself?

How was she supposed to respond?

"Hi, Dad."

Thank goodness. Havyn to the rescue. She nodded toward their dad and leaned toward him in an awkward hug.

Whitney stayed back a pace and kept her arms crossed over her chest. Watching.

Dad stood stiff, his hands at his side. Another awkward pause encompassed them before he spoke. "I should wish you a happy birthday. That is why I'm here after all." A forced smile now filled his face as he gazed from one sister to another.

"Thank you." Madysen motioned to a few chairs. "Why don't we sit down for a few minutes?" That was all she could offer.

He nodded and sat with her. The room filled with familiar faces and lively chatter kept her grounded.

"What have you been doing since you first came to Nome?" One breath at a time, one question at a time. They could have a reasonable conversation with him. Start over. Build something fresh. That was what she wanted, wasn't it? So why was it so hard?

Because good fathers didn't do what he did. The thought taunted her.

"Well, I knew you girls needed some time. And frankly, I did too. When your mother died before I got to make things right with her, I wanted to run away and hide. It hit me hard that we'd lost her."

She nodded. Because that's all she *could* do. She couldn't look at her sisters. They all had tempers, but Mama often said that Madysen's was the fiercest. Right now, she felt that. And this man was talking about their mother's loss as if he had some right to grieve along with them. He didn't have that right. And she wouldn't give it to him. Never. Clasping her hands together, she squeezed as hard as she could as the heat crept up her chest and neck, threatening to explode out of the top of her head.

No. She had to keep a lid on the anger. What would people think of her if she blew up at her long-thought-dead father at her own birthday party? Struggling to hold her composure, she bit her lip.

Whitney broke the silence. "Why did you come up here?" While there wasn't any anger in her voice, it certainly wasn't warm and friendly.

Dad swallowed, then leaned forward and put his hands on his knees. He took several breaths and swiped a hand down his face. "My main reason was to come tell you all the truth and ask for forgiveness. I wanted you to see the difference in me. But I had another reason as well. My brother-in-law came up here in '03. Supposed to come back home six months later, but no one has seen or heard from him. So Ruth—that's my sister-in-law—asked me to come find him."

"Your brother-in-law?" Madysen tried to keep her tone from being too clipped, but to hear Dad talking about this other family made her want to run away and hit something. Not a welcome feeling. But she forced herself to stay . . . she needed the truth more than anything else.

"Stan—Stanley Robertson. He's married to Ruth, who is . . . that is . . . she's Esther's sister." He took a shaky breath. "Esther is the woman who . . ."

Madysen held up a hand. It took too much effort to keep a lid on her emotions. Her words spilled out. "The woman you got pregnant before you supposedly died and left us."

"Maddy!" Havyn's sharp retort stopped her.

Dad's shoulders stiffened and he lifted his chin. "I know I

messed up. I failed. But I married her after that. She was my wife, and I would appreciate a touch of respect for her. She was a good woman." His voice caught.

"So was our mother. A better woman than you apparently knew." Madysen didn't even try to keep the accusation out of her tone. It left her with a sour feeling in the pit of her stomach.

"She was that. She was a saint. The woman had an endless ability to forgive. She never made demands on me."

"Maybe she should have." Crossing her arms over her chest, Madysen didn't care if her words stung.

He nodded. "I agree. Maybe if she had . . ." He shook his head. "No. I'm not going to try to make excuses. Your mother was a wonderful woman, but Esther was good too. She stood by my side and cleaned me up. If not for her, I wouldn't be here today." His eyes shone with a glaze of tears. "I would have died for sure with a bottle in my hand."

Madysen shifted in her seat. To hear her father's story, she'd have to hear about the other woman. Esther. She looked at her sisters. Whitney stood as still as a statue, her brow furrowed. Havyn looked like she might cry. Or be sick.

Madysen understood that feeling all too well as the taste of bile crept up her throat. But they had to get this over with. She swallowed. "Go on."

His face paled. "Esther passed away last year. It tore me up. But Ruth helped me with the kids. Even though she was having an awful time with her own brood with Stan being gone. So when she asked me to come up here, I couldn't refuse. Not after all she'd done for me. My other . . . well, my other kids are with her."

Other kids. Just like Maddy and her sisters had heard about . . . but now they seemed more . . . *real* as their dad talked about them. Madysen closed her eyes again for a brief moment and put her hand to her stomach before looking at him again. She could do this. "How many do you have?"

Pride filled his face, and his lips hinted at a smile. "There's three—other than you and your sisters. Matthew is eighteen, Elijah—we call him Eli—is fourteen, and then there's Bethany. She's twelve."

They had three more siblings. Three. The oldest of which was a mere three years younger than herself. That meant . . . she shook her head. She refused to think about what that meant. Heat crept up her neck.

Whitney turned in a swift motion and marched away. Madysen couldn't blame her. The look on Havyn's face wasn't shock—she'd known about their father's indiscretions since she was young—but the pain there was profound.

Dad's face fell. "I can see the wheels turning, Maddy—"

"Please, don't call me that as if we can just pick back up where you left off." She wouldn't look into his sad eyes. She wouldn't. He didn't deserve mercy or acceptance.

"Madysen. I'm sorry. I know what you're thinking, and you're right to think I'm an awful person. I was—"

She held up a hand and stood. "No. No more. It's my birthday, and it's supposed to be a celebration after all the grief we've endured. This isn't a good time."

He stood too and took her elbow. "Is there ever going to be a good time? This is hard on me too, you know. I lost Esther and now Melissa. And my kids are having to stay with their aunt while I'm up here."

Was he really comparing his pain to theirs? Wanting their sympathy? After all he'd done to them? "You're good at leaving your kids for someone else to raise, aren't you? Well, if you are feeling guilty about that, why don't you just go back to them?"

Havyn's gasp followed her as she turned and walked away as fast as she could from that horrible man.

Anger—one. Mercy—zero.

Two

adysen knocked on the Beauforts' back door. It opened, and she couldn't contain her smile when she saw her beloved friend. "Granny, I'm so glad you're back."

Granny, as she was known to everyone, wrapped Madysen up in her thin but strong arms.

She relished the warmth of the older woman's embrace. Her heart lifted just knowing Granny was finally back.

The tiny woman pulled away and drew Madysen into her home. The scent of cinnamon lingered in the air, while a fire crackled in the fireplace. It felt like . . . home. Like she was loved here and belonged.

Reaching for Madysen's hand, Granny studied her with eyes that had seen their fair share of the ups and downs of life. "My dear, I'm so sorry for all you've suffered this summer. Had I known, I would have returned from Seattle immediately."

Tears sprang to Madysen's eyes and ran down her face before she could bid them to stop. Swiping at her cheeks, she blew out a breath. "It's been almost more than I could bear at times. But God got us through. And John. What a blessing he's been. We couldn't have done it without him."

"John seems like the perfect husband for Havyn." Granny

gestured toward the parlor. "Let's sit so we can have a nice long chat."

"Oh, he is. And a wonderful brother to us, and a foreman of the farm. He's been Granddad's hands and feet and such a support." She pulled a hankie out of her pocket as everything threatened to overwhelm her at once. If she talked about all that had happened this summer, she might just spend the rest of the day crying. "Anyway, John told me you were back when we came into town to purchase supplies for our new venture. While he takes care of some errands, I had to rush over here and get in a quick visit."

"Well, let's have some tea. Then you can tell me all that's on your mind." Granny Beaufort led her to the settee.

Granny was still an attractive woman. She must have been quite the beauty in her younger years. Her sparkling gray eyes set everyone at ease as soon as they saw her, and the lines around them attested to the years of smiling and laughter. Everything about her exuded love, comfort, and happiness.

Granny was the perfect hostess and set out cups of tea and a plate of cinnamon cake. Then she sat down and lifted her eyebrows. "Well?" She leaned back and folded her hands in her lap. "I can see you are near to bursting."

It was all the encouragement Madysen needed. Her words spilled out. "Mama's passing was the worst part of a very trying summer. Between Granddad and the farm, we were all overwhelmed. But when she got sick . . ." She sniffed and swallowed against the tears clogging her throat. "None of us expected . . ." Oh, why did it have to hurt so much? Madysen cleared her throat. "It broke our hearts. I don't know how we are going to make it without her, she was . . . she was *everything*." She stiffened and tried to push the overwhelming grief aside. "I'm sorry. I didn't come here to talk about Mama, but I find it always comes to the surface." Madysen lifted her chin and wiped at her nose. "But that's not what is most pressing right now."

Granny patted her knee. "I'm here to listen whenever you need me. Grief is a crafty beast. Takes you by surprise at the most inopportune moments. So don't worry, we can talk about your sweet mother whenever the time is right. What is it that's troubling you?"

With a nod, Madysen took a sip of tea. The steam swirled around her face and calmed her. "Our father showed up the day Mama died."

The china teacup chinked against the saucer as Granny set it down. Her brows rose. "Oh, gracious. Child, I thought he died years ago."

"We did too." Embarrassment mixed with anger in her middle, which made the tea feel sour and unpleasant in her stomach. "But apparently after one of his drunken spells, our grandfather had enough. He found him in the street half-dead and made a plan. He offered our father money to sign divorce papers and disappear so that Mama could be free of him. Then he told everyone that Dad died. The whole town thought so." Madysen watched Granny's face, but after the initial shock, there was no reaction to the scandalous news. It helped to calm Madysen's nerves.

"Did your mother know?" Her voice was soft. Caring.

"I don't know for sure." Poor Mama. What must she have gone through all these years? "But I think she found out later that Dad was still alive." How could she even say it? It was so embarrassing. Best to just spit it out. "Dad had . . . well . . . he had another family. Apparently, at the same time he was with *our* family."

"I see." Granny sat back again. She never broke eye contact. Never made a face that showed she disapproved of her father's conduct. No condemnation. No horror. Just compassion and love. Her beautiful eyes shone bright with tears. "Go on."

"The woman he was . . . with—" Madysen cleared her throat against the uncomfortable conversation—"was pregnant with their third child when Granddad sent him off as dead." She rubbed her forehead. This was incredibly difficult to talk about, but she needed to get it off her chest. "This second wife is now dead. Dad came up here to find his brother-in-law and to try to mend things with us. But he arrived too late. Mama was already gone. He came to the funeral because he said we couldn't deny him that, but when Havyn and John married, we thought it was best to ask him not to come because we just didn't know what to do with this new situation."

Her words spilled out faster and faster. "Then I felt sorry for Dad and invited him to my birthday party. Which was a mistake because I don't think any of us handled it very well. Especially me. My parting words to him were quite ugly." She put a hand to her chest. If only she could go back and change so many pieces of the last few months.

Granny tilted her head, a sheen of tears glistening. "My dear, I am so sorry for your loss and all the pain you've had to endure. This hasn't been an easy time for you." She pointed a finger toward the ceiling and smiled. "But isn't it wonderful that the good Lord has given you a second chance with your father?"

Of course, Granny would see it that way. Maybe she should feel that way too, but she couldn't. Not yet. "I'm hoping to eventually have that perspective. But when he showed up and wanted to tell us everything . . . well, it made me mad. He betrayed all of us. He left us. Without a care."

She stood to her feet and wanted to stomp them, but resisted the urge. "The money and the drink were what was important to him. And apparently, his other woman threatened to leave him as well until she finally got him to sober up. It makes me wonder why *we* weren't good enough for him to sober up for? Why couldn't he have done that for his first family? And what do we do now? With the loss of Mama so fresh, I'm sorry, but it's hard to forgive him."

There, she said it. Then covered her face with her hands. She was so ashamed of how she felt, but she wanted to be mad. At him. It was all his fault. So she allowed the anger to build. She flung her arms out. "I know what you must think of me. Everyone always raves that I have the gift of mercy. 'Madysen's so merciful,' 'look at how merciful her heart is.'"

Mimicking the phrases she'd heard all her life made her want to explode. "Well, I'm *sick* of it because I can't even show it to my own father." Flopping back into her seat, she let her shoulders sag with the weight of all she carried.

Granny reached forward and grabbed both of Madysen's hands and sandwiched them between her own. She squeezed them tight and, with maternal chastisement, looked into Madysen's eyes. "Just because God has given you the gift of mercy doesn't mean that you'll always have it for everyone all the time. Mercy and forgiveness are two different things. And while, yes, I agree with what everyone thinks—gracious, you were always the one rescuing this animal or the other, or helping those less fortunate—you're not perfect." Granny leaned back and released her hands. "But I don't understand what it is that you're truly unable to forgive him for. I don't think you've told me everything."

Madysen could almost smell the musty scent of the mine. The cool, damp air pressed into her lungs. She closed her eyes against the memory of darkness, of being trapped and thinking no one would ever find her. Her heart picked up its pace, as did her breathing.

Granny's brow dipped low. "What is it, child?"

The story started to spill from her lips. All the anguish and fear of a little lost girl, and then her heroic daddy coming to save her. His promise to always find her. Always be there for her.

"He broke that promise! He left. He didn't care enough to be there or to come find me ever again."

"Oh, but he did. He's here, isn't he?" Granny's words forced Madysen's eyes open.

More than one emotion fought for control. She had longed for her dad to come and find her, even though everyone said he was dead. Her little-girl heart had yearned for her father. But too many years had passed. She'd lost faith in her earthly father. And now that he was back, it hurt even more to know that he'd never come to find her—any of them. Why hadn't they been enough for him to love? "It's a little too late, don't you think?"

"It's never too late, my dear. Never. Thankfully, we serve a God of second chances." The words were hushed, but firm.

Taking a long, slow breath, Madysen forced herself not to simply hear the words, but to allow them to sink in.

Granny watched her with a gaze that seemed to bore through to her soul. "I'm not saying that things will change overnight. This is going to take some time. You and your sisters and grandfather will need to sit down and have some serious discussions about it. You need to pray about it. Take the time that you need to heal." She pointed a bony finger in Madysen's face. "But don't waste the chance that God has given you to restore the relationship with your father. You'll always regret it if you don't."

Her words rang true, even though Madysen wanted to stay angry and hurt. But she shouldn't. She *would* regret it. Could she live with that? No. Time did heal wounds. Perhaps she simply needed to give Dad time as well. And spend a lot of time on her knees in prayer for her father rather than allowing the anger to fester. A sense of release filled her. Granny was right. It didn't have to happen right away. "It's hard to even think about."

"I know. But with the good Lord's help, we'll make it through. We will. You may never be close to him again, or even trust him, but you alone are the one to determine if you'll be at peace with him. I believe that once the shock wears off, you'll come around to extending him grace. I've always admired that about you, Madysen." She stood up and looked down, love shining from her eyes.

"I don't feel like extending him grace." Why did she feel like a petulant child as she said it?

"And maybe that's at the heart of this problem. Holding on to your anger goes against the very heart of your nature. It's worth considering." She picked up the tea tray and took it into the other room.

Madysen's conscience pricked. Her friend and mentor was correct, of course. But she couldn't deal with it right now.

The older woman returned and grinned at her as she took her seat again. "Now let's turn our minds to happier things. Did I tell you that my grandson has come back to us from the Yukon?"

Thankful for the change in subject, Madysen stuffed thoughts of her father aside. "No. How lovely." She forced a smile. "I remember we've often prayed for him."

"Indeed, we have. I'm hopeful that he'll stay with us and settle down. Maybe even raise some sheep."

"Sheep? Why sheep?"

"We had a sheep farm long ago, and Daniel loved it. I guess I'm hoping that he will find joy in life again. And if that involves a few stinky sheep, I think I can handle it." Granny glanced over her shoulder as she got to her feet. "Come help me clean up the kitchen, and I'll tell you all about it."

Madysen complied, eager to share about her own new venture. "*I* have sheep. I didn't get a chance to tell you. It started out as a rescue to keep Judas from selling them for slaughter. I actually stole them."

The look of shock and surprise on Granny's face made Madysen laugh.

"Well, that wasn't my intention, but I heard he was going to send them off early in the morning, so Havyn and I snuck into the place where he kept them and herded them home."

For the first time, Granny genuinely seemed speechless.

"I see I've surprised you. We didn't actually steal them, we paid Judas for them, I promise."

The older woman blinked several times. "I think I'm more surprised that they followed you. A stranger?"

"Well, not exactly. At least not at first. It wasn't easy, let me tell you. But a lot of grain and coaxing, and a couple of sticks, helped us get them home. Then we went to see Judas the next day, and he allowed us to buy them from him. He thought it very amusing that I went to such lengths to save some sheep." Warmth filled her chest. A good, satisfying feeling. "Turns out, I'm quite good with them. To make things even more adventurous, we discovered they were all ewes that were expecting, so now we have plenty of babies and milk."

Understanding lit Granny's face. She lifted her chin and nodded. "Ah . . . thus the new venture."

"Yes! We're going to make cheese." Madysen couldn't contain her excitement. At least something was worth celebrating.

"That is splendid, my dear. Did you know that we used to make a living with cheese production on our farm? Daniel knows far more about it than I do. He used to help his mother with the recipes. I'll bet if you ask him, he would share some insight and maybe even a recipe or two."

"Really?" Oh, praise be to God! Someone actually knew how to make cheese from sheep's milk. "That would be incredible. Do you really think he would help?"

"Oh, I'm sure he will." Granny's eyes twinkled.

"This is an answer to prayer. John and I were just talking about how we had a lot to learn. He knows how to make mozzarella from cow's milk because he used to help his family. He even taught us how. But we want to expand to make other cheeses."

"Then Daniel is your man." Granny began washing dishes, and Madysen took up a dish towel to dry. "So," Granny continued, "tell me all about the wedding and the marvelous shows you did at the Roadhouse. I heard that you Powell girls have been quite the hit."

Turning the topic to music was the perfect choice. Granny was right, once again. How many times had she told Madysen that it was best to think on the positive things?

THREE

D aniel Beaufort lifted a heavy crate and brought it to the front of the new display in the mercantile. "Here you go, and I hope that's the last one." He shot a grin to his father. "Because I don't know if my back can take any more."

Dad laughed as he limped around the crates. "You're young, and you haven't even broken a sweat yet. I doubt these are anything compared to what you carried up the routes to the Yukon. You haven't said much about it, but I've heard enough stories."

He'd thought to spare his family the details of his years away. Mostly because he didn't want to share the dark times. But he hadn't meant to shut his father out. "Oh, don't remind me. Just a year's worth of supplies weighed almost a ton. I don't have fond memories of hauling that over the ice and snow. Back and forth. Back and forth. Makes my back ache all over again."

Dad winced. "Makes mine hurt just thinking about it. How many trips did that take?"

Daniel tilted his head back as he tallied. "To be honest, it must have been a couple hundred trips over that same treacherous trail." He shook his head. "I don't know what I was thinking to take on something so daunting."

"Well, I won't require anything of that magnitude here. In

fact, that's the last of it." With a wink, Dad stuck his thumb out toward the counter. "Can you handle the register for me while I finish up the paperwork?"

"Of course." Daniel wiped his hands on his apron and surveyed the store. He'd been in Nome for six days and already things had settled into a nice routine. Dad and Granny hadn't pried. Just let him rest and dive into a new life. Being with family again fed his soul after the aching loneliness he'd experienced in the Yukon.

Running a mercantile wasn't what he'd dreamed of doing, but then again, did he even *know* what he wanted to do? When he was a kid, the answer was easy. Stay and farm with the family. But after Mom died and Dad got injured, Dad sold the family farm in Illinois and bought a mercantile in Seattle, and things were never the same.

Seattle hadn't been horrible, but it wasn't home. None of his friends kept in touch after he left, and all Daniel had to look forward to was working in the mercantile every day. Which wasn't anything to look forward to. At. All.

He grew more miserable with every month. So when he heard about the Yukon gold rush, he took off for adventure.

But he learned early on that adventure quickly turned into bone-wearying days, where his body ached from head to toe, and the rewards were few and far between. Not to mention the cold. And the lack of Granny's amazing food.

Then Dad and Granny moved up here to Alaska and bought another mercantile. Daniel didn't know their motives behind the move, but it had brought comfort knowing they were closer—even though he'd been too stubborn to come home.

Several years passed before he swallowed his pride and accepted that finding an easy fortune wasn't going to happen.

What a fool he'd been! But some things had to be learned the hard way. Good thing he was on the other side of it. Not a lesson he wanted to endure ever again.

At least he had decent work to do and a place to stay until he decided what he wanted to do with the rest of his life.

Of course, being in another gold-rush town wasn't exactly his first choice, but there seemed to be plenty of people making a decent living here without digging for gold. Look at Judas Reynolds. The man was very successful and respected in the town.

Now, that was someone he'd like to learn from. The man oozed charisma, and everyone seemed to love him. And he was probably the wealthiest man in town.

Daniel could see himself in a prestigious position like that. Being respected and well-known.

The bell jangled over the door, and he turned his attention to the customers.

A tall, dark-haired gentleman entered with a woman. His wife? Her dark red hair was something to behold. She wore it down—not something he saw on modern women often—and the curls spilled everywhere. Two pearlized combs held it off her face. Why did women always pull their hair back and wind it into a knot? It didn't make sense to hide it. Of course, he didn't have long hair, so what did he know?

The woman laughed at something the man said. Yeah, they must be married. Too bad.

He pasted on a smile. "Good afternoon, how may I help you today?"

"You must be Daniel." The man held out his hand. "Your father told us you were here, we just haven't had the pleasure of meeting you yet. I'm John Roselli, and this is my sister-in-law, Miss Madysen Powell. She just had tea with your grandmother."

Ah, so they *weren't* married. Good. Daniel's grin broadened. "Pleased to meet you both." He nodded to Miss Powell. The name sounded familiar, but he couldn't place it. Granny must have said something about the Powells.

45

"John!" His dad greeted the guest like old friends. Tucking his inventory paperwork under his arm, he headed over.

So much for Daniel needing to handle things.

"I see you've met my son."

"Indeed. I bet you are thrilled to have his help." Mr. Roselli seemed to know Dad quite well.

"Don't you know it. How are things out at the farm? How's Chuck?"

The customer began to answer his father, and Miss Powell pivoted toward Daniel. "As John mentioned, I was just visiting with your grandmother earlier today. She is overjoyed that you are here." The delight in her face drew him in like a magnet. She tilted her head a bit and looked like she was eagerly awaiting whatever he had to say.

His mouth went dry. But he couldn't pull his gaze away from hers. What was wrong with him? Forcing his mouth to work, he returned her smile. "Granny is pretty special. And I think that I'm the one who's overjoyed. I can't even begin to tell you how much I missed her cooking."

The pretty Miss Powell laughed, and it sounded almost musical. That was it! Dad and Granny had talked about the Powell family and their musical abilities.

"I can imagine." She smiled. "I had the privilege of having her cinnamon cake today. It was delicious. As always." She glanced toward her brother-in-law and then back to him. "How was the Yukon? I believe that's where Granny said you have been the past few years?"

He nodded. "Cold. Definitely an adventure, but not one I wanted to continue."

"I don't blame you. Gold rushes are never what they promise to be. Even here in Nome folks come thinking they're going to find gold nuggets just lying about—free for the picking."

Yep. He'd been one of those men . . . and not too long ago.

Dad led their customer back toward them and gripped his

shoulder. "Well, I better get back to work. I have a new peanut butter display to set up. Apparently, this product was all the rage at the World's Fair down in St. Louis. Although, I don't know what people will do with it or eat it with." Dad shrugged and continued to talk to himself as he went back to the display.

"What can I help you with today, Mr. Roselli?" Daniel looked between Miss Powell and her brother-in-law.

Dad's friend placed a hand on the counter. "Please call me John. We need to order a good deal of supplies."

"Of course. Let me get the ledger and books. Do you have a list of what you need?"

Miss Powell reached for the Sears Roebuck catalogue. "We do. Most of it is out of this catalogue right here." She pulled a list out of her pocket.

Daniel glanced over it and raised his eyebrows. It wasn't ordinary equipment. "What kind of farm do you have?"

"Dairy and poultry." John's deep voice expressed his pride.

"Humph." Miss Powell patted her brother-in-law's arm. "I'll thank you to not forget my sheep."

A guilty grin took over John's face. "I stand corrected, Daniel. Dairy, poultry, *and* sheep." He shook his head and laughed. "We're now making cheese, so we need the necessary kitchen and equipment to expand our process. We've used the house kitchen for several batches, but it's just not big enough. And now that we're venturing past mozzarella, we've decided to build a new kitchen just for the cheese."

With a pencil, Daniel started an order form. "That's quite a project. When I was younger, I used to help my mother make cheese from sheep's milk. It was quite good if I do say so." Daniel checked each item on the list and wrote it down.

"Granny said you would be the expert and might be willing to share a recipe or two." Miss Powell's words pulled his gaze upward. For a moment, he lost himself in the depths of her dark brown eyes. They held expectancy, joy . . . *life*. Such a difference from what he'd seen the last few years. The light in most people's eyes faded within a few weeks of being in the Yukon.

For some it happened sooner.

"We might need more than recipe help. Since you're an expert on sheep, we could use your suggestions and insight." John's eager voice pulled Daniel's attention back to the job at hand.

"Well . . . I wouldn't say I'm an expert. Just grew up on a sheep farm." Memories made him chuckle. "I enjoyed helping with the cheese part, but not so much with the sheep."

"But they're so cute!" Miss Powell's voice rose in pitch. "I'd *much* prefer working with them than doing the tedious process of working with the cheese."

It was fun to watch her become so passionate about her topic. The tiny Miss Powell's liveliness was a sight to behold. But he'd been staring too much already. Daniel looked back down at the order he'd been writing. "They might be cute, but they stink. And they bite. And they're not all that smart." He watched over the end of his pencil for her reaction.

"I'll give you that, yes, but their cuteness and sweetness should overrule those qualities."

John let out a hearty laugh. "Maddy, you think that because they all adore you and follow you around like you're their mama. Some of us have to deal with the not-so-nice ends of things."

Daniel joined in with John's laughter. "Exactly. That's why I enjoyed making the cheese." He finished writing the order down and handed the paper back to Miss Powell. John had called her Maddy. It suited her. He gave both his customers a smile. "It will probably take six weeks or longer—depending on availability. It might not make it in before the harbor freezes and shipping is curtailed. If you've got the extra money, we could send a telegram to St. Michael, and they can cable it to Seattle from there. That would allow them to put it on the next available ship north. Might get here inside of ten days. For sure by the end of the month."

"Let's do that, John." Madysen tapped her brother-in-law's arm. "We need that equipment, and there might not be six weeks of shipping left. I know they're thinking we won't be frozen in before November, but I've seen it happen in October."

"I'm sure if we telegraph it, we can make it work." Daniel would do whatever he could to make it happen.

"Then let's do it." John pulled several coins out of his pocket. "The building should be finished in a couple weeks, and we'd like to get started with the cheese making as soon as possible." He replaced his hat and tipped it at Daniel. "Good to meet you. We'd love to have you out to the farm sometime."

"Would be my pleasure." And not just for the sheep.

"Mr. Beaufort." Miss Powell gave a nod and followed her brother-in-law to the door.

"Nice to meet you both." In truth, meeting Miss Madysen Powell would probably be the highlight of his whole month.

"Oh, look!" She stopped by the post in the center of the store and stared at an advertisement Dad had put up. "Mr. Beaufort, do you know anything about this?"

He walked around the counter to her side. "Oh, that's the new group Mr. Reynolds brought in."

"'Merrick's Follies and Frolics,'" she read aloud. "'Singers, dancers, jugglers, magicians, and an Irish Tenor who is guaranteed to make you cry.'"

The bell jangled above the door.

"That sounds interesting." John leaned in closer, looking at the poster, and then turned to Daniel. "You say Judas brought them in?"

"I did, indeed." All eyes shifted to the voice at the door. Mr. Reynolds stood there, tall, smartly dressed, and with an air about him that demanded attention. A large smile filled his face. "Good to see you, John." He nodded. "And Miss Powell. How pretty you are in that green calico."

Daniel had thought so too, but of course hadn't mentioned it, or the way the gathered black band made her waist appear so very small.

"Mr. Reynolds." Miss Powell offered him a warm smile and stepped closer. "I was just reading the flyer about Merrick's Follies and Frolics."

He rubbed his hands together and wiggled his eyebrows. "I've seen how popular you and your sisters are at the Road-house and realized we needed more clean entertainment in our fine town."

"That's wonderful! I can't wait to catch a show myself." Miss Powell patted Reynolds on the arm as if they were long-time friends.

Reynolds's face turned serious. "How's the family? Everyone making it through this difficult time? And your grandfather?" The older man's tender tone conveyed great care for this family. They must have known one another for many years.

"Doing well." John shook the man's hand. "Thank you for asking. Chuck is improving every day, and we're ordering supplies for our cheese-making business. All of the ewes gave birth, so we will have plenty of milk once we wean all the lambs."

Reynolds narrowed his gaze "That's wonderful news. But can you get the shipment in before winter freeze?"

"We're having the store wire the order. It's expensive, but we're desperate to have that equipment before winter." John tapped his hat against his thigh.

"I'll see to it that they put the wire on my account." Reynolds's take-charge mode was hard to ignore. He looked to Daniel. "I have some things that need to be wired as well. Just charge it all to me."

"That's very generous, but unnecessary. You've done so much already." Madysen's expression was one of adoration.

"I insist." Mr. Reynolds's chest puffed out just a bit.

"You've always been so good to our family." Another one of those heart-melting smiles. If only it were aimed at him.

"It's my pleasure. You'll give Chuck and your sisters my best, won't you?" The man beamed at Miss Powell.

"Of course. Good to see you, as always."

The exchange between these people made him think that maybe it wasn't so bad to be in Nome. He could stay here, couldn't he? Find something to do that gave him purpose?

Miss Powell waved at him as she left the store.

"She's a beauty, isn't she?"

Daniel pulled his attention from the door to focus on Reynolds.

"You should hear them all sing. It's like listening to angels." And with that, the man turned for the counter.

Daniel would definitely look forward to hearing Miss Madysen Powell sing.

Who was he kidding? He'd do anything just to *see* her again. In the space of one encounter, the world looked brighter. One thing was certain. He wouldn't be able to get the redheaded Miss Powell off his mind.

FOUR

Very interesting. Judas pressed his lips together and squinted at the papers on his desk. So the Bundrant Dairy and Poultry yard were expanding into full-time cheese production. He shouldn't be surprised. He'd heard them speak of it, and they were definitely capable—especially with the sheep they'd acquired from *him*. And they'd done it all without his help.

Definitely not what he'd hoped.

The more the dairy grew, the more powerful that family became. In the past, it had all been Chuck. But when the old man fell ill, the Powell women didn't crumble. It had been the perfect opportunity to ingratiate himself to them. Yet somehow it hadn't gone according to plan. Oh, he still had their adoration and respect, but they didn't *need* him like they should. They'd even paid off all their debt to him! In record time.

They'd found a way to thrive. Without him. And that was unacceptable.

Now they were stronger than ever. Steady. Faithful.

Qualities that were overflowing and spilling out into Nome. *His* town.

He should have known that the Roselli fellow would be

trouble. But now that the man had married into the family, there was no getting rid of him.

Judas let out a long, low growl. His profits came from the chaos, crime, and depravity of the boomtown. He became everyone's hero. But if the town cleaned up, where would that leave him?

His reputation as a wealthy and respected man was well-known. But only a select few had learned, through their own stupidity, that he was also ruthless.

Those people were no longer in Nome.

He drummed his fingers on his desk. It was a pity he hadn't been able to work the situation this past summer more to his benefit. But once Chuck regained his senses after the apoplexy and was able to communicate again, he told his family and foreman where he kept his money. Apparently he still had plenty. They'd paid for the sheep, the chickens . . . everything. Now they didn't owe him anything.

Which meant Judas had no leverage.

He'd never been able to get that over Chuck Bundrant and his farm.

What was he missing? He hadn't come this far in this town not to succeed. Nome was his for the running. He could be mayor if he chose to buy the position for himself. But owning the main freighting service gave him far more power than the position of mayor. And since he'd added a passenger service that summer, he'd tripled his profits as hundreds, if not thousands, more men poured in to find their fortune in gold. As soon as they disembarked, his men were there to sell them claim sites and extra equipment.

There was also the hotel he'd had built and the beginnings of a proper docking system. That wouldn't be complete until next year, but he could require that anyone who wanted to use it pay a hefty rental.

All of it was his. So how did Bundrant and his beautiful

granddaughters elude his control? If the girls kept packing out the Roadhouse with their performances, they'd have even more sway trying to convince the men to clean up the town.

And that wouldn't do.

He couldn't charge them more for their orders or hold up any of their shipments. To hurt Chuck Bundrant and his grand-daughters would be like cutting off his nose to spite his face. So how to get them beholden to him—so deeply in need of his help that they couldn't turn away anything he asked them to do?

Everything he wanted was within his grasp. He'd worked years to make it to this point. He couldn't let one man and his piddly little dairy farm stand in the way.

Then there was Martin Beaufort. The man had been strug-gling financially for some time. Did his son have any idea how bad things were? It could be another avenue to exploit. Another business to get under his influence and power.

Looking into young Daniel Beaufort could prove beneficial. Perhaps there were more secrets to the family hidden away. All in good time.

He *would* have control.

The sun dipped low outside Chuck's window. He'd always loved this view. Exactly why he built the house positioned like this. Just never expected that he'd see so much of the view and for so long a time. Weeks of sitting in a chair or lying in bed. Unable to walk. Unable to talk.

The outskirts of Nome stretched out around him with the river valley gradually giving way to rolling hills. In the dis-tance were mountains, but from this vantage point, he couldn't see them. The ocean was to the south and west, and while he couldn't see that either, the effects of it were always present in the damp air and chilled breeze. Most impressive were the fogs that rolled in at speeds that baffled newcomers and had left more than one man lost in the wall of clouds.

He chuckled. He'd even gotten lost when a fog rolled in off the water. One minute he'd been walking a clear path made by the natives, and the next he couldn't see his own feet. The terrible loneliness, the isolation. . . . He shivered at the memory of it. Stuck there in that fog, he could believe he was the last man left on earth.

He'd never felt that again—until his apoplexy.

What happened to the days of health and strength of his youth? When did he get so old? It seemed to happen overnight. But then again, he'd ignored the signs. The headaches, pounding heartbeats, and shortness of breath. Why hadn't he paid more attention? Melly had probed about his irritation and being out of sorts, but he'd brushed his daughter's concerns aside.

Now she was gone.

His health was gone.

Doc had warned he'd been pushing too hard. When the first bout of apoplexy hit, he shouldn't have been surprised. But the second bout was much worse. And today he was paying the price for his stubbornness and pride.

And for the secrets he had kept.

Secrets that hurt his girls no matter how right he'd thought his reasons were at the time. And he'd lost Melissa before he could apologize. But she'd known the truth. When the girls found the box of letters Melly had written to them under her bed, he'd cried as they read them aloud. She knew about Christopher and his other family. And the fact that her husband wasn't dead.

Did she know that Chuck had orchestrated it to protect her and the girls? Why did she never say anything? Was she angry with him?

It tormented him. Especially at night.

Parents should never have to face losing a child. Parents were supposed to go first. His amazing daughter had endured a lot over the years. Rarely did she ever complain. She'd supported him and encouraged him through thick and thin.

But one question plagued him the most. Had she forgiven him?

He sure hoped so.

His chest ached and tears pricked his eyes. Not a man accustomed to tears, he'd shed a river of them this past summer. Losing his daughter was the worst pain he'd ever endured. Like someone took a hot poker to his heart and, instead of stabbing him, just let it burn. Long and slow. Never relenting.

There'd been no good-byes. He hadn't even been able to speak to her. Yet she sacrificed for him, taking care of him day and night. Never told him about the asthma. Then she contracted whooping cough. He hadn't been there for her in the toughest time of her life. And he'd always been there. That grieved him the most.

God, please forgive me. I know I don't deserve it. And I know that You already have forgiven me. But I feel this need to confess over and over again. How do I help my family now? Where do we go from here?

All this time Chuck had on his hands had led him to long conversations with the Lord. And plenty of Bible reading. He'd always thought that he had a good relationship with God, but it was growing. God had been doing a mighty work on his heart. Which he desperately needed. Even still, would he be able to make a difference with his granddaughters? He'd failed Melly. He couldn't fail them too.

He felt a new challenge in his soul. He'd faced death—multiple times. For some reason, the good Lord had given him a second chance. And a third. What would he do with it?

After Maddy's birthday party, she'd sat beside his bed telling him how awful she felt that she didn't want to forgive her father. Guilt riddled him over her anguish. The fault for that lay squarely on his own shoulders. Had he ever said a decent word about his son-in-law? The torment was what he deserved. The anguish his granddaughter was in was because of him.

And the longer he had time to think about it, the more it hurt—like a knife in his gut.

Not that he wanted Christopher to be a part of their family again. He'd moved his family to Alaska to get away from the man and the memory of him. Chuck flat out didn't want the guy around. But did he have a right to keep Christopher Powell from his own flesh and blood? The girls had a right to know their father—to forgive him if they chose to.

Christopher said he'd turned his life around. Shouldn't Chuck give his son-in-law a second chance? Just like God gave Chuck?

Chuck looked down at the paper and pencil in his lap. He'd gotten a lot better at writing lately and was beginning to utter some sounds—even words. But most of the time they couldn't understand him yet. Well, tonight, during the family meeting, he'd have a letter ready for them.

One that he needed to write immediately.

———

The fire in the fireplace crackled and popped. Madysen rubbed her hands together. "It's much chillier tonight. Please don't tell me the first snow is on its way." Taking her seat on the settee, she looked around at her family.

Chuckles echoed around the room.

"This is September in Alaska, Maddy." Whit shot her a smile and winked. "No guarantees."

Granddad sat in his wheelchair, and there was a good bit of color in his face. Madysen's heart lifted just looking at him. He'd begun to heal. Finally something joyful!

On his lap, he held his box, which contained paper and pencil so he could communicate with them all. He worked on exercises every day with John to regain his speech, and there had been marked improvement.

Whitney walked over to Mama's favorite wingback chair and curled up in it with her feet tucked under her. Havyn sat on the other settee cuddled next to John. The sight of the sweet love between them almost made Madysen long for a romance of her own. Something her family would love too, especially if she settled down here.

A lovely thought. Kind of what she'd always expected. But something inside her hadn't been satisfied for quite some time. In her dreams, she'd seen herself in fancy dresses, taking a bow in front of a concert hall packed with people. Was it selfish and prideful of her to dream of performing to the masses? Was it childish and silly to long to travel? Or was she just unsatisfied . . . with everything?

The past summer had brought all the unsettled feelings to the surface. She loved her family more than anything, and if she really thought about it, the idea of leaving them and this place they called home ripped her heart in two. So what was the answer?

What was wrong with her?

"Maddy?"

"Hm?" She focused on their faces. They all stared at her. "I'm sorry. My thoughts must have been elsewhere. What did you say?"

John gave her an understanding glance and put his arm around Havyn. "We're discussing the farm. Would you like to update everyone on where we are with the sheep?"

"Oh. Of course." John had implemented this new meeting each week since Granddad could join them now. They each talked about their respective responsibilities and brainstormed ideas for how to make things better. She cleared her throat. "Well, John and I ordered supplies this morning for the new kitchen. We're hopeful that we can get it in before the last ship and agreed to pay to telegraph the order, but Judas Reynolds included it with his wire free of charge. Since his freighting company is so large, he seemed assured that we would get it all in time since it's with his order."

Whitney tapped her pencil against her paper. "Certainly he's expecting his order before the harbor freezes, so we should be safe to plan on it."

"We should bake him one of those apple cakes he likes so much to show our appreciation." Havyn leaned forward and scribbled on the paper in her lap.

"Oh! What if we gave him some cheese?" Ideas popped into Madysen's mind faster than her words came out. "He loves the mozzarella we make, and Granny Beaufort suggested her grandson Daniel might be able to help us with some recipes for the sheep's milk cheeses. Apparently, he made a lot with his mother. I didn't have time to talk to him about it, but he said he would help us."

"Whoa, slow down." Whit could never keep up with her once she got going. But in her sister's defense, she did tend to talk too fast when she was excited.

"He *did* offer to help." John's support of her boosted her confidence.

"What a relief," Whitney said as she wrote on her paper, "to have someone else with knowledge should help us save time in the research department. Not that we really had time to spare for it anyway."

Havyn leaned forward and patted Madysen's knee. "Good for you, Maddy. If you can enlist Daniel's help, that should get us up and running even faster. Anything else about the sheep?"

"Gracious, yes." She bit her tongue to keep from sharing too fast. "All of the ewes have now given birth, some of them even had twins, so the flock has more than doubled. We're going to try and wean the lambs in thirty days—a new technique that John heard about—and then we will stagger the breeding so that we should have milk all year to keep cheese production steady."

"We've been doing that with the cows and found it successful, we just have to be very careful in the dead of winter." John tipped his head toward Granddad. "Chuck has been writing out details on what he'd like to see for our expansion as well."

"Oh!" Maddy leaned forward and pointed her hand to her brother-in-law. "Don't forget that you ordered a ram from Judas, which hopefully will arrive before the sound freezes over as well. If not . . . well, I guess we won't have to worry about breeding at all. At least until spring thaw."

"Good point. I've started building a creep pen for the lambs similar to the ones that Chuck made for the calves. That will aid us in weaning the sheep."

Whitney squinted her eyes—a sure sign she was thinking through all the possibilities. "How much cheese production are we expecting from the sheep?"

Maddy made a face at her sister. "That we're not quite sure about since we aren't sure how much milk production we'll have for certain. But we've already received orders, so we're hoping to keep up with the demand."

Her older sister nodded and turned to John. "And how much of the dairy milk will we be putting toward mozzarella?"

His brow furrowed, and he ticked things off with his fingers. "With all the new cows and calves, we're selling about eight hundred gallons of milk a week. In addition to that, we made fifty pounds of butter a week, and this last week, we did fifteen pounds of mozzarella. So that's my best guess for the time being."

"That is quite amazing. And we've had enough hands for all this so far?" Whit was always into the details.

Havyn beamed up at her husband, pride clear on her face. "John has hired ten more hands from Amka's people. They are hard workers and know the farm."

Hiring the natives was always their first choice, since the trustworthiness of men who came to town to dig for gold was always questionable.

"So far, so good," John confirmed. "But I'm sure it's going to get busier and busier. That's why it's good we're talking about each step. Just make sure that you each let me know how things are going and if you need any more help." John patted his wife's arm. "That brings us to the chickens. Would you update us, honey?" The look he sent Havyn made Madysen's heart soar. The man really loved her sister.

Havyn grimaced at her husband.

Madysen and Whitney laughed. They knew that face all too well. Someone must have mentioned raising chickens for slaughter again.

"John has ordered an entire gross of chickens that we will raise with the intention of becoming . . . fryers. I'm still not sure how I feel about this, but there will be roosters to fertilize the eggs, and we will keep raising this new herd separate from my girls. Other than that, my chickens are doing very well, with egg production at fifteen dozen a day. All of which we either use or sell on a daily basis. We could sell up to twice that many, but that would mean adding a *lot* of hens. Of course, winter is coming, and production will drop considerably if things go as they usually do."

"Do we have room for more hens?" Madysen tapped her chin with a finger. "Because if the demand is that high, I could see us adding to the flock. I mean, that's why we're having these meetings to talk about how we can increase production and make the farm even more profitable, right? More people are pouring into Nome every day, and those people have to eat."

"We do have the room, but let's see how we do adding chickens meant for eating, first. Obviously it will be better for us financially if we raise chicks from our own eggs." John seemed to be tempering his reaction. "Chuck, I need to get your thoughts on all of this. Financially, we are fine. And I know your desire is not for us to overwhelm ourselves with too much work, but you've built this farm into what it is, and we want to honor that. And as Madysen said, there are more people arriving every day. Gold fever has driven people out of the Yukon and into Nome. I'm sure we'll have the market for whatever we raise to sell."

Granddad gave a slight nod and wrote on the paper.

Let's talk about it in a few minutes. Whitney needs to update us on the dogs.

"We can do that." John turned to Whit. "Anything new to report?"

Their older sister straightened in the chair. "I've decided that Granddad's idea to train some of the dogs with the intention to sell is a very good idea. Everyone has always asked for my dogs because they know they are the best, but if I train them as sled dogs *before* I sell them, I can ask for more and be confident that their training is good. That would also help me to ascertain the real reason behind a lot of the requests for purchasing my dogs. An expensive, trained dog is less likely to end up in the fighting pits. The buyer will have to give a deposit for the dogs while I train them. And then wait for them to finish training. No rush jobs here."

John placed his elbows on his knees as he leaned forward. "Well, it sounds like things are in order all the way around. It's taken us a little bit to get it all straight, but I feel we're doing well. The workers are paid, all the debt to Mr. Reynolds is cleared, and we have plenty to move forward." He looked to Granddad. "Is there anything you'd like to add?"

Granddad made a noise and held out a paper.

Havyn took it. "You want me to read this?"

A nod.

Havyn unfolded the paper and began to read.

"There are some things that I've been needing to say to you for some time. But my pride and selfishness stood in the way. I'm sorry. God has made some big changes

in my attitude to get me to this point. He's humbled me. Not just physically, but spiritually."

Madysen stood up and went over to kneel by their grandfather. Whatever the letter entailed, she wanted to be by his side, letting him know that they supported him. No matter what. Havyn continued.

"Girls, I don't want you to hate your father. And I'm sorry I ever tried to turn any of you against him. At first, it was because I didn't think you'd ever find out he was alive, and so that was my excuse for talking negatively about him. Then it was my own pride that stood in the way. I knew you all loved your dad, even though he hadn't been the greatest father.

"Anyway, I know that he is in town and that he wants to spend time with you. I'm asking you to give him a chance. He is your father, and the Bible says that you need to honor him.

"Lastly, I need to ask for all of you to forgive me. I made excuses to myself and said that what I did was for your good—for your protection. But that wasn't the whole story. I simply wanted him gone so we didn't have to deal with him or the embarrassment anymore. I thought my daughter was too good for him. I'm so sorry that this had to come out the way it did, and I know this has been difficult for you all. I'm sorry. Please forgive me."

Madysen leaned over and hugged Granddad. It had been horrible what he did, but she understood why he did it.

Whit looked like a storm was brewing inside. "How are we supposed to honor someone who did the things he did? And I know you're partially guilty, Granddad, for convincing him to sign divorce papers and telling him to disappear. But he was the one who actually left. He didn't fight for us. Didn't plead to stay with us or to see us. Has he even written to you all these years to check up on us? Wouldn't that be what a *loving* father would do?"

The set of her jaw and red in her cheeks showed her anger, but a single tear slipped down her cheek. When Whit loved someone, she was a fierce protector, loyal, and compassionate. And when someone betrayed that love, it was almost impossible to regain her trust.

Havyn put an arm around their older sister. "I've asked the same questions, Whit. And I'm not sure I'm ready to forgive him for abandoning us. Or for starting another family while he was still married to Mama. Or for his drinking all those years. But I know that God would at least want us to give him a chance. To hear him out. Find out more about why he's here, and what he's done with his life since he left us."

Silence descended as they all looked to Whit. The seconds stretched.

"Fine." She swiped at her cheek. "We can invite him for dinner. But just because he seems different and said he hasn't had a drink in years, doesn't mean that it's true. It certainly doesn't mean that we have to invite him into our lives. As far as I'm concerned, our father is still dead."

FIVE

Daniel shoved his hands into his pockets and headed toward the parlor. Now that Granny was back, she wanted to have them gather in there each night and chat. Like they used to do. Before Mom died. Before Dad got injured. Before they left the farm, moved to Seattle, and then he left for the Yukon.

Before God turned His back on him.

Spending time with Granny and Dad wasn't the problem. But if he knew his grandmother, she would want to read Scripture too. And she'd probably pry into what was going on in his mind.

Neither of which he wanted.

Things could never go back to the way they were. It wasn't his fault. God could take the blame for that.

Changing direction, Daniel went out the side door and walked in the waning sunlight to the barn. He needed to get his thoughts straight before he went in to be with Granny and Dad.

They had hopes and expectations for him. And the thought of letting them down carved a deep hole in his gut, but he couldn't let go of the past and his anger at God. It haunted him at every turn.

Staring out at the last vestiges of light on the horizon, he fisted his hands in his pockets. Why couldn't he be happy?

When he was young, Daniel had loved everything about the farm. Yes, even the sheep. Life had been so good. It was hard to believe it had been almost ten years since Mom and Grandpa had passed. The cholera epidemic had been fierce in their little town in Illinois. And Daniel couldn't blame his dad for not being able to work the farm after a wagon accident injured his leg shortly after.

But he did blame God. After all, God was all powerful and all knowing. He could have stopped the horrible sicknesses and accidents from happening. He must have known how much pain such things would cause. And, since He had known and could have prevented it, that made Him heartless and cruel.

Daniel had only been sixteen at the time, but he'd decided he didn't want to have anything more to do with a God who would allow such atrocities.

And now here he was stuck in a home that wasn't his and a town he didn't like, but with a family that welcomed him with open arms, just like the prodigal son.

Problem was, Dad and Granny would ask questions about his years away. Daniel didn't want to admit that he had hated it. And he wasn't proud of many things that he had done. But none of that meant he wanted to get "right with God," as Granny put it. She'd push. He'd try to be respectful. But he'd probably have to leave again because he wouldn't be able to take it.

Was there no hope for a decent future for him? Where would he go now? It wasn't like he had the funds to buy a farm or a store or anything else that could make him money.

All this wasted time. He was twenty-five! He should be in a better place. Not starting all over again.

The bitterness put a bad taste in his mouth. He wasn't a bad person. He wasn't. Had he really become so hardened and cynical about life? About happiness?

He had to get rid of all that weighed him down. This wasn't him. Dad was thrilled to have him back, but Granny had seen right through him. She hadn't said anything, but she knew. Maybe that was why he was avoiding them.

He kicked a pebble and looked back at the dark sky. All the light from the day was gone. Just like his life.

No. The thoughts that had begun to darken his mind in the Yukon had to be stopped. He turned around and went back to the house. No matter if he agreed with his family or not, at least he could spend time with them. They were good, loving people. And he hadn't been around anything good for quite a while. Maybe things would look up now.

Perhaps he could save up and start his own business here. That way, he could still be near Dad and Granny. They wouldn't be around forever, and he loved them. They were all he had left.

Over time, he'd just have to let them know that he didn't want to talk about God.

Ever again.

"Daniel, is that you?" Granny's voice carried from the parlor as he stepped back into the house.

"It's me." He pasted on a smile, entered the room, and gave her a hug. "I took a little walk outside."

"Good for you. The fresh air is always invigorating to the spirit." She kept her eyes on her knitting as the yarn and needles seemed to fly effortlessly. "Martin, would you read for us?"

"Of course. I believe we were in John, chapter two?" Dad pulled out his Bible and put on his glasses.

Daniel bit his tongue, leaned back into the chair, and closed his eyes. Dad and Granny had good intentions. Good hearts.

But that didn't mean that he had to listen.

Pushing Granddad's chair back to his room, Madysen couldn't get her father out of her mind. The thoughts weren't very good either, which made her cringe. What did that say about her?

So she started chattering about the sheep. Granddad hadn't

gotten to see what they'd done with them yet. "I'm debating if I should name them all like Havyn names her chickens. But since the flock has already doubled, I'm not sure I could be creative enough to come up with that many names. Maybe I'll just number them."

She helped balance Granddad's weight as he climbed into bed. The process was getting easier all the time since he was exercising so much, but there was still a long road ahead of them.

He grunted and pointed to his box with his writing supplies.

"I'll get it." She grabbed the box that he had set in his chair and handed it to him. "Here you go." She pulled the covers up over his legs.

He immediately started scribbling.

What's bothering you?

"I'm fine. There's nothing bothering me." She pasted on a cheery smile.

Don't lie. I can see the wheels turning in that head of yours.

Letting out a long breath, she plopped down into the chair on the other side of his bed. "I should have known that I couldn't get past you." Madysen leaned forward and propped her elbows on his bed. "All this talk about Dad has my insides churning."

Granddad was devoid of expression. But then she saw the unshed tears. He looked down and wrote.

I'm so sorry for all the pain this has caused you. It's my fault.

"We've forgiven you. You know that. But how do we move forward?" She fidgeted with a loose thread on the coverlet. "I know, I know. I've always believed in giving people a second chance, but I don't know what to think or do about him. If he straightened his life out for this other family—why couldn't he do that for us? Why did he need another family anyway?"

Too many thoughts swirled around in her brain. "I mean, did he not love us enough? Did he not love *me* enough? Did he love any of us . . . at all?" Now that she opened the topic, tears flooded her eyes.

I'm sorry for what you are going through. But these are things you need to ask your father.

Not what she wanted to hear. Because talking to her father wasn't something she wanted to do right now. If ever. "I know, Granddad. He says he's different. And that he doesn't drink anymore. I want to believe it, but then that means that I have to acknowledge that he changed for them and not us." And there it was. All the hurt. All the anger.

Mistakes were made. A lot of them. I regret so many things that I did, but I just couldn't stand seeing Melly's heart broken over and over. She was strong and never said a bad thing about your dad, but I saw it. I wanted to fix it and make everything all right.

"To be honest, it was actually easier to think that Dad was dead. What does that say about me? I'm a horrible daughter. A terrible person." She put her hands over her face.

How could she be so awful?

Granddad laid a hand on her shoulder, prompting Madysen to lower her own. Granddad's eyes were filled with tears, and several streamed down his cheeks.

"I'm sorry, Granddad. I didn't want to make you sad."

He shook his head and looked down at the paper.

As he wrote, Madysen pulled in several breaths. How many times had she wished that they could redo the last few months? So Granddad wouldn't have fallen. Mama wouldn't have died. And Dad wouldn't have come back.

Guilt weighed her down for even thinking such things.

Granddad moaned, and she glanced at his paper.

It's my own doing that makes me sad. You didn't do that. We can't change the past. But we can do something about the future. Together.

She looked up and nodded. "You're right. I know. I just don't know what to do with all this turmoil inside of me."

Give it over to God.

Of course that was the answer. It was the answer to everything. But she hadn't been listening very well lately.

She gave him a slight smile. "Do you need anything? I think
I'll go out with the sheep for a while and sort through all this."

Go. I'm fine.

"Okay." She leaned over and kissed his forehead. "I'll see
you in the morning."

The night was beautiful. Not a cloud in the sky as twilight
hovered. But it was cold. There was plenty of daylight now,
but it would diminish quickly over the next couple of months.
Madysen breathed deep of the night air and filled her lungs
with the chill of the coming winter.

Everything seemed so clean and crisp.

Everything except her heart.

She'd made such a mess out of things. Especially the way
she'd talked to Dad at her party. If only she had a muzzle.

The cries and bleats of the sheep as she drew near made her
smile. She spent hours out here every day. Talking to them, singing to them. So that now, even if they were sleeping or napping
when she came out, they wanted to be near her.

She and her sister had teased Havyn for months about carrying on conversations with her chickens. And here Madysen
was, doing the same with the sheep. She blamed it on reading
chapter ten of John one morning. She'd been fascinated by Jesus
saying that the sheep knew their shepherd's voice.

In that moment, she'd wanted her sheep to know her voice
more than anything. And she'd done it too. Even the little lambs
came when she called. And she wouldn't have it any other way.

As she leaned on the fence and watched the sheep come close
and lie down in a giant mass of wool near where she stood, she
smiled at how that made her heart do a little flip. How could
she leave them?

For the first time, her two worlds seemed to collide. The world where she lived and breathed, and the world of her dreams. She couldn't have both. She couldn't stay here with her family and sheep *and* go travel and perform.

Life didn't work that way.

But if she left for a little while . . . she could at least escape all the turmoil with Dad. Experience living out her dreams just a little.

Common sense took over, and she giggled into the night air. There weren't any prospects for her to follow her crazy dreams anyway. Maybe dreams were supposed to be just that—dreams. Something fun and exciting to think about when life got dreary.

Tomorrow night when they performed at the Roadhouse again, she could just envision it was a fancy concert hall and sing and play her heart out to the masses.

It would just have to be enough.

Six

Buddy Merrick sauntered into Reynolds's Shipping and Freight. He tipped his hat to the receptionist and put on his most flirtatious smile. "Whom do I have the pleasure of meeting? Be still my heart, it's the prettiest lady in Nome."

The woman lifted one eyebrow at him. "You must be Mr. Merrick."

"Indeed, I am." He bowed deeply and then winked at her as he came up.

"Definitely a performer if I ever saw one." The woman shook her head. "I'll let Mr. Reynolds know that you are here."

As she marched off, Buddy laughed. She'd seen right through him. Plenty of people did. Especially stodgy, older people—and the receptionist was definitely one of those. But it was still fun to try to flirt his way into their good graces. He was a con man after all. And a good one.

He took off his hat and gazed around the room. Reynolds had good taste. Obviously the man had money, so how could Merrick's Follies and Frolics benefit most from him?

"Mr. Merrick." Reynolds's deep voice grabbed his attention. "Thank you for coming."

"It's my greatest privilege, sir."

Reynolds raised an eyebrow almost exactly like his reception-ist. Tough crowd. "Please. Join me in my office for a moment?" The man waved him over.

"Of course." Buddy entered and took a seat across from a large, impressive desk.

"Let me get right to it." Reynolds leaned back in his chair. "We'll have dinner at the Roadhouse in a few minutes, but I wanted to discuss a few things privately."

As if on cue, the receptionist closed the door.

"Certainly." Buddy shifted in his seat. Normally he took control of these conversations, but Reynolds didn't even give him a chance.

"I brought you here to make money. Plain and simple. To-night you will see that there are plenty of people in this town willing to pay a good deal for clean entertainment in dry estab-lishments. And since, sad to say, I didn't think of it first, Herb Norris has had the corner on that market. Oh, there are the occasional saloon performers, but nothing merits the attention and money of the Powell sisters."

Who were these sisters? Spinsters, no doubt. But it was worth investigating the competition. "I see. Well, as long as *I* make plenty of money, I don't mind that you do either." Hopefully the man got his hint. His show was *his* show.

"I've ensured that you will make plenty, Mr. Merrick. But this is *my* town. I brought you here. So you work for me." The tone was sharp, like the blade of a knife.

Ah, so the man thought himself to be in charge of all of Nome. That could work to Buddy's advantage. "Of course, Mr. Reynolds. I'm sure we will make excellent partners."

There went that eyebrow again. "I've had an outdoor stage built, just north of Main Street, for your use until the new building is finished. Which should take a couple weeks more. The issue we have right now is that even though the sun doesn't go down until about nine, the temperature has dropped quite a bit. It will probably warm back up, but this might affect our crowds."

"I highly doubt that, sir. We are known for bringing people from hundreds of miles around to see one of our shows."

"We're not in the city up here, Merrick. This is the Alaska Territory. We don't have people stretched far and wide. They'd die. But we do have twenty thousand or so people in Nome."

Obviously, this man was used to no one arguing with him. Buddy could play along.

Reynolds leaned over his desk, his dark eyes narrowed. "In addition to the stage, I've done a good deal of advertising with flyers all over town. None of which I did from the goodness of my heart—I expect my take of the show's profits, just as we agreed. Is everything still set for you to start tomorrow evening?"

"Yes, sir." Buddy kept his smile in place. No point in letting the man know he already despised him.

"And the accommodations for your troupe?" Reynolds shuffled through some papers on his desk.

He might look as if his attention were elsewhere, but Buddy knew better. "They are excellent. By the way, thank you for my room at the hotel. I don't stay with the performers."

"I know." The tone in which he said it made Buddy examine his new partner even harder.

Reynolds's impeccable reputation in town had caused Buddy to believe that the man who'd brought him up here was a goody-goody. Someone he could push over. Possibly swindle out of some gold. But now? He was in the presence of a master. Probably even another con man like himself.

"Why don't we head on over for dinner?" Reynolds stood and ushered him out the door. "A picture is worth a thousand words. Or in this case, a performance is worth even more."

Before they reached the establishment, Buddy could smell the food and hear glorious voices. Where on earth had the owner found such talent all the way up here?

When the door opened, the music that washed over him was far from amateur. Not only were three *young* ladies—beautiful red-haired ladies at that—singing with some of the best voices and harmonies he'd ever heard, but they were playing instruments too! Piano, cello, and violin, all played without flaw.

He blinked several times. Was this some sort of apparition? What had he walked into?

"They're pretty impressive, are they not?" Reynolds flashed a smile at him as a portly gentleman in an apron led them to a table.

"The special tonight is sourdough hots and reindeer sausage." An unlit pipe hung between the man's lips.

"We'll take two plates, please." Reynolds didn't even look at the man. "With butter."

"Comin' right up."

"Was that the owner?" Buddy couldn't help but watch the crowd. They were completely entranced. He took a cigar from his pocket and reached for a match.

"Yes. Herb Norris."

Reynolds reached over and pulled the cigar from Buddy's mouth. "They don't allow smoking here. It affects the girl's voices, or so they say. But their mother died of whooping cough made worse by a severe case of asthma. Since then the girls have insisted no smoking or they won't perform. Didn't you see? Even Herb just had it in his mouth—it wasn't lit." Reynolds smirked. "No smoking or drinking, and yet the man makes money hand over fist and pulls men in from far and wide."

"Where did he find such talent?" It was hard to keep the shock out of his voice.

"He's a friend of their family." Reynolds pointed to the stage. "Those are the Powell sisters. Well, I guess, one of them is married now and is a Roselli. But they are all the granddaughters of Chuck Bundrant. He owns a dairy and poultry yard outside of town."

For once, Buddy didn't want to fill the time with conversation. All he wanted to do was listen. There wasn't much conversation going on anywhere in the Roadhouse. The ladies on the stage had the entire room mesmerized.

Including him.

The song finished and the performers bowed. As the applause roared around him, he studied them. Two of the sisters seemed strong and sturdy. The one who played the piano had curly hair that escaped her long braid—curls sprang out at her temples and her neck. The one with the violin had straighter hair, neatly coifed into a beautiful design off to the right side of her neck. Probably because the violin had to be tucked under her chin on the left. But the one on the cello . . . she was tinier than her sisters. Dainty. Almost fragile. With that same dark red hair that spilled down her shoulders and back in a plethora of curls. Two combs held her hair off her face.

All three wore matching emerald green gowns. Nothing like the fashion of the city that he had to supply for the girls he hired. These were simple in their fashion with rounded but modest necklines, short puffed sleeves, and basque waists that dropped to a point just below their natural waistlines. The gowns had no fancy trim of any kind. No doubt they were handmade. And yet, these girls pulled it off as if they were adorned in the latest fashion from Paris. In fact, he'd bet the crowds wouldn't notice if the ladies wore potato sacks.

As the women started into a soft and slow ballad, their voices intertwining and floating around the others, he studied each of them. Only the cello accompanied, and it was probably the most beautiful thing Buddy had ever heard. No denying they were sisters. Perhaps since they dressed alike, they wore their hair in different styles so the audiences would know who was who? Clever really. But in reality, their instruments set them apart. When they sang, he couldn't pick their voices apart, their sound was so tightly woven.

He couldn't take his eyes off of them. "How often do they perform?"

The food arrived, and Reynolds didn't hesitate to pick up his fork and knife. "Thursday through Saturday evening. Earlier this summer they performed every night but Sunday, and while there was a large crowd each night, it took its toll on the girls. I think they cut back so that they could keep up with their chores at home."

"No Sundays?"

"No. They are religious." The man shoved a large bite of the sourdough pancakes into his mouth.

It made Buddy's mouth water. He took some of the butter from in front of him and slathered the cakes. Then poured a generous portion of syrup on top.

Reynolds pointed with his knife. "That butter is from the Bundrant farm. It costs extra, so enjoy it."

All Buddy could do was nod. Who knew that pancakes and sausage could be so satisfying?

"As I was saying, it was hard for them to perform every night, but they needed the money. Their mother fell ill, and their grandfather had a stroke."

"Did he die too?"

"No. Surprisingly enough, the old man is still going. Tough old coot. Their mother was a beautiful woman and as talented as her girls. She didn't perform for the public anymore. I'm not sure why. She was the most talented person I've ever met. I heard her play the piano once at the house. Amazing. She taught the girls. They had no other formal training."

"That's hard to believe." Buddy shook his head. "Yet talent like that must surely be a gift—something one is born with."

"Call it what you will. Norris is just pleased to have them coming as often as they do because his crowds triple whenever the sisters are here."

"I can see why." Buddy wiped his mouth with his napkin.

"So tell me, you said these girls work for tips? Their talent is wasted for that." He leaned back in his chair. Time to find out the whole story. The man beside him obviously had ulterior motives—a plan. Something long term, no doubt. "Why did you bring my troupe all the way up here when you could have just booked these ladies and demanded a small fortune for each performance? The crowds obviously love them."

Reynolds finished off his plate of food and wiped his hands on the napkin. "Because I am also a friend of the family. They started off performing a couple years ago to help out Norris—to bring more people into his establishment. The girls are very particular about who they do business with, and being the good friend that I am, I couldn't steal them from Norris. No matter how much money I could make. That wouldn't be appropriate, now would it?"

Did he detect a hint of sarcasm? Buddy squinted just a bit and studied Judas Reynolds. "I'm sure you chose the right thing. An upstanding gentleman like yourself."

Reynolds's smile told him more than he needed to know. It would be good to have this man as a friend and ally . . . and dangerous. Buddy would have to keep his eyes wide open. "Could you possibly introduce me to these fine musicians?"

"Certainly. They should be taking a break soon, and I'll arrange it." The gentleman rose from his chair and gave a tiny bow. "Enjoy the rest of your meal. I'll see to your request, Mr. Merrick." He gave an odd chuckle. "But watch out for the old guard."

"What?" Buddy shook his head. "Old guard?"

"Yes. Do you see the first two rows of old men—the ones who have made a half circle around the girls with their tables?"

He hadn't noticed it before, but he did now. "Yes. Who are they?"

"Friends of their grandfather. They watch over the girls when he can't be here. Guard them like banks guard their gold."

Judas broke into a grin. "If any particularly rowdy young man should approach, the old guard will take care of the situation. Those girls have better protection than the president of the United States."

Buddy could only imagine. "Then how are you going to get me an audience with them?"

Judas shrugged. "I'm practically family."

Buddy watched the man work his way through the room. It was quite apparent that everyone here had a lot of respect for him. Even the old guard welcomed him.

After several minutes, the girls exited the stage, and Reynolds waved to him from the front of the room.

The crowd turned boisterous when the entertainment was gone, and Buddy had a hard time moving through the mass of people. But when he reached Reynolds, Mr. Norris was there with him.

"Ah, so you are Mr. Merrick of the new show that's come to town." The man stuck out his hand. "It's a pleasure to have you in Nome."

"Thank you, Mr. Norris. Your establishment is wonderful, and the food scrumptious. I find myself completely entranced with your performers and simply must meet them."

Norris beamed a smile at him. "Thank you for the compliments. Can't say I've been told my food was *scrumptious* before, but you city folk have all your fancy words. I'll give you a moment to meet them."

As Reynolds ushered him toward the back, a tall, dark-haired gentleman stood outside the door. Was he the bodyguard?

"John." Reynolds nodded to the man.

"Judas." The man nodded back.

"Ladies"—his host held out his arms—"I'd like to introduce you to Mr. Buddy Merrick of the famed Merrick's Follies and Frolics. He heard you perform tonight and insisted that I introduce you."

The ladies looked up and met Buddy's gaze. They were even more beautiful up close.

"Good evening, Mr. Merrick, I'm very pleased you've enjoyed our performance." The first woman studied him with eyes that seemed to pierce his soul. She offered a slight smile, but not a genuine one. "I'm Miss Whitney Powell."

"You were the one on the piano, were you not?"

"Yes. That was me."

The next sister approached. "I'm Mrs. Havyn Roselli. It's a privilege to have you here." Her smile was brighter than that of her sister, but she too eyed him with an intense stare.

Then the cellist approached. A smile stretched across her face. "I can't tell you how excited I am to meet you, Mr. Merrick! I'm Madysen Powell." Now *this* was the greeting he was used to. She put a hand to her chest. "And how thrilling that you loved our show."

"I could take you three all over the world and make you stars. That's how talented you are."

The married one waved a hand at him. "You're being far too generous, Mr. Merrick, but we appreciate the compliment." She turned toward the back of the room and took a sip of water.

"Do you really think so?" Miss Madysen approached him, her eyes wide and dreamy.

Exactly what he was hoping for. "Heavens, yes. I haven't heard talent like the three of you in years. Years!" He tried to get the other sisters' attention, but they were glancing over music sheets. "Where did you study? Europe? New York?"

Miss Madysen laughed at that. "Our mother taught us."

So Reynolds was telling the truth. Even better. "I forgot that Mr. Reynolds said as much. I would have thought that you trained at the highest level of conservatory."

"Gracious. Thank you for such a wonderful compliment." Pink rose up in Miss Madysen's cheeks. Ah, she was an innocent. The possibilities could be endless with this one.

The other two ladies approached. Apprehension in their eyes. They looked at their sister. And then back to him.

The married one spoke up. "Our mother was a talented musician. She could play any instrument. A true virtuoso."

"I'm sure she was—just by the testimony of watching you three. And I was very serious in my statement. I could have you booked in concerts around the world, demanding the highest of fees from the most prestigious of audiences. You are that talented."

Mrs. Roselli wrapped an arm around each of her sisters. "Thank you, again. That is quite the compliment, but I don't think my husband and I would ever dream of leaving our family and Alaska."

The less congenial sister seemed a tad colder now. "Neither would I. This is home. But thank you."

Miss Madysen bit her lip but didn't respond. Just stood there within her sister's embrace.

"We need to get back on stage. It was very nice to meet you," Mrs. Roselli ended their conversation.

But Buddy watched the smallest sister. She appeared to be the youngest. And when they were walking away, she chanced a glance over her shoulder at him.

Bingo.

There was hope for him yet.

SEVEN

The Powell sisters were phenomenal. No two ways about it. More talented than anyone Daniel had ever heard. When Granny had encouraged him to come to their concert, he'd agreed and looked forward to seeing Miss Madysen Powell again. But it was so much more than he'd expected.

Yep, he was amazed. Just like Granny said. Of course, she was always right. At least, that's what she told him. Over and over. He chuckled.

The song ended, and he took a moment to study the men in the room. Chatter rolled through the large, open space now that the ladies weren't playing. The camaraderie and jovial enthusiasm throughout the crowd made him feel at home.

Home.

The past few days had helped to lift the dark cloud that seemed imprinted on his heart. Once he let go of the negative thoughts and realized his family loved him no matter what, it really was nice to be back with Dad and Granny. Neither one of them had pushed him to talk about anything spiritual last night, despite reading the Scripture and praying together. Out of respect for his family, Daniel kept his mouth shut and endured. All those years in the Yukon alone finally made him appreciate his relationship with his family.

It just took a long time for his stubborn self to admit it. Maybe now he'd be able to let go of the past.

As the sisters began another piece with all three instruments, he turned his attention back to the stage. The crowd hushed.

The haunting melody that the violin played brought up a lot of memories. When life was simpler and without all the pain of loss. Mom had always loved the violin. Said her dad played it. He'd always wished he could've known his other grandpa.

Since he was about eight years old, Daniel had followed Mom around the kitchen and helped her make cheese. Every day. She had high standards and worked him hard, but also gave him lots of affirmation. Dad and Grandpa took care of the sheep, and he and Mom made the cheese. Granny always kept the house warm and cozy and cooked all the meals. It was the perfect arrangement.

Until the cholera epidemic.

Losing Mom at the time in his life when he'd needed her most wasn't fair. Navigating those tough years into manhood without her had forced him into some dark places. Dad and Granny had been grieving as well and didn't know what to do with his struggles.

But things were different now. That much was clear. The years had given him a bit of wisdom and appreciation for the family he had left. For a long time, he'd said he never wanted to have anything to do with farming or sheep again. It hurt too much. But the thought of helping out at the Powells' farm was actually appealing. Funny how life came full circle like that.

Mr. Norris plopped a steaming plate of food in front of Daniel, and his mouth watered. He cut into the sourdough pancakes and took a bite. They practically melted in his mouth. The saltiness of the butter mixed with the tang of the sourdough and the sweetness of the syrup was a perfect combination. Now this was food he could eat again and again. Almost as good as Granny's.

He'd had some so-called butter in the Yukon on rare occasions. They'd put so much salt into it to preserve it that he couldn't tell if it had gone bad or not. Not like what he'd grown up with from his grandma's kitchen. And to be honest, this butter at the Roadhouse was some of the creamiest and freshest he'd ever tasted. Better not tell Granny he liked it better than hers.

Looking back to the stage, he watched the performers as they moved around. The woman who'd come into the store with John Roselli the other day sat on a chair with a cello in front of her.

One of the men whistled, then stood and put his hand over his heart. "You're my favorite, Madysen."

She glanced up and looked at the older gentleman. "Well then, Tom, this song is for you." A smile lit up her face.

She definitely knew how to handle a crowd.

Madysen Powell. What a charming lady.

In the next instant, her sister played a soaring introduction on the piano. Then Miss Madysen moved the bow furiously over the instrument's strings.

Daniel had never heard anything like it.

He leaned onto the table and watched her head bob with the bow, her curls bouncing with the rhythm. The cello seemed massive in front of her tiny frame, but she mastered it. The intense look on her face captivated his attention as she appeared to play with every ounce of strength within her.

Incredible. There were no words to describe what the music did to his soul. Maybe he should spend a bit more time around these talented ladies. Especially Miss Madysen.

"She's absolutely enchanting." A man's voice caught Daniel's attention. A guest of Mr. Reynolds, obviously, as they came to sit at the table next to Daniel's.

He wanted to shush them so he could listen, but the man continued. "I'm so glad you got me back there to meet them."

"It was my pleasure." Reynolds at least had the decency to keep his voice low. "I think you'll find the second half of the show to be even more moving than the first. I mentioned that the girls are religious. You'll find they'll have most of the old-timers tearing up as they sing hymns that remind them of home and their mothers."

The man chuckled. "We have a tenor who does that at the end of our shows. He sings folk songs rather than hymns, but he never leaves a dry eye in the audience."

Daniel watched the newcomer from the corner of his eye. It wasn't like he was eavesdropping. No conversation could be quiet in a place like this. But he didn't like the look on the man's face. A look that said he was interested. Too interested.

It took everything in him not to tell the man that he saw her first, but that would be childish. Every man in the room was mesmerized by the Powell sisters at the moment. As they probably were every night the women performed. What if Miss Madysen already had a beau? His heart sank a bit.

But it made Daniel think. Nome's appeal grew after he'd met Miss Powell. Perhaps he could settle down here. After all, his father and grandmother had no intention of leaving anytime soon. It would be nice to have them nearby, but he would have to find a place of his own to live.

His experience with sheep could get him a job on the Powell farm. Dad had even said that John Roselli just hired a new group of native men to help. Surely if Daniel approached him and offered to help with the cheese making, John would consider hiring him. Hadn't Miss Madysen even said she preferred working with the sheep themselves? Excitement built as he thought of the possibilities. Excitement he hadn't felt for anything for a very long time.

There was a commotion at the front of the room, but the girls never stopped playing. A man holding a large bouquet of hothouse flowers was trying to approach the stage.

"I love you, Whitney!" His shout rose above the music. "I brought you flowers."

Three old men from the front tables stood in unison and escorted the man back to his table. One of them took the flowers and said something to the younger man. He looked upset, but nodded.

While the girls continued to play, Daniel made up his mind. He would approach John as soon as the show was over. Hopefully that would allow them time to discuss the ideas going through Daniel's mind. Only one thing caused him hesitation—Mr. Reynolds had told the stranger the girls were religious.

He frowned and took a long drink of his now lukewarm coffee. Miss Madysen Powell was beautiful and talented, but he didn't need anyone else nagging him about his spiritual life. He glanced up to watch her playing away at the cello. The music she brought out of that oversized fiddle was quite something. She was like one of the fine china dolls his father had carried in the Seattle store. Maybe her religious views weren't as important as Reynolds thought. Maybe she was just following after her sisters. They appeared to be older than she and seemed far less approachable.

He smiled. That was probably all it was. She was religious because her family was. Daniel could handle that well enough. After all, he was in the same boat.

The show concluded to thunderous applause, and without warning, the stage was inundated with members of the audience. The men produced gifts and even more bouquets of hothouse flowers. Where on earth had those come from?

Daniel watched the strange production as the men attempted to pay court, while the old patrons who sat near the front formed a barrier and held them back.

"As you can see for yourself"—Reynolds's voice carried from the table next to Daniel—"these sad saps pay court to the girls every night. Even to Mrs. Roselli. They bring gifts, gold, and proposals."

"It's much the same for my leading lady and often for the chorus girls as well. Men are men. They are easily enthralled by the flash of a sweet smile and a hither-to look that promises more than they can even imagine. My ladies are quite adept at implying the possibilities. A few even carry through."

Daniel frowned. Surely the man wasn't implying that the Powell women did the same. It irked him more than he wanted to admit.

"Well," Reynolds replied, "as you can see, these young ladies are far more innocent and still the men do what men do. These men need little prompting. Of course, the girls always refuse the presents and proposals—if someone manages to actually get through to them—but they do it with such kindness that the fools actually walk away feeling as if they'd won something after all."

Daniel watched as John Roselli rounded up his musical family and exited the room, presumably for home. The other men went back to their tables and finished their meals.

Daniel paid for his food and made his way into the chilly night. The ladies had sung a mix of popular tunes, folk songs, and church hymns in addition to playing some lovely classical instrumental pieces. He could almost still hear their voices. It was said that music soothed the soul. At the moment, he agreed. It'd been a long time since he felt . . . peace.

Movement to the far right caught his attention. Madysen was hoisting her cello into the back of a wagon. How strange to find her alone. He made his way to her in six long strides and got there just in time to help her take her place beside the cello.

"Thank you for your assistance, Mr. Beaufort." She was out of breath and put a hand to her chest. "Sometimes it feels like my instrument weighs more than I do."

He didn't doubt that. "You were wonderful tonight. Granny told me I had to come hear you and your sisters. I'm glad I'm such an obedient grandson." He sent her what he hoped was a friendly look.

Madysen laughed. "It generally benefits us to listen to our grandparents." She settled her skirt and leaned back. "I'm glad you enjoyed the show."

"You're very talented. Where did you learn all of that?"

"Our mother. We've been singing or playing as far back as I have memory. Which is a great blessing because it connected me to my mother and sisters in a way nothing else could have ever done." She took a long look into his eyes, and Daniel's heart skipped a beat. "Do you have brothers or sisters?"

He shoved his hands into his pockets and shook his head. "It was just me. I guess that's why I have always been so close to my granny and pa. My mother and grandpa too, but they're gone." He couldn't hold her gaze, afraid that she'd see too much of his inner turmoil, so he looked at the corner of the wagon.

"It's hard to lose people we hold so dear."

Yes, she understood. All too well. He looked back to her brown eyes so full of compassion. "Granny said your mother just passed this summer. That couldn't have been easy to go in there and entertain folks with her being such an important part of it all."

Madysen's expression softened. "It is bittersweet to be sure. A part of me feels her presence every time I play, but it's like she's hidden behind a veil. I can't quite reach her, no matter how perfect I play or how much passion I put into it. It's like I can almost touch her again, but . . ." Tears came to her eyes and dripped down her cheek.

"But then she fades away and all that you're left with is the present and her very apparent absence." Daniel felt her pain mingle with his own.

Madysen's eyes widened. "Yes!" She nodded and wiped at

her tears. "Exactly that." She studied his face for a moment. "You understand."

"I do."

Daniel heard a commotion and turned. The others were coming from the Roadhouse. "I'd better go." He headed off before the others could join them.

He'd talk to John at another time. He wasn't at all sure he could manage a conversation with anyone else. Madysen's memories and raw emotions had stirred up his own bitter sorrow. If he were a drinking man, he'd head to town and drink it dry. Since he wasn't given to that habit, he'd just walk until he could numb those painful memories and force them back into their cages where they could neither be heard nor felt.

Rolling over for what must be the fiftieth time in the past half hour, Madysen gave up trying to sleep and slipped out of bed. She pulled on her sealskin pants to ward off the chill and a long *kuspik* that Amka had given her for her birthday. The hooded dress was part of the costume the native women wore. In summer it was lightweight, usually made from cotton cloth, but in winter it was heavier material—usually animal skins. Amka had managed to make this one from wool, dyed a dark burgundy, and Madysen loved it. Typical of the kuspik, it had large pockets and, just below the hip, a gathered ruffle of sorts that brought the length down to below her knees. Amka had trimmed it out in braided black cord. For a moment, Madysen studied the beautiful work. Maybe she could make something special for Amka. Not as fine as the kuspik, but something to show how much she cared—how much the whole family cared.

They'd relied so heavily on their native friends this summer.

As she walked to the back door, she brainstormed ideas to show their gratitude. But she was too tired, and her mind couldn't stay focused. Pulling on her warm seal mukluks, she then crept outside to join her sheep.

The sun had finally set, and the ebony skies hovered overhead like a shroud. Madysen pulled up her hood and spoke into the night.

"'The Lord is my shepherd; I shall not want.'" But she did want. She wanted so much, and everything she longed for seemed out of reach.

"'He maketh me lie down in green pastures: he leadeth me beside the still waters. He restoreth my soul.'" But He hadn't. Her soul felt crushed and broken. Her mother was gone. Her grandfather wounded . . . broken. And her father . . . her father had come back into her life as if to prove his heartlessness and lies.

"'He leadeth me in paths of righteousness for his name's sake.'" But lately those paths were unclear. Other paths were beckoning. Paths that would take her far away from her family and all that she knew.

She stopped, unwilling to go on with the psalm. She leaned against the fence. Why was everything at odds? Why did she feel torn apart?

Losing Mama had been so overwhelming, and yet they seldom spoke of it. It was almost as if there had been a silent agreement to say nothing—feel nothing. Mother was everywhere around them and yet gone.

"I'm not strong enough for this," she whispered in the darkness. "I'm too weak."

My grace is sufficient for thee: for my strength is made perfect in weakness.

Madysen heard the Scripture as if it had been spoken aloud. She couldn't recall where in the Bible those words were written, but at this moment they offered little comfort and no understanding.

Gazing heavenward, she tried to imagine her mother in heaven.

Her pain gone. Her body whole. She tried to think of the wonder that Mama would experience being in God's presence, but it was just too hard.

"You took her before I was ready, Lord." She gave a heavy sigh. God didn't make mistakes, so the deficiency had to be on Madysen's part. Tears blurred her vision. Would she ever feel whole again?

She had confided in Mama earlier in the spring that she might like to pursue a career playing her cello and singing. And not just at the Roadhouse. The idea wasn't at all a new one, although she'd not talked about it with her family until mentioning it to her mom.

They had a music book titled *The Songs of Jenny Lind*. The Swedish Nightingale had once impressed the likes of Chopin and Mendelssohn. She lived and sang long before Madysen's time, but she'd always stood as an inspiration for Madysen. Mama told them of a newspaper story that related how Miss Lind had performed before Queen Victoria, and the queen had been so moved by the singing that she threw a bouquet of flowers at Jenny Lind's feet.

Oh! To have people throw flowers at *her* feet! She wanted to sing and play and move people to such rapture that they couldn't keep themselves from adoring her. Maybe then she'd feel Mama's closeness again.

Madysen loved it when the men in the Roadhouse audience tried to approach with flowers and gifts. She loved that they adored her and she could share her talent from God with them. And maybe, just maybe, point them to Him.

"Perhaps that's why I'm so unhappy. So restless. Maybe it isn't just missing Mama, but also missing out on what I've been created to do." She drew a deep breath and squared her shoulders. It might be time to break out of her sorrow.

And embrace her true purpose.

EIGHT

Havyn straightened her husband's necktie and shook her head. "It's a shame you're so handsome."

John chuckled at her. "Oh, really. And why is that?"

"Because all the young women will be watching you rather than the show tonight."

"Oh, good heavens. I think your imagination has taken off with you." But he sent her a wink. "Let's see what kind of show Mr. Merrick has put together."

Havyn gripped John's arm a little tighter as they approached the outdoor stage that Judas had set up for this new show of his. She'd never been to anything like this before and wasn't quite sure what to expect. Lively music played, and the air was filled with the scent of something very sweet. As they moved a bit more into the crowd, she smelled popcorn, and it made her mouth water. She hadn't had popcorn since she was a child when they'd gone to the circus in Colorado.

Mrs. Simon walked by with her husband. "Blessings on your marriage, Mrs. Roselli." They'd just arrived back from Seattle and hadn't been at the wedding.

"Thank you." Havyn felt the heat creep up into her cheeks again. Being married to John was the most wonderful thing she'd ever experienced. It still made her a bit giddy when she thought about it, even after a month.

John leaned closer to her ear. "You look beautiful this evening, Mrs. Roselli. Have I told you that?"

"Twice. But I could hear it again and again."

"Oh, you two." Whitney took Havyn's other arm and laughed. "The constant compliments are quite sugary sweet."

"Well, I, for one, love it." Madysen stepped in front of them and walked backward for a few steps. "I think it's adorable and what every married couple should do." She turned around and barreled on ahead of them. "Hurry up, I want to get a good seat."

Havyn glanced at her older sister. "Guess we better hurry up."

As Whitney rolled her eyes, Havyn couldn't help but laugh. "Aren't we a mess? Sometimes I feel old and stodgy with all the responsibilities we have, but Maddy always seems to help me feel young again."

"Until she forgets what she's supposed to do and you have to holler after her." Whit laughed. "But I guess she does balance us out, doesn't she?"

Havyn watched their younger sister flit through the crowd, greeting people, smiling, laughing—as if she didn't have a care in the world. "Yes, she does. Life would be very boring without her."

Whitney elbowed her. "Hey, are you saying I'm boring? And what about John?"

The deep voice of her husband washed over her. "I'm fine with boring. Well, sometimes."

They enjoyed a laugh together and took in all the sights. Whatever was planned for the show, it must be quite grand. Especially for their little town on top of the world.

Maddy waved them forward. Of course, she had found seats up front. She was entirely too excited about this whole thing. What had gotten into her lately?

They took their seats and settled in for the show.

The chairs were packed into the grassy field. A huge crowd had arrived for this opening night. Even with quite a chill in the air, Havyn was warm with all the people around.

"Ladies and Gentlemen . . ." A booming voice sounded from behind the curtain. "Tonight, we hope to entertain and amaze you with Merrick's Follies and Frolics."

Applause sounded all around, along with some whistles and cheers.

Two entirely too skinny girls burst through the curtain. They were scantily dressed and went immediately into a tumbling and acrobatic routine. Bending and twisting and flipping all over the stage.

Havyn raised her eyebrows. How could they possibly move that way? And how could they perform wearing so little? Weren't they embarrassed? Cold?

She turned to Whit. Her older sister's jaw was dropped, and there was no missing the stunned expression on her face.

"Aren't they wonderful?" Maddy's loud whisper reached Havyn's ears.

That wasn't quite the word she would use. In fact, she was pretty sure that God never intended the human body to move quite like that.

"They're nearly *naked*." Whitney's whisper matched the disapproval on her face.

Applause and cheers erupted as the girls took a bow.

And then a short and pudgy man came through the curtain. Pulling three rings from behind his back, he showed them to the audience and then began to juggle. Another ring flew at him from the side of the stage. He deftly added it into the juggling mix. Then another. And another. Pretty soon, a large rubber ball was bounced toward him, and he proceeded to kick it up and bounce it on his knee while standing on the other foot and juggling all the rings.

The audience loved it.

At least he was fully dressed. The thought of the man coming out as scantily dressed as the girls made Havyn giggle. The audience of mostly men wouldn't have been nearly as enthralled.

The next entertainer walked to the center of the stage with her head down. She wore a stunning dress—the skirt was layers upon layers of some gauzy material. It hovered around her ankles in a great bell shape, while the top was tight and looked like a corset. It didn't even have sleeves. Underneath the skirt, they could all see a pair of pink satin shoes with ribbons wrapped around the woman's ankles.

The crowd hushed and many leaned forward as they waited for the young woman to do something. Then she lifted her arms and the music started.

Ah . . . she was a dancer.

She lifted up onto her toes, and the crowd gasped. A ballet dancer! Havyn had never seen one before. Such grace and elegance as the young woman moved about the stage. The music—played on a phonograph somewhere behind her—sounded like a full symphony orchestra. It was so familiar. And then it hit her. "It's Tchaikovsky," she whispered to John.

"You mean the music she's dancing to?"

"Yes. It's from *Swan Lake*."

"Oh. I don't think I've ever heard it before."

The music overwhelmed her senses as the dancer floated around the stage. Havyn didn't even want to blink.

It ended all too soon. Havyn took a deep breath. Now *that* was something she could watch for an entire evening. It was so . . . beautiful.

When the dancer left the stage, the pudgy man returned. Disappointment filled her. She wanted to ask them to bring the graceful dancer back.

But no. The man was back. This time with a box. For the next twenty minutes, he entertained them with magic tricks. If you could call it entertainment. Apparently a lot of the spectators thought it was.

She stifled a yawn. While the show was lively enough, she couldn't imagine sitting through something like this every night. Especially when there were so many chores to do at home.

The booming voice returned. "It's time for our intermission, folks. But make sure you are back in your seats in fifteen minutes."

The audience stood and moved around. She and John greeted a few friends from church and from the Roadhouse.

Mr. Cahill—their nearest neighbor—laid a hand on John's shoulder and smiled at her. "While this has been fun, I must say that nothing can hold a candle to your wife and her sisters."

John beamed a smile. "I quite agree, sir."

"Thank you, Mr. Cahill. Please tell Emily that I said hello." Havyn followed her husband and squeezed his arm as they walked among the crowd. "You *have* to agree with the man, you're my husband."

"No, I don't. I have to be honest. And you three"—he shot a look over her shoulder to Whit and Maddy—"are the very best. Your music is entertaining and moving. You are always adding new pieces and mesmerizing the crowds. So, yes, nothing can hold a candle to you. And I'm not just saying that because I'm partial. I'm saying it because it's the truth." He glanced around as if to make sure no one overheard him. "And you three do it with your clothes intact."

Havyn laughed out loud, causing everyone in a nearby radius to go silent and look at them as if they'd interrupted a Scripture reading. John grinned and rolled his eyes heavenward, which didn't help matters at all.

He led her back to their seats as the crowd began to quiet.

Whit leaned over and whispered in her ear. "I'm not sure what that was all about, but I'm ready to go home anytime. The ballet dancer was good, but let's hope the rest of this keeps me awake. My dogs will want to run at four tomorrow morning whether I've had enough sleep or not."

"I know." Havyn kept her words hushed. "Hopefully it will be over soon."

They all clapped as a tall and lanky man dressed in a fine suit walked to center stage. He stood for several moments while the crowd got so quiet, Havyn could hear herself breathing. Then as everyone seemed to be on the edge of their seats, he began to sing.

> "She is far from the land where her young hero sleeps,
> And lovers are round her, sighing;
> But coldly she turns from their gaze, and weeps,
> For her heart in his grave is lying.
>
> She sings the wild song of her dear native plains,
> Every note which he loved awaking;
> Ah, little they think, who delight in her strains,
> How the heart of the minstrel is breaking.
>
> He had lived for his love, for his country he died,
> They were all that to life had entwined him;
> Nor soon shall the tears of his country be dried,
> Nor long will his love stay behind him.
>
> O, make her a grave where the sunbeams rest,
> When they promise a glorious morrow;
> They'll shine o'er her sleep, like a smile from the west,
> From her own loved island of sorrow."

As he held out the last note, sniffles were heard throughout the crowd. Havyn couldn't resist looking around her. Handkerchiefs were in hand throughout the crowd. So the advertisement was true. The tenor definitely made everyone teary.

As gentle applause swept through the crowd, many people stood on their feet and wiped at their eyes.

Then the man held out his arms to quiet the crowd. And silence enveloped them once again.

After a very long and dramatic pause, he started again.

> "Did they dare, did they dare to slay Owen Roe O'Neil?
> Yes, they slew with poison him they feared to meet
>   with steel.
> May God wither up their hearts! May their blood cease
>   to flow!
> May they walk in living death, who poisoned Owen
>   Roe!"

The music hit Havyn in the chest. She'd always loved playing this piece on the violin but had never heard the words before. While it had a poignant melody, the lyrics were so . . . dark.

She closed her eyes and envisioned herself playing the violin, but the lyrics kept haunting her.

> "We thought you would not die—we were sure you
>   would not go,
> And leave us in our utmost need to Cromwell's cruel
>   blow—
> A sheep without a shepherd, when the snow shuts out
>   the sky—
> Oh! Why did you leave us, Owen? Why did you die?
>
> Soft as woman's was your voice, O'Neil! Bright was
>   your eye,
> Oh! Why did you leave us, Owen? Why did you die?
> Your troubles are all over, you're at rest with God on
>   high;
> But we're slaves, and we're orphans, Owen! Why did
>   you die?"

Once again applause erupted throughout the area. Accompanied by plenty of sniffing and clearing of throats.

One thing she could compliment Mr. Merrick on, he knew how to throw a variety show together. There was a little bit of everything to keep people entertained. But out of all of it, Havyn only wanted to see the ballerina again. The beauty and grace of her dance—along with the music—had stirred her soul. That was real talent.

While the crowd continued to applaud, a group of young ladies, also scantily dressed in chorus-girl attire, ran across the stage. They sang a fast tempo song with silly lyrics, all the while kicking their skirts up with their legs. This brought out a bit more raucous behavior from the men in the audience than Havyn appreciated.

John leaned toward her. "I'll go get the wagon ready."

"Good idea. Thank you. I don't think I can take much more of this." She tugged on Whit's sleeve as John left. "I think we should go."

"I couldn't agree more." Whitney poked Madysen and tugged at their younger sister's sleeve.

As they ventured into the aisle between the chairs, the song ended and the crowd cheered again.

Someone was speaking to the crowd and saying good night, but Havyn didn't slow. The sooner they could leave, the better.

NINE

Madysen climbed up into the wagon next to Whitney. "Whew. I'm glad that's over." Her older sister leaned back on the bench seat.

Havyn laid a hand on her husband's arm on the back of the seat in front of them. She looked over her shoulder at them. "Me too."

Madysen furrowed her brow. "I thought it was quite wonderful. Didn't you enjoy it?"

Havyn turned in the seat to fully face her. Then she glanced at Whit. "Well, I really enjoyed the ballerina. And the tenor wasn't bad either."

"But the skimpy costumes on those girls at the end were, quite frankly, scandalous." Whitney never did mince words.

"It's not like they walk around dressed like that all the time." Madysen tried not to sound like a petulant child. "It's a show. An act. Nothing more. And it looked like they were having fun entertaining the crowd." It was time her sisters took her seriously. She was an adult and entitled to an opinion.

"It's one thing to entertain with music or dance, but to be immodest and bawdy? I don't think that's necessary." Havyn turned toward the front again.

Madysen couldn't allow her sisters' opinions to be the last

word. "John, what did you think? Didn't you think the dancers were entertaining?"

He kept his gaze forward. "To be honest, Maddy, it made me uncomfortable. That's why I left to get the wagon. I don't believe it's right for a man to be looking on women who aren't dressed appropriately. It could cause impure thoughts. The Bible tells us that we are to guard our minds, and I aim to do that. It's different for you because you're a lady. But you must remember that men are often tempted by what they see."

"But what about the ballerina? Her attire wasn't all that modest either. At least at the top." Madysen tapped Havyn's shoulder. "And you said you really enjoyed it."

"I did. And you're right. It wasn't the most modest outfit, but I can see how constricting sleeves would be for her. Her performance was lovely."

"So why was hers lovely and the others' not?"

Havyn let out a long sigh. "That's a good question, Maddy, it is. But I think it's all about the intent. What the ballerina did was beautiful and graceful. It wasn't trying to entice anyone to look at her a certain way. . . ."

"But you're saying the chorus girls at the end had an ill intent?"

"Madysen Eleanor Powell." Whitney's tone sounded almost like Mama's. "That's not at all what Havyn was saying. But you have to admit that the atmosphere was different around the different performers."

Madysen crossed her arms over her chest. "But God doesn't look on the outward appearance, He looks at the heart. And I think it is completely unfair of you to judge the hearts of those women. I wouldn't mind learning to dance and travel the world performing."

The shocked looks on her sisters' faces wasn't quite what she was hoping for. But it did shut them up about the entertainers.

Was she wrong to think that it was okay for those girls to be dressed in risqué costumes so they could perform on stage? The more she thought about it, the more she cringed. She wouldn't want to wear something like that. She would feel exposed.

Maybe that was the point that Havyn and Whitney were trying to make.

So why did she argue so adamantly with them? Because her temper got the better of her? Or simply because she wanted them to start letting her opinion matter?

Silence reigned in the wagon as they reached their farm.

John helped each of them down. "I'll put the wagon and horses away."

"I'll get some tea going, and we can all sit in the parlor together." Havyn wrapped her shawl a little tighter around her shoulders and went inside the house.

Whitney stopped beside Madysen. "I'm not sure what's going on in that cute little mind of yours, Maddy, but I'm sorry we came across so judgmental earlier. That wasn't our intent. I hope you know that."

She wrapped an arm around Whit's waist and walked side by side with her. The bleating of sheep and the mooing of cows accompanied them as they strolled to the house. "I do. I just hope you are willing to listen to my hopes and dreams."

"Of course we are, silly. We're your sisters. And we love you more than anything."

Havyn greeted them at the door. And not with a smile. "Amka just told me that Dad is here. Talking with Granddad."

Whitney let out a huff. "All right. It's time we handled this head on."

"Whit—"

Their older sister held up her hand. "I'd appreciate it if you all would come with me."

Madysen glanced at Havyn and prayed that Whitney wouldn't say anything she regretted. Not that she was particularly excited about seeing their father either, but Whit could be fierce.

When they entered Granddad's room, both men raised their eyebrows. But Granddad held up a hand. "I"—he pointed to his chest—"him come." His words were few and far between because speaking still took so much effort, but hopefully Whit got the point.

"You asked him to come?" Whit put her hands on her hips. "Why?"

The two men looked back and forth between each other. Pages littered the bed. They'd obviously been talking for a good bit of time.

Dad took a deep breath and spoke up. "Chuck asked me to forgive him."

"Forgive *him*? For what?" The words flew out of Madysen's mouth before she could think.

"What on earth do you need to forgive *him* for?" Whit's posture stiffened. Shoulders up, chin raised. She wasn't about to let this be explained away.

Dad's face fell. Such weariness in his eyes. He seemed . . . defeated.

Granddad grunted and flailed his left hand. "Go . . . go . . . on." He wrote something down and handed it to their father.

Dad read, "'I need you all to sit down and please hear me out.'"

Madysen sat on the edge of Granddad's bed and took his hand, while Havyn sat in the chair next to him.

"Do we need to wait for John?" Havyn's voice lifted on the end. She was nervous.

"Don't worry, I'm here." John entered the room and went to his wife's side.

They all looked at Whitney.

"I'll stand, thank you." Arms straight at her sides, there was no mistaking the rigid set of her body.

Dad shook his head and fidgeted with his hands in his lap.

Maddy didn't think they could take much more. They had

been through so much the past few months. *Please, God. Help us to work through whatever this is.*

Why was Dad taking so long?

Another groan from Granddad.

Dad lifted his head and looked at him. "First off, Chuck, I want to say that, yes, I forgive you. It was my fault that this happened the way it did in the first place, so I need to carry the blame too." Then he looked at each of them, sorrow filling his eyes.

Madysen had the urge to cry, but she wasn't sure why.

"Chuck asked me to forgive him because the divorce agreement he had me sign all those years ago wasn't legal."

Havyn gasped.

Madysen frowned. What did *that* have to do with anything?

Dad went on. "Your mother never signed the papers. Chuck did. I should have realized that might have been the case because I knew he planned to tell Melly that I was dead. This means my marriage to Esther was illegal and my other children are illegitimate."

"They were illegitimate to begin with!" Whitney's words cut through the room like a knife. "Didn't this other woman have them while you were still married to *our* mother?"

As much as Madysen agreed with her sister's words, she couldn't help but flinch. Were any of them prepared to deal with this?

To his credit, Dad didn't lash out. "I know what you all think of me and what I did. I'm sorry. But I *did* straighten out my life. I married Esther. She was a good woman. Please. My other children don't know any of this. I need to tell them the truth, and that is going to be very difficult."

"So you're leaving again? Just like that?" Madysen spat the words and then clenched her jaw to keep the other angry words she wanted to say lodged in her throat. But it didn't work. "Fine. Go back to Colorado and take care of the children you obviously wanted more than us. Then we won't have to see you, and that's fine with me."

"Maddy!" Havyn got up from her chair.

Dad stood and held out a hand. "No. I deserved that. You three don't know me, and that's my fault. But no, I'm not going back to Colorado. I wasted enough years and missed out on too much with you all, so I'm staying in Alaska. For good. I'm your father, and I hope that one day you can forgive me, and we can get to know one another."

Havyn laid a hand on Madysen's shoulder. "What about your other kids?"

Madysen needed her sister's touch, and the anchor it gave her, because nothing made sense anymore. She reached up and grabbed Havyn's hand. Closing her eyes, she waited for what their father would say.

"I've sent for them. Ruth, Esther's sister, has arranged for her mother to stay with her children for the winter so that she can come up here and help me look for her husband. She's on her way now and is bringing Bethany and Eli with her. Matthew is in college, but I pray that one day you can meet him too."

A punch to the gut would have been more pleasant than the news Dad just shared. His other kids were coming here? They'd be a constant reminder that he hadn't been faithful to their mother. That he'd loved another woman. And *their* kids.

More than he'd ever loved them.

"I'm not sure we need to meet them anytime soon." Whitney's tone was a bit softer, but the intensity of her gaze meant they should all give her space to think this through.

Havyn squeezed Madysen's hand.

Dad took another long, deep breath. "Well, you're going to meet them. I asked Chuck if Bethany and Eli could stay here at the farm while I go look for Stan."

She and her sisters spoke at the same time. "*What?*"

Whit stepped forward, her hands fisted at her side. "Now wait just a minute—"

"No!" The emphatic word came from Granddad. Spittle ran down his chin.

Madysen reached over with a hankie and wiped it up while Granddad grabbed for his paper and pencil.

They stood in awkward silence while he wrote.

This is my house, and I told him they could stay here so they'll be safe. Do this for me. Please.

Whitney stormed out of the room.

Dad looked at Madysen, and his gaze bore through her. "I won't be staying here, if that's your concern. But I do hope that one day we can all get to know each other again."

He stood and walked out of the room.

John looked down at them. "I'll see him out."

"This is not going to be easy. For any of us." Havyn plopped down next to Madysen.

Madysen leaned her head on her sister's shoulder. "Those poor kids. Their lives are about to be turned upside down."

TEN

There were days that Madysen wanted to hug and love on every one of her sheep.

Today was not that day.

Looking at the field, she put her hands on her hips. Not only had they jumped a fence and gotten into the manure pit, but they'd also torn up several patches of grass and trampled through the weeds, which, of course, had little burrs on them that were now stuck to the sheep's wool coats.

Which was exactly why they'd kept the sheep out of this particular field. And why it was so tedious to prepare a field for sheep. If only she'd stolen a herd of cattle. Cows weren't so high maintenance.

Well, she couldn't do anything about that now. Besides, she loved her little critters. But somehow she had to get all of the sheep back into the other field. Then they'd have to be cleaned up. How exactly was she supposed to get burrs out of their wool anyway?

"Dumb sheep." She shook her head at them. As soon as she spoke, they all started heading toward her. *Now* they obeyed.

"You've made quite a mess of things, haven't you?" The little crowd of sheep around her grew. Along with the noise. Such a talkative group of animals. Though, what did she know? Maybe all sheep were this noisy.

She started counting heads and looked toward the other field. To get them there, she'd have to herd them all the way around to the gate. Which would take some time. But they'd never follow her back over the fence. Besides, she didn't want them thinking that it was okay to jump the fence.

She'd have to speak with John about building the fence higher. This field had been used for cows before. Cows didn't do anything crazy like jump fences. They just stuck their heads through the rails to eat the grass on the other side.

Madysen was the one who had wanted these sheep. What kind of harebrained idea was that anyway? What had she been thinking?

"Oh, great." She lost count. Probably shouldn't let her mind wander when she needed to focus. Starting again, she counted out loud in a singsong voice so that the sheep would stay near. For some reason, whenever she spoke or sang, they stuck close by.

One was missing. And she'd counted twice.

She glanced around the field. Better to get the sheep around her back into the appropriate field. Then she could look for the missing one.

It took a good half hour to get the sheep back into a pen, where she was sure they couldn't jump the fence. Best to keep them corralled until she got them cleaned up anyway.

A lot of bleating followed her as she walked away. They weren't happy that she left them. Or that she took them from the new field. Either way, they would have to stay put. One particular ewe began pitching more of a fit. Was its baby the one that was missing?

She went back to the field she'd found them in and searched. She even called out. But she didn't see a lamb anywhere.

The last place to look was the manure pit. Oh, joy. It rained this morning. And the sheep had already made a mess out of the pit.

The stench greeted her first. Good thing she was raised on this farm. Otherwise, she might've lost her lunch.

The pit was huge. As she circled it, she kept calling out.

Baaaaaaa.

The bleat was weak. Where had it come from?

She moved to the north end of the pit and crept to the edge. "Are you here? I can't find you."

Then she saw it. A manure covered blob moving in the deepest part of the pit.

It *was* one of the babies!

Lifting the bandana off her neck and up over her nose and mouth, Madysen took a deep breath and stepped into the muck. As she'd expected, the rain had turned it into a slimy, smelly pond. Her boots and sealskin pants could handle it. Hopefully. The poor little lamb would drown if she couldn't get to it. She'd sacrifice her clothing if she had to.

Squishing her way through the nastiness, she continued to talk to her sheep, hoping and praying it could move toward her voice. But it could barely keep its head above the sludge. The stench permeated the bandana, and for a moment, Madysen gagged.

Focus on the goal. Focus on the need.

She closed her eyes for a half beat of her heart, then set out again.

"Come toward me, little one. I'll help you out. Just come toward my voice."

Moving through the mess took every muscle in her body. But the closer she got to the lamb, the farther away it moved. Why was it going the wrong direction?

Could it not hear her anymore? Or were its eyes filled with so much muck that it couldn't see?

Up to her knees in the filth, she tried to move against the suction each step produced. Reaching for all she was worth, she tried to get ahold of the lamb's head. Another step. Two. Then the head disappeared under the thick, black sludge.

"No!"

She lunged for it and got hold of its neck. As she tugged it toward her, she felt movement. *Thank you, Lord!* Then she finally had the lamb in her arms. She tried her best to wipe the mess from its nose and eyes and held it close to her chest. Her clothes would probably need to be burned after this, but at least she got to the lamb in time.

A very small and tiny bleat came from the lamb as it rested its head on her shoulder.

It melted her heart.

"Do you need some help?" The voice from behind her made her jump, and she slipped and fell onto her backside.

The miry goo splatted all around her, and she felt some of it land in her hair as she began to sink.

Closing her eyes against the nastiness that covered her from head to toe, she growled rather than say the words that wanted to burst forth.

Footsteps sounded around the pit.

"I am so sorry. I didn't mean to scare you. Just wanted to help. That's all."

Who on earth was that? She opened her eyes and spied none other than Granny's grandson, Daniel.

What was *he* doing here?

"Please." Daniel stepped toward Madysen. "Let me help you." He reached out a hand. The smell was worse than almost anything he'd ever encountered, but he couldn't leave her there. Especially since it was partially his fault that she was in such a bad state.

Since she held a wriggling lamb in her arms, it was quite a feat for her to get to her knees. Then she slowly got up on one foot, then the other.

A quiver shook her shoulders. "This. Is. Disgusting."

"I know. I'm sorry. Again." Thank goodness he put on an old pair of boots this morning. He'd ventured out to the Bundrant farm thinking he might walk about the place with John and offer his insight. Then he spotted Madysen.

She took a slow step through the sludge about five feet from him. It was high up on her legs. It must take incredible strength to move through it.

He reached toward her. Not quite. "See if you can take another step toward me. I'll grab the lamb."

"Okay. But then you'll be covered in this mess too."

"Don't worry about me. Clothes will wash."

Her shoulders rose as she took a deep breath and nodded, moving ever so slowly forward a step. "I don't know. . . . This might not *ever* wash out." She leaned forward and stretched out the lamb to him. "Can you grab her?"

He reached and got hold of the slippery animal. Setting the lamb on the grass, he wasn't surprised to see it lie down. It was probably exhausted from trying to escape the pit.

He turned back to Madysen. "All right, reach out to me, and I'll pull you the rest of the way."

She nodded and reached her arms and torso toward him.

Daniel took hold of her arms and pulled.

Her left leg came toward him, but then she looked down at her other leg. "Umm, I think I'm stuck."

"On what?"

She gave him an exasperated look. "I don't know. It's not exactly like I can see through this stuff. I just know my leg won't move."

Great. "Maybe I need to pull harder."

"Whatever you do, do it quick. I don't know how much longer I can keep my breakfast from coming back up."

He laughed. "I'm struggling with the same dilemma, so let's get you out of there."

Daniel pulled with all his might—but she didn't budge. He, on the other hand, slipped and fell into the mire.

Madysen giggled behind her bandana. Then she held up a hand. "I'm sorry. I shouldn't laugh. Really. But now I know what I must look like."

He worked himself back to standing and couldn't help but laugh with her.

She managed to take a step toward him with her right leg, but now her left leg didn't budge. "Now I'm really in a bind." With her arms outstretched, she shook her head. "You're just going to have to pull hard, or I'll be stuck here forever. I can't hold this position for long, and *please* don't let me fall again."

Daniel wiped as much of the manure off his hands as he could, leaned forward, and grabbed her arms. But he couldn't get a grip. "Can you get ahold of my shirt sleeves?"

"Um, I can try."

"Just dig in with your fingers—you won't hurt me—and I'll do the same. I'll do my best not to hurt you."

"At this point, I don't care. Just get me out."

"All right. Hold tight. On the count of three. One . . . two . . . *three!*" He gritted his teeth and pulled.

A wet, sucking sound—and then he was falling backward. With a lot of force.

Madysen squealed. "My boot!"

They landed with a thud and a splat.

"Ewwwwww."

"My thoughts exactly." He got up and held out a hand to help her. "I think I've had enough manure experience for a lifetime."

"Me too." Once she was on her feet, she looked down at them. "My boot has become a permanent part of the manure pit."

"I'd like to be a gentleman about it, but sorry, I'm not going in after it."

She sputtered and then laughed. Louder and louder. "Would you look at us?"

"Yeah. It's pretty bad."

"What are you doing here anyway?" She shook out her arms and legs and drops of black muck flew everywhere.

"Well, I thought I'd come and check out your farm. See how I could help."

"Well . . . you *helped*. I'll give you that." Her eyes sparkled.

Maybe she wasn't too miffed at him. "I'm sorry. Truly I am, I didn't mean to startle you."

Her hearty laugh echoed through the air. "Don't worry about it. This is life on a farm." She picked up the lamb. "But I do have one request."

"All right."

"Promise me you won't say a word of this to anyone. Ever."

It was his turn to laugh. "As long as you promise the same." He stuck out his manure-covered hand.

She took it, and their hands squished as they shook on it. "Deal."

ELEVEN

What a mess. An absolutely, disgusting, nasty, horrific mess. There weren't even enough words in the dictionary to describe how bad she smelled. Not to mention how she must look.

Poor Daniel had excused himself and said he would find a remote place to clean up. She couldn't imagine him walking too far with the stench she herself faced. Madysen carried the lamb to the pond on the east side of their farm. There was no way she could go anywhere near the house like this. The pond wasn't used for anything, so she didn't feel bad for rinsing in it. Granddad hadn't fenced in any fields by the pond yet. He always said some things were just nice to look at. Though it wouldn't be pretty once she was done.

Looking around, she made sure none of the workers were near. At the edge of the water, she took off the one boot she had left and dunked it in the water. Brrr. It was chilly. Her one saving grace was the fact that the sun shone high and had warmed the day a considerable amount. But the walk to the house would be cold and miserable. With a breath, she clenched her jaw. Freezing on the way home was better than smelling like this. She carried the lamb into the pond and worked at getting it clean. At first, the animal didn't appreciate the cold water and wriggled around, but then it calmed down as she kept working her fingers through its wool.

Once the lamb was as clean as a pond-rinsed lamb could get, Madysen tucked it under one arm and began rinsing herself. She started with her head and dunked it back. How glorious to feel the water wash away the grime.

Once she got her face, neck, and hair clean, she swished herself, fully clothed in the water. Then moved over a few feet to cleaner water and did it again. Then again. And again. Until she rounded the pond two times. She was nowhere near clean, but it would have to do until she could get a bath. Hopefully she could get in the house quickly and get one drawn before anyone saw her.

Then she'd probably have to wash her clothes with enough soap for ten tubs of laundry to have even a chance at getting them clean.

She took the long route around the farm to deposit the lamb back in the pen and avoid seeing anyone. It was quite possible she looked like she had drowned, and she didn't want her sisters to worry. But if she got too close to anyone, they'd definitely smell her.

Lord, please help me get to the house quickly without anyone seeing me. Please.

As she rounded the corner of the house, she spotted a carriage that wasn't theirs parked near the front door. She stopped in her tracks, then rushed to hide behind the salmonberry bushes. Surely, they didn't have important visitors *today*? With a sigh, she peeked around the bush. No one seemed to be around.

She scurried to the side door.

"Madysen?"

Judas Reynolds's shocked voice made her freeze.

Whit's motherly tone was next. "What on earth happened to you?"

She didn't dare look, just blurted out, "Sheep . . . manure

. . . pond . . ." What was wrong with her? She couldn't even string a sentence together.

Havyn came out the door at that very moment. Her eyes widened.

Madysen held up a hand. "Not a word. Please. I need a bath."

"Of course." Havyn kept her voice low and looked over Madysen's shoulder. "We'll meet you all in the parlor a little later."

"That would be lovely."

A voice she didn't recognize.

Great. How many people were there to see her in this condition? Heat crept up her neck. She walked with her sister to the bathroom. "Do I even want to know who is here?"

"Judas brought Mr. Merrick out this morning. Apparently, the man was quite taken with our performance and, after meeting us, wanted to get to know us better." Havyn started to fill the large tub with the pump and then set water on the stove in the corner to boil.

Madysen couldn't have been more thankful that Granddad built this room especially for bathing. With four women in the house, it'd been imperative. Or so he said. She would never again take for granted the fact that she could so easily take a bath.

"While the timing of their arrival wasn't the greatest, I had to at least offer refreshments, so I came in to fix tea and sandwiches. But Whitney stayed outside with them to show them around." Havyn made a face. "Albeit reluctantly. You know how she gets when she's focused on her dogs. But it was Judas, and she seems to have a soft spot for him."

Madysen swiped a hand down her face. "I can't believe they saw me like this. I'm so embarrassed."

"Want to tell me what happened?"

"Not particularly. Maybe later. I'll just say that you should be thankful you are in charge of chickens."

"Hey, I helped you steal those sheep." Her older sister winked as she poured steaming water into the tub.

Madysen pulled a face at her. "It wasn't stealing. I prefer to think of it as saving their lives."

They shared a look, and Madysen couldn't resist laughing.

Havyn covered her nose and mouth. "You smell atrocious. Let's get you in that tub."

"I know. I can't tell you how many times I gagged. But please, hurry. Help me get cleaned up."

After more than an hour of soaking, scrubbing, and dousing herself with perfume, Madysen at least *felt* a little cleaner. But the smell seemed to be stuck in her nose.

"We better get to the parlor. You know Whit is not one to socialize for very long." Havyn tugged her arm.

"All right. Can you still smell it?"

"No. We drenched you in rose water, so there's no chance of that."

"I wish I could smell the rose water, but it still smells like there's manure up my nose." She scrunched up her face.

Havyn took several steps ahead of her and entered the parlor. Madysen followed and took inventory of the room. Her brother-in-law sat with their guests, but Whit was nowhere to be seen. She must have had her fill of small talk.

"John, I'm so glad you could spend some time with our guests." Havyn was back in hostess mode. Which was good because Madysen was weary from the struggle in the pit and the cleaning process.

"Of course. Whitney needed to get back to her dogs, so I took over the tour from there." He smiled at the men.

John really was wonderful. Not just for Havyn either. He was amazing with Granddad and taking care of the farm. Madysen couldn't have asked for a better husband for her sister. "Hello, everyone." She lifted her chin and walked over to the men. "I apologize for my earlier appearance. There was an issue with my sheep." Hopefully that explanation would suffice.

Mr. Merrick made a beeline for her. He stopped in front of her, grabbed her hand, and kissed it. "It is such a pleasure to see you again, Miss Powell."

"It's . . . ah . . . nice to see you too." She'd never been greeted in such a manner. The feel of his lips on her hand, the way he looked at her . . .

It made her feel fluttery.

Judas took his seat, leaned back in his chair, and crossed his legs. "Buddy here wanted a chance to tell you once again how much he enjoyed your performance. So as a friend of the family, I told him I could oblige. I hope that didn't put you in too much of a bind."

"Not at all." Havyn took a seat next to her husband. "We're glad that you were able to come visit us."

Madysen took a seat as well and studied Mr. Merrick. He was a handsome man, even if he was a good deal older. She could still feel the kiss on the back of her hand, and it made her heart pick up a beat.

Mr. Merrick sat again and perched on the edge of his seat. "I have to say, Mr. Reynolds was gracious to bring me out here, but I had an ulterior motive. You three are the most talented group of musicians I've ever had the opportunity to hear. And I can tell you that I've heard my fair share of fine performers. You could make a fortune if you came with me to the States to perform."

"Mr. Merrick, that is a high compliment." Havyn smiled at their guest. "But our home is here. Besides, we aren't performing to make money. We love it and love to help our friend Mr. Norris. He was there for us when times were challenging. That's what neighbors do, they help each other out."

Mr. Merrick put a hand to his chest. "I completely understand your loyalty and love your generous hearts, but I don't think you understand the type of opportunity I'm offering here."

The smile on Havyn's face looked a bit more forced. "Oh, I think we understand. Again, it is a wonderful offer, but we aren't interested. We could never leave Alaska or our grandfather."

Madysen couldn't believe her ears and watched the two volley words at each other, each getting a bit more intense as time went on. What was wrong with her sister? Didn't she grasp what an honor this was?

Enough. "Would it have to be all three of us?"

"What?" The shocked look on Havyn's face scared Madysen for a moment. Then she looked at Mr. Merrick.

"Of course not. Although the three of you together are incredible, even just one of you could become the next great star of the stage." His grin widened. "Bigger than Jenny Lind or Evangeline Florence."

"Madysen Powell!" Havyn switched into mother-hen mode. "You are not going to go traipsing around the country with a show that's filled with half-dressed women and a juggler! What about Granddad? And your responsibilities here? And your family? You must be joking."

Joking, was she? Wasn't it enough that her sisters bossed her around? She would not put up with them trying to take on the role of their mother. Especially since Mama had been so supportive and encouraging of their music. What was Havyn thinking to embarrass her in front of their guest? A man, no less, who was offering her a dream come true.

She lifted her chin and gave her sister a pointed look. "Let's not insult Mr. Merrick. And please remember that I'm twenty-one years old and can do whatever I want." The second the words left her mouth, she realized how childish they sounded.

"Madysen!" Now John looked shocked.

She cringed. Had she gone too far?

The bell rang from Granddad's room.

Havyn stared at Madysen for a moment. "I better go check on him. We'll talk about this later. Privately."

Why did her sister have to make such a big deal out of this?

Judas turned to John. "I'd really like to hear about the cheese making you will be doing with the sheep. It sounds fascinating."

John looked at Madysen. Then back to their guest. Several seconds passed, as if he was debating within himself about which conversation to address. "Of course, what would you like to know?"

Madysen let out her breath and glanced at Mr. Merrick. Would he think less of her because of what Havyn said?

He moved to a chair closer to her. "I would give you a contract on the spot if you agreed to join me." His words were hushed and calm.

Her hand flew to her throat. "Mr. Merrick, while that's very flattering, I'd need some time to think and pray on it. I just wanted you to know that I might be interested."

"Then why don't you tell me more about yourself?"

"I will, but I'd like to know exactly what you're suggesting. I'm not willing to run around in my undergarments like those chorus girls."

"Of course not." He gave a shudder. "I would never suggest such a thing. Have you ever seen women singers perform?"

"Not exactly."

"Well, it would be quite sophisticated. You would wear Worth gowns of considerable fortune. Surely you've heard of Worth?"

She tried to contain her giddiness and not sound like a child. "Everyone's heard of Worth."

"Since Mr. Worth's passing in 1895, his sons have taken charge, and in many ways, I believe they have improved the line." Mr. Merrick smiled. "But just imagine it. You gowned in Worth— I'm envisioning a lavender silk creation with a beautiful hat of tulle and feathers—perhaps tiny roses. Or maybe you'd wear a tiara in your hair, which would be beautifully arranged. You'd have long, white gloves and jewelry—diamonds and pearls."

Madysen closed her eyes and did indeed imagine it. Wouldn't

it be a wonder to dress in such a fashion? "It's a lovely picture to be sure, but I can't very well play the cello with gloves."

"You are right, of course, my dear. The gloves could be removed for that portion of the program. Anyway, as I was saying, you would glide onto the stage, where an audience of thousands waited to pay you homage. The orchestra would start up, and you would begin to sing an aria that would leave them all in awe. Then after another number or two, you'd play your cello. The audience would go wild."

Madysen could see it clearly. Hadn't she dreamed it a thousand times? So what if she was usually with her sisters in those imagined performances? She had a good enough voice to sing solo and had done so on more than one occasion.

She opened her eyes and met his gaze.

His expression turned soft. Almost . . . intimate. "I'm quite good at figuring these things, Miss Powell. I believe you would be an overnight sensation, and I'm quite willing to put up the money to make that happen."

This man—this handsome and wealthy man—actually believed in her. In her talent. It did funny things to her. "You would do that for me?"

"It's my job to find talent and introduce it to the world."

She took a calming breath. She needed to be level-headed about all this. Ask good questions. As if she'd thought it through already. "Where would I perform?"

"Where *wouldn't* you perform?" He chuckled. "Miss Powell, I don't think you fully understand. I've traveled the world, and as I go about my business, men and women always approach me to be discovered. Some are quite good. Others should reserve their singing for Sunday services—or worse still, the outhouse."

Madysen put her hand to her mouth, and he laughed again. "You are such a sweet dear. But as I was saying, I know this business well, and I know true talent when I hear it. You and your sisters are quite amazing. I could give you an incredible career. You would make thousands upon thousands of dollars."

While the thought of fame and fortune was enticing, Mama's face took over her memory. "The money isn't nearly as important as being able to travel and use my music to honor our mother. She's the one who developed our gifts. She gave us each a quality education in music, and I want the world to know it."

"See there, you've already made my job easier. I'll be able to advertise you as 'Mother's Little Darling,' the girl who learned at her mother's knee only to lose her tragically at a young age."

She held up a hand. "Let's not lie, Mr. Merrick. She passed away only this summer."

"It's not a lie. I wouldn't stoop to such things. You are still quite young. People will be moved by that kind of thing, for everyone has a mother."

Madysen considered his words. He seemed like an honest man. Genuine in his love of music. "It's quite a lot to consider."

"Well, please do. I would love for you to come with us when we leave Alaska." He beamed her a smile. "Now, tell me more about your life here."

They sat and chatted for the good part of a quarter of an hour while John and Judas talked about cheese. How incredible to have a man show such attention to her. And he was a gentleman. He held her gaze and paid her compliments. The more they talked, the more impressive he became.

"I know this might seem silly." His voice had lowered again, and he darted a quick glance at the other men. "But you have completely mesmerized me. I think I've quite lost my heart to you."

"Mr. Merrick . . . I . . . I . . ." Had he really just said what she *thought* he said?

He reached over and patted her hand. "If I can feel this way, then I know thousands of others will feel the same. I would give up all the others in my show if you would come with me. I could make you a star."

A blush rose up in her cheeks. Could he?

"Mr. Merrick, are you ready?" Judas stood with John over by the door.

"Yes. Thank you." Mr. Merrick got to his feet and nodded at Madysen. "It was lovely. Until next time."

"Yes." *Flustered* was too tame a word for how she felt at the moment. Before she could say anything else, their two guests left.

John stared at her, his brow crinkled and eyes concerned. Was he worried about her still?

No matter. It had been a lovely afternoon. Buddy Merrick had made her feel alive and cherished. And she liked it.

TWELVE

Judas strolled over to the new doctor's office. All of the other docs were in his pocket. He just needed to get this one on board with how things were done in Nome. A couple of the docs did their best to avoid Judas, but they couldn't very well do that since his freighting service was the only reliable one. Of course, that was because he'd bought off anyone else who tried to start a freighting business. But that was beside the point.

Judas approached just as the new man was hanging a shingle outside his door. He raised his voice to be heard above the din. "Good evening, Dr. Cameron." Nome's streets were always chaotic nowadays. Day and night.

The man stepped down from a ladder. "Good evening to you as well. How may I help you?"

"Judas Reynolds." He stuck out his hand.

"Ah yes. The owner of the shipping company. I've heard lots about you. I'm Dr. Peter Cameron." The man offered a smile. Seemed genuine enough. "Would you like to join me inside?"

"Thank you." He followed the doctor into the small building that had once been that sniveling Herbert Winthrop's office. It really was too bad that a patient's father had shot the man dead in the street. But it saved Judas from having to clean up the mess the man had made. "I wanted to offer you a catalogue of medicines and supplies that I can provide you. You'll find that I choose the best to ensure we are well taken care of here in our fine city." Judas held out the catalogue. He studied the man. Perhaps Cameron could take over pawning the fake medicines. He looked trustworthy enough—and those were the best kind for con men.

But the doc didn't take it. He glanced down and looked back to Judas with a nod. "While I greatly appreciate the offer, Mr. Reynolds, I brought all the equipment that I needed with me. And I won't be using a lot of stock medicines. I'm a naturalist and have found herbs to be much more useful in curing my patients over time."

Maybe the man was testing him. Surely he wouldn't say no so quickly. "Oh, then perhaps I can provide you with a catalogue for the items you desire. I'll just need to contact my suppliers."

"Again, thank you very much, but I've already connected with Mr. Beaufort at the mercantile, as well as the natives in the nearby village. I will acquire herbs and other items through them. And I'll have a hothouse where I will be able to grow almost everything I need." He pointed to the crates in the corner. "As you can see, I have enough to get me through this next year, but I'm much obliged to you for coming by. It was nice to meet you." The doctor shook his hand again. "Should you ever need my skills, I would be proud to act as your doctor." He held out a hand, showing Judas the door.

Dismissed. Just like that. Not what he was accustomed to.

"That's quite kind." He pasted on a smile and changed his tone so it was tinged with warning. "I think you'll find that I'm a good man to call friend." The doctor needed to learn the chain of command.

"I believe it's good to call all men friends until they prove otherwise." Cameron walked Judas to the door this time. His actions making an emphatic statement. "Good evening, Mr. Reynolds."

"Good evening." So the man thought he could tell Judas no and be done with it. That wasn't how things worked around here. The good doctor just needed some coaxing to get into Judas's corner. If he knew what was good for him, he wouldn't take too long.

Never mind. The new doctor could wait. There were more pressing matters on his mind. Like what he was going to do about the Bundrant farm.

The visit today hadn't born any fruit, sadly. While he pretended the visit was about showing Merrick the farm, his real objective had been to check things out for himself. How had Roselli come in with all that gold and paid off the debts? He would have preferred the family stay beholden to him. Like almost every other person in Nome.

Did Chuck have that much gold lying around? Or were they finding more? Perhaps on Chuck's large acreage?

He'd teased John when he'd brought in the bag and asked if he'd been panning for gold. But the young man had simply laughed. "When would we have time for that?"

Judas wasn't fooled. That *had* to be the case. After all, Chuck's property had the river running through it, with plenty of other creeks and tributaries on it. No wonder the family had stumbled into gold.

It was only fair that Judas have part of it.

Or all.

The next morning, Judas studied Garrett Sinclair as he slouched in the chair across from his desk.

Judas leaned forward. "I have a new job for you. One that is going to require some planning and serious thought."

"Okay. Sure." The man shrugged his shoulders.

"Go get yourself cleaned up. Look respectable. Shave. Use your manners—I know you have them. And then find a way to get in at the Bundrant dairy farm. Find out if they're panning for gold out there."

"What makes you think a dairy farm has gold?" Skepticism showed all over Garrett's face.

"Because of this." Judas dumped the bag of nuggets onto his desk. "I'll give you half if you do this job well for me."

Sinclair sat up. "Sure thing, boss."

"Just remember, you need to figure out where the gold is coming from. Endear yourself to them, do whatever it takes. But don't cause any problems. Got it?" Sinclair was a handsome man. Surely he could get one of the girls to talk over time.

"Got it."

"Good. The family considers me a dear friend. They are devout churchgoers and honest people. Don't screw this up."

"Yes, sir." A sly grin filled his face.

Whitney sat at the kitchen table with Havyn. Her responsibility to steer their younger sister had grown heavier since Mama was gone. Madysen had barely said a word to either of them for two days and had gone to bed early.

It was troubling.

Whitney wrapped her hands around her mug of tea and shook her head. So far she wasn't doing a very good job of helping Madysen. "I can't believe it. I can't believe she would consider leaving."

"Something about that man seemed to almost bewitch her," observed Havyn. "It was strange, and when I said something, I came across as her bossy older sister who didn't want her to have any fun or follow her dreams. *Ever*." Havyn pinched the bridge of her nose. "I'm not that horrible of a sister, am I? I mean . . . I want her to follow her dreams. But I couldn't believe how protective I felt. We can't let her leave, right? John said he was worried because she talked to Mr. Merrick privately for a good while in the parlor. John was in there with them, but Judas wanted to know about the plans for making cheese, and so they ended up talking the whole time."

Whitney stared at her cup. They'd always been so close. And yes, they'd bossed each other around, but Mama always had the final say. What would *she* do in this situation? Whitney had no idea how to help Maddy. Her sister saw the world in vivid colors, while Whitney saw it in black and white.

"You're not a horrible sister. I probably would have been much, much worse. Madysen has always flitted from one thing to another. This is probably just a passing fancy. She's young." Would her words comfort Havyn? Because they weren't comforting her.

"For some reason, that makes me feel ancient. We're not that much older than she is, Whit." Havyn reached across the table and grabbed her hand.

The gesture was sweet, but for some reason, Whit felt nothing but guilt. Maybe if she were a better sister, a better example . . . If only she were more like Mama.

Logic seemed the only course of action. "I know, but she's the baby. Maybe we've encouraged this all these years because we have handled her with kid gloves. I'll talk to her tomorrow. After things have settled down. She was probably just flattered and didn't think it through." The thought of Maddy leaving them made her chest catch. Whitney didn't want the family to be split up. "Especially since Mama just passed. I can't imagine she'd be willing to leave everything and everyone she's ever known." She prayed it was true.

And feared it wasn't.

Havyn took a deep breath. "I don't know, Whit. She dreamed of playing and singing on bigger stages long before this. And you know how dramatic and flamboyant she can be. She loves people. And social events."

"But she also loves those sheep." Whit pointed over her

shoulder. "She's almost as bad with them as you are with your chickens."

"Hmph." Havyn gave her a look. "What about you and your dogs? You're pretty fierce when it comes to anyone helping with them."

"But that's different. I don't talk to them and name them and treat them like they are babies."

"Oh, you do too. I've heard you talking to them many times. And you've given *all* of them names!" Havyn narrowed her eyes as she laughed.

"Only because I'm training them, and they have to have names so they know who I'm giving the order to. Not because they are like dolls at a tea party." Her frustration came out with the barb. "My dogs work hard and may well save your life someday. I'd like to see your chickens do that."

"I'm going to ignore that because I know you're hurting, Whit." Havyn took a sip of tea. "My chickens might not pull a sled—although now that I think of it, wouldn't that be a wonder?" Havyn set her cup down and giggled. "Teams of chickens pulling little sleds."

"Good grief." Whitney tossed her head back, and some of her irritation melted away. Havyn was always good at calming the situation. And as much as she wanted to defend herself and her dogs, there really wasn't any difference. Other than the fact that she was much more serious about her work with the dogs. It wasn't like the chickens or sheep could pull a dog sled, despite Havyn's wild imagination. They couldn't provide transportation or help in an emergency like her dogs could.

"Admit it. You talk to your dogs just as much as we do with our animals. Even if you are more bossy." Havyn lifted her brows.

Was that a challenge? Well, Whitney couldn't deny it. She began to laugh. "You're right. I'm just as crazy as you two are."

Havyn reached across the table and grabbed her hand again.

This time she squeezed, and Whitney felt a surge of warmth. "You're the best of all of us, Whit. You're strong and loyal, smart and stubborn. You don't take anyone's guff. You get things done. You stand up for what you believe in, but—" she choked on her words—"Maddy's not like that. She's so full of tenderness. She'll be too naïve out in the world beyond our little town here. Something horrible could happen to her. We've got to stop this." Tears shone in her eyes.

Whitney didn't have a good answer. "How do we do that without pushing her away in the process?"

"Havyn," John called from the door. "I could use a hand. Can you spare some time?"

"Of course." Havyn got to her feet, then glanced back at Whitney. "Just think about it, sis. We need to figure out what to do."

Whitney dipped her chin. She'd been thinking a great deal already. Madysen was just one part of the problem. Granddad had made great strides, but he was never going to be the strong man he'd once been. And that changed all the plans at the farm.

And then there was their father. How could Granddad ask them to forgive their father and get close to him? Granddad had to know what an impossibility that was.

Her father. A drunk for as long as she could remember. Yes, he'd been lively and even fun when he was drunk. And he made big promises and plans. She'd clung to those promises like life rings. Every time he talked of them having a big house with a white picket fence and a garden, Whitney had believed. For herself and her mother. Mama always said how wonderful a garden would be. Wherever they lived, Mama and Whitney always tried to plant a few things to help with their food supplies. But mining towns had poor soil for growing anything.

There had been other promises as well. Promises to stop drinking, to settle down and get a good job rather than always looking for a way to get rich overnight. Whitney had often heard her parents talking late into the night. Usually her father was intoxicated, which made him particularly imaginative. Once—how old was she then? Five?—he talked to Mama about starting a cattle ranch in Texas. How they would buy a nice big piece of ground and get a small herd that they could breed and expand until they were one of the biggest ranches in the state.

Oh, how she'd believed that dream. She'd imagined them all having horses to ride. She used to fall asleep dreaming of that plan—certain that their father could make it happen. Even all these years later, it was still a dream in the back of her mind. But now it was her dream. Not one that came from a drunkard, whose promises meant nothing.

Walking out to where the dogs were, Whitney tried to push all her thoughts aside, but Dad kept coming back to mind. All he'd said and done over the years. Granddad had made his disdain for the man clear when she was young, and Whitney took on those feelings quite easily. With every broken promise—every lie and exaggeration—Whitney hated her father more. He was the reason for every unhappiness.

When they'd all thought he was dead, it was easier. Because he could be banished from her mind. But now he was back. And so were the memories and feelings.

As she approached the dog pen, the dogs' yips and barks brought her attention back to the present. They knew if Whitney was there, they might have a chance to run or eat. They wanted nothing more than her attention so that they could get their fair share.

Was that what Madysen was doing? Did she want her fair share of attention? Maybe they could let her perform solo more often. It wouldn't hurt to showcase their baby sister's talent more. And quite frankly, Whitney didn't mind a bit. She had lost the joy music had once given her.

All it did was remind her of her loss. How was she supposed to go on without Mama? They had been so close. Before Havyn and Madysen came along, it had been Whitney and Mama. They were never separated. No matter where her father dragged them off to, Whitney and Mama had been together. Her first lessons were on Mama's lap. She could read music before she could read letters. Music had been everything to Whitney because it was everything to Mama and it connected them. Now it was fading away. As if when Mama died, the music had died with her.

Whitney stared off across the yard, blocking out the sounds of the dogs. She had never felt more alone. Havyn was married, and no doubt she and John would one day have children. Madysen wanted to leave, and she'd probably never return if she did. Granddad was a broken man with a nearly impossible recovery to occupy him.

It was so strange. She'd always figured to stay single and care for Mama in her old age. Whitney started life with Mama and figured to spend the rest of her life with that precious woman. No one understood her like their mother. No one spoke wisdom that resonated better than their mother.

How could she be gone? And why did it have to happen so fast? They had no time to talk, to say good-bye.

Whitney bit her lip until she tasted blood. She wasn't going to cry. Never wanted to cry again. Without Mama, she had to shoulder the weight and responsibility of life on her own. Tears were wasted on sorrow. It brought no relief and granted no insight. Tears showed weakness and nothing more.

The dogs had worked themselves up into a frenzy. The only relief now would be to run.

"All right"—she went for the harnesses—"who's going with me?"

THIRTEEN

Emotions Daniel had buried while up in the Yukon now stirred as he headed out to the Bundrant farm. Memories flitted in and out.

Working with Mom on the old homestead . . .

Making cheese, the reward from their labor . . .

Working with the stubborn sheep . . .

It all brought a smile to his face.

For so long, he'd shoved the memories aside because they hurt. But something had changed. He couldn't help but want to assist the Powell family. Dad heartily encouraged it. Probably because he and Granny were determined to convince Daniel to stay in Nome.

At this point, it wouldn't take much to convince him to stay. Madysen was enchanting—even under the most disgusting of circumstances. For the first time in a long time, his heart didn't feel like a dead rock inside his body. The Yukon had made it easy to just avoid people. There he knew where he stood. Folks had only wanted him for one thing: his gold. If, on the slim chance that wasn't their focus, there was one other thing they might want: his ability to work. He'd done his fair share of that. When his search for gold came up empty, he tried his hand at just about anything else. He'd even built coffins and laid rails, but something always was missing.

He'd told himself it was the gold. Every man there had gold fever. It had worked its way into their souls, demanding they leave hearth and home for the unknown. But that wasn't why he went.

An old gold miner accused him of hiding. After Daniel shared his anger at God, the man spat at the ground.

"God don't exist in the Yukon." The man squinted. "The devil took up residence there to cool off from hell, and God let him keep it."

Those words resounded in Daniel's mind. Over and over. The Yukon had been a good place to hide from the memories of his family and their lives together.

And from God.

But far sooner than he anticipated, he didn't want that hard, cold heart. And now, he longed for family. Warmth. Hope.

Daniel flicked the reins of his horse. It didn't have anything to do with God. No need to ponder spiritual matters.

It would be nice to simply spend time with Madysen today and learn more about her. That is, if he had the chance to see her.

As he rode up to the sheep pens, his heart lifted when he spotted her kneeling on the ground, rubbing a sheep's belly.

"Good morning." He dismounted and stood there, holding the reins.

She peered over her shoulder. "Good morning to you." Her smile was just like her. Warm and genuine. Did she smile at everyone like that? Her wild curls were pulled back with a ribbon, but he loved how it all cascaded down her back.

Focus.

Fidgeting with the leather in his hands, he cleared his throat. "I came out to offer my assistance—meager as it might be— with the sheep. John mentioned in the store the other day that

I should stop by. My first attempt was a bit of a disaster, so I thought I'd better try again. To stop by. So I did." Why was he rambling? "So what are we up to today?"

Her laughter floated over to him. "How long did it take to get the stench out of your nose?"

"It's still there." He scrunched up his nose.

"Me too." She shook her head, curls bouncing this way and that. "Well, it's generous of you to sacrifice time for us. We really appreciate it." Madysen stood and took the towel from her shoulder and wiped off the sheep. "I'm sure we could learn a lot from you. I sent off for a book about raising sheep, but learning from someone who has actually done the job is so much better. How long are you here?"

For her? Forever. He cleared his throat. "I can stay all day if you need me to."

"Oh, well, in that case . . . we're not performing at the Road-house tonight, and I know John was hoping you could help us with some recipes. As well as any guidance you could give us on weaning, cheese making, or just sheep in general." She shrugged her shoulders. "I love the sheep, but I must admit I have a lot to learn."

Such sweet innocence.

She took off her work gloves. "Let me go get him."

"I'll walk with you." He wrapped his horse's reins around a fence post.

Walking side by side with her, he shortened his gait. She was a tiny thing, and his legs ate up far more distance than hers. "Have you made any cheese before? I can't remember if I asked."

"We have. We've made quite a bit of mozzarella. John was raised on a dairy in Italy, so he knew how to make that. My sisters and I have all gotten pretty good at it, but we need to learn about cheese from sheep's milk. Is it a lot different?" She clasped her hands in front of her as they walked.

Their conversation was easy. She felt like a longtime friend.

And he liked that. "I can't imagine that the process is entirely different, but I remember my mother saying that sheep's milk has more solids in it than cow's milk."

"What happened to her—if you don't mind my asking?"

He winced. Not exactly his favorite topic. "She and my grandpa both died of the cholera when I was sixteen."

Her head bobbed. "I'm sorry. I think I remember now that Granny mentioned it when she told me about her husband. I confess, I didn't think about your mother then."

"She was a wonderful woman."

Silence accompanied them for several moments.

"My mother was the only constant in my life . . . well, except for God." Her words were soft. "Granddad has been there for us, but it's not the same, especially since he hasn't been well. Mama was always there to hear about our day and quell our fears. We talked about everything with her. As we got older, she was our closest friend too. I don't know how she did it all. She was so encouraging . . . and now that's gone."

Here he was feeling sorry for himself, and he'd completely forgotten about her pain. "I'm sorry, Madysen. That was insensitive of me to talk about my mother."

"I brought it up." The half smile she gave him spoke of her sorrow. How was she so sweet with such grief weighing on her?

"Still, I should have been more conscious of it." He slapped his leg with his hand. "There are days that feel like she's been gone forever, and then on others it seems like just yesterday." He looked at her. Sorrow etched her face. Better change the subject and quick. "Tell me about playing at the Roadhouse. How'd that get started?"

"Granddad and Mr. Norris dreamed it up." She shrugged.

"Is that a heavy schedule for the three of you?"

"We love it so much, it doesn't feel like work. Although I must admit, we do get tired." There was a tint of sadness to her tone. "But my music reminds me of Mama."

"You are very talented. I've never heard anyone sing or play like you."

Her smile was back. "I want to keep performing, to honor Mama. I just keep thinking of all the places and people I could sing for. How I could tell them how my mother brought me to them—that it was her dream for me."

"Your mother wanted you to travel and perform?"

She frowned. "Well, not exactly. Her dream was for each of us to use our talents to serve God and bring joy to others."

"Serve God? Why would God care if you sang or didn't?"

"Well . . . I suppose He doesn't exactly care about what I do, so long as I serve Him."

He shook his head. "That's a bunch of hooey. Preachers talk about us serving so we'll help get things done at church or in the community, so they don't have to. I mean, imagine if the congregation stopped tithing and serving—the preacher and his family would have to do it all. And in the end, if God is all powerful, then He could just do it Himself and leave us to live our own lives."

Madysen stopped walking and placed her hands on her hips. "Daniel, do you not believe in God?"

Great. He'd said too much. Why'd he have to open his big mouth?

"Well?"

Her face held an expression he couldn't interpret. It wasn't judgmental and it wasn't pity. So what was she thinking? Could he be honest with her? Maybe he should try to smooth things over. "Of course, I do. I was just suggesting that maybe you should make the decision based on what makes you happy rather than what God wants. It's not like God doesn't know what's going to happen."

They walked for several seconds in silence. He must have offended her. He'd have to dig himself out of this one.

"You have an interesting way of looking at things, Daniel Beaufort." She didn't look at him.

"Does that mean you're not mad at me?"

Those wide eyes looked at him. "Why would I be mad at you? I like my friends to speak their minds."

Then why hadn't her smile come back?

"Good." Awkward silence accompanied their steps. "Oh, that reminds me. Granny asked if you wanted to come for lunch tomorrow."

"Let her know I'll be there." She looked in the other direction. "I've been needing to talk with her anyway."

His comments about God hung in the air like an ominous cloud. How did he get past this? He shoved his hands deep into his pockets. "I'm excited to work with sheep again. It's been a long time, and ever since John brought them up, I've been thinking about it."

"I thought you didn't enjoy the sheep." One side of her mouth lifted in a grin.

He grinned back, glad that she was letting his previous comments drop. "Ah, so you remember. Well, I might have been too hasty in my reply."

"Even after our debacle in the manure pit?"

He stopped, turned to her, and crossed his arms over his chest. "I thought we weren't ever going to talk about that again."

Her laughter filled the air and broke the tension. "You're right. I made you promise. But it should be okay between the two of us. That's not exactly something you can forget."

Opening the barn door for her, he couldn't help but let his smile grow. "No. I don't think I will ever forget that. Or the smell."

"I'm so glad you could come for lunch today." Granny pulled her best china out of the cupboard.

Madysen counted the dishes. "Will Daniel and his father not be joining us?"

Granny shook her head. "No. It's just us girls. The menfolk went off to deal with a new shipment."

"I'm glad." Oh dear. She hadn't meant to blurt that out. She looked at Granny to see if the woman was offended, but she just smiled.

"Sometimes it's nice to have some time for just the women-folk." Granny brought a tureen of soup to the table. "Given the chill, I thought this might warm our bones. I have sourdough bread too, and of course some of your butter. I hear tell we can expect cheese before too long."

"Yes, we're working on it." Madysen placed her napkin in her lap and waited for Granny to take her seat.

"I'll offer grace." Granny bowed her head. "Father, we thank you for food and shelter and the love of good friends, Amen."

"Amen." Better bring up the subject that wouldn't leave her alone before she lost her nerve. "Granny, I have a question to ask. What happened with Daniel and God?"

Granny's brow dipped as she buttered her bread. "You picked up on problems, did you?"

"We were talking about something, and I just got the impression that he wasn't . . . well . . . that maybe he didn't believe in God."

"Daniel believes all right, but he's angry. He has been since his mama and grandpa died. He was devastated to lose them, and he blamed God for allowing it. We had always stressed that God was in control of everything."

"He is."

Granny tilted her head and glanced out the window. "Yes, but to Daniel God being in control seemed to mean that, because we were Christians, we would always have a good life without problems. It was our fault for not helping him see early on that in a fallen world, bad things happen. Even to God's children. Do you know the verse, 'In the world ye shall have tribulation: but be of good cheer; I have overcome the world'?"

"John sixteen, verse thirty-three. Mama had us memorize that when we were living in Colorado."

"Yes, well, Daniel believed Jesus was telling us we could be of good cheer because nothing bad would touch us. So when his grandpa and mama died, it was clear to him that God had lied."

"How sad." Imagine thinking God would lie. He'd never lie to His children. He loved them more than anything.

"Maybe I shouldn't be telling this"—Granny shook her head—"but Daniel decided that God no longer cared, and because of that, he wouldn't care either."

"That makes sense. Well . . . not to believe that way, but his attitude makes sense. He must hurt an awful lot to push God away like that. For me, losing Mama made me cling all the more to God. And now . . . I think God is leading me in a way that I never expected."

"And what would that be, child?"

Madysen swallowed and drew a deep breath. "I think God wants me to perform for people, to honor my mother. With each performance, I would tell the people that my mother had taught me everything and that I was dedicating my performances to her."

Granny smiled. "I think that's a lovely idea."

"You do? Because I'm not sure anyone else will."

A frown furrowed Granny's brow. "Why in the world not? God gave you the talent, you should use it."

Madysen sat up straight and met Granny's gaze. "Because it means leaving Nome."

"Leaving? Why?"

"To sing on other stages. Maybe travel all over the world. Buddy Merrick believes he can make me a star. And what better way for me to honor Mother's memory? He wants me to go to the States with him—well not with *him*, but rather with the troupe."

Granny showed no sign of judgment, so Madysen continued.

"He wanted all three of us girls, but of course Havyn is married and Whitney . . . well . . . Whitney is Whitney. But I was intrigued. I've always wanted to perform for larger audiences, and Mr. Merrick believes that he can make that happen. He's very fond of me."

"I see." Granny took a bite of buttered bread.

"You can't say anything to anyone else, but he told me he was very taken with me. I think he might even be falling in love with me."

Granny ladled soup into Madysen's bowl. "And how do you feel toward him?"

"I'm not in love. I hardly know him. But I am thinking hard about what he's offering. We talked about it a few times, and he told me it wouldn't make me much money at first. He was very honest about the fact that he'd be putting up a lot of his own money to buy me gowns and to hire musicians to accompany me, as well as to pay advertising fees and the rent where I'd be singing and playing. He hasn't tried to tell me I'll be rich and famous overnight. But I wouldn't do it for the money anyway. I want to honor Mama and God."

"Well, it's all very interesting."

A slight lilt in Granny's voice told Madysen she didn't approve. "I wouldn't be traveling alone with Mr. Merrick. He has an entire group of performers, and many of them are young women. I haven't heard all the details of course, but I can't say it doesn't appeal to me. Especially when I think of playing music all over the world. Don't you think Mama would be proud?"

"Your mother was always proud of you, my dear. But she was also a very practical woman. I don't know that she would approve of you traipsing off with a group like Merrick's Follies and Frolics."

Her words hit Madysen hard. Of all people, she'd thought Granny would understand.

"My mother was practical—but she was also encouraging,

and she wanted the best for me. My sisters are caught up in what's best for them, and no one finds fault with that. Now that I find something that seems good for me, no one understands." Even to her own ears, she sounded whiny. But why couldn't anyone be on her side?

"Child, I understand." Granny leaned forward, leaning her elbows on the table and resting her chin on her hand. "But what about your father? You've just learned he's alive. Don't you want to know him better?"

"Why? So he can leave me again?" Madysen folded her arms against her chest. "I won't give him the opportunity. No, Granny, if anyone is going to do any leaving this time, it's going to be me."

"Well, well," Daniel walked into the dining area to find Madysen and his grandmother still sharing lunch. "I figured you two would be done by now."

Granny got up and started clearing her dishes. "We got caught up in conversation. How did things go with the new shipment?"

"Just fine. There's another boat coming on Friday." He looked at Madysen. "It might very well have part of your order."

"That would be wonderful." Madysen got to her feet. There was no sparkle in her eyes. No smile on her lips. "Thank you for lunch, Granny. I need to be going."

"Take some of my cookies home with you. I know your granddad would like them." Granny hurried to wrap cookies in a dish towel. "Send our best regards."

"I will."

Madysen didn't even look at his grandmother. What on earth happened? The tension between the two women was clear.

He caught Madysen's gaze. "Did you walk here?"

"No, I rode my horse."

"Perhaps I should ride along with you." Maybe it would allow him a chance to find out what was wrong.

"That would be wise." Dad came into the room, wiping his hands on his apron. "Looks like it's going to rain."

Madysen took the bundle of cookies Granny offered and nodded. "Thank you."

Daniel wasn't quite sure whom she was thanking, but he'd take it. "Great. Let me get the horse saddled. It'll only take a moment."

He hurried to the barn and threw on the blanket and saddle without much thought. A few minutes of time with Madysen would make his day brighter. It always did. She seemed to understand him, and while he wasn't sure what she thought of his comments on God, her kind nature seemed to make it impossible for her to treat anyone badly.

He brought the horse around front and found her waiting beside hers. "Ready?" He helped her up. She was as light as a feather.

Madysen eased her horse alongside his as he mounted. Daniel smiled to himself. "Did you and Granny have a good visit?"

"It was all right."

Her words didn't match her mood. Daniel waited until they were beyond the outskirts of the town before continuing the conversation. "I don't mean to pry, but it didn't seem like things were quite all right."

Madysen gave a heavy sigh. "We were talking about my father."

"He's come to town as I understand it."

"We thought he was dead."

"Dead?" Daniel slowed his horse. "Why did you think he was dead?"

"Because he let us think he was. He and Granddad arranged it that way so that our father would no longer be a part of our lives. It's a long story. Suffice it to say it's not pleasant."

So someone else had secrets. It shouldn't be shocking, but he couldn't help but raise his eyebrows. "Do you want to talk about it?"

She shook her head. "Not really. But I wouldn't mind a leisurely ride with you back to the farm."

Daniel smiled. "I'd like that too. If it starts to rain we can hightail it to your place."

"I don't even care if it rains." The melancholy coming from her didn't fit. She was usually so lively.

"I've been told I'm a good listener." He leaned forward in the saddle until he caught her eye.

When their gazes locked, she pulled her horse to a stop. Her eyes welled with tears. "Do you ever feel like no one understands you?"

More than he cared to admit. "Yeah, I do."

"How do you handle it? I mean, you don't have sisters like I do . . . who know everything about you, work with you, perform with you, live with you. And it's really hard being the youngest and longing for their respect." She looked down at her hands as they worked through her horse's mane. "But now that I'm ready to stretch my wings, they're not listening to my dreams or opinions."

Everything in him wanted to fix it. But how? Especially since she seemed to still be processing her own thoughts. So he waited.

She lifted her shoulders and then they sagged. Was she feeling defeated too? He opened his mouth to respond, but she started talking again.

"And add to that all the stuff with our dad. . . . I don't think anyone understands how I feel. Is it so wrong of me that I don't just jump in and forgive him? Not that Havyn and Whit are ready to let bygones be bygones either, but since I'm the 'merciful' one, they're shocked at my behavior." She turned her face toward him and then covered her mouth with her hand. "I'm sorry. That was completely inappropriate for me to say to you."

With a flick of the reins, he moved his horse closer. "You know, I figure since we shared what was probably the most disgusting event in either of our lives, that we can feel comfortable talking about anything. Who cares what society thinks? Or anyone for that matter? Aren't we friends?"

Leaning her head to the side, she studied him. Then she tapped her chin with her finger. An endearing gesture. "You're right. We *are* friends, Daniel Beaufort."

"So share anything you like." He put his hand over his heart. "I promise not to betray your confidence to anyone, and I won't think less of you. We've got plenty of time and nothing but the great outdoors to hear us."

FOURTEEN

Judas Reynolds looked over the claim deeds he'd managed to amass over the last few months. When people couldn't make ends meet, they gave up their claims and sold them off to the highest bidder before leaving Nome. It was the only money they walked away with in most cases.

He liked the way he ran things. He could appear for all to be the savior everyone needed. That one true friend who could make good on his promises and always be there for the disadvantaged.

Of course, there were those who had found out exactly what he was. Too bad they weren't around anymore to tell anyone.

He smiled and stacked the deeds. Another ship was in harbor, and as soon as the barges and smaller transports brought the passengers and cargoes into Nome, Judas would put his men to work. His office would soon be flooded with eager men looking to make their fortune. They'd come seeking claims, and Judas would show them the map where three miles east of town the biggest deposits had been found. He'd talk about the millions of dollars' worth of gold that was going back to the States on the very ship they'd come in on. He'd tell them how he'd added additional ship service just to keep up with all the gold. He might even point out that some folks were simply gleaning gold from the beach sand, although they weren't making anywhere near the money that the claims did.

He chuckled. It was all too simple. Controlling everyone and everything.

Except for Chuck Bundrant and his family. Judas frowned. Even sick, the old man had managed to remain solvent. In fact, the family had flourished all the more. For years, Judas tried to figure out a way to get the upper hand by being their friend and champion. But things were changing in Nome. He didn't need the goody-goodies eroding all his hard-earned efforts, especially when more and more of them seemed to find homes here. Maybe it was time to change how he played the game. Show them his true power.

Ticking down a list of families in his mind, Judas looked again for ways to get leverage. Ah, the Beauforts. They owned the mercantile. And Granny Beaufort was close to the Powell women, and from what his sources had told him, the Beauforts were well respected.

Martin already owed Judas a substantial amount. Especially after his last big order before winter. Maybe Judas should offer to loan the man more money. After all, it wouldn't serve him to let the livelihood of the mercantile owner be threatened.

Yes, that could be a source of increased pressure.

"Boss, the first groups are nearly to shore."

Judas turned to find Garrett Sinclair in the doorway. Judas sneered. "You know what to do."

He tucked the claims into his desk drawer and settled back in his chair. He had a feeling it was going to be a very good day for business.

It was merely the first of October, but already the ground held a dusting of snow, and the temperatures had settled in the thirties at night with the days warming up only to the upper forties at best. This came as no surprise to Daniel after all his years up in the Yukon, but how did the newcomers deal with it? The tents lining streets and streams wouldn't be enough for the winter, would they? Thousands of people lived that way.

Alaska was an unforgiving land. One mistake could kill a man. The territory was a test of endurance, and only the hardiest could master it. And that included the animals.

The wagon jolted and bumped its way along the rutted road to the Bundrant farm, bringing Daniel back to the moment. The past couple of weeks had been incredible. He'd worked to help John and Madysen as much as he could with the sheep. The more he worked with them, the more he enjoyed himself. Which had been a surprise.

So much of his sheep knowledge and experience came back to him. Amazing, considering how long it had been since he'd worked with them. He could almost hear his granddad at his side, instructing him.

"Remember Daniel, if we care for the sheep properly, they will pay for themselves in wool and milk. If we make cheese for sale, then they bring us a profit. Add to that selling off lambs, then we're triple blessed."

And now he was working with sheep again. Madysen told him how she stole her sheep from Mr. Reynolds in the dead of night, how she struggled for hours to get them back to her family farm. He could just picture her antics.

Daniel couldn't keep the smile off his face. Madysen was so easy to talk to. They'd talked for hours that night as he saw her home. Since then, they spent a good portion of each day discussing life. He couldn't wait to spend more time with her—and the family, of course.

He looked over his shoulder at the wagonload behind him. Three guys waved at him. It was a good thing they'd been able to come along. He'd been so excited about the Bundrant order coming in that he hadn't thought it through. He would never have been able to load the heavy stove all by himself, nor could he unload it, so he'd asked a few men to help out.

He wound the wagon up to the new milking shed John had built for the sheep. Had John finished the new attached kitchen? He was pretty close last week when Daniel visited.

Madysen waved as she came down the lane, hair flying behind her as she ran. She had a ribbon between her teeth and was wrangling her curls so she could tie them back. That done, she put both hands to her throat. "Is that what I think it is?" She bit her bottom lip in excitement.

Daniel set the brake and hopped down. "It sure is! By the first of October too. I was sure it would take longer."

She ran toward the wagon and gripped the sides. "I can't believe it! This is what we've been waiting for." She clapped her hands, and the sound filled the air.

Whitney and Havyn came running from other areas of the farm, with John not far behind. Madysen skipped over to greet them, and though he couldn't discern what they were saying, Daniel heard their delighted squeals.

The thought of pleasing Madysen made his heart soar.

John ate up the distance between them with his long strides and held out a hand to him. "Good to see you, Daniel. I hear you've brought our order."

"I think the people down in Seattle might have heard everyone's excitement." Edward, who drove the other wagon, made the men laugh.

"True." John shook his head. "These ladies are quite *resonant*."

Daniel quirked an eyebrow up.

John stepped closer and lowered his voice. "It's a musical term. Just go with it. I've learned too many of them now, I can't help but use them all the time."

With a slap to John's back, Daniel laughed. "You might need to teach me some of that."

"Will do." He surveyed the wagons. "I'm sure to owe you a favor after all of this."

"Is the new kitchen finished?"

"Yep. Finished it three days ago. We're all ready to go."

"Then let's unload." Daniel rubbed his palms together.

Between the three ladies and the five men, they had the two wagons unloaded in half an hour. Daniel pulled the bandana from his pocket and wiped sweat from his face as he surveyed the situation.

"You guys take the other wagon and head back to town. I know you have work there. I'll settle up with you tonight." The men nodded and were on their way before Daniel had even turned back to John. He put his hands on his hips. "Where do you want to start?"

John gestured to Madysen. "Well? You're in charge of the sheep, thus in charge of this project too. So you just tell us what to do, and we'll be your hired labor."

Havyn grabbed Whitney's arm. "We'll go make lunch while you work on it."

"Sounds good." John called over his shoulder.

Madysen led them back into the cheese kitchen. "We should probably make sure the stove gets up and running properly, then we should set up the tables, shelves, and workspaces. Then sort through all the other supplies."

"All right. I'll work on the stove while you two work on the tables and such. Just beware, there will probably be some smoking since it's never been used." John looked at the monster of a new stove and rubbed his chin.

Daniel crossed his arms and watched Madysen move about the room, tapping her chin. It made him want to chuckle. Stepping this way and that, she mumbled something under her breath. Then she touched her forehead. "I completely forgot! I made a diagram. I'll be right back."

"Hey, Daniel, come help me move this just a couple inches forward." John had his arms on one side of the stove.

"This thing is massive. I hope we can do it by ourselves." Daniel found good arm holds and looked to John.

"On the count of three, move it toward the wall. We only need a little bit."

He and John grunted as they moved the cast-iron beast an inch. Huffing and gasping for air, they leaned over the stove.

Daniel eyed John. "That enough?"

"It's going to have to be." John let out a whoosh of air. "Because I don't want to do that again."

"Got it!" Madysen chimed as she came back into the kitchen. "I paced off the space the other day so I would know where to put things."

"Very smart." Daniel tried to look at the paper over her shoulder. Even after all the heavy lifting, he was eager to help her. "Where do you want to start?"

Taking several steps, she counted out the length. "This is where we'll put the main worktable."

They worked together until all the tables were in place, then he hung the shelves where she wanted them. Soon, all that was left was to sort the supplies. Getting down on their knees, they started unpacking all the crates.

"I better get back to the cows. I'll see you for lunch at the house?" John patted the stove. "She seems to be working just fine, but holler for me if you need me."

"Will do." Daniel lifted sacks of salt out of a crate. Then he turned to Madysen. Why was it that his heart did a flip every chance they had to be alone together? "Have you figured out how to work your schedule? I know you were worried about that last time we talked."

"I have." She let out a long sigh. "Thankfully, Amka has found us a few more people to help with all this new work. In-uksuk and Yutu are two of the men who will come three times a week to help. And then Amka's sister Kireama will help out two days a week as well."

"That is wonderful news. And have you started to wean the lambs?"

"Yes. And oh my goodness, isn't that just heartbreaking?" She let her shoulders sag for a moment. "It's hard to hear them wailing for one another."

"You'll get used to it." Her compassion was endearing, but Daniel loved her feistiness too. More than once, he'd gotten her riled just to watch. "And you know it's for a purpose."

"Cheese!"

"Yes, lots and lots of cheese."

"Apparently word has gotten out around town because we're already getting more orders. They don't even care which kind of cheese it is, they just know they want some."

Daniel gave her an embarrassed grin. "Should I not have been telling people about it? Dad already agreed to sell it in the store, so I thought that meant it was public knowledge."

"Oh, it's fine." She shrugged. "But I have to admit that it did make me feel a little worried and unprepared. What if we fail at this?"

"You won't fail. You guys are legendary."

"Really?" Her expression said she didn't believe him.

"Really. Why is that such a shock to you?"

"I don't know. Because we're just normal people. A regular, hardworking family."

"Sure. A regular, hardworking family that also happens to have the only dairy and poultry farm in town, and probably has the three most beautiful and talented musicians in the whole country." He stacked cans on one of the shelves and looked at the wall. He needed to rein in his mouth.

Light laughter tempted him to look, but he kept stacking. One at a time.

"Do you really think we're the most talented in the whole country?"

His neck felt hot. "Of course. I wouldn't say it if I didn't believe it."

They continued working for several minutes. Then she came up beside him and helped empty a large crate. "It was very kind of you to say. I guess I would rather not talk about myself right now. But Granny had a lot to say about *you* at lunch the other day."

He groaned. "She probably told you everything there is to know about my childhood. Hopefully there weren't any embarrassing stories?"

"No." She patted his arm and stacked some clean towels on a shelf. "She thinks the world of you."

"It's mutual." But the more he thought about it, the more he worried that Granny had probably told Madysen the truth. About a lot of things. His heart sank to his feet. "She told you I'm not walking with God anymore, didn't she?"

Her hands stilled. "That's not why I brought it up, Daniel. I promise. But yes, she told me. You and I had already touched on some of your thoughts, so it didn't come as a shock."

Tension entered his throat. Best to prepare for the worst. "Does that mean we can't be friends anymore?"

She scrunched up her face and swatted at his arm. "Why on earth would you ask that? After all the conversations we've had?"

"Because most people who call themselves Christians don't want anything to do with a person who once knew the Lord and now wants nothing to do with Him."

She sat on the floor and gave him her full attention. "I find that hard to believe."

"It's sad but true."

"That's terrible. And not at all what Jesus told us to do."

He sat on the floor facing her. "Let me get this straight. You're fine with being friends even knowing what you know? You're not judging me?"

"Of course we can be friends. And no, I'm not judging you." Her feisty voice was back. "I *can't* judge you. I don't know your heart. Only God does."

"All right then. Let's not talk about it."

She held up a hand. "Now that's not fair. Especially if we're friends. Look, I don't want to offend you, but as friends—and I truly mean that, you are a good friend—getting to know you has made me think about something."

"Dare I ask?"

"It sounds like you had a wonderful family. Your heart was broken when your mother and grandfather died, and you were young. Your relationship with God was still in its infancy. You, like all of us when we're young, probably based that relationship on the relationships the members of your family had with God. So when you got angry at God for what felt like Him taking away your family, you thought you couldn't have a relationship with Him anymore. How could you without a strong faith of your own to fall back on? You didn't know what to do, so you walked away."

"Yes, I walked away. I trusted God. Put my faith in Him. And He let me down." As much as he tried not to allow it, agitation filled his voice. A change of subject was in order. "I don't want to talk about that anymore. I hear you all went to see the new show in town?"

Madysen tilted her head and studied him for several seconds. Her soft look changed to hurt, and she looked down at the floor, then back to him. Her smile was different now. Forced? "We did. And I thought it was absolutely brilliant."

"Oh. Well, Mr. Merrick has been in the store several times, and he does nothing but sing your praises. It's almost like he wishes you were part of his show." The thought was ludicrous.

Her eyes brightened. "Really?" She put both hands on his

arm and got to her feet. Daniel rose as well. "Oh, wouldn't that be glorious? To sing and play for different crowds all around the world!"

He rolled his eyes and turned back to the inventory.

"I saw that, Daniel Beaufort." Her tone had changed. She was miffed at him. Good grief.

"Saw what? I didn't do anything." He placed the last few items on the shelf. No matter what he said, he couldn't make this better. Especially since she seemed enamored with that silly show.

"I saw you roll your eyes. You obviously don't think much of Mr. Merrick and his show."

The conversation wasn't going the way he wanted it to go. "Let's not talk about that. Do you know how to milk the ewes?"

"You like to change topics, don't you? It might help if you gave folks a list of what they can and can't talk about with you. Is that the way you always work with your friends? If so, maybe we can't be friends."

Whoa. Where had that come from? "Now wait a minute."

"No, *you* wait a minute. You may think it's acceptable to go around sulking and brooding because God didn't make your life all roses and cherries. You may even convince yourself that you have a right to ignore Him because of it. You may also think that Mr. Merrick or his show isn't worth a second glance, and that's fine. I am of a firm opinion that everyone is entitled to think whatever he or she chooses. But when you desire friendship with me, that doesn't give you the right to dictate to me what I can and can't talk about or care about. Understand?" She put her hands on her hips, her expression fierce.

No one had ever been bold enough to push back with him. Even Dad backed away when Daniel demanded he not talk about God.

Demanded.

He had been making a lot of demands lately. "I'm sorry.

You're right. I don't have the right to dictate what you can talk about."

"Friends ought to be honest with each other and talk about anything. Sometimes lingering on the uncomfortable places in your life will help you get over them faster. Sometimes *not* talking about them will actually make the problem bigger. I know because I have a lot of uncomfortable things going on right now, and I think I've made a bigger mess of them by burying them." Her expression softened. "I like you, Daniel. Your friendship has been an unexpected surprise, and I cherish it. Your help with the sheep has been wonderful too. But I won't walk around on eggshells trying to figure out what I can and can't say to you. So if you want to be my friend, and I hope you do, I would like you to try trusting me with those uncomfortable places in your life."

He dared a question of his own. "Will you trust me with yours?"

Madysen didn't hesitate. "It may seem silly, but yes. I will."

"All right then, I'll trust you."

"And you won't try to shut me up or storm off when you feel out of sorts or annoyed?"

She was asking for more than he'd ever been willing to give, but somehow it seemed right, and he knew she would guard his heart and not seek to damage him further.

"I promise. It might be hard at first, and you'll have to be patient with me."

She nodded. "And you with me." She grinned. "I can be very trying at times."

He laughed out loud, and the heaviness of the moment passed. "I'll bet you can be."

"Now what was that you asked me about the sheep?"

He had to pause a moment to remember. "Oh, do you know how to milk the ewes?"

She wiped her hands on her apron. "No, I can't say that I've learned that yet."

"Well, since we're done here, why don't we head over to the milking shed, and I will help you learn. With the lambs being weaned, you're going to need to know."

They walked out of the kitchen and around to the milking side of the building.

He was looking forward to this. "I was quite an expert at milking the sheep when I was younger."

She laughed. "Oh? Well, how hard can it be, right? I know how to milk cows. Should I go get a stool?"

He chuckled at her. "No stool. But we will need a head gate. It will keep the ewes from maneuvering around while they're being milked. Otherwise you'd have to tie them off and hope for the best."

"That sounds a bit challenging."

"Don't worry. I'll help John build one. And if we build a ramp up to the head gate, that will help so the milker can have the ewe at a height that won't require bending over."

She walked to the far end of the milking shed. "Would this be a good place for it?"

"Brilliant! That's the perfect place for it."

A wide grin filled her face. "I'm actually full of brilliant ideas. What do you need to build it? Do you think we could get it done today?"

"Build what?" John entered the shed. "I came back to let you know lunch is ready, but if we need something else built, you'd better tell me quick. Supplies will be hard to get once the harbor freezes."

Daniel explained everything he'd told Madysen. John nodded and scribbled on a notepad. "I'm sure glad you're here, Daniel. There's a lot we need to learn when it comes to Maddy's sheep. I'll grab the supplies from the other barn after we eat, and we can start right away."

Madysen bounced on her toes. "Will there still be time for you to teach me how to milk them today?"

"Sure, we can definitely get started once we get the gate and ramp built." Her excitement was such a delight.

"Oh, this is going to be so much fun!" She came over and gave his arm a pat. "Thanks for all your help with my sheep. I know you haven't exactly had the greatest experience with them—or with me."

He grinned. "But you're worth it."

She blinked several times, then looked away. "Once we get the milking under way and all the lambs weaned, how long will it take for cheese production?"

"Not too long. Just depends on the variety of cheese and how long you want to age some of them."

"How many varieties do you think we should do?" John stepped next to Madysen. "Or should I ask, how many do you think we'll be *able* to do with the number of ewes and amount of milk that we will get?"

Daniel thought through the numbers in his mind. "Possibly three varieties to start. Then hopefully move to five."

John seemed to weigh this information. "You up for this, Maddy? Sounds like a lot of work—"

"Miss Powell?"

They all turned around. A man stood there, just outside the barn door.

Madysen recognized him first as he removed his hat. "Mr. Merrick! How lovely to see you again. What brings you out to our farm today?"

"Why, I came to see you, Miss Powell."

She giggled and wiped her hands on her apron before she took his arm. "You're just in time for lunch. Will you join us?"

Daniel felt gut punched and turned away as if to find something that needed his attention. Unfortunately nothing did, and he was forced to turn back toward the couple.

Merrick nodded. "That would be awfully nice."

Madysen turned to John and Daniel. "Would you please tell

my sisters that I will be in for lunch, shortly? And that I'll be bringing a guest? I'm going to take a moment and show Mr. Merrick my new kitchen." She looked back to Mr. Merrick. "Unless, of course, you'd rather not."

"I'd be delighted." The man was all smiles and manners. Dressed in a fancy suit and shiny shoes.

Daniel didn't like him.

Not one bit.

The two exited the milking shed, and Daniel glanced at John. "I guess she doesn't need me to teach her how to milk the sheep today after all."

John shook his head. "We can still get things built though, so we're ready." Disapproval flashed across his features.

"I take it you don't like Mr. Merrick any more than I do?"

John's frown deepened. "I have to say, after seeing the show and spending a little time with the man, I think he's nothing but trouble."

"And Mr. Merrick is vying for Madysen's attention?"

"I hoped it was just a passing fancy, but he does appear to be doing so. And of course, Maddy thinks he's charming and loves to hear all his stories about traveling the world and all the famous people he knows. But I suspect it's all a façade."

"Don't you think Madysen would be too smart to fall for someone like that?" Daniel swallowed down his doubt.

"While she is very intelligent, just like her sisters, Madysen sees the best in people. It doesn't help that she's got it in her head that she's always wanted to travel and perform in all the big cities. Thinks she can make some sort of memorial to her mother that way."

"I thought she loved all of this? Especially the sheep." His stomach fell like a rock into his shoes.

"She does. But after her mother died, she came up with this idea. She believes that God brought that man here. My wife thinks her feelings have more to do with the turmoil of all that's happened. It's been a lot for each of them to process."

"I see." Daniel took a couple of the boards from John. Maybe he shouldn't stay in Nome.

Looked like God had it in for him again.

FIFTEEN

Chuck wriggled himself to the edge of the bed. The exercises were making him stronger every day, but he still couldn't make his right arm and leg do his bidding. He prayed he'd be able to do that soon. Being confined to that wheelchair was making him go crazy. And his speech. How long before he'd be able to talk again? Thankfully, he could write well, but how he longed to voice his thoughts and answers again.

And to sit around the dinner table with his family, feed himself, and talk about the goings-on of the farm. Was he destined to spend the rest of his life watching from the outskirts? That wasn't acceptable. The doc said that the only way to improve was to put all the effort he could into his exercises.

So here he was again. Working on the repetitive movements for the fifth time today. And it wasn't even lunchtime.

But if determination could win the battle for him, he'd get there. Soon.

"Knock, knock." Whitney stood at the door with her hands on the jamb. "I didn't want to startle you, but I thought we could chat a few minutes before I took you to the table."

He waved her in with his left hand. "I'd . . . luf . . . dat." Wasn't perfect. But it was better than last week.

"You probably have it figured out by now that I'm thinking through a lot of different things."

He nodded.

"And I really just need someone to listen. With Dad's kids coming up here, everything seems off. It's hard enough that he's back. And on top of that, I don't know why, but I've been thinking about what it means to settle down. I mean, Havyn and John are perfect for one another, and I am so happy for them. Then Madysen declares she wants to go off and leave the family—I don't think I'm ready for that. And here I am, the oldest, and have I pushed everyone so far away that there won't ever be someone for me? Am I that hard and icy?" Tears made her eyes glisten.

"I don't want to be cold. I don't want to push people away. But that's what I find myself doing over and over again. Except for you and my sisters. Why am I like this? It's not who I want to be."

He waved at her and pointed to his box of paper and pencils. She got it off the side table and helped him into the chair. With a deep breath, he started to write.

You have always been the strongest of my girls. My beautiful granddaughters. Steadfast. Stubborn, yes. But we're all stubborn. Do you remember when you were little and one of the mines collapsed?

She nodded.

It felt like an earthquake. We were standing in the middle of the street, and you fisted your little hands at your sides and just stood there. Your mama said that you refused to be shaken. You were like that on the playground . . . and thankfully, in life. Don't let the changes shake you. You are Whitney Powell. You are a beautiful, talented, and powerful lady. Don't forget that.

As she read, a tear slipped down her cheek. She reached over and gripped his hand. "Thanks, Granddad. I guess I just didn't realize what losing Mama would do to me. I miss her. I figured she'd always be here."

It was his turn to cry. A parent should never see one of his children die. It wasn't right. He was supposed to go first. And yet, he was still here.

"I guess it's just a new season of life. Lots of adjustments. Lots of change. And as the oldest I feel responsible for everyone." She folded her hands and gave him a smirk. "I must admit that I wasn't happy with you for hiring John. I know you know that, but I was wrong. He's the perfect foreman, the perfect choice for Havyn, and the best at running this farm. So you deserve an apology. I'm sorry. And yes, I just admitted that I was wrong. But you're not allowed to tell anybody."

He lifted his mouth in what he knew was only a half smile since the apoplexy. But it was better than nothing. "It . . . be . . . our secret."

"Well, why don't we get you ready to join us all for lunch?" She stood up. "Thanks for listening."

He gave her another nod. But her words troubled him. It was the third time someone had mentioned Maddy leaving. He couldn't allow his youngest granddaughter to go gallivanting all over the world with who knew who. It was preposterous.

All the more reason to get stronger quickly. And he needed to make sure John and Havyn were on his side.

Someone had to talk some sense into Maddy.

***

After a rather tense lunch, Madysen had suggested she and Mr. Merrick take a short walk. Why did her family dislike him so? They acted as if they expected him to steal her away at any given moment. Even Granddad watched him with a guarded look in his eyes.

Mr. Merrick, however, had been the perfect gentleman. He didn't seem to notice anything was wrong.

Stopping by his mount, he fished something out of the satchel hanging from the saddle horn. "These are for you. And please, I'd like you to call me Buddy." He held out two packages. One was a box wrapped with a beautiful ribbon, and the other was wrapped in paper and tied with twine. "Go ahead and open them."

Madysen looked at him, her heart pounding. "All right."

She took the ribbon-wrapped box first and untied the satiny bow. "Oh! They're chocolates!" Each piece was a beautiful creation all on its own. The scent drifted up to her nose. "They smell so good."

"They're from the finest chocolatier in all of Seattle. They'll be divine, I promise." He passed her the other package. "Now, open this one."

She tucked the box of chocolates under her arm and wondered what it could all mean. Normally chocolates meant something special. Like courtship or engagement . . . but that couldn't be, could it? She undid the twine on the other package. The size and weight made her think of a book. As she carefully opened the paper, she saw the title, *More Songs of Love*, and she wanted to gasp.

"It's poems." He stepped a bit closer.

"How . . . lovely." She put it to her chest. It must mean what she thought. . . . "Thank you, Mr. Merrick."

"Please. Call me Buddy."

"Buddy." Her voice sounded raspy. Breathless. She needed to pull herself together.

"I must admit, Miss Powell—might I call you Madysen?"

"Yes, of course."

"I must admit, Madysen, that you are all I can think about."

Drawn in by his mesmerizing eyes and smile, she hung on every word. Not only was he handsome and dashing, but he also loved music. He knew literature and poetry. And he'd seen the world. She'd made a list several years ago of everything she hoped for in her future husband. So far, he fit perfectly.

"In all my travels, I've never met anyone like you."

"Thank you for the compliment, but I believe you are trying to flatter me." She tried not to blush, but it happened anyway. She and Buddy had spent a little time together here and there, but could he actually be fascinated with her? Out of all the faraway places he'd visited and all the famous people he'd met, was it farfetched to think he could pick her? Plain and simple Madysen Powell?

"You sell yourself short, sweet Madysen. I know you must think me ridiculous, being drawn to one as young as you."

She started walking again and crossed her arms over the packages as she hugged them to her chest. "I don't think you're ridiculous at all." Even if she had thought it, she would never have said as much.

"Truly? That makes me glad. So many other women might take my intentions the wrong way, but I knew you would understand." He sounded so eager to please her. Was this what love was like? She should ask Havyn.

"You have so much to offer, and when I think of you being a part of my life . . . every day and night . . . it excites me in a way I cannot explain. I've never had reason to believe I would ever find someone to fill my heart and soul."

"I . . . uh . . . I feel the same way." Should she have said that?

"The future holds so many possibilities." He touched her cheek. "I just know that there's nothing we can't accomplish together. When we—the troupe—leave Alaska, Madysen, I want you to come with us. With me."

For a moment Madysen thought he might kiss her. She'd never been kissed before, and the thought intrigued her. Should she let him? Mama would tell her to wait for her engagement, but wasn't he, in fact, proposing with such bold declarations and asking her to go with him? It was all a bit too much.

She started to ask for clarification, but he pulled her into his arms and gave her the briefest of hugs. "I can see I've overwhelmed

you. Just know my heart is true." He released her and climbed
into the saddle. "I have much to prepare for my performers."
He smiled down at her. "I lingered entirely too long as it is, but
I couldn't resist."

"I . . ." Words escaped her. No man had ever talked to her
like that before.

He leaned down and placed a finger over her lips. "Shhh.
We'll talk again soon."

And with that, he rode away.

Clutching the gifts to her chest, she watched him. Thoughts
competed for an audience, but she tried to push them aside and
just linger in the moment. A man had expressed his interest in
her. Possibly he had proposed. She frowned.

Or had he?

"Well, that was interesting."

She jumped. *Daniel!* "What are you talking about?"

"I didn't realize you were betrothed."

"What makes you think that? Mr. Merrick and I have only
known each other a short time. In fact, I met him shortly after
I met you."

Daniel crossed his arms over his chest. "Well, you certainly
haven't embraced me yet."

He saw that? What must he think? "I didn't embrace him.
He embraced me."

"I see. So should I just jump in?" He stepped toward her
with open arms.

Powerful heat rushed to her face. "Daniel Beaufort! How
dare you spy on me like that and tease. I don't need to explain
anything to you." Did she? Oh, but she had just admitted to
accepting an intimate gesture from a man she barely knew.
But Buddy loved her . . . wasn't that what he said? Or meant?
And, they might be engaged. Or not. And the gifts. She should
mention those. "He brought me these lovely gifts." She tilted
her arms to show them to him.

"Ah, chocolates and love poems. Is that what it takes to earn the affections of the lovely Miss Powell?"

One look at his roguish smile and the glint in his eye made her fury burn. "You're teasing me. And I don't find this amusing at all." She spun on her heel and stormed toward the house. "I won't speak of it with you."

"Hold on. We agreed that we wouldn't give each other lists of things we couldn't talk about."

She turned back around and narrowed her gaze at him.

He raised a brow and crossed his arms against his chest as if to dare her to tell him he was wrong.

"Oh . . . oh . . . you're infuriating. I had a lovely moment, and you had to ruin it."

"If it was truly that lovely of a moment, nothing I say or do could dampen it."

He turned to head to the kitchen, leaving Madysen to watch after him. She stomped to her room as fast as she could, wanting to be alone. This must be love, right? Otherwise, why would she be embarrassed, joyous, and excited all at once?

"Maddy?"

Placing the gifts on her bed, she steeled herself. When she turned, she found both her sisters at the door.

"What's going on?" Havyn came over and took her hand. "You don't stomp unless you're quite furious."

Madysen wanted to yank her hand away. Her sisters would just talk to her like she was a child. Again. Little Maddy . . . always forgetting to do her chores. Little Maddy . . . needing mothering. She was sick of it. Maybe it was time to tell them how she felt.

"I'm tired of being treated like a child."

Whit and Havyn both looked at her with wide eyes and then exchanged a glance.

When neither one said a word, Madysen continued. "Buddy has given me some very personal and beautiful gifts to show me his intentions."

"What?" Whitney stepped close and lifted her chin. "His intentions? We just met the man! Maddy, neither one of us thinks of you as a child anymore—you are certainly of marrying age—but this . . . *man*, he's entirely too old for you. And I think it's a bad idea to let him think that you want his attention. Gracious, he's not even going to be here very long."

"I think you need to mind your own business." Madysen straightened her shoulders. "I've never had anyone interested in me like this, and it makes me happy. Granddad and Mama kept us—me especially—too protected, and I've never even had the chance to get to know any suitors. I don't need anyone telling me what to do."

"Maddy . . ."

Oh no, she didn't. Havyn's soothing voice—the one she used on Angry Bird when she was trying to calm the chicken down—wouldn't work on her.

"We're not trying to tell you what to do."

"Yes, we *are*." Whit's lips pinched together. "That man isn't good enough for her."

"No"—Havyn sent a long look to their older sister—"we're *not*. But we are your sisters, and we love you. We don't want to get in the way of your happiness, but the last couple of months have been crazy. We all have a lot of hard things to work through. Good heavens, I feel like the world is completely topsy-turvy." She let out a long breath. "I'm sure this is creating upheaval in you too. Especially with the interest of a remarkable man like Mr. Merrick."

Madysen held up a hand. "Just stop right there. I don't want to hurt either of you. But for the first time, I feel cherished and adored. And Buddy believes I have many opportunities. Opportunities that I thought were silly dreams a few weeks ago. But now I intend to live my life the way *I* want to. I will honor God and hopefully see my dreams come true all at the same time."

"Live your life the way you want to?" Whitney's voice was

eerily hushed now. "Does that mean you intend to leave Alaska with this . . . Buddy?"

Madysen looked between her sisters. The thought hurt. But at the same time, it was exciting. "Maybe. He has asked me to go with him when he leaves Alaska."

Ignoring the gasps of her sisters, she turned around and let her fingers slide over the gifts from Buddy. Expensive and intimate. Surely it meant his heart was true for her.

It had given her the courage to speak her mind to her sisters, but . . . was she brave enough to actually follow through?

SIXTEEN

Buddy surveyed the crowd. The show had been going strong for weeks, and it was a huge success. Reynolds had been smart to bring him in. Not that Buddy wanted to admit that to the man.

"Mr. Merrick."

Speak of the devil. Judas had come to stand next to him.

"What did I tell you? The people love it."

"I assured you we could bring in the crowds, Reynolds. That's what a good show does. And I'm an expert at putting such shows together." He couldn't let the man or his performers take all the credit.

"You did, indeed." Judas turned a keen eye to him. "I've got a business proposition."

"Oh?" Buddy pulled a cigar out of his pocket. This would be fun. Maybe get the man to squirm just a bit.

"I'm impressed at how much money can be made with this venture, so I'd like to buy you out and keep the show in Alaska. Over time, I could change things up and add other performers—and I'm sure your people are capable of doing other things as well?"

"Yes, of course. They are multitalented." Not entirely true, but he wanted to see how high he could jack up the price. The longer he kept Judas talking, the more this could be to his advantage.

A plan formed. An ingenious one, if he did say so himself.

"Good. Well, I will make it worth your while."

Judas was so confident that the deal was already done. Did anyone ever tell this man no?

Judas might be a shrewd businessman, but Buddy conned shrewd men all the time. "Well, I did hand-select this group. And then I trained them for several years to prepare for touring."

"Of course. Name your price and we can negotiate."

Buddy held up a hand. "Wait just a moment. I'm open to selling, but there's something else I would require beyond just the purchase of my troupe."

Reynolds quirked an eyebrow. "And what might that be?"

"Miss Madysen Powell."

"Mr. Merrick—"

"Hear me out." He held up both hands this time. "I will sell you my show for a *discounted* price if you can assure me that Madysen Powell will go back with me to the States. I'm certain that with her as the main star of my new show, I'll be able to make a fortune." He lowered his voice and leaned in. "I also think she'll be a good diversion on long nights."

Judas let out a long breath and squinted at him. "You do remember that the Powell women are all quite religious—otherwise I would have been seeking them for my own diversions."

"That's the deal. I'll only sell my show to you if you can guarantee her as part of the payment." He stuck a stogie between his lips.

Judas didn't seem fazed by his request. "Have you considered proposing marriage to the girl? As I said, she is religious, and you've already been wooing her."

"I'm not the marrying kind." Buddy made a show of picking at a piece of lint on his lapel. "I'm the moneymaking kind, and that girl's talent is going to make me a lot of money. If I happen to get more in the deal, then so much the better." He grinned. "I'm usually lucky in love. . . ."

Reynolds laughed. "You are quite the bargainer, Mr. Merrick. But Miss Powell is not going to be easily persuaded. I can guarantee that she will go and do whatever you like—if you make her fall in love with you and promise her marriage. As for the rest, your terms are acceptable. Before I agree to anything, however, I need to hear this discounted price."

Buddy leaned closer. "Let me work on the details. For one thing, I'll need you to agree to keep everyone on at their regular salary for at least a year. If and when you are through with them, you'll also give them passage back to the States."

A slow smile eased across Judas's face. "I think I can manage that." He stuck out a hand. "I'll wait to hear your price, but Mr. Merrick, I think we have a deal."

The handshake was all Buddy needed. "Wonderful. Let's get it done. I want to be on the last ship before the Sound is iced in."

"That gives me several weeks. Plenty of time." Judas walked away with a wave. "I presume you want Miss Powell to be of a cooperative heart in this matter."

"Just get her on the boat with me. I can convince her of what I feel for her. It's merely a matter of getting her away from that possessive family of hers. They guard her closer than the bank is guarding gold."

"Very well." Judas dipped his chin. "I will have papers for our transaction drawn up immediately."

Buddy admired the man as he disappeared into the crowd. Good looking, powerful, he carried himself with a confident air that also oozed comfort so people would trust him. How did he do it?

He'd have to study the man a bit more. Maybe use Reynolds to create his new persona in his next location.

Oh, this was going to be fun.

The dogs yipped and howled around Whitney. They jumped up and down in the barn.

"I know you want to get out there, but we don't have enough snow yet. We'll have to practice with the cart, okay? You can't run as fast, but it will at least give you some challenge. Oh, and you should know there are a few more buyers coming by today, so be on your best behavior." Good grief, she really *was* as bad as Havyn and Madysen.

Of course, her little talk did no good. The jumping and howling increased as she pulled out harnesses. It would take the better part of the morning to exercise all of them. Good thing she'd gotten out here early.

As she rounded up the first group of dogs, the ache of losing Mama hit again. Sometimes she had everything under control, and then it came like a kick to the stomach. Grief was such an ugly beast. And she had no idea how to control it.

Whitney snapped the leash on Aurora. Control. That was the problem. As long as she had everything under control, she functioned just fine. But when she lost it?

Look out.

Whitney shook her head to clear her thoughts.

Baaahaaaah!

She turned and watched Maddy herding some ewes into the milking shed. Good thing they were bringing in a steady income, because sheep were messy and stupid.

The dogs pulled on the lines, drawing Whitney's attention back to them. "Do those strange wooly things look yummy to you?" Whitney snapped another leash in place. "Because I'm certain you all look like wolves to them." One of the pups gave a mournful cry, and Whitney shook the last clip at him. "Have a little patience. We're going to run. I promise."

She snapped the clip in place, then gave the signal to go. The dogs stayed in formation and ran as a team. In fact, the long lead lines that she held were a bit slack, which was a good sign. This group was ready. They knew what to do, when to do it, and how to do it. Together.

It was beautiful to watch.

She called out commands and they obeyed. Perfect. Every time.

"Whoa." She spied her first customer of the day and gave a little wave to Amka's brother Ben. She never demonstrated the dogs without one of the workers or John to stand as her protector. Ben grabbed his rifle and stood guard off to the side. Be there four-legged attackers or two, Ben would be at the ready.

The customer approached. "Hello der, Miss Powell. I'm Nils Andersson." His Swedish cadence made her smile. It was almost musical. "I come to see de dogs."

"Of course, your brother made an appointment with me. I can exhibit them here with the cart instead of a sled. Let me show you what they can do." This was her world. Her comfortable place of refuge. If only she could stay right here.

She demonstrated for Mr. Andersson, and then a Mr. Meyers showed up. He was only looking for one dog, but he was very particular about the animal he needed. They'd met before and hadn't made a decision. After an hour of discussion with both men, Whitney knew exactly which of her animals would suit their needs. They struck deals and shook on it. It was still hard to part with any of her dogs, but she had to do her share for the family.

After she'd made final arrangements for delivering the dogs and the two men left, she turned and smiled at Ben. "Thanks. I think it's safe to go back to John now."

Amka's brother nodded, slung his rifle over his shoulder, and headed toward the dairy barns.

Time to get the dogs unharnessed and fed, then go to work cleaning up after them. "Good dogs." She walked over to them, laughing at how they wriggled and squirmed to get her attention.

Unconditional love. That was what her dogs gave her. It was so much purer and more honest than people's love.

She hated to be such a cynic, but after what she'd seen as a child, who could blame her?

Dad wasn't all bad. She had some good memories of him, but they were few and far between. What she remembered well was the weight of carrying a full-grown man on her six-year-old shoulders as she dragged him home from the saloon while he stumbled and sang off-key. Not what a small child should have been doing.

Her sisters didn't share those memories. Even Mama hadn't known everything.

Whitney had protected her too.

And now there was Maddy to protect. What had gotten into her? Why would she even consider leaving the family to travel off to who knows where? It didn't make sense.

True, Madysen was full of life whenever the three of them played and sang together. It was almost magical. And it was understandable that Mr. Merrick's visits and gifts had enchanted her baby sister. But why didn't the man ever stay long enough to visit with the rest of the family? Except for that one awkward lunch and the first time he offered to employ them all to sing in the States, he'd shown very little interest in anyone but Madysen.

Whitney shook her head. None of it added up. If Mr. Merrick truly wanted to become part of their family, wouldn't he want to get to know them? To get their approval?

Of course, let her or Havyn bring up concerns about Mr. Merrick to Madysen, and their sister's eyes shot sparks.

It was too much like it was with their dad. Madysen had always defended their dad when Whitney said something negative. Madysen always took a stand for those whom others disliked.

If only she had more of Maddy's compassion. Perhaps then she'd know how to help her beloved sister.

"Excuse me, Miss Powell?"

The deep voice caused her to turn around. "Yes?" She studied the handsome man before her. Where had she seen him before?

"Name's Garrett Sinclair." He removed his hat and stuck out a hand. "I hear you have the best dogs around, and I'm in need of a new team."

She didn't shake his offered hand and fidgeted with the dogs' lines instead. Why had she let Ben go back to the dairy barn so quickly? They rarely had unannounced visitors to the farm. They were too far out. But they were always careful around new men. Nome had become a haven for ne'er-do-wells. Shoulders tight, she pulled her dogs closer. "What happened to your other team?"

The man looked down and fiddled with the brim of his hat. "They've been loyal for many years. But they're aging." His voice was full of compassion.

A man who cared about his dogs like that must be safe. Her shoulders relaxed a bit. "So you've been in the north quite some time."

"Yeah. Love the cold." He smiled and stuffed his hat back on his head.

"Well, I do have several buyers interested. I insist that all of my buyers train with any dog they wish to purchase."

"That sounds wise. That way you know what kind of people they are—if they will take care of the animals." He crouched down in front of several of the dogs. Let them sniff him.

This guy said all the right things. She narrowed her gaze at him. "What do you do for a living?"

"I mine a claim outside of town."

Hm. A gold digger. "And are you financially able to take care of a team of dogs? They aren't cheap to feed."

"I'm well aware. Like I said, I've had my other team for years.

They're like my family." He seemed sincere enough. Then he smiled. The dimples in his cheeks made him even more hand-some, but she wasn't impressed.

Whitney took a deep breath and studied him. "Are you will-ing to go through the training? It will take several weeks."

"Of course. Like I said, I heard you were the best."

"All right, then." She stuck her hand out this time.

He shook it. "I have to admit, I never expected for the owner of Powell Sled Dogs to be so pretty."

Men. Why did he have to say that? "My price is set. There will be no negotiating or flattery. If you want someone to sweet talk, there are plenty of girls in town." Her words sounded harsh even to her own ears, but she wasn't about to be coaxed and cajoled by a man.

Mr. Sinclair's deep laugh echoed through the air. It made the dogs bark. "No negotiating. Got it. I'll be back."

Whitney gathered up the next set of dogs and made herself *not* watch the man walk away. Why would she? He'd had no effect on her.

None whatsoever.

SEVENTEEN

"All right, are you ready to finally learn how to milk the ewes?" Daniel grinned at Madysen. Her fun-loving personality was so invigorating.

"Yes, I am." She put on a clean apron and then held out a piece of paper. "There's a few more things that we need to order. Unless, of course, you have them in stock. I don't know what we would have done without you, Daniel. I've been so busy in the cheese kitchen—again, thanks to you—that John hasn't had the opportunity to teach me. But I know he's grateful you taught him. I guess I should say that I'm grateful too. These are my sheep, after all, and you two have helped all of this be possible." She covered her mouth and giggled. "Sorry, I tend to ramble when I'm excited."

"And you're excited to milk a ewe?" He took the paper from her and glanced down at the list.

"Yes! And I'm excited about other things as well. I may be leaving soon." The hint of a smile hurt.

He frowned. "Leaving Nome? For where?"

She shrugged. "Wherever I can perform. Buddy Merrick believes I can make a name for myself on the stage. I'm quite excited to consider it." Her smile stretched, and she swayed back and forth.

"I didn't think you were seriously considering it. And your family is all right with this idea? I mean, you don't even know this man and yet you'd consider running off with him?"

Madysen's countenance fell. "You make it sound risqué."

"Well . . . isn't it? This man shows up in town a matter of weeks ago—you don't know him from any of the other strangers who came on the same boat, and now you're ready to leave with him. If that isn't dangerous, I don't know what is." Why on earth did he allow himself to care about her? Then he took one look at her and knew . . . because she was Madysen. He wouldn't change her, not even to keep her.

"You don't know him like I do." Her chin lifted a tiny bit, and he noticed the spark of challenge in her eye.

Daniel put the list in his pocket. "Tell me about him. Where's he from? Who are his parents? Does he have siblings? How old is he?"

Rolling her eyes, she let out a dramatic sigh. "Ugh. Everyone is always worried about his age. I don't know how old he is. And just because he's older than me doesn't mean we aren't suited for each other. I don't know where he's from. I know he loves music and believes in me. He has handled a lot of performers and believes he can make me a star."

"That still doesn't tell me anything about who he is." Daniel kept his tone even. "A girl can't just go off with the first man who comes along and tells her she's pretty and sings well. Not if she's smart."

Madysen drew a deep breath and planted her hands on her hips. "I thought you were going to show me how to milk the ewes."

He could continue to fight her on the issue of running off with Buddy Merrick—which he wouldn't win if the set of her jaw was any indication—or he could be her friend. Maybe what he needed to do was give her a reason to stay.

"I want to teach you. I like helping you out here. And I think we have a couple of the things on your list at the store. But we may have to order the rest. Of course, there's no way of knowing if we can get it in before the freeze."

"I understand." She calmed and offered him a smile. "I didn't mean to get carried away. Let's forget about it and get down to business. We can have a pleasant afternoon. What do you say?"

He shook his head as he laughed. "I don't know how pleasant it will be, but I'm happy to try and make it that way."

"I'm sure we'll have a very pleasant time of it. And I just want you to know how thankful we are for you. I'm glad I have help coming next week. Otherwise, there's no way I could keep up."

"You're welcome. Remember, I volunteered to help. I forgot how much I loved this until I came back, so I should be thanking *you*."

"That's what friends are for, right?" Her earlier frustration was replaced by a smile. It lit her face and made her even more beautiful.

If only she trusted him the way she did Buddy Merrick. All this time out at the Bundrant Dairy around Madysen was making his head spin. Hearing her laugh, watching her scrunch up her nose as she concentrated, and getting to know all her little habits was a joy. What if all that was taken away?

"What do I do first?" She glanced around at the ewes.

"Grab a clean cloth and a bucket of water."

"Got it." She picked up the items.

"Now lead the sheep over to the head gate we built."

"That's quite a contraption." She eyed it as if inspecting it for flaws.

"Yes, it is. But you've got to get her in it. Put a little hay in front of her to keep her occupied, or you'll end up with a mess. Sheep are not as easy as cows." As fascinating as she was to watch, he forced himself to focus. He was here to teach—not gawk.

"Oh boy. Is now the time to tell you that I never thought cows were easy?" Her grimace was comical.

Oh, she could make him laugh. "You'll do fine. Just watch me. First give me the water and cloth."

Madysen handed over both.

"Okay, so this is how you wash the ewe once she's secured in the head gate." He straddled the sheep. "You'll notice that this breed of sheep has longer tails, which help to keep them warm in the winter, but they do make birthing and milking a little more messy." He looked up to make sure she was watching and then studied her. "You know, we're going to need to build another ramp for you."

"Why is that?"

"You're . . . well, you're more petite, so you won't be able to straddle the ewe. My mother always preferred straddling because it offered her more control over the animal, but we can adjust. You'll have to stand over here." He moved her into position. "All right, take the pot and start milking. Very similar to cows, just be vigilant in watching the ewe because you don't want her going to the bathroom in the milk."

"It can't be *that* difficult." Madysen went to work, but because of her height, she was at a weird angle. "Nothing is happening."

The ewe must have sensed Madysen's frustration and kicked the pot over.

"I know, I know. I'm trying." She picked up the pot and went back into position. "You are my sheep, you know my voice, so this shouldn't be a problem for you."

Daniel did his best to not laugh. Between Madysen trying to convince the sheep that she knew what she was doing, and the ewe completely not caring, it was like watching an awkward dance between milker and sheep.

The sheep now had her leg in the pot. Which didn't seem to please her very much.

"Be still. I'm trying to help you." Madysen knelt beside the sheep.

Daniel couldn't contain his mirth any longer. His laughter spilled out. "I'm sorry. I just wish you could see this. It's almost as funny as—"

"No, don't say it." A smile split her face. "Remember, you're not supposed to bring that up ever again." And then she started laughing along with him.

He stepped up to Madysen's side and got her in position once again. This time, he put his hand over hers on the teat and showed her how to press high into the udder. "Most lambs butt up against the udder when they're feeding, and this simulates that so the ewe relaxes to give milk." Their close proximity made him very aware of her. Her scent. The softness of her skin. Her hair tickling his face.

"Oh, I see. Look! Milk!" Her enthusiasm fed his soul.

He stayed close with his hand on top of hers as she continued to milk. "You're doing great. I think you're getting the hang of it."

"I am!" She turned, and their faces were mere inches apart.

Oh, to stay right there, gazing into those brown eyes. But he pulled back and smiled. "You did great. Now you just repeat that one hundred times or so."

She pulled out the pot of milk and laughed. "It's a good thing we have help. Otherwise, I *would* be in trouble."

"Ready to try again?" He released the ewe from the head gate and rubbed down its sides.

"Excuse me."

They turned to find a kid in the doorway.

"I was told to come here to find a Miss Madysen Powell?"

"I'm Miss Powell." Madysen brushed off her apron and went toward the boy.

"These are for you." He pulled a bunch of hothouse roses from behind his back. "And here's the card." The boy gave a brief smile and, after Madysen took the gifts, ran out the door.

Daniel held his breath.

She read the card and then put it up against her chest. "How romantic." Turning to face him, her smile practically lit up the room. "They're from Buddy."

"So it's *Buddy* now, huh? He sure is trying hard to impress you."

"I know you think it's premature and that I don't know enough about where he was born and who his parents are, but . . . I think I might be in love with him."

Daniel didn't like the sound of that. He made a bit too much noise as he put things away. "If you were really in love, you wouldn't think it 'might' be . . . you'd know."

"That's not true. I'm new at this. And he's only come to visit a few times, and don't go getting mean again. I don't want to fight." If she stuck out her bottom lip, she'd look like a little kid.

Maybe she needed a little push. "Okay, so what does your family think about him? They know you better than anyone else."

"They don't know him very well. Not yet. When he visits, he usually has enough time to see me, and that's it." She leaned in and sniffed the flowers.

"So he hasn't spent any time with your family? Don't you find that a little odd?"

With a huff, she marched right up to him and tapped his chest with her finger. "No. I don't. But what I do find odd is that you seem determined to stick your nose into the middle of my business."

"I thought that's what friends did? Because they care." She could aggravate him like no one else. "Would you rather I just let you do whatever you want? Not care if you go off and make stupid decisions?" He swiped a hand down his face and clenched jaw. Perhaps that was over the line. He really needed to tame his mouth sometimes.

Too late.

"You think I'm stupid?" She stepped even closer and had to tilt her head back to look at him. "How *dare* you, Daniel Beaufort. Maybe we shouldn't be friends after all."

Several days of snow had kept Madysen from doing what she wanted to do, which was to talk to Granny. While Whitney was thrilled with all the white stuff on the ground, Havyn and Madysen weren't quite ready. They still had lots of preparation to do for their animals, and the weather was quite pleasant before the snow fell.

But late fall was here with its chilly temps. And snow.

She found Havyn in the kitchen, stirring some fish stew. "I'm going to head over to Granny's for a visit."

"Please give her my love."

"I will."

"Maddy?" Havyn set the spoon down and walked over to her. "Are you all right? It seems we haven't talked a lot lately, and we're all so busy . . ." Her words drifted off in . . . disappointment?

Tears sprang to Madysen's eyes, and she went to her sister and hugged her. "I love you, Havyn. And I love you for asking. We were all so close before Mama died. Nothing has seemed right since we lost her. It's like we're simply existing—getting through each day as best we can. And yet, you're married now, which has changed things. I guess we haven't had the time or energy to deal with everything." She pulled back. "So to answer your question, I think I'm all right. But half the time, I don't understand what I'm feeling."

Havyn grabbed her hands. "You do realize that if you left us, we'd never be the same. I don't know if I could handle you not being here. You're precious to me, Maddy, and I don't want to lose you too." Tears streamed down her sister's cheeks.

"You're not going to lose me, Havyn. But there's this little dream I've had of touring and performing in honor of Mama. I want the world to know about her and what she did for us—with us. I want the memory of her to go on and on." And why would God have brought Buddy along at just the right time if she wasn't supposed to go? It only made sense that God had given her this open door, no matter how hard it would be to walk through.

"But it will, Maddy. With us. We're the ones who will keep her memory alive. We're the ones who will honor her name. The world won't care about her. They might come to hear you, but they won't remember her."

Madysen frowned. "But *I* will. Is it wrong for me to try and keep her memory alive?"

"Of course it's not wrong to want to keep your love for her alive. But, Maddy, that's something few can appreciate. Just us who knew her. Strangers will never care about Mama." Havyn gave Maddy's hands a squeeze. "Is that what you really want to do?"

Was it? She looked out the window. "I honestly don't know, Havyn. But I do know that I want to be loved. And I want to look forward to the future. Right now, it's hard to see through the fog." Whenever her sisters questioned her on this, she dug in her heels. Was it only because she wanted to stand up to them? Wanted them to respect her?

"Grief has a funny way of doing that to us, doesn't it?" Havyn said. "I'm sorry if I haven't been there for you. I know we've all had so much change that we're not quite sure what to do with ourselves, but we should sit down and spend more time with each other." Havyn leaned in and hugged her.

For a moment, Madysen closed her eyes and stayed in the embrace, and it felt like Mama was hugging all her troubles away. "You mean our practicing music doesn't count?" Madysen hoped the teasing would cheer her sister up.

"I guess it counts a little, since we're technically together, but we haven't done much more than prepare for our concerts at the Roadhouse."

A fun idea popped into her head. "What if we were to hold a small concert here? For Granddad! We could have it as a celebration of sorts since he's getting stronger all the time. And invite his close friends."

"Like a party!" Havyn smiled.

"Yes. Wouldn't that be fun?"

"Oh, it would. But when would we have it?"

"Right away. And I can invite Buddy to join us as well. Daniel too."

An hour later, Madysen was on her horse, on the way to Granny's. It had been fun to plan something with Havyn. Just like old times. Maybe her sister was right. Maybe it would lift all of their spirits and get them out of the cloud of sadness they all seemed to be in.

So why didn't anyone want to talk about it?

At Granny's, she hopped off her horse, tied him to the post, then went to the door and knocked.

"Well, Maddy, what a joy to see you today. Come in, come in." The older lady waved her in. "How are you doing?"

"I'm doing well, how are you?" She took off her gloves and cape.

"Enough of the chitchat, I can tell you have something on your mind." Granny bustled into the other room. "Tea?"

"Yes, please." One of the things she loved about Granny—she always got to the point.

Granny returned in short order with a tray of goodies and steaming cups of tea. "All right now, what seems to be troubling you?"

Madysen took a cup of tea and glanced around. "Are we alone?"

"Of course. The men are over at the store."

She let out a breath. "Oh, good."

"Child, come now, let's hear it."

"How do you know when you're in love?" There. She'd said it.

"That's a tricky one, my girl. There's the affectionate kind of love that you might have for a baby or a pet, but I doubt that's the kind you're asking about. Then there's the lusting kind of love, which makes you feel things that are reserved for married couples. And of course there's the crush kind of love where you feel attracted to someone, or an idea of someone, and want love simply for the idea of love. But then . . . there's the deep abiding, unconditional love that you want in a marriage partner. It grows over time even though you don't see how it could because your heart is so full. But it does. Is that what you're talking about?"

Granny's words sank into her mind. She desperately wanted that deep, abiding kind of love. "How do you know if it's the unconditional love you talked about?"

"Have you examined First Corinthians chapter thirteen?"

"No. I don't think so. Although the passage is familiar."

Granny reached over to the table beside the settee and picked up her Bible. "It says starting in verse four,

'Love suffers long and is kind; love does not envy; love does not parade itself, is not puffed up; does not behave rudely, does not seek its own, is not provoked, thinks no evil; does not rejoice in iniquity, but rejoices in the truth; bears all things, believes all things, hopes all things, endures all things. Love never fails.'"

She tapped the book in her lap. "I would examine every one of these qualifications of love and ask yourself if that is what you feel. And does that man feel the same for you in return?"

Leaning back in the chair, Madysen folded her hands in her lap. Was that what she felt for Buddy?

No, it wasn't. But she didn't know him well enough yet, and

he seemed to fit her list. Didn't that count for something? And didn't lots of people get married without fully knowing their spouse? God had blessed many marriages that way. As long as they were joined in their faith—

Were they? Where did Buddy stand with God . . . and why hadn't she asked him about it?

And how could she know if he felt that unconditional love for her? He'd given her fancy words and gifts, but nothing that helped her know anything about the man deep inside. Daniel had been right on that account.

Daniel. Oh, that man could get her angrier than a stirred-up hornet's nest. But he had been a true friend. Even though he probably wouldn't come near her ever again after their heated words. *Her* heated words. So where did that leave her?

"Is there someone in particular you want to talk about?" Granny's eyes twinkled.

"Hm?" She blinked several times.

"I said, is there someone in particular you want to talk about?"

Daniel. No, Buddy. She gave herself a mental shake.

She could deal with her argument with Daniel later. At least Granny wouldn't judge her or condemn her for her feelings about Buddy. "Yes, there is." She took a deep breath. "It's Mr. Merrick. He's shown me a lot of attention and has given me some lovely gifts. I think maybe he loves me—maybe that he's even thinking of proposing. Something he said recently sounded an awful lot *like* a proposal." She looked down at the table. "But I'm so inexperienced, I wouldn't know if it was unless he just spoke it plainly."

"And shouldn't he . . . speak it plainly?" Granny tapped the table with an arthritic finger. "Shouldn't he tell you exactly what he's feeling and thinking?"

Madysen nodded. "He should, but maybe he feels like I do. I don't know *what* I'm feeling."

"How would you describe it?"

"Exciting? New? It makes me feel special when he brings me gifts and comes out just to see me."

"How well do you know this man?" The older woman took a sip of her tea.

"Like I said, we've spent time together, but there's still a lot of conversations to be had." Daniel's words came back to haunt her, and the more she said things out loud, the more she doubted herself. "I think we need to spend a lot more time together."

"Does Mr. Merrick want to settle down in Nome? I thought he was a traveling performer?"

"No. And he is. He's talking about taking me on tour so I can sing and play my cello in front of larger audiences. He thinks I'm very talented."

Granny tilted her head and smiled. "You don't need Mr. Merrick to tell you that you're talented, Madysen Powell. You know very well that God gave you and your sisters an abundance of talent."

"I know. I guess I'm just wondering if this is all there is? Is this what I want out of life? To stay here and be with my family in Nome. To continue playing at the Roadhouse. Take care of my sheep. Help Granddad with the farm . . ."

"Why do you sound so disappointed?"

"I don't know. That was all I ever wanted before . . ."

"You've suffered a great deal of turmoil and grief." Granny patted her hand.

"I guess I don't really know *what* I want anymore. What if this is God's will for my life? It's not like I went looking for this door to be opened."

"Why don't we pray about it? The only way to know the truth is for us to bring it to the throne of grace."

Yes, of course. Granny was right.

Madysen helped Granny down to her knees and then knelt beside her.

Granny started. "Father, we come to You for direction and

understanding, but first we come in love and praise. As Jesus said before raising Lazarus from the dead, we thank You that You have heard us. What a blessing to know we can come to You and that You hear us."

Madysen clutched her hands together. Why hadn't she already prayed about this? She had worried over it, pondered it, and even discussed it with others, but she'd avoided bringing it to God. How very immature of her. No wonder her sisters treated her as they did. If she wanted to be respected as an adult, she really should handle things in a mature manner. That meant getting everything straight with the Lord.

"Lord, in the situation of Madysen and Mr. Merrick, we know that love is a powerful thing and should never be treated lightly."

Had she treated love too casually? She thought of the gifts Buddy had given her. Trinkets that suggested deep, intimate feelings. His words hinted at such feelings, but he hadn't really shown her anything of himself. Gracious, Daniel and her sisters were right. She knew nothing about this man, and yet she was considering leaving the protection of her family to go away with him. What had gotten into her?

"Keep Maddy from making poor choices. Lead and guide her. And help us to understand and accept her decisions. As a grown woman, we need to accept that there may be a path for Maddy that isn't one we might have chosen for her. If You are truly leading her away from Alaska, then comfort us. Put our minds at peace."

Tears stung Madysen's closed eyes. When Granny was done, she lifted her face to heaven. "Lord, please show me what You would have me do with my talents and abilities. I want to glorify You. And please protect my heart. Help me to understand Your unconditional love."

"Ahem." Someone cleared his throat behind them.

Madysen looked over her shoulder.

Daniel.

"I'm sorry to interrupt, but some of the earlier items you and John requested came in on the *Corwin* today. I'll be taking stuff out to your farm as soon as . . . I can get help."

"I can help. I was about to head home myself. Or do you need someone stronger than me?" She lifted Granny to her feet.

"No, Dad and I can load it. I just wasn't sure if there would be anyone there to show me where you wanted everything." He wouldn't look at her, and he sounded . . . nervous.

Drat her angry tongue. "Daniel, I need to apologize for—"

"Don't worry about it. We can talk about it later." He let out a sigh. "I just didn't know how to tell you."

"That our order has come in earlier than expected?" She furrowed her brow.

"No." He looked to his grandmother and then back to her. "Your father's . . . family came in on the boat too. They were asking how to get out to your farm. But then your father came, and he's loading them up to take to your home."

Eighteen

Daniel sat next to Madysen on the seat of the wagon. She hadn't said a word to him since they loaded up, tied her horse to the back, and headed out of town. He glanced at her again. What must she be thinking?

"I see you looking at me again, Daniel Beaufort." Sitting ramrod straight, her hands folded in her lap, she looked like a tiny statue that could topple over with a good gust of wind.

"I'm just worried about you. You haven't said anything."

"Maybe because I don't know what to say."

Pink crept up her cheeks. Was she mad? Hurt? What? "Well . . . have you prayed about it?"

She let out a huff. "Prayed about *what*?"

He shifted his gaze straight ahead. So she was going to make him force it out of her. "The situation with your father and his other family."

"Oh, that." Out of the corner of his eye, he saw her shoulders slump a tiny bit. "No, I haven't. At least not lately. I guess I don't know what to say to God about it either because I don't know how I feel about it."

"Seems like you don't know how you feel about much these days."

Madysen stiffened but said nothing. Apparently he'd hit a nerve.

"You've got to feel something." He slowed the horses so they could take the time to have this conversation. Madysen needed it. Whether she admitted that or not.

"Oh, I feel lots of things, I just don't think any of them are good things." Her words dripped with disdain.

"Well, then, you should pray about it." He shrugged.

She turned toward him, eyes wide.

"Don't stare at me like that. I was stating the obvious. You should pray about it."

"But why are *you* encouraging me to pray? I thought you were angry with God?"

"I was. I mean, maybe I still am. But ever since you and I talked about it, I've tried to have conversations with Dad and Granny. They've been patient, but it's not like they have answers for me. They said that I have to find the answers on my own. Which doesn't make any sense, so I guess I'll talk to John about it."

"What about me? I thought I was your friend too? Even though I said we shouldn't be friends. I didn't mean it."

He chuckled. She really was adorable. "We are friends. I just wasn't sure you wanted to talk to me about it."

Madysen shifted on the seat so she was almost facing him. "Of course I want to talk to you about it, Daniel. That's the most important part of my life—my relationship with God. I will always want to talk about that."

"Don't go preaching at me now." A small grin lifted his lips. "I was simply asking if *you* had prayed about your own struggles."

"Oh, you're impossible." She started to touch his arm, then pulled back. "You just had to bring it back to me, didn't you?"

"Well, it is about you. That's how this conversation started. Besides, I like hearing you talk about yourself. I like getting to know you better." Might as well be honest.

"Okay, fine. I guess I don't know what to expect. It's hard to imagine having other siblings. It's been me, Whit, and Havyn for all these years. Now they're here, and I'm still having a really hard time forgiving Dad." She waved her hands in front of her. "Everything has changed so much I just want to scream." After all the words were out, she slumped even more. "And now you probably think I'm a raving lunatic."

"Never." He took her hand and squeezed, then let go and took the reins in both hands so he wouldn't be tempted to do it again. It was entirely too pleasurable to touch Madysen Powell. "May I ask you why you are so angry with your father?"

She tucked her hands up under her skirt and sat on them. Keeping her head down, she started, her voice low. "I was seven years old playing with my friend Jeb in an abandoned mine. . . ."

Daniel sighed as he listened to Madysen's story. For her to go through all that at such a tender age . . . that was awful. But to have her father come and rescue her had been so sweet and special. Then his promise to never leave her.

A promise he broke.

Daniel wasn't sure he would be able to forgive the man either.

"And when we heard the whole story—the story how he thought it was fine and dandy to leave his family and start over somewhere else—the anger built inside me. It would have been easier if he *had* just been dead."

As they pulled up to the farm, Daniel was speechless. No wonder she was angry. And no wonder she was struggling with all her feelings. What a painful season they'd had to endure.

It suddenly made sense why she was swayed by Buddy Merrick's wooing. She needed some sort of bright spot in her life to take her mind off of the chaos that had become normal. She needed a purpose and a place to belong. If only he'd been the one to woo her first.

"Thanks for listening, Daniel."

He helped her down off the seat, wanting to do so much more for her. But what? "You're welcome."

"I'll be praying for you." She sent him a sad smile.

With a nod to her, he watched her walk away. Now that he knew what was going on, he realized Madysen didn't want to leave. Not really.

She just needed her world to turn right-side up again. He could help her do that. Before that Merrick fella did any more damage.

Whitney maneuvered the sled over the fresh snow. This was the perfect run for Mr. Sinclair to see what her dogs could really do.

When he'd shown up that morning, she hadn't been keen on taking them out since he hadn't made an appointment and her schedule was quite full. Plus, she and her sisters were performing at the Roadhouse tonight, which meant they needed a good chunk of time to practice the new songs they'd put together.

She glanced at the man riding in the basket. Normally, she would have asked John or Ben to join them on another sled so she wasn't alone with a stranger, but they were busy today too, and she didn't want to take them away from their work for an unplanned run. Besides, her dogs were protective of her, and she always carried a gun. Not that she was really worried. Mr. Sinclair seemed honorable.

"Your dogs are amazing," Mr. Sinclair shouted over his shoulder to her.

"Thank you." She commanded the dogs to the right, toward the river. Should be a beautiful drive home that way.

"Hey, would you mind if we stop for a bit? I've got an injured leg that needs stretching."

Reaching inside her coat, she checked the watch pinned to her shirtwaist. "We don't have a lot of time, but I think we can manage it for just a little bit." Once they were on a nice level patch by the river, she called out, "Whoa."

The dogs came to a stop, and she set the hook to keep the sled in place. She dismounted the back and went to check on her dogs. Their yipping and bouncing told her all she needed to know—they loved this as much as she did.

Mr. Sinclair climbed out of the basket in the front of the sled, stretched, and limped over to her. "They look great. I'll be happy to own some of your fine dogs."

"I'm glad you are pleased. There's still a good bit of training you need to go through with them so that I can ensure you understand their care and commands, but if you are willing to commit to it, I don't think we will have any problems finding you the dogs that you need for your team."

He moved even closer and looked down into her eyes. "I'm sorry if I offended you the last time we met."

"You didn't offend me." Bells went off in her mind. Where had the limp gone? "We should go."

He closed the gap between them in an instant and gripped her in his arms. Then he tried to cover Whitney's mouth with his own.

Shock-fueled adrenaline surged. She slammed her boot into the top of his foot.

"Ow! What was that for?" He frowned down at her, but his arms stayed clamped around her.

She met his gaze head on and spat out her words. "Let me go, Mr. Sinclair! I have no interest in whatever you have planned."

"So you like to play hard to get, huh?" His smile turned into a sneer.

The look in his eyes shook her to her core. He wasn't going to stop. "No, I most definitely do not!" She turned her face away to avoid his kiss, but he pressed his lips to her throat instead.

She had to break free! She squirmed, but her arms were pinned against her sides.

He chuckled.

She was trapped. *Lord, help!*

Pepper, her lead dog, growled.

"Stop it, right now, Mr. Sinclair."

"Oh, you know you like it." He gripped tighter and tighter as his mouth roamed her neck and face.

"Stop it!" She screamed in his ear.

His face turned red. "No. You want it. Scream all you want. No one will hear you."

The pulsing of her heart pounded in her ears. *No!* She wouldn't let this happen. She wasn't strong enough to stop him, but . . .

She had one chance. She lunged at Sinclair and bit his ear.

He let out a holler and let go of her. She flew backward and hit her head on the cold ground.

"You stupid . . . wait until I—"

She pushed herself up and shouted, "*Attack!*" Her dogs lunged toward Sinclair, yanking the sled and its anchor out of the snow.

Her docile, happy sled dogs were now vicious protectors.

In a flash of snarls and fur, they were on the man and took him down. Growling and chomping.

He covered his face with his arms. "Get them off me!"

She was in no hurry to comply, but she didn't want to risk him hurting one of her dogs with his frantic punches and kicks.

"Pepper, come!"

The dog did as commanded, and the other dogs followed their alpha back to where she stood. She forced her trembling fingers to steady as she unhooked Pepper.

Sinclair struggled to sit up. "You'll pay for this!"

Fists at her side, she walked up to the man who dared to take what wasn't his. Pepper never left her side. She bent down over his face. "You do realize that if I give the command, they will rip you to shreds."

His gaze fixed on the growling dogs. "Keep them off of me."

"Why should I?"

"What's your problem, woman?"

Her problem? The man thought he could terrorize any woman he wanted? A terrible shaking started in her stomach, but she forced herself to be strong. "Pepper, stay. Guard." She walked backward to the sled and grabbed her rifle from its sheath. "You are the problem, Mr. Sinclair. And men like you, who do this to unsuspecting women."

She carried it back to where Pepper kept watch. The other dogs were still growling and snarling. A few had bloody mouths.

It wasn't their blood.

She leveled the gun at him. Something about holding the gun helped calm her nerves. She was a crack shot. The man couldn't harm her. Not anymore. "This is what's going to happen. You will find a way back to your horse and get off my property. And if you *ever* return to this farm—ever—well, let's just say I can't promise your safety. Now, I am going to get back on my sled, and my dogs and I are going home. If you even *think* about harming one of them, I'll shoot you."

"You can't talk to me that way. You're nothin' but a woman." He spat at her.

Aurora growled and got in Sinclair's face, teeth bared.

"A woman who won't hesitate to shoot a hole straight through you. Now git, and quick. You don't want to be here when the sheriff comes. And you can rest assured that I will speak with him about your behavior."

Whitney's heart pounded in her chest. How had she not seen what a sleazy man Garrett Sinclair was? To think that she'd actually thought he was handsome. Her eyes burned, but she wouldn't cry. Not yet.

"Start walking."

Sinclair got to his feet keeping a careful eye on Pepper and the team. He picked up his hat and dusted it off. Pepper growled. The other dogs followed suit.

"If I were you, I'd run." Whitney didn't waiver.

Sinclair looked like he wanted to say or do something more, but at another snarl from Pepper, he turned and trudged out across the snow. Whitney waited until he was a good quarter mile away before lowering her rifle and rehitching Pepper.

On her sled, she kept the rifle trained on Sinclair, who was heading for the main road. She'd take the back way and come into the farmyard from the south so she didn't have to risk seeing that monster again.

"Let's go!" The dogs took their positions. "Hike!" They took off running. A couple of them looked back.

The tears finally came and Whitney wanted to scream. Never had she been touched and kissed by a man. And it had been so violent and awful. Her skin began to crawl, and she wanted to rip it off. Everywhere he'd touched she wanted to burn with fire. But she couldn't. As her body finally calmed down, the emotions took over. Would she ever feel clean again?

The shaking started in her middle again and spread to the rest of her body. It wouldn't stop.

Every bit of confidence and strength that she'd felt was gone. How could one man steal that from her?

The dogs ran fast, which was fine with her. They probably sensed her urgency to get home. When they ran up to the area of their kennels, John was there waiting for her.

She just stood there with her feet on the runners, one hand gripping the sled, the other on the rifle.

"What's wrong, Whit?"

She shook from head to toe.

"What happened? Are you hurt?" His face went ashen as his brow furrowed. "Havyn!" He yelled toward the chicken yard. "Whit, please talk to me. Whitney? *Whitney?*"

But nothing would come out.

Havyn ran toward her. "What's wrong? Oh my goodness, Whitney, what happened to you?" She turned to her husband. "She's white as a sheet."

And then the sobs started. Clutching the rifle to her chest, she dropped down to her knees in the snow.

Havyn was at her side, wrapping her arms around her. Comforting, safe arms. "John, something's terribly wrong."

Tears poured from her eyes. "He . . . he . . ."

"Sinclair?" John stepped closer. "What did he do?"

"He tried . . . he tried . . ."

Havyn gasped and held her tighter. "John, take care of the dogs, please, and make sure that man gets off this property permanently."

John's words came out cold and furious. "I'll get Inuksuk and Yutu from the sheep's milking barn. When Sinclair comes for his horse, we'll take care of him."

Havyn's gasp rattled through Whitney's brain as she clung to her. Her sister might be worried about Sinclair's life, but Whitney didn't care what her brother-in-law did to the man.

"We won't hurt him. We'll just make sure he knows to never come back." The words ended on a growl, unlike anything she'd ever heard from John.

Havyn lifted Whitney to her feet and held on with a fierce grip. "I'm going to take Whitney inside."

John breathed deep. "Just a moment. Whitney, did he . . . did he hurt you?"

She shook her head. "I stopped him."

The intense look on John's face made her feel safe. There *were* good men in this world. Men who would protect women. Men who would do the right thing.

Havyn put her forehead against hers. "Come on, Whit, let's get you inside."

She tried to move her legs and arms, but they wouldn't obey her mind's commands. If Havyn hadn't been holding her up, she'd be a puddle in the snow.

Havyn just held her while Whitney watched John unhitch the dogs from the sled. He held the lead line, but her dogs whimpered and whined and tried to get to her within their harnesses.

As their noses poked at her and they all wriggled as close as they could, she relaxed. They'd saved her. "Good dogs. Good . . . good dogs."

John caught her eye and seemed to understand in an instant what had happened. He nodded at her. "You trained them well. I'm glad you are all right."

That was when the shaking kicked up a notch. Tremors shook her to her very core. But once she saw her dogs safely ensconced in their enclosure, she nodded to Havyn. "Please. Let's go inside."

"Okay. John will make sure you're safe."

"I know." Her legs felt like they wouldn't hold her weight, but the more steps she took, the stronger she felt. "I was so . . . so foolish. I should have known . . ." She couldn't finish the sentence. What could she do? Women who were attacked like that were usually blamed. After all, she *had* gone out without a trusted escort.

As they made their way to the house, a wagon with several people in it was coming up the lane.

No, no, no! She couldn't deal with people right now.

"Don't worry about it. Madysen and I will take care of them."

"Who is it?"

Havyn let out a long sigh. "It's Dad. And his other family."

NINETEEN

Madysen paced the hallway outside her sister's room, her stomach churning. As soon as John told her what had happened, she'd raced into the house.

She should have been there. She should have done something to stop it. Guilt wrapped around her shoulders like a wet woolen coat.

John said he would keep Dad and the others outside and occupied after he got rid of Sinclair. But what were they going to do with company in the midst of this horror?

A noise at the door made her look up. Havyn exited Whitney's room and closed the door behind her. She took Madysen's elbow and leaned close to her ear. "I think she's okay. Just in shock. Thankfully, it wasn't as bad as it could have been, but you need to tell Dad that now is not a good time."

Madysen pressed a fist to her aching heart. "Are you sure she's all right?"

"Yes. At least physically. But this didn't just affect her outwardly." Havyn wrapped an arm around her shoulders. "We've got to be strong for her. And I don't think we should have that party anytime soon."

Madysen nodded. Then she looked toward Granddad's room. "Has anyone told him?"

"Not yet." Havyn shook her head. "But Whitney asked me

to go do that so he doesn't worry. Especially with our guests here."

"Oh, Havyn. What are we going to do? There's no place for those kids to stay except here." There couldn't have been worse timing for them to show up at the farm. "We can't turn them out in the snow."

"I know, but I can't deal with that at the moment. Whitney is in no shape—"

The door opened, and their older sister poked her head out. "As loud as you two are, I'm sure the entire household has heard you." Whitney lifted her chin. "Don't worry about me. I'm fine. We had planned to let them have Mama's room anyway, so just get them settled in." Whitney turned to Madysen. "But would you mind sharing my room with me for a night or two? I don't think I'm comfortable enough to be alone." The words were so formal, so distant—and so unlike Whitney.

"Of course." Madysen wanted to say something more to reassure her sister, but the words wouldn't come. Whitney closed the door, and a sigh escaped Madysen's lips.

Havyn lifted her shoulders. "All right then. I'll go tell Granddad and make sure that there are clean linens in Mama's room. I'll meet you in Whit's room tonight so the three of us can talk."

Madysen nodded. "I'll go greet the . . . family."

Why was it so hard to say that word? These were her father's children, same as she. But *family* conjured up images of the people whose photographs rested on the fireplace mantel. Or whose names were embroidered on Christmas stockings. The people with whom she'd shared twenty-some years of memories.

Her father's children were strangers.

Same as John had once been.

Madysen nodded at the thought. She'd had no trouble welcoming John to the farm. She'd had no dread, felt no need to find fault with him. So why did she feel those things now?

She hugged herself. She could do this. Be hospitable. It wasn't like she'd need to put up with them for long.

Her heart began to pound. Could she leave Nome? Leave her sisters when everything was in such turmoil? Was the loss of her mother still so hard to bear that she was looking for a way to escape Mama's empty room?

Buddy painted a beautiful picture of what their life together would be. And she needed more *life*. Not all the grief and sadness. Winter was always difficult, but with Mama gone, the cold pierced Madysen to her bones. Everything seemed drab and gray. The only warmth was her time with Buddy and the rosy future he promised.

Was it selfish to want to go, to leave the relentless grief of home?

She continued pacing the hall. Answers eluded her. Instead, the questions chased each other in an unending circle inside her brain.

If Mama were still here, what would she do?

Madysen stopped cold.

The answer was easy. Mama would love like Jesus loved. Because that was His command, to love as He loved the world. And He was willing to sacrifice Himself for everyone.

Madysen inhaled and repeated to herself, "Love as Jesus loved. Love as Jesus loved. . . ."

She kept it up as she went down the hall, out the door, and past the empty wagon to the big barn where voices sounded.

Her dad looked at her as she approached. "Maddy." He cocked his head to one side. "Is everything all right?"

She pushed her emotions to the farthest corner of her heart. "It's been a trying day, and we had an unfortunate event." It sounded frosty, even to her own ears, but how else could she explain it? "Nothing for you to worry about, though. Did John show you around the farm?"

"He sure did." Dad beamed. "Didn't he, kids? Won't this be a great place to stay?"

The two kids behind him were almost as tall as she but with far less meat on their frames. Their lips were pressed together, but they couldn't hide the occasional tremble.

Madysen put on a smile and stepped forward. "Hi, my name is Madysen, and I'm the youngest . . . well, I guess I'm not the youngest anymore. But I'm the youngest of the three of us . . . that is. Um . . . your older sisters." Oh, help. What had she gotten herself into?

The boy stepped forward and stuck out his hand. "I'm Elijah. But everyone calls me Eli. I'm fourteen. And this is my sister, Bethany. She's twelve."

Madysen shook his hand. "It's nice to meet you both." Funny, neither one of her new siblings had red hair. They both had brown.

Probably because Mama was the one with red hair. Her heart twinged. *Oh, Mama, we could use you now.*

"I'm Ruth." A woman stepped out from the barn with John right behind her. He carried a couple of suitcases—they probably belonged to the woman.

"I heard you say that you're Madysen. My, how beautiful your hair is. I have always loved red hair, and just look at those curls! How lovely that you wear it down."

Was that a compliment . . . or something else? Something with an edge? Madysen reached back to tame her tresses. "I get horrendous headaches if I pull it up. It's awfully heavy." Why had she gone on like that? She didn't have to defend herself to this woman. "I was just noticing Eli and Bethany have brown hair, like Dad."

Ruth nodded. "They take after my sister."

Madysen forced a smile. "Well, let's go get you settled in the house."

Bethany clung to their father and whispered. "Do we have to stay here? Can't we go with you?"

The ice in Madysen's heart melted. She knew what it was

like to be deserted by this man. How could he do it again? He'd promised things were different, yet here he was, proving to be the same selfish father. The blood in her veins heated. She turned around and marched toward the house. They needed some privacy, and she needed space to keep from breaking her vow to love as Jesus loved less than five minutes after making it.

John caught up with her. "How's Whitney?"

"I'm not real sure. Havyn is with her now."

"I could have strangled Sinclair when he came back for his horse. Had it not been for Yutu and Inuksuk standing there with their fierce looks and crossed arms, he probably would have picked a fight with me. He looked raving mad. I wouldn't have minded teaching him a lesson, but I could hardly deal with him with your family standing there waiting for attention."

"At least he left." Madysen hated that people could be so evil. "Are you all right?"

"Not exactly, but I don't really have a choice."

"Maddy?" Dad's voice made her turn around. He and the children were just a few feet away. Ruth had positioned herself to one side, as if to give them privacy.

Madysen stopped at the porch steps. "Yes, Dad?"

"I think maybe it's best if I leave now. It might be easier on Eli and Bethany to adjust, and I just got a lead on Stan. I sure would like to find him so that I can come back and take care of the kids." He kept an arm draped around each one of his newly arrived children. "And of course reunite Ruth and Stan." He seemed so genuine. So truthful.

How should she respond? She finally managed, "Of course."

"Give me a minute to say good-bye."

Madysen turned and climbed the steps, John close behind her. He put the suitcases by the front door, then moved to the far side of the porch to give the little family as much privacy as possible. Madysen followed him, her arms tight around her middle. What could Dad say to Eli and Bethany that would make this situation right? Madysen had been so young when Dad had supposedly died. The pain, however, had been of grown-up proportions.

Dad sat on the steps and bid Bethany and Eli to join him. Bethany threw herself into his arms and cried.

"Please don't go."

Madysen pressed her teeth together so hard her jaw ached. Hadn't she said the same thing at her father's coffin? His *empty* coffin! Bitterness burned her throat. She loved Grand-dad, she did, but how could he have thought that was kinder—better—for Mama? For her and her sisters to pretend Dad was dead? A girl needed her daddy. How could anyone think otherwise?

"You need to be brave, Bethany." Dad's voice carried in the silent yard. "Remember your aunt Ruth and your cousins. They need me to find Uncle Stan. They need him, and we can help."

Madysen pressed her palm over her lips. Everything, from the tone of his voice to the love shining out of his eyes, said he was sincere. But how could she—how could anyone—ever trust the word of a man who'd caused so much hurt?

"But why must we stay behind?" Eli's question twisted Madysen's stomach. "We could come and help you."

"The mining camps are no place for children."

Madysen stiffened, her arms jerking straight down. They'd been good enough for his *first* set of children. He'd dragged her and her sisters from one gold camp to another.

"There's too much danger at the camps and way too much fighting. I couldn't bear it if something happened to you."

But he didn't mind those things happening around *them*. Madysen clenched her fists. Could he even hear what he was saying? Staring at the man she once adored, she wanted to shake some sense into him.

Then Bethany sniffed. A single tear trailed down her cheek. Eli put his arm around her.

Every argument and every disappointment swirling inside Madysen's spirit halted. Took second place to these poor children. None of this—absolutely none of it—was their fault. They loved their father. Had lost their mother too. Just like Madysen and her sisters. Madysen drew in a deep breath and let it out. Relaxed her fists.

John gave her shoulder a pat.

"It will get easier," he whispered.

Bethany buried her face against Dad's chest. "I'll be brave, Papa."

He whispered something to her, then kissed the top of her head.

Sitting beside their father, Eli seemed all gangly arms and legs, but he nodded as Dad talked to him. Then he smiled, and the threesome got to their feet and embraced.

Dad had hugged Madysen and her sisters like that once. Long ago. She remembered it as though it were yesterday. His love had meant so much to her. She'd played the memory over and over in her head like a piece of music. Seeing him do that now was both sweet and bitter.

She didn't want to share that precious memory.

Dad turned to Ruth. "I'll be back as soon as possible. I promise you, I will find him."

"Remember, Chris, even if it's the worst . . . I want to know." Ruth lifted her chin. "And . . . if he's . . . if the worst has happened, I don't know what I'll do. I always thought we'd be buried side by side in the family plot. But I don't think I want to return to Colorado without him."

Ruth was taller than Madysen by at least five inches, but she suddenly seemed small and fragile.

"We'll cross that bridge when we come to it." Dad gave Ruth a hug.

Madysen bowed her head. Here she was wrapped up in her feelings about Dad, and this poor woman didn't even know if her husband was dead or alive. Had it put an edge in her voice? One that Madysen misread in her own distrust?

Madysen opened the door with her left hand and beckoned to Bethany and Eli with her right. Ruth and the children deserved her compassion and understanding even if Dad didn't . . . but did he deserve her mercy and forgiveness?

Did anyone *deserve* it?

The question echoed in her head as she ushered the children inside. John waited for Ruth to precede him into the house, then they all walked to the window.

Dad waved. They all waved back.

Lord, keep him safe. And help him to find Ruth's husband. She ought to ask for something more, maybe something about changing her heart toward her dad, but whatever else she needed from her heavenly Father was overshadowed by the pain of what she hadn't received from her earthly one. *Lord, teach me how to pray.*

Dad turned and climbed up into the wagon, maneuvered the horses back down the snowy lane, and slowly disappeared.

Eli worried his lower lip while Bethany wiped at her tears. They both looked so weary.

"Why don't we go into the parlor for a little bit and warm by the fire?" The poor things had been out in the cold the whole time she and Havyn had been seeing to Whitney.

Whitney. Her heart ached for her sister. Why was this world filled with such cruelty?

Madysen led them into the parlor, and their eyes widened at the expansive stone fireplace. They just stared for several moments.

Taking Bethany's shoulders, she directed her to the settee so they could sit and watch the fire. "That's my favorite part of this room—other than the musical instruments."

John tapped Madysen's shoulder. "I'll go get some tea started, then I'll need to check on Daniel. He's been in the cheese kitchen trying to help you out by getting everything unpacked and sorted."

"Oh, I completely forgot. Thank him for me, will you?" Her brother-in-law was so thoughtful. Protective. Kind. And to think that Daniel was here too. "Would you tell Daniel to please come have a cup of tea and some cake before he heads out?"

John nodded and looked at their guests. "I put your bags over there." He pointed to where they were placed by the side door.

"Thank you." Ruth tucked her hands in her lap. "It was so nice of you to carry them. I'm afraid we're all a bit worn out. The boat journey here was so long."

John grinned. "Remind me to tell you all sometime how I arrived by dog sled."

"Dog sled?" Eli's tone showed his interest.

John laughed. "Yup. It was quite the ordeal. But for now, I'll go put the water on for tea, and then I have to get to work." He left them, whistling as he went.

Madysen smiled at Ruth. "We're going to put you in my mama's room. There are two small beds for you and Bethany and a cot for Eli. Maybe later we'll figure other arrangements since it's not exactly ideal."

"It's a roof over our heads, which is more than we had." Ruth rubbed a spot behind her ear. "Nome is a difficult place to find refuge."

Madysen nodded. "The hotels are almost always full. Mr. Reynolds just built a new one, and he says there's never an unrented room. Most of the folks who come here just live in tents, however."

"Even in the cold and snow?" Eli seemed even more interested in that than the dog sled.

Madysen widened her eyes and smiled. "Yep. Even then. It's amazing what people endure for the promise of gold."

Ruth nodded. "I'm sure Stan gave the cold little thought."

Eli took a seat by the fire. "Our dad told us that you thought he—our dad . . . um, your dad—was dead."

Goodness! That was direct. Madysen cleared her throat to

give herself a second to come up with a response. How much had Dad told them? And how was she supposed to respond when she still didn't know how she felt about it? "Yes. We thought he was dead for many years." She kept her tone as free of emotion as she could. "Until he arrived a few months ago."

"And you didn't know anything about us?"

Madysen shook her head. "No. Well, that's not entirely true. My sister Havyn knew about you, but she didn't tell us."

"Our mother"—Bethany peered up at Madysen—"was a wonderful woman."

"I'm sure she was." She swallowed the growing lump in her throat. She didn't want to cry or make a scene, but it broke her heart that Bethany—who up until now hadn't spoken directly to Madysen—felt it necessary to defend her mother. It forged a small bond between them.

Girls who had loved and lost their mothers needed to stick together.

"Look, I know this is very difficult for you. But we are family now. Our mom passed in July, and our grandfather has been very ill, so things are difficult around here, but we can weather these storms together, right?" The words definitely weren't her own. *Thank you, God, for giving them to me.*

Eli and Bethany nodded.

Ruth offered a slight smile. "I told them on the boat that maybe God had brought us here for a time of healing and hope."

Madysen's heart softened a little more. What must Ruth be going through? She'd left her own children at home and endured a difficult journey in hopes of finding her lost husband. If she could have a good attitude about this, shouldn't Madysen?

After tea and cake, and an extensive conversation about the Nome area, Madysen stood. "Just leave your dishes and I'll see to them. I'll show you to your room. You can get settled and have a rest. Then we'll have supper around six. Does that sound good?"

"It's perfect." Ruth covered a yawn. "I'm sure we'd all appreciate some time to ourselves."

Eli and Bethany nodded.

Conflicting emotions flooded through Madysen as she walked down the hallway to Mama's room. They had two beds set up in there, which brought back all the memories of sleeping in here with Mama while she coughed and struggled to breathe.

Madysen shook her head against the thoughts. She didn't want to share this sacred space. But Mama would. And she would encourage them to enjoy the life and laughter of the children. No matter the circumstances. So Madysen straightened her shoulders and opened the door.

But once Madysen stepped into the room, she couldn't get outside fast enough. "Why don't you get settled, and I'll meet you back in the parlor in a little bit?"

She stayed just long enough to be polite before fleeing, nearly slamming the door in her haste to escape. Everything about this situation was painful.

Everything.

Her younger siblings were in pain. Ruth was in pain. Havyn and Whitney were in pain. She was in pain. Granddad was in pain. Mama was still gone. And though Dad was back, he had left again, which caused even more pain.

But who had it worse, her or Bethany and Eli? The father she remembered was very different from the one who'd just left.

Dad had changed. He wasn't a drunkard and womanizer anymore. He wasn't focused on his own selfish needs and wants.

But the change was too late. Too late to make it up to Mama. Too late to make their childhood right.

When she walked in the door to the cheese kitchen, she wasn't exactly sure what she needed, but Daniel stood there smiling.

She broke into tears.

He walked over to her and stood there looking oh-so-understanding. "What is it? Can I help?"

She shook her head, then wrapped her arms around his waist and sobbed into his shoulder.

He cocooned her in his arms. "Shhh. It's all right. Want to talk about it?"

She couldn't answer. Tears flowed from the fount of ache within.

So he stood there and held her.

After several minutes, she pulled back and wiped at her face with her sleeve. "I'm so sorry. That was inappropriate and presumptuous of me. It's just . . ."

The compassion and concern on his face undid her. She let it all spill out. "Whitney's hurt, and I'm not sure what to do with my father's other kids. I want to hug them and love on them, but I keep remembering how we got to this place, and I get angry all over again. Eli and Bethany don't deserve my anger. They're just kids. Innocent kids. And I want to be their big sister. I've never had any younger siblings. But I had to give them and Ruth Mama's room, and it just hurts to remember my last moments with her. And Dad already left to find his brother-in-law, and I don't know when he will be back, and it's all just a big mess." She'd said everything so fast that she gasped for air and started crying all over again.

He gripped her elbows. "It's okay. Messes are a part of life. Especially family messes."

She put her head on Daniel's shoulder. She felt safe. Comfortable. Warm.

"I'm here, Maddy. Whatever you need." He rubbed her back lightly.

She smiled against his shoulder. "I think that's the first time you've used my nickname."

He paused for several seconds. "Is it all right if I call you that?"

"Yes. I like it." And then her heart did that thing where it felt like butterflies were inside her.

The longer Daniel held her, the more she realized she wanted to stay right here.

With him.

They stood in the middle of the kitchen for several minutes while he just rubbed her back. Gentle. Caring. Loving.

She pulled away. What was she thinking? "I'm sorry." She wiped at her face again. "I shouldn't have cried all over you."

"That's okay, Maddy. I want to be here if you need me. I'm your friend, remember?"

She nodded. But at that moment, there were a lot of feelings that made her think of Daniel as more than a friend. No wait. Those feelings were reserved for Buddy. Weren't they?

She heard footsteps outside and took another step away from Daniel. What was going on with her? Why had she fallen apart on him like that?

"Hey, Daniel." John walked into the cheese kitchen. "Oh, Madysen, you're here. You must have already told him."

Her brother-in-law looked back and forth between them. "Everything all right?"

Madysen wiped the last traces of wet from her cheeks. "Yes, I just needed a bit of a cry and didn't want to have it in front of the kids."

"Understandable. Well, I've got to go check the cows before dinner. Are you going to be all right?"

She nodded. "I think so."

"Just let me know if you need me, okay?"

Another nod.

John turned to Daniel. "Havyn told me to invite you to stay for supper."

"Thank you, I'd like that very much."

"Great. We'll see you then."

After John left, Daniel picked up a bucket of sheep's milk. "Why don't you let me finish up here, and you go splash some cool water on your face. I bet that will make you feel better."

"I'm sure it will." She forced a small smile. "Thanks for listening."

"Anytime."

"Maybe we can all gather around the piano tonight—" She gasped. "Oh no!"

"What?"

"We're supposed to play at the Roadhouse!"

———————

Madysen hadn't wanted to add to anyone's burdens, but she had to remind her sisters of their commitment.

"I can't play at the Roadhouse. Not now." Whitney shook her head and paced in front of the fireplace in her room. "I'm sorry. I can't."

"Well, maybe it could just be the two of us, Havyn?" Madysen looked to her sister.

"I think someone should be here for Whitney, as well as the children and Ruth. We can hardly drag them along. They just got here." Havyn tucked her hands into the pockets of her apron.

"You've always wanted to perform on your own." Whitney sounded almost flippant. "Why don't you go do that?"

Madysen looked back and forth between her sisters. Should she? "I guess if you think I should. . . . I don't mind at all. If John will come with me, then I'll do it. I can explain to the audience that we've had some unexpected problems, and I'll give an abbreviated show."

"I don't know. . . ." Havyn's words faded as she looked to her husband. "What do you think?"

He shrugged. "At least this way we won't completely disappoint the folks by not showing up at all. Maddy can get a taste of what it's like to perform alone, and no one should be any worse for the wear. Besides, I need to talk to the sheriff about what happened to Whitney."

"No!" Whitney shook her head. "No one must know."

"You can't be serious, Whit!" Madysen stared at her sister. What had gotten into her?

"Whit, he *attacked* you." John's face looked like a storm.

Whit held out both of her hands. "Yes, but I've thought on this a great deal. People will say it was my fault. They think women are nothing more than objects to be admired or scorned. Our reputation is the only thing we have, and if this gets out, mine will be ruined."

John stepped closer and fisted his hands. "I understand, but we can't allow Sinclair to get away with this."

"No sheriff. Not a word to anyone—not even Dad. I don't want anyone else knowing what happened." Whitney put her hand to the back of her head.

"Are you all right, Whit?" Havyn moved in faster than a mother hen.

"It's my head—my neck. I hit hard when I pushed away from that man." Her older sister looked so weak and discouraged.

Havyn wrapped an arm around her. "You should see a doctor."

"No. I don't need anyone." Whit's tone was resolute as she curled up on her side. "Please just leave."

Madysen shared a glance with John. Fury filled his eyes. As the man of the house, what must he be feeling? And here she would be taking him away from the farm tonight. Would he be able to resist hunting down Garrett Sinclair?

She put a hand to her throat. What if one of the men tried the same thing with her? Performing alone lost its appeal. Sure, John would be there to protect her. And the old guard. But was that enough?

She fled to put her music together for the evening. She could do this. Wasn't it what she wanted to experience?

She'd better get used to it. Because if she left with Buddy, she'd be performing all alone.

All the time.

Madysen took the stage and offered up her explanation, then broke into a lively tune on the piano. Good thing Mama made sure all of them could accompany themselves on the piano. But she wasn't near as good as Whit.

The men began to clap. They didn't seem to mind at all that Madysen was alone.

But it wasn't the same. At all. Together, she and her sisters created a beautiful painting of music. Alone, Madysen was like haphazard brushstrokes and skeletal shapes. Was that how it would be if she went off with Buddy Merrick?

She played through several songs, her discontentment growing. The men seemed rowdier than usual. Did they sense something was wrong? Or was she imagining things because today had been so horrid?

Each song became more like a chore than a joy. Her head began to pound. What were Havyn and Whit doing right now? Had they gone to bed early? Was Whit all right?

For the first time in her life, Madysen wanted to cut a performance short. She breathed her relief when she finished the tenth song.

"I'm going to take a little break, but I'll be back in a few minutes." The applause was lackluster. Whatever their earlier enthusiasm, it had waned, and she couldn't blame them. Her heart wasn't in it.

John and Daniel met her at the foot of the stage steps.

Daniel took her elbow. "Are you doing all right? You don't look like you're enjoying yourself."

She wanted to fall into his arms again. Tears stung her eyes. "I—"

Crash!

She turned to investigate the cause of the noise, but Daniel and John closed in behind her, practically pushing her into a small storage closet.

"Stay here." John's voice brooked no argument.

Madysen nodded, too tired and disappointed with herself to put up a fight.

Daniel gave her a rueful smile from the doorway. "What were you about to say?"

She shook her head, the moment gone. "Nothing. I'll be fine."

He gave her a searching look, opened his mouth, then shut it again. "I'll leave you in peace." He closed the door a few inches. "I'll be right outside if you need me."

"Thank you." What a good friend. So reliable and caring. The remembrance of his embrace earlier brought warmth to her cheeks.

She waited until the door was closed to lean her head back and let out a long sigh. Her fingers ached. She rubbed her right hand and then her left as she took deep breaths.

"She needs a few minutes alone, Mr. Merrick." John's voice was a bit muffled through the door.

"I understand that completely." Buddy swung open the door. "I simply wanted to bring her a present or two." He held out his offerings. More candy and hothouse flowers.

"How kind of you." Madysen held up a hand to refuse. "But I must decline. We make it a point to never accept gifts from the audience on performance nights. If we start it with one, we have to keep it up with all the others."

"How very noble of you." He handed the candy to John and the flowers to Daniel. With their hands occupied, they were unable to stop him when he stepped inside the small closet. "I understand." Buddy picked up her hand and patted it. It didn't soothe her the way it usually did.

It wasn't even close to how much better she'd felt inside the comfort of Daniel's arms.

Heat crept up her cheeks again. What a terrible, disloyal thought. Buddy was her future. She had no business thinking of Daniel.

"You're quite amazing you know." Buddy picked up her other hand, trapping both of hers between his. "Your performance has been splendid. Why, you must see that you don't need your sisters. You are a star all on your own."

She gave a sidelong glance at John and Daniel, who couldn't help but hear the man. She tugged her hands free. "It's not the same without them."

"No indeed. It's infinitely better."

"She needs to get back on stage." John moved his bulk into the closet between them.

"Of course, of course. We can't keep her audience waiting." Buddy reached for her shoulder and patted it, but John guided her out of the closet, away from Buddy's touch. "It's not your fault that you bear the weight of talent. Your sisters have had a good turn with you to anchor them, but now is the time for you to grab hold of your destiny. *Our* destiny."

Somehow the words weren't as appealing as they had been yesterday. And what was with all the patting? It was annoying.

Tapping his fingers on his desk, Judas thought through the next part of his plan. It shouldn't be that difficult to convince Madysen that she should take off with Buddy. He'd seen the way she looked at the man—as if he could fulfill all her dreams. And apparently Buddy had done a fine job wooing her with gifts and praise.

"Mr. Reynolds." Garrett Sinclair stood at the door.

Judas frowned. It was nearly eleven in the morning. "Come in." He waved him in. "Close the door."

"Yes, sir."

"It's a little late in the morning to be showing up for work, isn't it? You've been mighty scarce. I expected a report before now."

"There was some trouble." He offered nothing more.

"There's always trouble of some sort. Do you have anything to report?"

Sinclair made himself comfortable in one of the chairs. He crossed his right leg over his left and then picked at his teeth with his finger. "There isn't any gold on that property. At least, not that I could see. There's no cave or mine, no panning or sluicing going on. Nothing."

"Then how do you explain where all that gold came from?" Reynolds narrowed his eyes and leaned over his desk.

"Probably from the fact that their farm is thriving. They're smart. And they've got enough dogs, cows, chickens, sheep, and whatever else to produce a lot more gold than that little bag."

Judas nodded. "All right, you need to get back out there and get hired. Find out how they operate—"

"Nope." Sinclair stood. "I'm done. Keep your gold. I'm not going back out there. Just wanted to let you know." The man left, slamming the door behind him.

What had gotten into him?

It didn't matter. Judas would deal with him later. Besides, he could find out what he needed another way.

The clock chimed.

Mr. Beaufort was late. That was odd, the man was usually quite punctual.

His secretary came to the door. "Mr. Beaufort is on his way, sir."

He gave a slight nod. "Show him in."

Several moments later, Martin appeared at the door quite breathless. "Judas, I'm sorry to be late."

He put on his most welcoming smile. "Not a problem, my friend. Not a problem." He waved the man into his office and pointed to a chair. "Is everything all right? You seem quite flustered."

The merc owner sat down and took a few deep breaths while

he fidgeted with his tie. "I'm sorry. I hate to be late, but I was going over everything in the books to see if there was any way I could have made a mistake."

"Oh? Is there a problem?" Judas used a compassionate tone. One he'd mastered over the years.

Martin sighed. Long and heavy. "I don't know what happened, but I won't be able to make my arranged payment. And I find that I'm not even adequately prepared for the winter."

Judas stood and walked around the desk and then sat casually on the edge, folding his hands on his lap. "Don't worry about it, Martin. I'm your friend. We'll get through this together. Times have been tough for many. How can I help? Do you need more money?"

The man was good enough to look embarrassed, but he held his gaze. "I'm afraid I do. Can we amend our agreement to increase the loan? I don't want to burden my son or my mother with such financial woes."

"Of course, we can. How much do you need? I can give you as long as you need to pay it back."

The man leaned back, relief clear on his face as he relaxed. "I can't tell you how much I appreciate it, Judas."

"What are friends for, Martin? The Good Lord above didn't bless me with all this not to share it with those in need. Let me help." He leaned forward and gave Martin's shoulder a friendly squeeze, then walked back to his chair, opened a drawer, and pulled out the agreement.

It only took a few minutes to amend the contract and for them to sign it.

Mr. Beaufort walked out the door with full pockets and a spring in his hobbled step.

Judas got up and closed his door with a chuckle. The fool. He probably didn't even read what Judas amended to their agreement. And the man would probably be back for more money. Again.

That was fine with him.

It wouldn't be too long before Judas owned the mercantile too.

Not too shabby for only eleven o'clock in the morning. The day was looking up.

TWENTY

Whitney gritted her teeth. Garrett Sinclair had fooled her. Her! She was famous—at least within her family—for being cautious, particularly where strange men were concerned. And the one time she let her guard down? She'd been attacked.

Lesson learned. No more trusting men. Ever!

She went to check on the dogs. They carried on as usual, ready to run, but today she didn't have the stomach for it. What if Sinclair was waiting for her? John suggested she take someone with her and exercise the teams two at a time, which was a great idea except for two things. First, it wasn't fair to take John or the others away from their own work. Second, and more important, she shouldn't have to do it.

Whitney leaned down and stroked Pepper's thick coat, taking comfort in the feel of his fur against her fingers. "I admit it," she whispered in the dog's pointed ear, "I'm afraid of Garrett Sinclair. And that gives him power over me."

"I hope I'm not disturbing you."

Whitney jerked upright.

Ruth Robertson stood a few feet away. She wore a scarf around her head and a long coat, but both were too thin for the Alaska cold. Under normal circumstances, Whitney would offer to loan the newcomer one of her thick coats and fur hats. Under normal circumstances, she'd make small talk to befriend a woman new to Nome.

But these were far from normal circumstances.

The only way she could survive however long it took to heal from her attack was to put up walls. With everyone.

Ruth stepped forward. Tentative. "I don't mean to intrude, and I don't mean to pry, but I overheard a few things . . . and I pieced together what happened. It's a horrible thing to go through."

"What?" Whitney swallowed and coughed to clear her throat. "I don't know what you're talking about."

"You were assaulted by a man, weren't you?"

Whitney shook her head. A little too fast. This woman had been welcomed into Whitney's home, and she had the nerve to eavesdrop? "I'm not sure what you heard, but I'd rather you say nothing about it."

Ruth nodded. "I understand but, if I may, I'd like to offer you a small bit of advice. Don't shut friends or family out of your life."

How did this woman know what she was feeling?

"I . . . had a similar experience."

Whitney sucked in a breath and held it.

Ruth looked away. "I was sixteen. I was walking home to the farm, and a man rode up out of nowhere. He asked me for directions. I gave them to him, and the next thing I knew, he was off his horse and I was on the ground. Fortunately for me, my friend, Stan, was fishing nearby. He heard me scream and came to my rescue. But even though he wrestled off my attacker and tied him up for the sheriff to deal with, my scars remained."

"What happened to the man who attacked you?"

It was a long moment before Ruth shook her head. "He said I'd . . . I'd . . . *wanted* his attention. That I was embarrassed when Stan came along, so I changed my mind—as women and girls were known to do. Nothing could be proved in court. It was my word and Stan's against a man with powerful friends."

Whitney hated how that made her feel. Helpless. Worthless. "No one cares. We're just women. We mean nothing."

"Well, I mean something to Stan. He is good to me." She cleared her throat. "I just wanted you to know that I understand."

"How long was it before you stopped looking over your shoulder?" The question was out before Whitney could stop it.

Ruth shrugged. "I still do."

Whitney looked to the barn rafter. Would she have preferred false comfort over the truth? Maybe. But then again, no. She summoned her courage with a deep inhale and looked at Ruth. "Then how did you get . . . beyond it?"

"It was something Stan told me. 'Don't let that man have one more second of power over you.'"

Ruth was lost in her own story. "Stan was right. By hiding in my parents' house, I was giving that man control over my life. My family didn't really understand why it was so hard to move on, but they supported me. After years of working at it and praying about it, I finally felt strong enough to travel alone with Chris's children."

Whitney moved to one of the other dogs and scratched his ears. "My sisters say I'm cynical. I'm afraid this has only made that worse."

Ruth reached out and patted Whitney's arm. "A little cynicism is healthy. Especially after what you've been through. Were you . . . hurt in any way?"

Whitney rubbed the back of her head. "When I got out of his grasp, I fell backward and hit my head. It's a bit tender, but I'll be fine." Those were the outward scars. The inward ones were too raw, too undefined to put into words.

Ruth's small smile said she'd heard what Whitney hadn't

said. "Just remember that you have someone to talk to who's been through it. If you ever need it."

"As winter comes on we'll keep the sheep penned up here and feed them hay and grain and other things they need." Madysen showed Bethany around. For the last two days, the girl had been her constant companion. And she'd loved it. It hadn't taken long for her younger siblings to carve out a place in her heart.

"We didn't have sheep on our farm, but we did have chickens and cows." The girl was tiny for her twelve years, but she was smart and observant. "I like working with the animals."

"The sheep can be difficult at times. They aren't the smartest of animals. I suppose that's why the Lord so often spoke about us being like sheep." Madysen pointed out into the pen. "I mean, just look. They're outside in the cold and snow when they could be in here keeping warm. They're free to come and go as they like, and yet there they are."

"I like the snow, so maybe they do too." Bethany grinned. "I'm looking forward to going on one of Whitney's dog sleds. She said she'd take me sometime."

"I'm sure she will, and won't that be fun? I love riding on the sled with her. Let's go check on the cheese. We're making something Daniel called feta. It's in the brining stage."

"I like cheese, but Eli doesn't. He likes meat." Bethany tucked her hand into Madysen's as they walked.

Emotions stirred that Madysen hadn't felt in a while. She wanted to protect the sweet girl and keep her young and innocent forever. "We get plenty of meat too. Fish mostly, but often beef and musk ox, which is absolutely delicious. People do a lot of trading up here. Our native friends bring it to us sometimes in trade for eggs and milk. They bring us other things too. Dried salmon, berries, and vegetables they've grown. And sometimes seal, which I'm not at all fond of eating."

Her younger sister scrunched up her nose. How cute! Havyn and Whit always teased her about making the same expression.

"Can I call you Maddy like the rest of the family does?" Bethany swung their arms as she stuck out her tongue to catch a snowflake.

A day or so ago, that might have upset Madysen, but today it was endearing. "Of course. I'd like that."

They checked the cheese and made certain nothing else was needed before heading back to the house. Bethany had grown rather quiet.

"Is something wrong?"

Bethany shrugged. "I miss Papa. I know he has to help Aunt Ruth find Uncle Stanley, but I wish he didn't have to go. I'll bet you miss him too since you just found out he wasn't dead."

Discussing Dad wasn't her first choice, but what could she do? "I'm still trying to . . . handle what happened."

"You mean that he was alive and lived with us?"

The light snow that had been falling since dawn grew heavier. Good thing she started early on her chores. Still, a part of her wished she could dismiss Bethany and go off to do something more.

"I won't lie to you. You're twelve and old enough to know that lies really hurt people."

"But Papa said he thought it was best for everyone. He knew he'd made his family miserable by drinking all the time."

Madysen looked away. At least he hadn't tried to hide that truth from them and make himself sound like he'd been the one wronged. But Bethany probably knew nothing about Granddad's part in it. Which raised up a whole different swirl of emotions in Madysen. Why didn't she feel as angry toward Granddad as she did Dad? Granddad had been more deceptive. He had instigated the entire lie about Dad being dead, but for some reason, it was easier to forgive Granddad than her father.

Later that night, Madysen couldn't get rid of the question.

Outside was clear, and the stars shone from every corner of the sky. She loved to stare at them, but tonight it couldn't calm her spirit.

Despite the colder temperatures, Madysen took a seat on the porch swing. She could hear the others laughing and talking inside the house. Everyone seemed to be having a lot of fun with the game John started.

The door opened and Havyn came outside. "I thought I saw you come out here. Aren't you cold?" She pulled a heavy wool shawl around her head and shoulders.

"I'm warm enough for now." Madysen patted the swing. "Can I talk to you?"

Her sister laughed. "Of course. Isn't that what sisters always do?"

Where should she start? "Well . . . after I got the kids settled in Mama's room that first night, I was overcome with emotion, and I ran off to the sheep kitchen. Daniel was there. . . ."

"Oh?"

"Promise me you won't be critical?"

Havyn crossed her heart. "I promise. I've never meant to be critical, Maddy. I'm sorry."

"You have to promise that you won't say a word to anyone."

"Madysen." Havyn gave her a pointed look. "Seriously? This is me. The sister who keeps all the secrets."

"I know, I know. This is just awkward. . . ." She looked down at her hands. It would be so much easier if she had her cello and bow in her hand. That was when she felt the most comfortable.

"Go on. I promise I won't say a word. Get it off your chest."

"I've been thinking that I might be in love with Buddy Merrick. I know for sure that I care for him. He comes to see me regularly, his faithful attention and sweet gifts make me feel special. He ticks off everything on my list that I ever wanted . . . well, almost everything. Plus he promises adventure and plenty of stages to perform on . . ." The words fell flat and hung in the air.

"But?"

Madysen took a deep breath. "But when I was so upset, Daniel held me while I cried. He's been such a good friend to me. And . . . I felt new things for him. Intense things. Things I haven't felt with Buddy. I'm so torn, Havyn. I want to stay in Alaska and be here with all of you, but with Mama gone and Dad back, it all just feels so strange. And then there's my dream of performing and honoring Mama. What do I do?"

Havyn lifted her face to gaze at the stars. "That's a question only you can answer, Maddy." She turned toward Madysen. "Love shouldn't be taken lightly. Yes, Buddy has been very sweet and attentive to you, but do you feel toward him what you should feel toward a husband? Or is it simply that the idea of marriage is appealing because he can give you what you want— a bigger stage to perform on?"

"Don't we all want that?" Madysen spread her hands to encompass both Havyn and Whitney, who was still inside. "I thought you and Whit loved performing too."

"We do." Havyn's face lit up in the moonlight. "The music is in our bones. But do you want to travel the world and be in a different place every couple of days just so you can play music? I know you pretty well, Maddy. You have a heart for people, especially family—"

"—and animals." Madysen gave her sister a wry smile.

Havyn giggled. "What were we thinking, stealing those sheep? Whose idea was that anyway?"

"Oh, stop." Madysen swatted her sister's arm. "We gave them a good home." Her laughter turned into a pinched feeling in her heart. Leaving her sheep wasn't a pleasant thought, and leaving her family? The more she thought about it, the more it hurt.

"I think performing in a new city every few nights might be thrilling for a while, but you'd get tired of it pretty quick."

Madysen tucked her hair behind her ear. "I know. I've thought of that. But then I get all excited about seeing audiences stand and applaud because they love my music. Grand stages and concert halls. It sounds very prideful, even to my own ears. But I must admit, performing without you and Whit . . . It wasn't the same."

Havyn reached out and wrapped an arm around Madysen's shoulders. "Mama wanted us to use our talent to glorify God. I don't remember that she cared about the size of the stage or the audience. I remember her caring that we did our best because we were playing for Him—and Him alone."

Her sister was right.

Havyn shivered and tucked her hands under her shawl. "So now I'm going to ask the tough question. Have you prayed about it?"

"Humph. Daniel asked me the same thing. I've been planning to, just haven't yet."

Havyn laughed. "People often have plans that never come to fruition. You have to put them into action."

She snuck a glance at her sister. "Mama used to say that to me every time I forgot a chore or something I was supposed to do." Sweet memories washed over her.

"And your answer was always—"

"I was planning to," they said in unison.

She looked at Havyn and laughed.

Now was as good a time as any. "Would you pray with me?"

"Of course I will." Havyn took hold of her hand.

Madysen lifted her face to the sky and poured out her heart to the Lord.

———

Whitney buried her face in the pillow to muffle her moans. Her head felt as if it would explode.

"Whit?" Madysen opened the door to her room. "Whit, are you all right?"

"It's . . . it's just my head." She began to sob. Which was the last thing she wanted. It made her head pound harder and—even worse—guaranteed that her sister wouldn't leave her alone.

Sure enough, Maddy came into the bedroom. "It's nearly dawn. I'm going for the doctor."

"No." Whitney closed her eyes against the exploding pain inside her head. "I don't want anyone to touch me."

"I know you don't, but you must." Madysen sat down on the edge of the quilted bedspread. "Something is terribly wrong. You must see a doctor."

Whitney pressed her palms against her throbbing temples. "I can't bear the pain."

Madysen got to her feet. "I'll get John. He can go, and Havyn and I will help you get through this."

"Tell him . . . make him promise he won't say what happened."

Her younger sister nodded. "I'll make him promise."

Hours passed, or maybe it was only minutes, before John returned with a man Whitney had never seen before. She gripped the edge of the bedspread, pulling it tight against her chin. Her heart beat fast. As fast as if she were running beside her dogs. Even faster when he approached the bed where she lay helpless.

Why had she agreed to this? "No! Go away! I'm fine!"

"You don't look fine." The stranger took off his coat and draped it over her bedpost, as calm as though she'd invited him to tea rather than yelled at him. "I'm Dr. Peter Cameron. I understand you took a bad fall and hit your head. Sometimes the effects of such an injury don't show up right away. I fell out of a tree once when I was a youngster, and for days I thought I was just fine." He set his bag beside her on the bed and pulled out a bottle. "Could someone bring a pitcher of warm water and a basin?"

Whitney's heart rate slowed a fraction. His casual nature and gentle tone were soothing.

"Now, why don't you tell me exactly what happened?"

Exactly? No! But neither would she lie. "I . . . I was working with my dogs . . . I raise sled dogs." She glanced toward Madysen and John. "I . . . uh . . . I pushed away from something and . . . and . . . I fell backward. I hit my head, but it didn't feel that bad."

He nodded. "And where is the worst of the pain?"

She put her hand to the base of her skull. "It starts here and comes up over my ear. It doesn't always hurt. It comes and goes."

Havyn returned and handed a basin of water to the doctor. He took it from her and walked to the dresser.

Whitney watched his every move.

He placed the bowl to one side and poured water into it.

He took out a bottle from his pocket and poured some into the water and thoroughly washed his hands.

Deep breaths. The inevitable was coming. The man was going to want to touch her.

And she would have to let him.

He took the towel Havyn offered and walked toward the bed, drying his hands.

Whitney began to shiver.

"All right. I will need to feel your head. Do you feel good enough to sit up?"

Her head? Just her head? She could handle that much. She had to. She pushed off the pillow, careful not to disrupt his black bag.

He smiled. "Perfect." He took the lighted lamp beside her bed and pulled it closer, waving it in front of one side of her face and then the other. Replacing the lamp on the nightstand, he held up his index finger. "Without moving your head, follow my finger with just your eyes."

What kind of doctor was this man? She'd injured her skull, not her eyes. But he wasn't touching her, so she obeyed.

Dr. Cameron dropped his hand to his side and smiled. "Very good. Now I need to feel your neck and skull."

Whitney sucked in a breath and leaned away from him. Dr. Cameron never took his gaze from hers, his expression filled with compassion. He knew. She didn't know how, but he knew. Had John told him? No, Madysen would have made him promise, and he wasn't one to break his word.

The pain struck again and she grimaced.

Dr. Cameron lifted his hands slowly, like a horse trainer showing an unbroken stallion a saddle before daring to touch him with it. "I'm going to turn your neck back and forth, and you tell me if anything I do makes the pain worse or better." But he didn't move. Was he waiting for her to give him permission to touch her?

Whitney looked around the bedroom. Half her family was here. If this doctor, as comforting as he seemed to be, tried anything, John would drag him from the room and beat him to a pulp. She took a deep breath and prepared for revulsion. "All right."

But when his touch came, it was so gentle that Whitney relaxed.

She cried out when he pushed her head toward her chin.

"I'm sorry." He released his hold. "However, I believe I know the problem. You have what some call railroad spine."

Whitney frowned. "What?"

"I know. There aren't any trains even close by." He smiled. A very nice, nonthreatening smile. "But people were often whipped around during locomotive rides, injuring their necks. Hence the name. When you fell, your neck snapped back and forth. There is now swelling, and that's causing you pain."

"What can be done?" John asked before anyone else.

Dr. Cameron straightened. "Many doctors would confine the neck, but I don't believe that is in the patient's best interest. I will prescribe some herbs that can be made into tea. This will help to relax the muscles and reduce the swelling. I will also give you a tonic I made from other herbs that will help when the pain is most severe. There are some plasters that can help if applied on the neck and some special massaging that will also ease the misery." He looked at Havyn and Madysen. "I can show you how to manipulate the muscles for your sister." He looked back at Whitney. "Lastly, there are stretches that you can do yourself."

He raised his eyebrows. "In time your body will recover whether you do these things or not. However, you will heal faster if you follow my directions."

The pain was already easing, as it always did after a while. Whitney closed her eyes for a moment and then met his gaze again. "I'll do whatever I have to. I have a great many responsibilities to my dogs."

The doctor nodded. "That's right, you raise sled dogs. Do you sell them and teach others how to manage them?"

Whitney started to say no, but something about this man put her at ease. "I do. But I must warn you, I require a lot of training."

"Well, that would suit me just fine, since I know absolutely nothing about driving a team. But I'm going to have to get around in the winter. I've promised the native villagers that I will treat their sick and injured."

What manner of man was he? "Most doctors wouldn't care about the natives."

This brought a chuckle. "I think you'll find, Miss Powell, that I'm not like most doctors."

Madysen went out to help Havyn make breakfast. Neither she nor Havyn seemed to have the energy to talk, so Madysen spent the time in prayer for Whitney—and for herself. She presented the most important issues to God.

Daniel was a wonderful friend. Should she explore what she'd felt when he'd comforted her?

Buddy was a good and decent man. His intentions seemed honorable and his feelings clear. Should she take to the stage and travel? Did God want her to do that for His glory?

One thing became clear. She needed to have a conversation with Buddy and see what his plans were. To make sure they lined up with her own priorities.

She had time. Nothing had to be decided right away. Well, at least not until the last ship was ready to pull out of Nome.

Havyn stirred the eggs in the pan. "I can manage this. Why don't you see if Whit needs anything?"

Madysen nodded and went to check on her older sister. Whitney was sound asleep. She'd be miffed with herself for not being up to run the dogs, but that was just too bad. She needed rest. No doubt John and Ben could take care of the dogs.

Madysen made her way into the parlor and grabbed her cello and bow. It was the perfect time for a little practice as everyone dressed for the day.

Taking her chair, she moved it over to the fireplace and settled into it with her instrument.

With a deep breath, she closed her eyes and thought about her favorite piece—the piece that Mama had given her when she was fifteen. Bach's Cello Suite no. 1. It fed her soul in a way nothing else could. Not needing any accompaniment or any other instrument, she felt it was the song that truly showcased her beloved cello.

Placing her bow, she played G, D, B, A, making it dramatic and slow, and then took off into the brisk tempo of the running sixteenth notes that continued throughout the prelude. She let the notes wash over her as she played from her heart.

For a moment, she could almost envision Mama sitting in her favorite chair, smiling as she played.

Mama had been such a talented musician. *She* should have

toured the world and played. Granddad often said that she had offers, but she declined them all to raise her girls.

A tear slipped down Madysen's cheek as she continued the piece.

Was that why she had come up with the idea of traveling the country in honor of Mama? She hadn't thought of her mother's dreams before now. What had it cost Mama to decline those offers? Had she longed to go on the stage and perform? Had her situation kept her from being able to live her dream?

"Nothing was ever more important to me than you three girls," Mama once told Madysen. *"You are my life, and I'm so blessed to be your mother."*

No. Those weren't the words of a woman who regretted her choices. But what if she had? What if that longing was always there, but their mother kept it buried deep inside?

Madysen closed her eyes as the music built. It gave her a sense of taking flight—of bursting through a cloud into the warmth of bright sunshine—of spreading her wings to soar over the earth. She put aside her worries and focused on the moment. Rich melodic tones filled the room as the fire popped and crackled.

She finished the piece in a flourish and smiled.

"That was beautiful."

Madysen opened her eyes. Bethany stood there, a sweet look of awe on her face. "Thank you. It's my favorite piece."

"What's it called?" Bethany tilted her head.

"Bach's Cello Suite no. 1."

Bethany scrunched up her nose and frowned. "That's not a very pretty name. It needs a name like 'Butterflies in Flight,' or something else that sounds like the picture the music paints."

What a surprising and insightful comment. "That's actually a very interesting thought. You're right. The title is quite bland." She stood up and took her cello back over to its case. "And I always think of flying when I play it."

"It sounds like that, or like running and twirling." Bethany gave a whirl.

Madysen couldn't help but chuckle. "Is breakfast ready?"

"Yes." Bethany stopped in midtwirl. "Havyn sent me in here to tell you, but I got all caught up in the music. You are so good."

"Thank you. I've practiced for many, many years. I don't know what I would do without music. Do you play any instruments?"

Bethany shook her head. "Could you . . . teach me?"

Madysen loosened the bow hair before putting it in the case. "Are you willing to practice every day?"

Her little sister's eyes lit up. "Yes. I will practice all the time. I've always wanted to be able to play music."

Madysen laid her hand on Bethany's shoulder, and they walked to the kitchen together. "What instrument strikes your fancy the most?"

"I thought it would be piano. Until I heard you play the cello just now. I think I want to learn that." A full smile covered the girl's face.

Madysen turned Bethany to her so they were face-to-face. "How about both?"

Her little sister's eyebrows shot up. "Really?"

"Really. That's how I learned. Maybe after we get all the chores done today, we can start."

"I'll do whatever you want me to do. I'm good at chores. Can we go now?"

Madysen laughed. "And skip breakfast? You must really want to learn."

"I do, I do!" Bethany clapped her hands and twirled around several times.

Her sister's unbridled joy made Madysen want to twirl around with her. And to think, she had almost denied herself the chance to know her other siblings. "Good, because we have lots of chores to do around the farm before we can play."

"But we can start today?"

Madysen's heart melted a little more for this sweet girl. "Yes. We will start today."

Bethany took off for the kitchen skipping and singing, "I'm going to learn muuusic!"

She'd done that—brought joy to a twelve-year-old. That's what music had always done for Madysen.

She stopped at the doorway as her breath caught. What if she left Nome? Wouldn't she trample the sweet girl's dreams?

How could she live with herself if she did that?

TWENTY-ONE

Daniel slowed his horse as he neared the Bundrant family farm. Snow sparkled across acres of rolling hills, and in a distant valley, Daniel could just discern the edges of the frozen river.

Beautiful.

There was peace here, a peace Daniel needed but couldn't quite wrap his fingers around. Madysen said it was because he had relied on his parents' and grandparents' faith, so when it was tested, he'd run away.

Was she right? Or was he ready to believe anything she said because he was halfway in love with her?

Maddy. Her name was as beautiful as her home. She had let him call her by her nickname, and she'd walked into his arms and let him comfort her.

What would life be like with her at his side?

He smiled and kicked his horse back into a steady clop.

As much as he wanted to explore the enticing possibility, Maddy was in love with Buddy Merrick. At least she thought she was.

Besides, if Daniel was ever going to deserve the love of a woman like her, he needed to resolve his bitterness toward God.

John had also lost his parents, and yet he lived at peace. How had he done it?

As Daniel neared the house, he waved at Whitney. She returned his wave but didn't smile. That wasn't like her. Maddy said her sister had been injured. The doctor had come, but maybe whatever medication he brought wasn't strong enough to dull Whitney's pain.

A crunch turned his attention.

Amka, the native woman who often helped on the farm, struggled to wheel Mr. Bundrant through the ice-crusted snow.

Daniel dismounted and tied his horse to the hitching pole. "Should he be outside?"

Amka stopped pushing the wheelchair and sighed. "You know Mr. Chuck. He's determined to inspect the farm now that he's feeling just a tiny bit better."

Chuck pulled the plaid blanket over his legs closer to his waist. "My job."

Amka came around to the side of the chair. "Your walking is getting better, Mr. Chuck. Why don't we wait until you are up on your feet?"

"No." Chuck lifted his chin. "Now."

Amka looked heavenward and shook her head.

Daniel grinned. Nice to know the man had some faults. His granddaughters described him almost as a saint. Who could live up to that?

"All right, you stubborn man." Amka returned to the back of the wheelchair. "But I now have a witness that I warned you this was a bad idea."

Chuck grunted.

Daniel trudged closer. "Let me help."

She gave way with a smile. "Thank you."

"Where are we headed?" Daniel looked to Amka.

She pointed at the same moment Chuck said, "Barn."

Although the older man had hollow cheeks and his coat

looked about two sizes too big, pushing him through the uneven patches of snow and ice had Daniel sweating by the time they reached the barn door.

"Thank . . . you." Chuck sounded out of breath, as though he'd been the one pushing the wheelchair.

Daniel turned to Amka. "I need to find John, but I can come back to help you with him later."

She shook her head. "I appreciate it, but I can manage." She pointed to her left. "Mr. John is over there checking the cattle."

"Thanks." Daniel picked his way through the snow back to his horse and mounted up. He inhaled the scents of farm life. He'd missed it. Which was as surprising as it was comforting. He'd run far, disdainful of his life before his mom and grandpa died, as a way of distancing himself from the good memories. He'd focused on the pain, the hardship, and the stench of farming. But after his first encounter with Maddy, even the smell of manure made him smile. She had a way of making everything better.

Even God.

Daniel reined to the left. It was time to stop running away from what he didn't want and start running toward the things he did want. He didn't want to run a store, he didn't even want to live in town. So that left . . .

Farming.

He laughed aloud. He'd run all the way to Alaska to get away from the one thing he wanted most in the world. If that was God's idea of a joke, it was a pretty good one. Was He, as Maddy and Granny insisted, far greater and more loving than the distant, uncaring God Daniel had decided He was?

The issue needed to be settled.

Daniel spotted a large herd of cows huddled together near the river. John was riding around the edge of the herd. He lifted a hand in greeting and steered his horse in Daniel's direction. "Good morning, Daniel. Good to see you."

"You too. Checking the herd?"

"Yep. Since we started year-round breeding techniques, I've got to keep a closer eye on things. The demand for milk and cream is up, so the extra work is paying off."

"Seems like you might need more help." Daniel scanned the horizon.

"You volunteering?" John cut a look at the cheese kitchen. His tone of voice said he was teasing.

"Well . . ." Daniel left his thought unfinished. He was here to ask John about God, not about a job.

"Are you saying you'd come work here?" John leaned forward in his saddle. "Because I've got my hands full, and we just talked about hiring someone to be my right-hand man. This cheese business looks to make a tidy profit, but we need good help."

Daniel gripped the reins tighter in his hands. It was the same work he'd grown up with, but running it in the Alaskan climate was far different. Working on a farm as successful as Chuck Bundrant's, learning how to handle the long, bitterly cold winter, might be the difference between success and failure. Then maybe one day, he could own his own farm.

He relaxed his grip. "I'd like to think about it, if that's all right."

"Please do. I'll need an answer by next week, though."

Daniel nodded.

"Which reminds me, I need to check on this morning's milking. The regular milkers are used to the cows, but since we've added the sheep, the process is much slower. Want to go with me?"

"Sure, but I was hoping we'd have a chance to talk."

John clicked his tongue at his horse. "What can I do for you?"

Daniel shifted in his saddle as they moseyed along the river, letting their horses take it slow. This is what he'd come for, but now that the moment was here, his heart was beating like he was pushing that wheelchair again. He took several breaths to calm his heart rate. "Can I ask you about your faith?"

"Most certainly."

"I know you lost your parents when you were young." Daniel looked John in the eye. "Did that make you bitter toward God?"

John sat up straighter. "No."

Daniel huffed. This farm was full of men who were saints. Men who, unlike him, hadn't questioned and run away and . . . He blinked several times to clear his mind's eye of the things he'd done in the Yukon. Maybe God hadn't answered his prayers to save his mom and grandfather because He knew the terrible things Daniel would do.

"I was hurt, obviously." John's low words carried a hint of sadness. "I grieved for a long time, but Nonno—my grand-father—kept telling me that just because bad things happen doesn't mean that God doesn't care or see."

"And that made losing your parents okay? Just like that?" He rubbed his forehead.

"Hardly." John shook his head. "I was a sad, mean kid for a long time because I missed my parents so much. But Nonno reminded me that the Bible says we'll have tribulation in this world. And Jesus said that we were to take heart because He had overcome the world. That was what I clung to."

Daniel sighed. "Granny shared that verse with me too, but I guess I'm missing the point. If God has enough power to over-come the world, shouldn't He use it to protect His children from harm? Isn't that what a loving father should do?" The resentment Daniel thought he'd put behind him seeped into his words.

John looked down for a moment. When he raised his head again, there was compassion in his brown eyes. "You could ask those same questions of a hundred different people and get a hundred different answers. I'm no theologian, so I can only tell you what makes the most sense to me."

"That's all I can ask for." It was all anyone could ask for, but Daniel wanted more. He wanted a solid, unmovable answer that satisfied him to the core. Because the distance between him and God had escalated from an occasional annoying itch to a relentless unquenchable thirst.

"Let me start by asking you a question." A gust of wind blew John's scarf across his face. "But let's ride closer to the cheese kitchen while we talk."

Daniel turned his horse so he and John could ride side by side.

"Should God have saved His own Son from harm?"

Daniel felt his eyes widen. "I . . . I don't know."

"I think you do, but it doesn't fit your presumption that God should save His children, so you don't want to answer."

Harsh. But true. The Bible stories and lessons learned at his mother's knee flooded Daniel's mind. "Then, no. If God had saved Jesus from the cross, there'd be no forgiveness of sins." And even if no one else on earth needed forgiveness, he did.

"Which is how God overcame the world." John cut a glance at Daniel. "He didn't overcome it with power. He overcame it with sacrifice."

Daniel felt his heart crack open a sliver. Bitterness began to dribble out.

But John wasn't done. "Let me ask you another question. Once a person accepts Jesus' sacrifice for sins, should he go immediately to heaven?"

The question was rhetorical, so Daniel didn't answer.

"Of course not. We're here to draw people to Christ. It's our job. Now I don't know about you, but I've worked a lot of jobs, and I never made friends with the people who were high above me. I made friends with the men who were shoveling the same muck I was."

Daniel started fitting pieces into place. "So if God's children don't have to shovel muck too, how can they talk to the people around them about Christ?"

"Exactly." They reached the cheese kitchen. John drew his horse to a halt.

Daniel reined his mount in so they faced one another.

"Like I said, I'm no theologian"—John leaned down to pat his horse's neck—"but it seems to me that God needs us to show the people around us what a difference having a relationship with Him makes when we face the same hardships they do."

Daniel stared at the ground. "I'm starting to see that God didn't take my mom and grandpa because He hated me, but I don't know what to do with this anger I've carried around for the last nine years." He looked up at John. "I'm tired of it. I want it gone, I just don't know how to make that happen."

"Have you ever asked Christ to take it from you?"

The simple question shattered what was left of the shell around Daniel's heart. "A thousand times, but why would He? I've done horrible things that—"

"I'm cutting you off right there." John raised his left hand, palm out. "Too many people think there are big sins and small sins. But there's just sin. It means missing the mark. In the book of Romans, Paul calls it falling short of the glory of God."

"But that's an impossible standard."

"Exactly." John shrugged. "And it gets worse. The consequences of sin are death—both physical and spiritual."

Daniel had heard his whole life about Christ's sacrifice to pay the penalty for sin, but for the first time, it wasn't some theoretical idea. It was real. "So since Jesus lived the perfect life, He was the one person who didn't deserve death and could, therefore, pay the penalty so I don't have to."

John nodded. "Now you've got it."

"But how do I do this? How can I be forgiven and put God in charge?"

"The Bible says you need to believe." John smiled. "Sounds ridiculously simple, I know, but Romans ten says, 'That if thou shalt confess with thy mouth the Lord Jesus, and shalt believe in thine heart that God hath raised him from the dead, thou shalt be saved.'"

The words washed over him. Words of absolute truth. "I do believe Jesus is Lord and that He died on the cross for my sins." Daniel's eyes dampened, and he let the tears fall. "I believe that He rose from the dead—that God raised Him."

John smiled. "Amen."

Daniel froze. It was gone. The enormous weight he'd been carrying inside . . . was gone.

God had already freed him.

He bowed his head, and for the first time he could feel God's presence. It was wondrous.

I'm yours, Father. I'm sorry it's taken me so long to get here. I'm sorry I let the world stand in between us. I'm just so sorry. Please forgive me.

Warmth rested on his head, and Daniel had to look up.

The sun had just broken through the clouds.

After supper that evening, Granny stacked the supper dishes to one side and eased back in her chair while Dad took up his Bible as he always did.

"We're reading from Luke fifteen this evening." Dad flipped through the pages.

Daniel spoke up. "Dad, I have something to say before you read tonight's verses."

Dad put the Bible down and nodded. "Go ahead."

"First, I want to say thank you for never giving up on me. I know you've worried about me for a great many years, and I'm sorry that I put you in that position. I've listened to the things you've said, and I've taken them to heart. Today John Roselli helped me make myself right with God."

Granny's eyes filled with tears. "Oh, Daniel, that's wonderful!" She reached across the table to squeeze his hand.

Dad wiped at his cheeks. "You've brought us great joy, son.

But the even greater joy is God's and all of those in heaven. You'll see what I mean when I read our passage."

He picked up the Bible again. "'What man of you, having an hundred sheep, if he lose one of them, doth not leave the ninety and nine in the wilderness, and go after that which is lost, until he find it? And when he hath found it, he layeth it on his shoulders, rejoicing. And when he cometh home, he calleth together his friends and neighbours, saying unto them, Rejoice with me; for I have found my sheep which was lost. I say unto you, that likewise joy shall be in heaven over one sinner that repenteth, more than over ninety and nine just persons, which need no repentance.'"

Granny took out her handkerchief and wiped her eyes, while Dad closed the Bible and looked to Daniel with great love in his expression.

"Heaven is rejoicing with us tonight, for the lost has been found. Welcome home, son."

Madysen finished milking one of the sheep. She wasn't very good at it yet. Thankfully their workers were better, because without milk there wouldn't be cheese.

She carried her buckets into the kitchen and sighed. Surely she'd get the hang of it in time.

"Just the person I was looking for." Daniel came into the room, a spring in his step. What was he so pleased about? "It's snowing great huge flakes out there."

"That's why you came looking for me?" Madysen grinned. "To tell me it's snowing?"

"No, actually, I came to tell you something of great importance."

There was something different about him today. He seemed— what? Younger? Lighter? She couldn't quite put her finger on it, only that he was smiling with his whole being, and it made her smile right along with him.

"I wanted to share it with you yesterday, but you were nowhere to be found."

"I'm sorry you couldn't find me. Yesterday afternoon I gave Bethany a cello lesson." She placed her buckets on the counter.

"I am found." His grin widened. "Like that little lamb in the manure pit, I've been pulled out and cleaned up."

"We aren't supposed to mention that." She chuckled. "Wait—say that again?"

"I made my peace with God."

Her eyes widened. "You did? Oh, Daniel, that's wonderful." She ran to him and wrapped him in her arms. "I'm so happy for you."

"I'm happy for me too." He returned the hug. "Nothing has ever felt so right."

She pulled back to look into his eyes. "What convinced you?"

"You. John. Granny. Dad. God." His expression grew serious, but he didn't let go of his hold. "I was so blinded by my sorrow . . . by the certainty that God no longer cared. Now I can see that was Satan's ploy to separate me from the only One who truly did care."

"I'm so glad you saw the truth of it."

"I went to talk to John yesterday, and he helped me to get things straight, but you, just living your faith, convinced me as well. Granny's never-ending prayers for me and Dad's Scripture readings and encouraging words about God . . . all of it worked together to show me the truth. I just want to say thanks for not turning away from me when I spoke so angrily against God. Thank you for caring enough to keep being my friend."

"I will always be your friend, Daniel." She rested her hand against his chest. It felt right to be in his arms once again. Like she was home. And safe. Buddy gave her gifts, but Daniel gave her comfort.

Their lips were only inches apart. Was he going to kiss her? She certainly wanted him to—

Goodness! Where had that thought come from? This was about celebrating Daniel's coming to God, not him kissing her.

She eased away. "I'm so thankful for our friendship and all that you've taught me." She smiled. "This is one of the best days of my life! I've never been a part of someone coming to God. It humbles me and thrills me all at the same time to know that God would use me like that."

"You're an amazing woman, Maddy. I hope you know that." He was looking at her the way John had looked at Havyn on their wedding day. Maddy's heart began to pound so hard, she could hear it. "There's something else I want you to know."

"Madysen!" Bethany's call drifted to them. "Madysen!"

Oh, how she didn't want to answer. But she had to. "I'm in the cheese kitchen."

Bethany ran inside huffing and puffing. "Havyn said to tell you to come to breakfast. Oh, and Papa's back." Bethany gave Daniel a quick wave then turned and disappeared. The dear girl was probably anxious to see her father again.

But Madysen wasn't. She was far more anxious to know what Daniel wanted to tell her. What that tenderness in his face meant. Was it just gratitude that she'd helped lead him into a relationship with God?

She wanted there to be more.

She looked at Daniel again. "You were saying?"

He smiled. "It will wait for another time."

TWENTY-TWO

Madysen swallowed down her disappointment. "I guess we'd better go in for breakfast."

Daniel shook his head. "I should leave. I can come back later when—"

"No." Goodness, that was rude. What had gotten into her? "I mean, you're already here. There's no sense in taking the long trip back to town just to repeat it later today."

"Are you sure?" Daniel cocked his head to one side. "I'd think you'd want some time with just your family now that your dad is back."

"You're practically family." It was true. And it put another huge smile on Daniel's face. Madysen squeezed her hands into fists to keep from reaching for him again. "You're here almost every day, and you've helped with the sheep, and we really owe you so much and . . ." She was jabbering on like a magpie. "Just come on."

He saluted her. "Yes, ma'am."

She stuck her hands on her hips. "Are you calling me bossy?"

"I would never do such a dangerous thing."

She loved his tone of voice and the glint in his eye. She chuckled. "Smart man."

They walked out of the cheese kitchen. Dawn brushed the

sky with pink light. The days were getting shorter and shorter. Fall was brief in Nome. Soon, the deep freeze of winter would set in. The sun would appear for mere hours. Madysen breathed in the crisp air, the faint scent of cinnamon announcing that Havyn had been baking this morning.

John opened the door to the house and stepped onto the porch. "I need to talk to you for a moment."

"Which one of us?" Madysen climbed the steps.

"Both." John waited for Daniel to follow Madysen onto the porch before drawing them away from the front door. John rubbed his index finger under his nose. "Whitney is having a bad morning."

Oh no.

Daniel looked between her and John. "I've noticed she hasn't seemed like herself lately. Is she sick?"

John raised his eyebrows and looked at Madysen, a question in his eyes. "I think we need to tell him. He's practically family, don't you think?"

Madysen would have laughed at the repeat of her identical assertion a few minutes ago but couldn't get past the worry to do so. Whitney had said she only wanted family knowing she'd been attacked. Madysen winced. If the mere thought of what happened to her sister made *her* heart hurt, how must Whitney feel?

John raised his eyebrows a fraction higher, a silent repeat of his earlier question.

Madysen nodded.

He turned his attention to Daniel. "I told Whit that the men on the farm needed to know so we could protect her. She was hesitant, but she agreed." John paused and his jaw clenched. "Please make sure that no one else hears of this, all right? Last week, Whitney was attacked by a man."

All the light went out of Daniel's face. "Who?"

Madysen almost shivered. She'd never heard that hoarse tone from Daniel before. Rage—pure and simple.

John shook his head. "She's asked us not to identify him. It was someone she knew and thought was safe."

"It's made her leery of all men." Madysen put her hand on Daniel's forearm. His scowl eased a fraction. "She might lash out at you, or she might ignore you completely."

John lifted one shoulder. "Or she might be very pleasant, if a little cold."

"I get the idea." Daniel covered Madysen's hand with his. "Are the ladies safe here? Or do you think he might return?"

Her heart warmed at both his question and his touch. *God, what do these feelings mean? Should I stay here? My family needs me, and I'm beginning to think I want more than just friendship from Daniel.* But what about Buddy? Hadn't she accepted his gifts and courtship? How did she really feel about him? She felt heat creep up her neck. She focused her attention back on her brother-in-law, who had continued talking while she was praying.

". . . the other reason I wanted you to know." John jutted his chin toward the cheese kitchen. "When you're here, I need you to look out for anyone who doesn't belong on the farm."

"Of course, I will." The hard edge was back in Daniel's voice. He'd once told her he'd done things when he was over in the Yukon that he regretted. For the first time since she'd known him, she saw a glimmer of the man he'd once been. But he'd changed, and he was a new creation in Christ.

Why was it so easy to see Daniel as forgivable but not her dad? Or Garrett Sinclair? The easy answer was that Daniel had never hurt her or someone she loved. But she felt God nudging her to go deeper. If only life would slow down so she could catch her breath and *think*.

"We should go inside." John gestured for Madysen to precede him into the house.

She took her hand off Daniel's arm, regretting the loss of his warmth. She went straight to the kitchen to help Havyn and

Whitney carry plates of eggs, sausage links, and cinnamon rolls to the dining room.

Bethany and Eli were speaking one after the other, telling their dad about their adventures on the farm. Granddad looked happier than Madysen had seen him since before his stroke. But she noticed Ruth's face was pale, the chords in her neck visible over the high collar of her gray dress.

After Madysen set down the plate of cinnamon rolls, she took her place between Whitney and Ruth at the table.

John waited for Havyn to sit next to him before taking her hand and saying grace.

Amens echoed around the room, then food flowed as freely as conversation.

It came to an abrupt halt when Granddad lifted his left hand. "Do you . . . have . . . news?"

Ruth went stiff.

Madysen put down her fork and took Ruth's cold hand. The poor woman. If Dad had found her husband, he should have told her by now.

"Not really. I thought I had a lead. I talked to a man who actually knew Stan. Said he'd been working the area next to his mine, but he hadn't seen him in about six months."

"Did he have any idea of where he might have gone?" John placed his elbows on the table.

"No. Looks like he helped out at various mines. Doesn't have his own claim. I checked that first thing." He looked to Ruth. "I just wish I had better news." Dad wiped his mouth with his napkin. "I've searched up and down the beach, asking anyone if they've seen him. I even talked to that Reynolds guy at the freighting office to see if maybe Stan had taken a job with him. He hadn't, but Reynolds gave me the idea to check the outgoing passenger lists to see if Stan had headed home and we missed each other. He hadn't. So I'm at a loss of where to look next."

Ruth sniffed. "He's got to be here. Where else could he be?

What if something has happened to him?" She took a deep breath. "I'm sorry. I appreciate you looking for him. I'm determined to remain hopeful."

Madysen couldn't imagine what it must be like to face the unknown like that.

"He can't care much about you if he hasn't been in touch for all this time." Whitney's words were soft and ruthless.

Ruth broke into great sobs, got up from the table, and ran toward the door.

"Whitney! Where's your compassion?" Dad's yell made Madysen jump.

Eli and Bethany didn't move.

Whit took a sip of water. "If I'm lacking compassion, I learned it from you." She plopped her napkin over her untouched plate of food, stood, and walked slowly down the hall.

Silence engulfed the table for several moments. Madysen looked around the table and stood. "I'm sorry for Whitney's comment, but she's suffered a lot the past few days. I'm sure she didn't mean it." She turned to her dad. "You had no right to scold her like that. You have *no* idea what she's been through. And the upheaval that all of this has wrought on the family. If you'll please excuse me."

As she walked away, she heard Havyn explaining that their elder sister had been injured. Madysen wanted to defend Whitney, but the truth of the matter wasn't pretty. How would their younger siblings feel if they knew Whit had been attacked?

Attacked. The very word made Madysen cringe. That was something those kids didn't need to hear.

She went to Whitney's door and tapped. "Whit, it's me."

Nothing.

She tried the knob and it turned. Entering as quietly as she could, she looked at her sister and then closed the door.

Whit's face was drenched in tears. "I'm so ashamed. I should have never said anything like that to Ruth. I don't even know what came over me for such awful words to come out of my mouth. Ruth has been nothing but kind to me. I actually like her."

Madysen moved to her sister's side. Whit was someone who needed to talk things out, so Madysen would give her space and be content to listen.

But Whit didn't move a muscle or say a word.

Madysen moved closer and put an arm around her sister's shoulders.

Whit stiffened. "I'm so full of anger. I can't believe the way that man put his hands on me. I feel used and dirty and hurt. Why didn't I see it?" Strong, stoic Whitney collapsed onto Madysen's shoulder. Deep sobs shook her. "If the dogs hadn't been with us, I don't know what I would've done. All I want is love and acceptance, but now I'm going to think that every man I meet intends to take advantage of me."

Madysen struggled to keep her composure. She needed to stay strong. How many times had her older sister sheltered her, comforted her, and held her up when she was hurting? Too many. It was time to return the favor. But how? All she wanted to do was curl up and cry right along with Whit.

She wrapped her other arm around her sister and let her cry. *Lord, give me the words to say, because I don't have any.*

Whit sat up straight and sniffed. "I hate men." She reached for a hankie. Her face hardened and was streaked with tears.

"But all men aren't like that, Whit. Just look at John." Madysen put her hands on both sides of Whit's face. "Just because one man did this doesn't mean that they are all bad and deserve your hate." She pushed some of Whitney's curls off her face. "What about Daniel? And Mr. Norris and the old guard at the Roadhouse? If they knew what Sinclair did, I shudder to think what they would do to him."

A few more tears escaped Whit's eyes. "Then I wish they knew. I just want him to suffer like he's made me suffer."

"Whit, you don't mean that. You've never wished harm on another person like that."

Whitney leaned back on her bed and put her hand over her eyes. "The sad thing is . . . I do mean it."

Madysen studied her sister. How could one man inflict so much pain and instill such fear and hatred in Whit? "There are good men who love you and who would protect you with their lives. I'm sure there are even some good ones who would protect you even though they don't know you. Not all men are given over to such vile actions."

"I used to believe that, but teaching my heart to accept that now seems impossible."

There were no words that could mend the wound. Madysen took Whit's hand. "Why don't we ask everyone to go outside and do chores, and you and I can play one of Mama's favorite pieces together?" It had always helped in the past.

Whit sat up and shook her head. "No. I'm sorry, Maddy. I feel like all the music within me has died."

That couldn't be true! No wonder Whit was so torn up.

"And you're talking about leaving. I'd never demand that you give up on true love just so you could stay in Alaska—that would be too selfish. But are you sure it's even love? It scares me to think of you out there all alone . . . with only him to protect you."

"Don't worry about me." This wasn't the time to discuss all the thoughts and doubts she'd been having.

"It's my job. I'm your big sister. Always have been, always will be." Whit rubbed the back of her head.

"Is the headache back?"

Whitney closed her eyes. "Yeah, most of the time it's dull, but then it turns into a sharp stabbing pain every once in a while and takes my breath away." Tears formed in her eyes, and she slumped. "I was so horrible to Ruth. I need to apologize to her. And to the kids too. They are probably frightened of the monster that is their oldest sibling."

"Maybe you should lie down for a while. We can talk to them later." Should she get in touch with the doctor? It didn't seem right for Whitney to suffer so much.

Her sister stood. "No. I need to do this now."

No sense arguing. Once Whit made up her mind, that was it. "All right. Let's go together."

Whitney pulled a hankie out and mopped up her face. Then with shoulders squared, she marched out of her room.

When they made it back into the dining room, no one said a word. Ruth had returned and sat eating.

Whitney fiddled with the hankie. "Ruth, I am very sorry for the way I spoke to you. I didn't mean a word of it, and I should have never said such a nasty thing. It isn't true. You've been a good friend to me, and I've been cruel. Please forgive me." She turned to the kids. "Eli and Bethany, please don't think that's the way I act all the time. I'm so sorry."

Ruth stood and came over to hug them both. She whispered, "I acted the same way. This isn't your fault."

Madysen shot a glance at her sister. What was that about?

Whitney ducked her chin and took her seat.

Madysen looked around at everyone. The tension had eased, but awkward silence prevailed. "Anyone need more coffee or milk?"

"I don't, but I would love another cinnamon roll . . . or two." Daniel gave Madysen an unrepentant grin.

"I'll take some coffee and a cinnamon roll." John lifted his cup. "Oh, I haven't had a chance to make this announcement, but Daniel has agreed to come to work for us full-time. He'll start next week."

"You look miserable."

Granny interrupted Daniel's thoughts. He looked up at her. "Good morning to you too."

"All right. Let's have it. What's bothering you?" Granny sat in her chair and rocked back and forth. "I thought you got everything straight with God."

He'd forgotten in the Yukon what it was like to live with family—and to have them always in his business. But he didn't mind. Not anymore. It showed him that they cared.

"I did. It's not that." He gave her a look.

"Oh . . . I see. It's a girl." She pointed a bony finger in his direction. "I know that expression."

He held up both of his hands and smiled at her. "I figure you're the best one to talk to about love. It's Madysen. I can't stop thinking about her, and I'm worried that if I don't tell her how I feel, then she'll leave forever with that slick Buddy Merrick."

"Oh."

"Don't even start, Granny. I can see those matchmaking wheels spinning in your head. But I didn't tell you so you could interfere. I just can't compete with Buddy. He sends her expensive presents almost every day and he tells her all these smooth rehearsed lines." Daniel stood up and paced in front of the rocking chair. "To top it all off, he's at the Roadhouse every time she performs— and I know because I'm there too. It's ridiculous. He's not even at his own show, because he's *there* watching *Madysen*."

"So what's the problem?" She folded her hands in her lap and leaned back. The chair stilled.

"I've fallen in love with her."

"And how exactly is that a problem? I think it's wonderful." Her face beamed and her eyes twinkled.

"I know you think that's wonderful, but not if I can't win her heart. I can't compete with Merrick, and I don't want to. But I'm going to have to talk to her before she makes her decision. If she leaves with him, then I don't think I'll ever see her again." He knew what he had to do, just not how he was actually going to do it. What if he said the wrong thing?

"Long have I prayed that you would find a godly woman, Daniel Beaufort. Maddy is a strong believer. I don't think she will do anything rash. Mr. Merrick has definitely swept her off her feet, but that doesn't mean she's chosen him. She's sensible. And you two are friends. Why don't you talk to her tonight after they're finished at the Roadhouse?"

"Tonight?" His voice squeaked. Most of the time, Granny's suggestions were good. And made him feel better. But this time, not so much. It made his stomach feel all squirrelly. He put a hand over the offending part of his abdomen and sighed.

"Yes, tonight. In a few days, you'll be working out there full-time. Don't you think you ought to have it resolved before then? It might make working on the farm mighty uncomfortable."

Granny was right. He'd better do it soon. "Fine. I'll talk to her tonight."

"Good boy." Granny started rocking again.

Was that a smile on her lips?

"Don't forget to let me know how it goes." The twinkle in her eye as she winked at him made him shake his head.

The day had passed far too slow. He'd worked in the store for a couple of hours and couldn't help glancing at the clock every few minutes. Dad had been consumed with the books and seemed worried. But every time Daniel asked, Dad said it was nothing, so he'd headed out to the farm.

He'd thought maybe he'd have time to speak privately with Madysen, but she'd been busy teaching Bethany, and he didn't want to interrupt. So tonight was it. He'd offered to stand watch at the Roadhouse with John, which would give him easier access to Madysen after the show. He would ask to take Madysen home. Then . . . he'd tell her how he felt.

Him and every other man in town.

He let a heavy sigh out between his lips.

When evening finally came, the Roadhouse was packed as

usual, and the food was phenomenal. John had been glad for Daniel's offer. This was Whitney's first night back, and no one knew exactly how she would do.

Offering up a quick prayer for her, he watched the crowd. Whitney's attacker wouldn't dare show up, would he?

The sisters began to play. Whitney was at the piano, her hair tied into a tight knot at the back of her neck. She wore a shawl over her dress, she didn't smile, and her color was a bit pale. He felt sorry for her. No doubt she'd be on guard all evening.

The ladies were soon caught up in their performance, and Daniel began to relax and enjoy the show. It was beautiful—*they* were beautiful. Thank goodness nothing was amiss.

The usual quiet of the audience was disturbed by some rude fellows at the table not far from where he and John stood. The man in the middle was all smiles as he told raucous stories to the other men.

Daniel tried to tune it out, but as soon as one of the men remarked about the lovely Miss Whitney Powell, the man in the middle laughed and declared that he had been intimate with her.

The other men clamored for more.

Rage washed over Daniel and he looked to John—to find that John had moved closer to the stage. Daniel ate up the distance to the rowdy table with long strides.

"She isn't as stuck-up as she seems, gentlemen." Garrett Sinclair sent a grin to his audience. "She just needed a little strong persuasion."

Daniel grabbed Sinclair's collar and punched the man in the face. "Shut up!" His throat burned.

Sinclair put a hand to his bloody lip and narrowed his gaze. "We can take this outside if you want, but it's not lies. I ain't got nothin' to hide."

He gripped the man's collar tighter and pushed him up against the wall. "Shut. Your. Lying. Mouth."

Sinclair sneered. Then he pushed Daniel away and threw a punch of his own. Daniel dodged it and swung back.

The whole table of men came at him.

One punch after another landed to his gut and head then—Blackness.

"Daniel? Daniel?"

Madysen's voice called him. Where was she?

"Daniel, are you all right?"

Wha . . . Something wet was on his face. He reached up and grabbed it. Ah. A wet cloth.

He opened one eye. Madysen was like an angel hovering over him.

She leaned back a bit. "Oh, good, you had us scared."

"I'm fine." He sat up and winced at his throbbing head. And his aching jaw. What happened?

"Everyone go back to your tables. He's fine." Madysen put her arm around Daniel as he got to his feet. "What was the fight about?"

Daniel looked around. Sinclair and his crude friends were nowhere to be seen, and the stage was empty. "Where are your sisters?"

"Taking a break. John's with them. Tell me what you were fighting about."

"Sinclair said something horrible about your sister to a table full of men. I couldn't help it. I punched him and told him to stop lying. He punched me. I punched back. Then his friends jumped into the fray."

Red tinged her cheeks. "Sinclair? I didn't see him. What did he say?"

He shook his head. "It's not for a lady's ears."

She stiffened. "If it was truly that bad, you *need* to tell me. She's my sister."

With a grimace, he told her the conversation.

Madysen's expression fell. "Oh no. If this spreads, it will ruin her reputation. She'll be devastated. She wouldn't even let John go to the sheriff for fear of people blaming her."

"I don't think Sinclair is inclined to keep his mouth shut."

"Look, don't say anything to Whitney. After we're back on stage, tell John what happened, please. He'll know what to do." Madysen glanced back as her sisters returned to the stage. "She's been through so much already."

"Don't worry, Maddy. I'm sure John and I can handle this."

"Thank you." She grabbed his hands and squeezed. "I better get back up there."

He nodded. "You'll do great."

But her expression told him she knew as well as he did that their lives were about to get a whole lot worse.

TWENTY-THREE

I'm going to kill him."

Daniel had never seen John so furious. But he wasn't serious, was he? John was too good a man. God-fearing.

"I wanted to do the same—believe me." Daniel fisted his hands just thinking about it. "This is not a good situation. I'm worried about the ladies. This town is full of despicable men. If even one of them believes Sinclair's lies, who knows what they'll try." Daniel stood with John at the back door. The girls were loading their things in the wagon and probably thought it strange that he and John weren't there to help.

John swiped a hand down his face. "I knew we should have told the sheriff. Whitney figured everyone would think she encouraged the advance. With Sinclair telling his lies . . ."

"Her fears may come true."

John looked like he *could* kill Sinclair.

Daniel put a hand on his friend's arm. "I'm sure Sinclair or the men he was with have told this story to others. How can I help?"

John stood there, flexing and unflexing his hands at his sides. "I don't know. But thank you for telling me. We'll have to pray about this and see what unfolds."

"I'll be glad to help in any way that I can."

John gripped his shoulder. "Thanks. You've done a lot to help this family out already, and we really appreciate it. Hope you know that."

He did. And it gave him a sense of pride. "Would it be all right if I drove Madysen home tonight? I'd like to talk to her."

"Of course." John turned back to the wagon. "But let's not say anything to Whitney just yet, all right? She's fragile enough. She doesn't need to know what the ruckus was about."

"You got it." Daniel walked with John to the wagon. Madysen was just about to climb up. "Can I drive you home, Madysen?" Daniel shoved his hands deeper in his pockets. Why was he so nervous?

She looked to the others and shrugged. "Sure. Are we going to ride double?"

"No. Dad let me borrow his sleigh. I think you'll find it very comfortable." He grinned. "And warmer than the horse."

He helped her climb up into his sleigh, then got in and settled a blanket over her lap. "I'm betting you'll stay nice and toasty."

She laughed. "I'm sure. It looks like more snow might be on the way." She tied the ribbons of her wool bonnet. "Thank you again for defending Whitney's honor tonight. I just hope nothing awful comes out of that man spreading his lies."

"I hope so too. But we better prepare ourselves for the worst. Men like that enjoy the attention."

"Can we talk about something else?" She waved a hand in front of her. "I'm sorry. But it's beginning to make me feel sick to my stomach."

"I understand. Besides, I had a couple of things to discuss with you." Two major issues weighed on his heart, but which one should he bring up first?

"Oh?" Shifting in her seat, she turned toward him a bit more. "About sheep?"

He laughed. "It's always about sheep with you. You sure do love those critters."

"It's not *always* about sheep. Sometimes it's about music." She giggled.

"I stand corrected." Their laughter filled the night air and made him comfortable just sitting with her in companionable silence.

"So?"

"Oh, sorry. I wanted to talk to you about my becoming John's assistant. Are you all right with me working full-time at the farm?"

"Why wouldn't I be?" She squeezed his arm. "It's absolutely wonderful. I readily admit that I don't know much about sheep, although I'm trying to learn. Knowing you're going to be there for us and with us, well, you have made my week so much better."

If only he could make more than just her week better. But they had such a good friendship, he didn't want to mess anything up. Except . . . if he didn't say anything to her about how he felt, she might leave forever. Was he willing to take that risk? "So tell me about Buddy. Any more thoughts about leaving Alaska?" If only he had the nerve to say what was really on his mind.

"You know, I appreciate you asking. Since Buddy hasn't had time to get to know my family too much, I feel like they aren't giving him a fair shake. Yes, he's a little flashy and flamboyant, but most performers are. Behind all of that is a man who really sees me. He understands my dreams. And he seems to care about me a lot."

Not what he wanted to hear. "And it sounds like you are considering his offer?"

She gave a little shrug and tilted her head. "We've discussed the possibility. Buddy feels he can make me a star."

"But what about the rest? What about his . . . feelings for you?" Daniel cleared his throat. "Are you thinking . . . of, uh, . . . of marrying him?"

Madysen shrugged as if the question were about nothing

more important than the price of eggs. "I am, but he hasn't exactly asked me. Not yet."

How could he talk to her about this? He couldn't just tell her that she was making a huge mistake. Could he? They rode in silence for several seconds. He couldn't let this opportunity go to waste. "Maddy, can I ask you a question? And you understand that I'm not judging you, just like you were so kind not to judge me when I told you about my anger toward God?"

She squinted at him. "Sounds ominous. But you're my friend, and I know you care about me, so go ahead." She straightened a bit and folded her hands in her lap.

The horses pulled the sleigh along and swished through the snow. Daniel could hear his heart beating. Hopefully she couldn't. "Well, have you thought about the fact that maybe this is just a crush you have on Mr. Merrick? Could it be that you are in love with the idea of being in love? Or maybe it's the idea of performing?"

She sat silent for several moments.

Had he gone too far?

"I don't think it's a crush, although I must admit I'm not sure. Yes, it's exciting to think about getting married and traveling the world and being famous—" she took a deep breath— "but I would like to think that I am sensible enough to not be swayed by the *idea* of it all. Hopefully I would be sensible enough to actually care for someone for who they are." By the time she was done, she sounded aggravated.

"I'm sorry if I—"

"No, I'm the one who's sorry." Her shoulders dropped a bit. "Here I told you I would listen, and I didn't. You're my friend and are just expressing concern. My family has been expressing concern too. But I feel like everyone just needs to get to know Buddy. Give him a chance."

What he wouldn't do for this woman. But giving Buddy Merrick a chance wasn't appealing.

"It's hard to give a chance to someone who doesn't exactly make himself available. From what I've seen, Buddy Merrick shows up, pays you court for a few minutes, and then takes off before anyone can speak to him."

"He's a very busy man."

"But an honorable man would make time for the family of the woman he loved. He would spend time getting to know the family and put their minds at ease. Let them know he is trustworthy. He would maybe even go to church with them, but I've never seen Buddy Merrick at church."

Raising an eyebrow, she pointed a finger at him. "You seem awfully opinionated and judgmental, Daniel Beaufort, when you'd promised you wouldn't be."

She was miffed at him. Again. Great.

"And besides, not that I'm making excuses for him, mind you, but they *do* perform quite late into the night on Saturday. There are two shows you know."

Daniel shook his head. "Things like that don't matter when you're in love."

"You sound like you're an authority on such things," Madysen snapped. "Just how many times have you been in love, Daniel?"

"Once." For all the good it would do him. "Just once."

At the farm, John walked up to the sleigh as Daniel handed Madysen down.

"Daniel, Chuck would like to speak with you. Do you have a few minutes, or do you think tomorrow would be better?"

"Tonight's fine." He hopped down from the sleigh and handed the reins to John. "Just leave them tied up here for a bit."

Maddy had already said good night and gone inside. What could Mr. Bundrant want to speak to him about?

Havyn greeted Daniel inside the door. "You know where Granddad's room is?"

"No, I don't believe I do."

"I'll show you." Eli waved him down the hall.

"Thanks."

Eli stopped in front of an open door. "Here it is."

Daniel nodded at the young man.

"Come in." A husky voice greeted him.

The man in front of him sat up in the big bed, propped up by numerous pillows. The lines etched in his face attested to years of hard work, lots of laughter, and plenty of grief.

"Good evening, Mr. Bundrant." Daniel took off his hat and gloves. "I hear you wanted to see me?"

"Yes." He motioned for him closer. "Close door."

"Oh, certainly." Daniel felt his heart accelerate at the seriousness.

Chuck held out a piece of paper.

It's wearisome to try to form all the necessary words, so this will have to do. Do you know anything about this Buddy Merrick fellow?

Daniel passed the paper back. "No, sir, I'm sorry, I don't." It rankled him. A lot. Especially considering the conversation he'd just had with Maddy. Did *anyone* know the mysterious Mr. Merrick?

Chuck wrote for several seconds and handed the paper back.

No one seems to know much. Which disturbs me greatly. The man hasn't even come to meet me or speak with me . . . which seems awful strange because I hear he visits Madysen all the time.

"It is strange." The paper went back and forth. "In fact, I just talked to Maddy about it, and now I think she's peeved at me."

I had a feeling you would say that. John tells me you might be interested in my Madysen?

"I . . . well, that is . . . I think she's wonderful . . ." he swallowed and cleared his throat. Best to just come clean. "That is to say, yes, I care for her a great deal."

Chuck shifted a bit and wrote again.

I've always admired your father. He could have given up when that wagon crushed his leg, but he didn't. Instead, he found something else he could do. That's admirable.

Daniel had never thought of it that way. "Yes, sir. You're right about that. Dad's not one to give up. Neither am I."

John tells me he's asked you to come on permanently?

"Yes, sir. He has."

Please call me Chuck. Have you given John an answer?

"I agreed to come."

I'm glad. Would have hated to have to chase you down and talk you into it.

Daniel smiled. He liked Chuck. A lot. The man must have been quite the force to be reckoned with. The older man continued to write, then handed the paper over to Daniel.

Well then, that's that. I want you in charge of the cheese making from the sheep's milk. Madysen is in charge of the sheep. That should give you plenty of time together and lots to talk about.

Daniel laughed. "We just had a tiff, so who knows how long that will last. But I find it entertaining that you're playing matchmaker."

I'm good at it too. It worked with John and Havyn. Why wouldn't it work with you and Maddy?

"I would hope that she could come to care for me on her own." He tilted his head back and forth as he considered the conversation they'd had on the ride home. "Then again, I'll take all the help I can get."

Smart man.

Chuck smiled, but it was only the left side of his face that lifted.

"I guess I should go." Daniel stood. "Unless you wanted to discuss anything else?"

You need to understand Madysen. She hates to think some-one is being false. And until her father came back, I didn't think she was even capable of not believing in people. So this is a tough time for her. You need to woo her. Try to win her heart. But just be you.

"That doesn't exactly sound easy."

Love never is, my boy.

Twenty-Four

S now fell in fat, giant flakes from the sky above as they drove to church. Madysen stuck her tongue out for a moment and caught a few. It made her feel like a little girl, so she did it again. She and her family were piled into the sleigh on this chilly Sunday morning, which at least made it feel a bit warmer. John, Havyn, and Whitney were in the front, while Maddy, Eli, Bethany, and Ruth sat in the back.

"I like to do that too." Bethany tugged on Madysen's sleeve, then demonstrated.

"It's fun, isn't it?"

Bethany snuggled up closer to her. The freckles on her nose made her look younger than she was. "Can I start helping you with the sheep? I've been watching for several days, and I think I could handle it. Eli's helping John with the cows. I want to help too."

Madysen held back a grin. Bethany was a veritable fount of questions all the time.

"Aren't you helping Havyn with the chickens?"

"Only in gathering eggs. And that doesn't take all day. Besides"—she dropped her voice to a whisper—"I want to spend more time with you."

Madysen's heart melted. She'd given Bethany a few music

lessons so far, but the young girl hung on her every word and followed her around. Everywhere. Maddy put an arm around Bethany. "I would like that very much. Unless Havyn has given you another job."

"No. She suggested I ask you anyway. Something about how your hands were full to overflowing."

Laughing, Maddy nodded. "She's right. Sometimes I wonder what I got into when I stole those sheep—"

"You stole them?" Bethany pulled back, her brow furrowed. She crossed her arms. "You're not supposed to steal."

Madysen giggled and told Bethany the tale.

It even made Ruth laugh—something that hadn't happened since the confrontation at the dining room table. And each time Dad came back with no news about Ruth's husband, she grew quieter. At least she talked on occasion to Whitney. But she worked herself to the bone, even though they'd all told her it wasn't necessary.

Whitney seemed quieter too and had started having terrible headaches at night. Madysen and Havyn were both urging her to see the doctor again, but Whitney didn't want to see anyone.

The sleigh came to a halt. They'd reached the Roadhouse. Everyone climbed out and went inside. Would they ever manage to get their own church built? They'd been collecting money for over two years and had hoped to do it yet this fall, but John told her the lumber they ordered had been used to build Judas's newest hotel. It was a mistake, but it nevertheless delayed any chance to build the church before winter set in. Herb Norris assured them it wasn't a problem, and they could continue to meet at the Roadhouse. It wasn't an ideal set up, but it was good enough.

Voices hushed as Madysen and her family headed for a row of chairs. Why was it so quiet today?

No one spoke to them. How strange. Normally the ladies flocked together near them, and they all caught up on the news. But today . . .

Something was wrong.

Madysen took a chair and looked around the room.

"Miss Powell?" Buddy's voice captured her attention and made her smile. "Might I sit with you this morning?"

See? The man was at church after all. Where was Daniel? Did he see this? "Why, Mr. Merrick. I certainly didn't expect to see you here."

"Of late, I've been quite lonely. I found I missed church too much not to come today." He gave her a smile. Was that the same smile he gave to the crowds each night? For some reason, she longed to have him share something special with just her. "When I was a boy, I was part of a choir. It really was one of my favorite things."

She shook off the negative thoughts. He was here. That was what mattered. "How wonderful. It pleases me to no end that you are a churchgoing man. I had an inkling, to be sure."

"My religious beliefs are important to me, but certainly not something that I wave around like a flag. They're too deep and personal."

Madysen couldn't contain the smug feeling. "How refreshing. As you know, my faith is very important to me too."

"Yes, it's one of the very things that attracted me to you."

"Of course it is," a deep voice said.

Madysen turned to Daniel, who stood on the other side of her pew. When did he arrive?

"Daniel, good morning." Even though she was still a bit angry with him for not taking her side, she gave him a pleasant greeting.

"How are you today, Madysen?"

Madysen beamed a smile. "I'm just fine." After Daniel's questions the other night, she had prayed about the situation. Unequally yoked marriages were no good. Just look at what had happened to her mother and father. So she'd been praying harder for Buddy, and here he was in church today.

"Good morning, Miss Powell. Mrs. Robertson." Daniel smiled as the others took their seat in the row in front of Madysen and Buddy. "And good morning, Eli and Bethany." Then he waved to Havyn, John, and Whitney at the other end. He looked down at Madysen and grinned. "Might I sit with you today?"

Buddy frowned. "I don't think—"

"We would love to have you join us." Madysen spoke at the same time.

"Thank you." Daniel moved past Buddy and Madysen and sat on her other side. He winked at her.

Well, this was interesting. Of course, Daniel had greeted the whole family. Buddy was here just for her. That made her feel special. And he was in church. That was good. And yet . . .

Her family didn't like that Buddy didn't know any of them. How could that happen if he didn't make an effort? Maybe she should talk to him about that. Might help ease everyone's tension.

But the tension grew during the service. Buddy and Daniel both held out hymnals to share with her. Then, during the sermon, Buddy fidgeted with his hat. Daniel seemed to get closer with every breath he took. But maybe she was imagining things.

When the service was over, everyone stood. She wanted nothing more than to go outside and take huge, gulping breaths of the cold air. The two men confused her. A lot.

Buddy blocked her path. "Miss Powell. Madysen." His voice was low, and he stepped closer. "Might I speak with you privately outside, before you head home?"

"All right."

He offered his arm and whisked her out the door and to the rear of the Roadhouse. Then he glanced around. "I'm hoping we won't be interrupted."

She raised her eyebrows. "Oh?"

"Oh, sweet Madysen, I would never do anything untoward.

I simply brought you out here so I could ask you to marry me."
He didn't get down on one knee, but his eyes sparkled. Was
that love she saw there?

She covered her mouth with her hand.

"I find that I can't think of my life without you. I've been,
as I mentioned before, so lonely. Being with you has filled an
emptiness inside that I'd tried to fill with so many things. Even
the show and the constant moving from place to place."

Poor man. What it must have been like to lead such a lonely
life. And to think that she could bring him happiness!

"I find that when I'm with you that void is gone. More than
anything, I want you to be on my arm—to be my wife and
take that emptiness away forever. And I will make you famous
and can arrange for concerts all over. You are so very beautiful
and talented."

"Thank you . . . but—"

"Please don't answer just yet. I know that you need to think
about it." He smiled down at her. "But let me give you this."
He pulled a large sparkling ring out of his pocket. A grand
diamond surrounded by red and blue jewels.

She'd never seen anything so beautiful in her life.

He put it in her palm. "Think about it, please, Madysen. I
pray that you can come to love me as I love you. I'll give you
everything you've ever dreamed of. But sadly, we will need to
leave before the Sound is frozen. And the last scheduled ship
heads back to Seattle in a few short weeks. Please don't send
me away alone."

The elation she felt a moment before dropped to her toes.
"You want an answer and for us to be married in a matter of
weeks?"

"No, my dear. Don't stress. We need to be married in Seattle
so that my dear, sweet mother can be at the wedding. I'm on
the road so often that it will break her heart if I don't allow
her the honor of being at our wedding."

"I don't know. . . ."

"Madysen." Havyn's voice caused her to turn around. Her face was covered in tears.

Buddy looked at her sister and nodded. Then turned back to her. "Think about it." He closed her hand over the ring and walked off without a word to Havyn.

Madysen shook her head. What had just happened? But one look at Havyn's face said something was terribly wrong. "What is it?"

"You noticed how it was so quiet when we walked into the service?" Her sister looked mad and hurt all at the same time.

"Yes?"

"Someone has spread a horrible rumor that Whitney is a . . . is a . . . loose woman."

The ride home had been eerily silent. When they got back to the farm, Dad was there waiting for them.

He had his hat in his hands and looked furious, which was not a good sign.

Havyn and Ruth took Whitney inside with the kids. All Madysen could do was watch.

Dad looked at her. "Tell me that what I just heard in the mining camp isn't true." His face was red.

So it was all over town.

"How could you even begin to think that your daughter would . . . would . . ." Madysen couldn't even voice it.

"I punched three different men in the mouth. I couldn't believe it would be true. But I need an explanation, and I need one right now." Spit flew from his mouth.

"Chris, you need to calm down." John joined them and took him by the arm. "Let's go inside. Whitney needs to tell you what happened."

When they entered the parlor, Whitney was sitting in Mama's

favorite chair. Back ramrod straight. A distant expression on her face. "Everyone has heard, haven't they?"

Madysen knelt in front of her and grabbed her hands. "We're not going to stand for this, Whit. We're not."

Whitney looked at their father. "If you knew me, you'd know it's not the truth."

Havyn cleared her throat. "I think I should explain. I shouldn't have told you only bits and pieces of the truth. When I said that Whit was injured, I was trying to spare you the details. Garrett Sinclair came out here under the guise of purchasing dogs. Whitney took the dogs for a run to show Mr. Sinclair how they handled. He . . . tried to take advantage of her."

Dad's face had gone ashen. He looked at Eli and Bethany. "Go to your room, please. I'd rather you not hear what I have to say."

The two children nodded and got to their feet and left. Dad turned back to Whitney. "I'm truly sorry this happened to you, but you must be honest with me about what he did to you."

Her older sister shivered. "He touched me and kissed me. He had me pinned and started . . ." Whitney lowered her head.

Havyn went to her side. "It's all right, Whit. Just take your time."

"I pushed him away and fell. I stopped him . . . well . . . the dogs did. I'd taught them to attack on command. If I hadn't . . . I don't know if I would have escaped." She looked up, and there were tears in her eyes. "I got my rifle. I think I would have killed him if he hadn't left."

Dad jumped to his feet. "Someone needs to teach that man a lesson. And I intend to do it. No one touches my daughter like that. And then to spread such lies!"

"Sit down, Chris." John put a hand on Dad's shoulder. "I agree that Sinclair needs to be confronted, but we're not going to do anything rash. Whitney didn't want anyone to know—not even the sheriff because of the way women are treated when these things happen. We went along with her wishes to save her reputation, but obviously things have changed. We need to involve the sheriff now, so he knows the facts of the situation."

"It's not going to do any good, you know." Whitney stood. "People have already formed their own opinions. My reputation is ruined. End of story." She walked toward the door. "Please don't bother me. I need to be alone." She rubbed the back of her neck as she left them. No doubt her headache was back.

After Whit was gone, everyone started talking at once. They all wanted to come to Whitney's defense. But the more everyone talked about it, the angrier they became. The noise was deafening.

Madysen sat frozen in her chair. She could scarcely breathe for the pain clutching her heart. If she were capable, she'd find the man and punch him in the nose herself!

The cacophony in the room made her want to scream. Madysen stood and clapped her hands together, the way she did to get her sheep's attention. "This is not helping. Whitney needs us. We need to restore her reputation. But we can't go flying off the handle with Sinclair. More than anything, we better get down on our knees and pray for God to show us what to do. I know we're all angry and would like to beat that man to a pulp. But that's not what we should do."

She stomped out of the room and headed to the sheep pens.

Good thing Garrett Sinclair had stayed clear of their farm, because she might be small, but she was strong. She could make him pay.

She had seen that same fiery anger in everyone in that room.

The bleating of her sheep calmed her heart a bit. A little manual labor would be good for her soul, even if it was Sunday.

John and Daniel had finished the elevated creep pen in the middle of the large pen. It allowed the lambs and ewes to see each other while keeping the weaned lambs from trying to nurse. Now that they were milking the sheep every day, it was a wonderful solution. All because Daniel had taken the time to come help them.

Daniel . . .

She pulled Buddy's ring out of her pocket and sat on a bale of hay. What was she going to do? She had never thought of how lonely Buddy must be. Day in and day out, he was surrounded by hundreds of people, and yet he still felt so alone. She could understand that, and her heart ached for him. If she had the power to save him from that misery, shouldn't she do whatever she could?

"Care for some company?"

She looked up when she heard Daniel's warm, deep voice.

She gave him a weak smile. "Sure. That would be nice."

"So you're not mad at me anymore?"

Squinting her eyes at him a bit, she pursed her lips. "I'm not sure. But I'll think about it."

A light chuckle accompanied his footsteps as he came closer. "Don't think about it too long. I miss you."

His words did funny things to her insides.

He came close and sat beside her. "What do you have there?"

Madysen held up the ring.

"Wow. That's impressive. I take it Buddy proposed?"

"He did." With her head down, she just stared at the ring. Any girl should be overjoyed with such a prize.

"And?"

"I didn't answer. Needed time to think about it." Twisting and turning the ring, it caught rays of sunshine coming through the windows. "The last ship to Seattle is set to sail November tenth, so I need to make up my mind by then."

"Oh." He stiffened. "That's only a couple weeks away."

"I know."

"So shouldn't you make up your mind before then? I don't know much about these things, but doesn't it take a while to plan a wedding?"

A wedding. That her family would miss. It wouldn't be anything like she'd dreamed. "He wants to marry in Seattle so his mother can be there."

"What about all of your family here?"

She shrugged. "We were all together for Havyn's wedding. . . ."

"And they will want to be a part of yours, Maddy. You are loved and cared for here . . . by lots of people. Is it wise to go off with a man you're not married to? What if he never intends to actually marry you?"

She held up the ring. "Would a man give me a ring like this if he didn't intend to marry me?"

"He might." Daniel grabbed her hand. "If . . . the girl is naïve enough."

"I am not naïve, Daniel Beaufort. How can you even say such a thing?" She tugged at her hand, but he held tight.

"Maddy, you have a huge heart. You really do think the best of everyone, but what do we know about Buddy Merrick?"

"Why do you keep asking me that? I know lots of things. Things like . . . well, for instance . . . oh, you've flustered me and I can't think." She shot him a look. "You're not being a very good friend right now."

She tried to yank her hand out of his grasp again. But he held fast. "I think I'm being a better friend than anyone else has been to you, because I'm speaking truth. I care about you. That means I want the best for you. And if that means, Buddy . . . then so be it. But I don't think it does."

"Well, then, what do you think *is* the best for me? Because I have no idea. I want to be hopeful again. Joyful again. I want to be happy and loved."

"But Maddy, you *are* loved. Why can't you see that?" He reached up and touched her cheek. "Maybe . . . you have a friend who wants to be more than friends."

She got lost in his touch. Was he saying what she thought?

Twenty-Five

D aniel hefted another crate and passed it to his dad. He wanted to get out to the farm as soon as possible. Bethany had interrupted his discussion with Madysen yesterday, and he wanted to try to talk to her again. To make sure she knew how he felt. Before it was too late. "You sure you'll be okay without me here?"

"I'll be fine. You'll be missed, but if you can spare a half hour every day to help with some odd jobs, I'll be perfectly content."

"Not a problem. I'm sure I can manage that." He rechecked the inventory. Yes, he'd done it correctly. Lately, it had been hard to keep his mind focused on the task at hand. "You've seemed a bit worried lately, Dad. Everything all right?"

Dad waved him off. "Everything's fine. I've just made a few mistakes in the books. Once I get it all figured out, things will be right as rain." His smile looked forced.

"Need me to help?" Daniel walked over to his dad. "I'm pretty good with numbers."

Dad put a hand on his shoulder. "Don't worry about it, it's no big deal. You go on out to the farm and help."

Granny entered the mercantile and brought him a paper bag. "This is for everyone, so I expect you to share."

As soon as he took the bag, the scent of cinnamon overtook his senses. "Your cinnamon cake." He closed his eyes. "Granny, you spoil me."

"Of course I do, that's my job." She patted his arm. "Now what's got you all fired up this morning?" The look of innocence on her face didn't fool him.

"You know exactly what, Granny."

"Hey, maybe *I* don't." Dad crossed his arms over his chest. "What's she talking about?" He grinned.

"Oh, you two are impossible. There happens to be a red-headed girl who might perchance be on my mind."

"Which one?" Dad quirked a brow.

"You know perfectly well which one."

Granny went to the penny candies and straightened the jars. "So you've made up your mind about her?"

"I have."

Dad came over and elbowed him.

Daniel shook his head. "Like I said, you two are impossible."

"You know what you have to do to make that happen, don't you?" Granny poked him in the belly. "I don't want to wait forever."

He rolled his eyes. "Yes, ma'am. I know."

The bell over the door jangled.

"Oh, good. People." Daniel went to the front to greet them.

Christopher Powell and John Roselli entered, expressions serious. Chris's jaw looked like it might explode, he had it clenched so tight.

"We're going to find Sinclair and confront him. We'd appreciate it if you would come with us."

"Of course." Daniel took off the apron he used in the store and called out, "Dad, I'm going out to the mines before I head to the farm."

Dad came up behind him and wiped his hands on a towel. "Sinclair's not working any mining anymore." He looked at

Daniel. "Sorry, I overheard. He's working for Judas Reynolds. I made a delivery to Judas not more than thirty minutes ago, and Sinclair was there."

Judas put the last of the deeds for his newest claims in the safe. He'd no sooner straightened than he heard a commotion in the outer office. What in the world was going on? He went to the door and found his receptionist arguing with a trio of men. Men he knew very well.

"John." Judas nodded as he stepped out. "Daniel, and I believe this is Mr. Powell, if I'm not mistaken. To what do I owe this visit?"

"It's not a pleasure call, that's for sure," Powell all but growled.

"Step into my office and tell me what's going on."

The men followed him and waited until he was seated. "Please, sit."

"We don't have time for that." Powell ground out his words.

"Judas, I'm afraid I have some news about one of your employees that you won't like to hear." John glanced over to Powell and Daniel.

"Go on, Roselli. You know I trust you to be honest with me."

Judas listened as John told the whole sordid story. He should've known that Sinclair would do something stupid. The man was entirely too arrogant for his own good.

"He didn't rape her, but only because Whitney somehow got the upper hand with the help of her dogs. They attacked Sinclair, and she got her rifle."

"Bad enough what he did to her"—Powell skewered Judas with a fiery glare—"but at the Roadhouse Saturday night, he was talking it up. Making like he had been intimate with her and was proud of it. Like she'd invited his advances. Folks were talking about it at church on Sunday."

Judas might have laughed had the men not been so serious.

What did women's reputations matter? Now *his* reputation, that was important. Speaking of which . . .

He might be able to use all this.

Judas squinted his eyes and pressed his lips into a thin line. "How dare that man smear a lady's reputation like that!" He pounded a fist on his desk.

His secretary came running through the door. "What do you need, Mr. Reynolds?"

"Have Burt come see me immediately. You should be able to find him in the warehouse."

"Yes, sir." She ran from the room.

He straightened, putting on his best moral outrage. "Gentlemen, rest assured that I will take care of this."

"We don't need you to take care of it." Powell leaned over the desk. "We can take care of it ourselves. We just need to find Sinclair."

No, they didn't. It wouldn't help Judas at all if they did. "Look, I understand how you feel, but beating the man senseless won't change what he's done. In fact, such a reaction from you might convince people that what he said was true. His very public besmirching needs a very public retraction. You can't provide that, but I can."

Powell straightened.

Ah, capitulation. He loved it.

"How?"

He held Powell's gaze. "You said Sinclair announced his falsehoods to his friends at the Roadhouse. I will ensure he makes another announcement there. And at the Follies. *And* at church. The reverend and I are well acquainted, and I'm sure he will be more than happy to see a sinner confessing his wrongdoing."

The trio stepped back and discussed it among themselves for a moment. Judas could hear that they were concerned about how Whitney would bear up under this very public reminder of what had happened to her.

Judas leaned back in his chair, schooling his features into the picture of concern. "Our dear Whitney is humiliated by a lie. We must bring out the truth. It sets us free, as the Good Book says." Judas got to his feet. "Don't worry about a thing. Sinclair *will* make his apologies, and Whitney will be vindicated. By week's end."

Or Sinclair would be dead.

It took a full day for Burt to locate Sinclair. When the oaf was finally seated across from Judas, he looked completely confused. "What did you call me in for? It's my day off."

Judas narrowed his gaze. "You stupid fool. How could you have been so careless as to make such declarations about a prominent lady in our town—someone you know is a family friend of mine. Especially without even having the pleasure of doing what you insinuated. You really are an idiot! Now I have to clean up your mess. No, I take that back. *You* are going to clean up this mess. And you are going to do exactly what I say."

Sinclair leaned back in his chair and grinned. "It's not that bad. I don't see why you are so worked up about this."

Judas came out of his seat and around his desk in a flash. He grabbed Sinclair by the collar and pulled him to his feet. Once Judas had him standing, he punched Sinclair in the nose, knocking him to the ground. "This isn't a grinning matter. Now, do I have your full attention?"

Sinclair got to his feet. His nose dripped blood onto his shirt. He seemed momentarily stunned.

Good.

"Answer me."

"I'm listening." Sinclair took out his handkerchief and tried to stanch the flow of blood.

"Let me make myself very clear, Mr. Sinclair. I own you. I know things about you that would get you hung. And I'm not a man who merely threatens. If you don't do exactly as I say, you won't live to see another sunset. That's a promise." He straightened his vest and jacket. "I don't have room for men in my business who can't follow orders."

The fool straightened in his chair and dared to lift his chin. "Yes, sir. I'll do whatever you say."

Judas spotted a green dress and flash of red curls out the window of his office. "You're going to have to leave out the back, Sinclair. Make sure you aren't seen. Don't go into town. Don't speak to anyone. Is that understood? You will wait until I tell you what to do."

With a nod, Sinclair left out the side door of his office.

Judas took a breath, then hurried to the front of the building to call after the retreating figure. "Miss Powell!"

Madysen turned and smiled, then came back. "Mr. Reynolds, how nice to see you. I was just in town with John to check on our orders. The time is narrowing fast for getting in product."

"Indeed, it is. That's part of the reason I wanted to talk to you. Won't you join me in my office?"

She followed him inside and gave a nod to the receptionist.

"Sit down, please. Can I offer you anything?"

She took off her coat and sat in the same chair Sinclair had just vacated. "No. I'm fine. What can I do for you?"

"Well, I heard that congratulations are in order?" He pasted on his best smile.

Her brow creased. "For what?"

"You and Buddy Merrick, of course!" He walked to the front of his desk and leaned against it. "What a fine match you two will make."

"Oh, well . . . you see—"

She didn't look at all like a blushing fiancée.

"You deserve to perform on a larger stage, Madysen, and Buddy will take fine care of you. Oh, and won't your mother be smiling down from heaven?" He clasped his hands in front of him. "Now . . . what would you like for a wedding gift? I want to spoil you."

———————

Havyn picked up her violin and tried the concerto again. By measure twelve, she was distracted and missing notes. Why did some people have to be so awful? The thought of people around town spreading rumors about Whitney . . .

It was so wrong!

Putting the violin back in its case, she let out a long, shaky breath. It was a good thing she sent a note to Mr. Norris saying they couldn't perform for a while. None of them were up to it. Nothing would be right until the lies about Whitney were rectified.

But would that encourage everyone in town to believe the lies? She hoped not.

Movement out of the corner of the window caught her attention. Maddy was back.

Her sister came in the room, taking off her gloves. "Where is everybody?"

"Ruth is doing schoolwork with the children, and Granddad is sleeping. And I presume John returned with you from town."

"Yes. He and Daniel are unloading."

Something in her sister's face told her that she needed to talk. "What's going on?"

Madysen took off her bonnet and tucked her gloves inside. "I'm going to get Whitney. There's something I need to speak to you both about."

No smiles or wave of her hands. It must be serious. Then again, everything was serious right now. "I'll put on some tea."

A few minutes later, they were all gathered in the great room. The place where they'd played music, opened presents, held family celebrations, and watched the fire crackle during deep conversations and secrets shared. Many lively games had been played in this room. Havyn closed her eyes for a moment and could almost hear Mama's sweet laughter.

Would the ache of losing her ever fade? Or would they have to deal with the waves of grief for the coming years? Opening her eyes, she looked at her sisters. Madysen seemed weighed down. Whitney sat stoic and quiet.

Just a few days ago, she'd hoped to share some happy news in this room. But things had changed since that horrible man had tarnished Whit's reputation.

Maddy scooted to the edge of her seat. "I'm glad we could all be together like this." She took a deep breath. "I guess I better just come out and say it. Buddy Merrick has asked me to marry him and join his troupe."

Havyn watched her baby sister. For some reason, Maddy didn't seem all that happy about her news. Which was fine with Havyn, but she counted to ten before allowing herself to respond. "A few days ago, it seemed this was what you wanted. Have you changed your mind?"

"No." Maddy looked down at her hands. "I don't know. You all don't know him like I do."

Havyn tried to keep her tone loving as she repeated the question. The last thing she wanted was to push her sister away.

"I thought I did . . . but now . . . I'm not so sure. I'm torn between the dream and my life here. It's hard to think about leaving my sheep and . . ."

Had she been about to mention Daniel?

"It's hard to think about leaving all of you. What do you think?" Maddy's gaze bore into hers.

"Oh, Maddy. It seems to me that if you really loved him, you'd be thrilled. Dancing around the room and full of joy."

"Well . . . I . . ." Maddy bit her lip.

Havyn sent a look to Whit, but their older sister didn't say anything. "I can't imagine life without you here. With us. I love you so much. And I can't see that Buddy loves you like a husband should love a wife. Not that I'm comparing him to John, but you know what I mean. Does he even have a relationship with the Lord? And what about when you start having children? Are you going to continue traveling?" She paused and stood up. "I'm sorry. But I can't say that I think you should marry him." Had she said the right thing?

Maddy nodded and sniffed. Was she crying? "I need to make a decision soon because the ship leaves on the tenth. Buddy wants us to marry in Seattle so that his mother can attend the wedding. Buddy is her only child. So . . . you all would miss the ceremony."

"Oh my." Havyn plopped back down in her chair. "I don't even know what to say. Whit, help me out here."

"I think you should go." Whitney spoke up from Mama's chair. The only place she sat nowadays. "And I think I should go with you."

"*What?*" Havyn couldn't help how loud her voice came out.

Whit looked at her. The sadness in her eyes almost broke Havyn's heart. "You've heard what people are saying. Saw how they treated me at church. At *church* of all places. My reputation is ruined, and even though everything I love is here, I don't see how I can stay. I'd rather shrivel up and die." She looked back to Maddy. "If you'll have me, I'd be forever grateful if I could go with you. That way we could perform together, and I can get away from this horrible gossip. Maybe after time, I'll be able to heal from what that man tried to do."

It was like someone had ripped Havyn's heart out of her chest. How could her family be falling apart like this? *Lord, what are You doing?*

Madysen looked disappointed. Not exactly an excited bride-to-be. She tilted her head at Whit. "Are you sure?"

Whitney fiddled with a thread on her apron. "Yes, I think it's best. I think you and I should leave Alaska."

Twenty-Six

Nothing had gone as she'd expected the past few days. Madysen herded the new lambs back into their pen. And she wasn't sure what to do anymore. She couldn't ignore that the feelings she had for Daniel were more than friendship, but after Whitney declared they should leave Alaska together, Madysen couldn't exactly tell her sister no. Not after all she'd endured. Guilt twinged every time she thought about *not* wanting to leave. Maybe God had given them this opportunity so that Whitney could get away and heal. Was Madysen wise in thinking that? And then, of course, there was Buddy. He loved her. He was lonely and empty without her. She didn't want to cause him pain . . . but maybe she understood a little more about love and her own heart now. *God, what do we do? I'm so confused.*

At first it had seemed like a good idea to ask Buddy if they could hold off on the wedding for a while, and she and Whitney could start performing and see how it went. But that would be pretty insensitive of her. Would he even be willing to wait? The presents came twice a day now.

Bethany brought in some new straw. "Dad just rode up. Is it okay if I go out to see him?"

"Of course, sweetie." How precious it had become to have

her younger siblings here. No matter the circumstances, God had brought them all together. As a family. That probably meant she should show her father mercy. She just wasn't sure how.

She began to spread the new straw.

"Maddy?"

Turning around, she saw Dad standing there. "Bethany went to see you."

"I know. I asked her to go inside and wait for me. I need to talk to you."

"Okay." Madysen kept working. It had become harder and harder to cover her feelings when Dad was around. And she wasn't sure either one of them was ready to actually deal with it.

"Could we just sit for a moment?"

Madysen straightened and set the pitchfork down. "All right, but not for long." She went to a bale and plopped down, digging her fingers into the straw as if to hold on. Dad sat across from her.

"I know you're angry with me, and you have every right to be. I was a horrible person, a terrible father. I made mistakes, and I'm still a sinner. I'm so grateful that, as a child of God, I'm saved by grace. But last night I was reading my Bible in Matthew chapter five. Jesus said that if we know someone is holding something against us, we must go to that person and be reconciled."

Madysen stared at her father. She couldn't move or say anything. He wanted reconciliation? That was impossible.

"I want more than anything to mend our relationship. Even if we can't ever be close again as father and daughter. I want to beg for your forgiveness. I'm sorry. I let you down. I should have stood up to your grandfather all those years ago, even though he was just trying to protect you all in his own way. But he was fierce and threatening, and I was a coward who deserved to be threatened. I would have done the same thing if it was my little girl being treated the way I treated Melly." He looked down at his shoes.

Madysen couldn't even feel the straw between her fingers. It was like she was glued in place. "So your whole apology is to blame Granddad?"

"No." He held up his hands. "No. I shouldn't have even mentioned him. As a parent, I completely understand what he did, and *I* did this. Me. No one else. Through it all, I think God was trying to protect you. And He was waiting for me to come to Him. But I was afraid of God.

"I was afraid of everything, so I sought strength in alcohol. I was afraid of failing, of loving, and especially of being a father. I'm sorry I didn't stand up for you. And I'm sorry that I left you. I remember what I promised after I found you in the mine. It has haunted me ever since."

The tears started then. How she longed to go back and be that little girl again. The little girl who adored her daddy and knew that he would always come find her. "I want to forgive you, but I don't understand. We loved you. Mama loved you. Yes, Granddad can be formidable, but we were your children and Mama your wife. You had *our* support." She shook her head. "Why did you leave us? Why did you go to another woman?"

Dad bowed his head. "I don't know. It just seemed to happen. I was drinking one day, and Esther was there. She could see the pain I was in and started talking to me. She cared about what I was feeling, and it seemed no one else did. Whenever I tried to talk to your mother, I was either too drunk or Chuck would make a scene. He didn't want us to reconcile, and I can't really blame him."

Madysen thought about that for a moment. Granddad had already admitted these things, so why did it hurt so much to hear them from her father? Would they have remained a family if Granddad had stopped interfering? Anger at the older man filled her heart. If Granddad hadn't tried to save them from Dad, he might have found the strength to stop drinking. For *them*.

"When Chuck decided I should let you all think I was dead, I gave up. I guess a part of me knew I wasn't good for you girls. And Chuck had a lot of friends who wouldn't have minded seeing me dead."

"You thought Granddad would kill you?" Madysen tried to imagine the man who'd done so much for them taking the life of another. It didn't seem possible. But on the other hand, none of what Granddad had already admitted to doing seemed possible for the man she knew. Perhaps she was just a poor judge of character.

"I hate to say it, but Madysen, he threatened just that. You can ask him about it. I think he would be honest. Anyway, I was too scared to fight back and took what he offered. I'm sorry."

She put aside her confusion about Granddad and turned to her father. "I think I can understand that—especially with a threat of death hanging over you. But . . ." She drew a long breath and let it go. "Why were *they* important enough to change for and we weren't?"

Dad's brow furrowed and he shook his head. "I'm not sure I understand."

"You stopped drinking and became a good man for Esther and your new family. Why couldn't you have done that for us? Weren't we important enough? Didn't you love us enough?" Tears came to her eyes. "When you died, I thought we must have been really bad—maybe God was punishing us by letting you die. Then when I found out that you were alive and you had another family that you'd cleaned up your life for—well, obviously we must have lacked something."

He look . . . crushed. Then shook his head. "You never lacked anything. None of you did. The lacking was all mine. I wasn't a good man, Maddy. I certainly wasn't walking with God. I guess when your granddad made it clear I had no other choice, I saw it as a way out—a way to end your pain and that of your sisters and mother. It was a coward's way out. I knew it then and I know it now.

"When I agreed that Chuck would tell your mother I had died, I laid low. I was beaten up pretty bad, and Chuck got word to Esther. She came, and he told her the plan. She was horrified to find out I was married, that I had children, but he gave her a great deal of money and promised I would marry her. Esther agreed to take care of me and move away. I was so bad off I don't even remember the move. Esther managed most of it. She nursed me back to health, but the realization of what I'd done to you all those years made me want to give up and die. I wanted liquor to consume me . . . to take away all of my pain. I hated myself so much."

Madysen shook her head. It still didn't answer her question. "But you didn't keep drinking."

"Sadly, I did drink. A lot. Tried to drown myself in my guilt. But then Esther said she'd had enough and we were going to move in with her parents in Colorado Springs. I said no. Esther made it clear my answer wasn't the right one." He glanced down at the floor. "I told her to leave without me, and I thought she would. But the next night, I got drunk so bad, I probably should've died. A guy beat me up and took everything out of my pockets. Esther was loaded up and ready to go. She had two men throw me in the back of the wagon and off we went. She gave me whiskey while I was healing, but gradually watered it down to wean me off.

"As I recovered, she told me what I had done to you all was abominable, but now that it was done, I needed to make a decision. Either give up the bottle and start fresh with her or stay with alcohol and die alone. You see, the doctor had told her that my body couldn't handle the amount of liquor I'd been drinking. He said if I continued it, I'd be dead inside of six months."

"How awful."

"It was. I guess I'd thought by doing what Chuck wanted, death wouldn't be a threat. But here it was again. I was scared, but Esther promised to see me through it. She made me pledge to never take another drink. No one had ever done that before. All I had left was my word on this one thing. I couldn't turn back."

"So you didn't do it for them. You did it for yourself."

Dad nodded. "Chuck always told me what was wrong with me. I thought it was just a father being overly critical of his daughter's husband. I didn't care about fixing what was wrong because you girls and your mother accepted me as I was and continued to love me. And, for a while, Esther did too. But then she saw that it was taking my life. She told me she wasn't about to stick around and watch me die.

"Then one day, when there was a tent revival, I just happened to be coming by that way after work. I heard the preacher talk about Jesus coming for the lost, the wounded, the sinner. I can still remember him saying, 'If you and the world have given up on you, just know that Jesus never will.' I'd heard religious stuff from your mother and Chuck, but this man was speaking to the very heart of who I was. I went home and told Esther about it, and we went back every night while the revival was in town. We got saved there, and God took away my desire for liquor. He transformed me—and then I was broken for an entirely other reason. Sober and saved, I realized I needed to make things right with your mother and you girls. But I thought it was too late. You already had new lives."

He took out his handkerchief and wiped at his tears. "Esther's parents got us in church, and our lives were turned around. I decided the only thing I could do was be a good father to the family I still had. And that brings us back to the present."

He tucked the handkerchief away. "I am so sorry for the way I failed you and your sisters and your mother. I can't undo what I did, but I'm begging you to forgive me."

Madysen considered all that he'd said and fought back her own tears. What a tangled mess. Sinful actions wrapped up with more sinful actions. Lies complicating lies. She sighed. There had been so much hate on Granddad's part. Madysen couldn't let that hate continue in her heart.

She got to her feet, and Dad did likewise. "I appreciate that you told me the truth. It hurt so much to lose you. You promised to always be there for me and then suddenly you were gone. I *hated* you for leaving me, but . . . not anymore." Madysen went to her father and wrapped her arms around him. "I'm sorry. I'm so, so sorry. I forgive you, Dad."

"Just like that?" The shock in his voice shook her to the core. Then he finally wrapped his arms around her, and she felt him release a long breath.

Nodding against his shoulder, she sniffed again. "Just like that. Isn't that what Jesus did for each of us? Mama taught us that forgiveness was a decision we had to affirm or deny—we had to choose it—but once made, it's a process that will take place with healing and come a little more each day."

"Your mother was a wonderful woman. I didn't deserve her."

She pulled back and looked into his eyes. No more anger filled her chest when she saw him. "I need to forgive you completely and start anew. Especially since Whit and I will be leaving Alaska soon. You need to be here for Havyn and Eli and Bethany."

"What are you talking about?"

She told him about Buddy's proposal and how Whit wanted to go with her to get away from the rumors.

"Your mother always dreamed that at least one of you would follow in her footsteps and make her way as a professional musician. But Judas promised that Sinclair is going to make this right. There's no need to run away from it."

"Whitney doesn't see much hope for staying here." The weight of the decision tore at her insides. Why was this so hard? But she had to do the right thing for her sister. And if this is what she needed, then so be it.

"I don't like this, Maddy. I don't know the man at all." He stepped back and frowned.

"To be honest, Dad. I don't know you very well either. But you just asked me to forgive you and start a new life with you."

"It's completely different. Please, let's talk about this some more. Maybe with the whole family. What do they think?"

She took a deep breath and sat back down on the bale of straw. "I think this is the right thing for Whitney, Dad. And I think I need to do it. I don't mind sacrificing if it will help my sister heal."

"But is it the right thing for you? You can't just marry someone because you think it will make everything easier. Is this really the life that you want? Do you want to marry that man?"

"I don't know. But I'm not sure I have any other choice."

Daniel leaned against the outside of the sheep pen. He hadn't meant to listen in on Maddy's conversation with her father—but now his heart was pounding so hard it threatened to burst out of his chest.

Her comments about leaving Alaska felt like a knife wound to his gut. But then to hear her own desires of wanting Whitney's pain to go away—for her to be healthy and whole . . . he could see Maddy sacrificing her own wants and desires for her sister.

No longer was he convinced that Buddy had won Madysen's heart. So now he needed to win Maddy for himself. But how?

God, I need Your direction. I'm not sure how to fix this, but I know that You have provided a way and that You have overcome. Show me. Please.

"Granddad?" Maddy whispered as she entered his room and then closed the door. Lifting her shoulders, she prepared herself for the conversation they needed to have.

He opened his eyes and blinked several times. "Maddy . . ."

"There are some things that I need to say, okay? I need you to listen." Whew. It was hard to tell the main authority figure in her life to listen. No matter what, she deeply respected and loved him.

He pushed himself up a bit with his good arm. "'Kay."

"I forgave Dad. And it feels really good. Now I need to forgive you." Her heart squeezed tight in her chest, and she felt the sting of tears in her eyes. "Since first learning about Dad being alive, it was easier to blame him than to hold you responsible for your part. I know why you did what you did. Dad having another family was horrific, and you had to keep that hidden from us for a long time. I've been afraid to be honest with you . . . to tell you what you did back then made me angry when I found out about it. I've been harboring that anger deep inside. I'm sorry. I'm sorry I was angry and didn't come talk to you about it. Yes, life with a drunken father was horrible, but Mama loved him despite his faults. And so did we. But Granddad, *God* needed to change him. Not you." She took in a shaky breath. "I can't believe I actually said that out loud."

"Glad . . . you did. . . . I'm . . . sorry."

She threw her arms around his neck. "I forgive you. And I hope you'll forgive me too."

"I do." He struggled against tears and had to work hard to speak. "Anger blinded me. Just like love blinded your mother."

"Love is a better blinder than anger, isn't it?" Maddy shook her head, then her heart skipped. "I've been dealing with that one myself." She leaned in and kissed Granddad on the cheek. "I'm sorry, but I've got to go."

She needed to talk to Daniel.

Now.

Daniel wasn't anywhere with the sheep. So where could he be?

Maybe Havyn knew. Madysen trekked up the hill through the snow to the chicken yards.

Giggles and laughter floated down to her. What was going on?

"Maddy, come see the new chicks!" Havyn waved her over.

Bethany had about six of the fluffy chicks in her arms, while Eli had more on his shoulders and in his lap.

"Where did these come from?" She looked to John.

"I ordered them for our . . . um . . . *unnamed* chickens." He looked a tad uncomfortable.

Bethany looked up at Maddy. "He means that these are the ones that will start the new flock to be fattened and killed. These are the fryers."

The fact that her twelve-year-old sister could say such a thing was a bit of a shock. Must be more farm girl in her than they realized.

"We're about to move them into the barn where they can stay warm." Havyn smiled.

"And you're okay with this?" Madysen wasn't sure what to think of it all, because Havyn was notoriously protective of her chickens.

"I am. And I think Bethany and Eli will be able to manage this flock beautifully." Havyn looked to John, and he nodded at the kids.

"Really? They can be our responsibility?" Eli's voice squeaked. Poor kid, his voice was changing, and it was hard to hear him go from little kid to young man every other sentence.

"Really." John tousled his hair.

The love of this family—the bond they shared—it made her want to cry and hug all of them right then and there. How could she leave? She closed her eyes against the sting of tears and then focused. She had someone she needed to see. "Hey, I've been looking for Daniel. Have you seen him?"

"He just brought the chicks, so he must be around here some-where." Havyn picked up another fluffy chick.

They were all enamored with the new babies. She wouldn't get any more information out of them. "Thanks. I'll keep look-ing." Madysen went back to the sheep barn. Maybe she should clean the kitchen. It might do her good to get out some of this nervous energy before she talked to him anyway.

Scrubbing the worktable for all she was worth, she prayed for God to show her what to do. She couldn't leave without knowing what Daniel actually felt for her. She'd never want to abandon Whitney in her time of need, but maybe things could be different with Buddy. He'd offered her a contract after all, hadn't he? Did that *have* to mean marriage? Or would he be heartbroken and cancel the contract if she turned him down? Then what would that mean for Whit? The only choice seemed to be to accept his proposal, start performing, and get Whitney established somewhere else. Maybe one day, her smile and love of music would return.

"Hey there. What did that table ever do to you?"

Daniel's voice made her jump.

She looked down. She'd been scrubbing the same spot for several minutes. "Sorry, I guess I've got a lot on my mind."

"Care to talk about it?" He leaned up against the wall, so casual and calm.

She loved that about him. "What did you mean that you might want to be more than friends?"

"Maddy." He took slow steps toward her. "You've got to be blind if you can't see how much I care about you."

"It's hard to see things when a person won't just be outright . . . honest."

"Honest. You want *honest*?" He closed the distance between them and took her in his arms. "I adore you, Madysen Powell. With every fiber of my being." He leaned his head down, closed his eyes, and put his lips on hers.

Fire lit in her belly. And her breath caught.

He deepened the kiss, and she lifted her hands, running them through his hair and down his neck.

She almost fell over when he pulled away.

"Was that honest enough for you?"

She gripped the table as he walked out of the kitchen.

He was gone.

Twenty-Seven

Madysen looked at the ring Buddy had given her, but it was Daniel she thought of. She didn't feel for Buddy the things she felt for Daniel—that much was clear.

Especially since that kiss. She could scarcely think of anything *but* Daniel.

The ring caught the sunlight as Madysen walked out across the yard. It was rather gaudy. At first she'd been impressed by it and all its lovely gemstones, but as she considered wearing it the rest of her life, Madysen felt less enthusiasm for the ring.

Or maybe it was just that she felt less enthusiasm for its giver.

"What am I going to do?"

She heard a team of horses approaching and came back around toward the house.

Buddy.

She needed to speak with him and to finally sort through her feelings, but she honestly didn't want to do it.

When he gave her a wave, however, Madysen knew it was too late to make any other choice but to go greet him. What was she going to say? She tucked the ring in her pocket and whispered a prayer.

"Father, I don't know what I'm supposed to do. Please help

me. I don't love Buddy the way I love Daniel. But can I turn down Buddy if that destroys Whitney's chance of healing? Aren't we supposed to lay down our lives for one another? Is that what I'm supposed to do?"

Buddy stopped the sleigh and jumped down to greet her. "My dear Madysen. I kept trying to get my work done and focus on our show closing up to head to the States, but you were all I could think of. How lovely you are today."

She glanced down at one of her oldest wool coats and long skirt. His comment would be laughable, if not for his sincerity. "You are kind to say so, but these are my work clothes, as you might have guessed."

"Just think how very different your work clothes will be when you begin your singing career with me." He smiled and extended a new gift. "I saw this and thought of you."

Madysen opened the little box. Inside was a pair of diamond teardrop earrings. "They're beautiful." She closed the box. "But I can't accept them. They are much too costly."

"But you'll soon be my wife. I think such a gift is more than appropriate."

"I haven't given you my answer yet." Why was she stalling? *Lord, help. I don't want to say yes, but I feel I must.*

Buddy smiled and took hold of her gloved hand. "Haven't you?" He gave her fingers a squeeze. "I know this is daunting, but we have our entire lives ahead of us. You have such amazing talent and will be the finest performer ever known to grace the stage."

How strange that he was focused on the performance aspect of their future rather than their marriage. Why wasn't he speaking to her of his love and inability to imagine a future without her at her side as his wife—not a singer. Why hadn't she seen this before? So maybe she could turn down his proposal and still sign a contract to perform.

Buddy sandwiched her hand between his. "I came out here

today because the last ship out of Nome has been moved up to the day after tomorrow. We need to arrange for your stateroom and some travel clothes. I can buy you all new things in Seattle, including a wedding dress."

This was happening too fast. The ship couldn't be leaving that soon, could it? "Um . . . I'm not sure I'm comfortable with any of this. My family won't like the idea of me not marrying here. If I say yes, there shouldn't be any reason we couldn't have a small private ceremony here first and then have a wedding for your mother in Seattle."

He shook his head. "I wouldn't be comfortable with that. It would be like lying to Mother."

His answer was a poor excuse. "But as a single young lady, traveling with a man to whom I'm engaged but not married would surely put a stain on my reputation."

"Who cares about what other people think?" Buddy took her hands. "We'll know the truth. God will know the truth. The rest is completely unimportant."

"My sister Whitney wishes to join me if I go." Madysen couldn't wait to see what his response might be.

"She's the unmarried one—the one who usually plays piano?"

"Yes. She's also the one the entire town is talking about, so please don't tell me reputations don't matter. She's devastated and thinks leaving Nome might be her only hope of recovery."

"I would love to have her join the troupe. The two of you playing and singing would be marvelous. I know we could make a lot of money."

"And that's important?" Madysen became more uncomfortable. Buddy had still shared no real thoughts on their life together. It was all about the show.

"Of course money is important, you little goose." He pinched her cheek. "Money will allow me to keep you in a comfortable lifestyle with plenty of beautiful things."

"Love is much more important."

He frowned. "Well, of course it is. Women are such creatures of emotion. Love will always be important."

There was an edge of irritation to Buddy's voice that she hadn't heard before.

"So Whitney would be welcome to join us?"

"Of course. She would be an amazing asset to the show. Does that mean you'll accept my proposal and come with me to Seattle?"

Madysen thought again of how heartbroken her older sister had been since the rumors spread about her supposed lack of virtue. What choice did Madysen have? Whitney needed this—needed Madysen.

"I don't know about the proposal, Buddy."

"But—"

"No buts." She held up a hand. "My family has been through a great ordeal, and if you push me, I'll lose my temper. There will be no marriage unless you're willing to say that we can have a ceremony here with my family before we leave." Well. That felt good. Like she was finding herself again. She lifted her shoulders and stared him down. "Let me talk it over with my family. I want to do what's best for my sister. If she wants to go, we'll come be a part of your show."

"All right. I won't push. Another reason to put off any wedding until Seattle." He pulled her into his arms and gave her a rather awkward kiss. It was nothing like Daniel's kiss.

Nothing at all.

Thank heaven Buddy made it quick.

"There, now we've sealed it with a kiss. Soon we'll be on our way for Seattle, and you and your sister will become stars—rich and famous."

Madysen frowned. "I thought you wanted to *marry* me?"

"Oh, I do, my dear. Of course." Buddy laughed. "Of course."

"She's agreed to marry me."

Buddy's smug tone was almost as irritating as the smirk on his face. Judas didn't give him the satisfaction of a reaction. He just watched the man as he perched on the edge of his desk.

"And, get this. Her sister Whitney is so devastated over her reputation being ruined that she wants to go too. I'll get two for the price of one."

"And exactly what is that price?" Judas leaned back in his leather chair.

Buddy laughed. "I discussed your desires with my performers, and most are willing to remain in Alaska, but a few wanted to return to the States because of their families."

He could live with that. Judas inclined his head. "So long as the stars remain, I can always train other performers."

"Yes, exactly." Buddy flicked lint from his suit sleeve. "The last ship leaves the day after tomorrow, as you well know. We should conclude our transaction tonight. I will need cash or gold, and then the show is yours."

"You still haven't given me a figure." Judas eyed the man. Merrick was obviously crooked, but so far he'd held up his part of all bargains.

"Five thousand dollars." Buddy held up his hands as if certain Judas would protest. "That's the amount of money I could have made in the time it will take me to train a new group of performers. See what a deal I'm giving you? I'll actually make little or nothing. But the fact that I'll have Madysen at my side, as well as her sister, makes me feel generous."

Judas nodded. "Five thousand sounds reasonable." He'd been keeping track of the take for the show's admission price and number of performances. It wouldn't take long to make that back.

Buddy seemed surprised that he was so agreeable but said nothing. He extended his hand. "Then let us shake on it, as gentlemen do."

Judas shook his hand. "Oh, I wanted to thank you again for helping me with my little presentation tonight. Whitney may be going to Seattle with you, but Mr. Sinclair's apology will send her off with her reputation restored."

"I think it's a brilliant plan to make the man apologize at the Follies."

"He'll do so at the Roadhouse, as well as at church tomorrow morning. By the time he finishes, there won't be a soul in a hundred-mile radius who doesn't know what he did and that Whitney was innocent."

Buddy angled a look at him. "Why are you doing that?"

Judas frowned and looked down his nose at the fool. "Why wouldn't I? A young woman has her reputation to recommend her, nothing more. I won't see those girls abused this way. So now you have what you want, and I have what I want."

Judas let his cold smile tell Merrick which of those two facts actually mattered to him.

Good. The Powell girls and other family members were in the audience of Merrick's Follies and Frolics. Judas had gone to Chris Powell and explained exactly what he had planned, and Chris had assured him they would be there for the Follies, as well as at the Roadhouse and, of course, church.

Where he'd found aggression and strong arming to be a means of controlling others, the Powell ladies had remained loyal because of his kindness. Now, however, two of them were going with Buddy Merrick. Judas didn't really care for that idea and hoped that by having the very public apologies, Whitney would change her mind.

If that didn't work, he'd think of something else to convince her to stay. Because he'd had a revelation. There *was* a way for him to get in on the profits made by the farm. It was surprising he hadn't thought of it before.

Marriage.

That was the answer.

And since Whitney would be the only daughter left to woo, he needed her to stay. How else could he become her hero . . . her savior . . .

Her debtor.

He smiled. He really was clever, if he did say so himself.

Whitney wasn't happy about making a public appearance, but her sisters had convinced her this was important. She might as well brave the crowd and hear the apology Sinclair was supposed to give, and then she'd be done with Nome. It was almost a relief that the ship was leaving so soon. When Madysen left to marry Buddy Merrick, Whitney would be at her side and would never have to face these people again.

Madysen reached over and took Whitney's right hand, and Havyn did likewise with her left. It was only them and John. Everyone else had opted to stay home and take care of Granddad.

And save Whitney further embarrassment. She had no wish to subject Eli and Bethany to the horrors of whatever Sinclair might say.

Mr. Merrick came out to open the show and asked everyone to quiet down. "It has come to my attention that a great injustice has been done to one of the most beloved families in Nome. To one family member, in particular. It's a terrible thing when rumors are allowed to rule the day and ruin the lives of such precious people."

Whispers echoed around her. Whitney kept her head low to hide the red that was surely creeping up her cheeks.

Could it get any worse?

"So without further ado, I invite Mr. Garrett Sinclair to come forward and make right the wrongs he has done this very honorable and beautiful young lady, Whitney Powell. Mr. Sinclair."

She didn't want to see him! But with her sisters holding her hands so tight, she couldn't get up and leave. Whitney forced herself to sit straight, lift her chin, and look at the man walking onto the stage.

Sinclair had trimmed his beard and mustache and cleaned up. Had Judas lent him the suit and tie he wore?

Sinclair cleared his throat. "Ladies and gentlemen, I'm here to tell you that anything you've heard about Whitney Powell being a woman without moral values is wrong." His Adam's apple bobbed as he swallowed and lifted his chin. "The fact is, I tried to force my attention on her. She did not invite or accept my attempts and did, in fact, protect her virtue with the help of her dogs and a rifle." There were several hoots of laughter from a group of men at the very back of the audience.

Sinclair fixed the men with a glare. "It's not a laughing matter. I was wrong, and the young lady put me in my place. I admit being refused made me angry, so I spread lies about her. I am here tonight to set the record straight. Whitney Powell is innocent. All this gossip being said about her, the wrong actions that day, it was and remains my fault."

Heat filled every inch of her body. Had he really said that? Would anyone believe him? She wanted to cry and cheer all at the same time.

He walked from the stage, and Buddy returned clapping. The audience began to clap in turn, and soon it was a thunderous response.

Whitney was grateful that no one had pointed her out, and once the chorus girls came out to get the show started, she was even more grateful that her family ushered her away without a word.

Only once they were all back in the sleigh and headed to the Roadhouse did anyone speak up.

"I thought he did a good job of taking responsibility," Havyn declared from where she sat beside her husband. "Hopefully people will take to heart what he said tonight."

"I have to admit, I'm shocked that he told the truth. But will it even matter to most of them, I wonder?" Whitney pulled her scarf around her neck as the horses started down the road.

"It matters to us. You've been vindicated and needn't be ashamed. You never did anything wrong." Havyn looked over her shoulder to where Whitney and Madysen sat. "I'm so thankful Judas was able to put the fear of God in that man."

Madysen linked her arm with Whitney's. "Yes, we need to thank him once again for his kindness. And now those rowdies also know your dogs will attack and you carry a rifle."

"Not that it will matter for much longer."

"Speaking of which"—John scratched his neck and tilted his head toward Whit—"since you're leaving with Madysen, what are you going to do about your dogs? None of the rest of us handles them much."

"I have buyers for the various teams." Whitney couldn't keep the sadness from her voice. "Except for my personal team. I'm going to teach you how to take them over. I'll need you to spend a lot of time with them before I go." John would be great with the team, and when she returned for a visit, Whitney would be able to see them again. Especially Pepper. "If that works for you."

"I'd be honored," John replied. "I just wish you'd reconsider leaving—"

"The boat leaves day after tomorrow."

At Madysen's low voice, everyone turned to look at her. Whitney's heart thundered in her chest. "*What?*"

Madysen was *not* leaving Nome.

Daniel would do whatever it took to keep her there.

She knew that he was in love with her. And *he* knew she felt the same for him. Grief had simply clouded her reasoning. And no wonder. Hadn't she been through enough? She also loved her sister and wanted to take her away from the embarrassment borne in Nome. He couldn't blame her for that either. Then there was Buddy's lure of fame and fortune. Daniel certainly couldn't compete with that. Nor did he want to. He shouldn't have to. Love should be enough to make Maddy rethink what she was doing.

"She doesn't love him." The sheep he'd been milking looked at him, a piece of straw dangling from its mouth. "Well, she doesn't." Daniel fixed the ewe with a glare.

He was just about to turn the animal loose when Madysen walked into the sheep shed. "John told me you were in here."

"Well, I figured I'd better start helping out more with them so they get used to me being their master. You won't be here much longer."

Madysen nodded. "That's why I wanted to talk. I'm supposed to leave tomorrow. I didn't want to go without explaining."

He let the ewe return to the flock and gave her his full attention. "So explain. But you can skip the part about being in love with Buddy Merrick because I know you aren't. You're in love with me."

Madysen flushed red and looked to the floor. "A person can love a lot of different people."

"Yes, but they can't be *in* love with more than one man at a time. It just doesn't work that way."

"So now you're an expert on love?"

Daniel shrugged at her haughty tone. "Seems to me I know a whole lot more about it than you do."

"Oh!" Madysen stomped her foot. "I came here out of the goodness of my heart to share my feelings and thoughts, and you've got no respect for either."

"Fools don't deserve respect."

"Daniel Beaufort, you take that back. I'm not a fool. I am very concerned about Whitney. She wants to go with me and escape the embarrassment of living here."

"Sinclair apologized yesterday at the Follies and at the Road-house. Then this morning he stood in front of your entire church and apologized again. I heard many of the congregants apologizing to Whitney for believing the worst about her. All that gossip is soon to be behind her."

"Maybe so, but as far as I know, she still plans to go with me."

"And you still plan to marry a man you don't love." His words struck home. Madysen's face fell, and Daniel took advantage of the moment. "There, see. I knew I was right. You don't love him."

"But he loves me, and he's so lonely. He's been very kind to me. I'm sure in time I could fall in love with him."

"How are you going to do that when you're in love with me?"

"You're making a supposition that you have no right to make." Her cheeks tinged pink. "I never said I was in love with you."

He crossed the space between them. Madysen had to lean back to look him in the face. "So tell me that you aren't."

"Aren't what?" She licked her lips.

She was clearly stalling.

"Tell me that you aren't in love with me, Madysen." He inched closer.

She opened her mouth, but nothing came out.

"Here you are."

Drat! Daniel glanced at Whitney, who was entering the shed.

"I've been looking everywhere for you." Whitney crossed the room, studied their faces, and then raised her brows. "Looks like you two are having an argument. I don't want to interrupt." She looked at Madysen. "Just come see me when you're finished."

"No, that's quite all right. We're finished here." Madysen sidestepped Daniel and went to Whitney. "What is it you need to see me about? You can talk in front of Daniel. He was just about to leave anyway."

Whitney looked from Daniel to Madysen. Madysen wasn't

fooling her sister one bit. "Well . . . you see . . ." She frowned. "I've been talking to Ruth and Havyn, and I've changed my mind about going with you to Seattle."

Madysen's mouth dropped open. "But I thought . . . I thought it was important to you to get away."

Whitney shrugged. "I'm not going to run from that man and the gossip of a bunch of ninnies. My reputation is restored, and I am not going to be tormented by what others believe."

He couldn't help but smile. "Good for you, Whitney. I'm so glad to hear it. Otherwise, you might have spent the rest of your life running. That's a terrible thing to do. I know. I've done it, and it gets you nowhere. Even when you think it might all work out to your benefit, it never does."

Daniel looked at Madysen full on. "I'll leave you two to discuss the details of how this affects *your* trip, Maddy. I have cheese to check on."

Early Monday morning Madysen tossed in her bed. Today was the day the last ship would leave Nome. She hadn't talked to Buddy since church on Sunday, but he'd told her to be at the dock by eight.

She hadn't slept a wink last night. The whole family had gathered after Daniel left. While there had been a lot of discussion around her, it hadn't taken much for her to make up her mind. How could she leave the man she truly loved and marry a man she didn't love?

There was no need to sacrifice her own life for her sister's. And as much as she loved performing, the thought of leaving Alaska no longer held any appeal. She got up and dressed. No one else was up yet. Good. If she didn't get off the farm before they woke, she'd have way too many questions to answer. Better to answer them after the fact.

Madysen snuck downstairs, made her way to the barn, and saddled the horse. *Thank You, Lord, for helping me along the way. I know I strayed a lot as I journeyed through the grief, but You kept shepherding me. Thank You for keeping me from going down the wrong path, and for setting things straight for Whit. God, please help her to heal. She's been hurt so much. I praise You for bringing Dad back to us, and for bringing Ruth, Eli, and Bethany. I'm going to need Your help speaking to Buddy. Give me the words to say. Help him forgive me.*

The ride into Nome seemed to take forever. The darkness made Madysen a little leery. She hadn't thought to bring a gun. What if she ran into a wild animal or highwayman? There were always desperate men around gold camps. She urged the horse to go a little faster, though they had to be careful on the snow-packed road.

When she reached the edge of town, bustling activity greeted her. Madysen breathed a sigh of relief.

"God, please give me strength to do what I must."

She reached the boarding docks and tied off her horse. She had plenty of time before the last steamer would take passengers out to the ship, but already there was a lot of commotion. A lot of people wanted to escape being imprisoned over winter in the frozen north.

Madysen took a seat and waited for Buddy. He hadn't said what time he'd arrive, but she felt certain he wouldn't be the last aboard. Buddy struck her as the type who liked to be settled in early on. He liked having full control of his life and the things that affected him.

The wait continued as a hint of dawn showed on the horizon. That couldn't be. How strange that he hadn't come. What time *was* it? When a rather well-dressed man passed with an equally fashionable woman, she asked for the time.

"It's a quarter after eight." The man nodded and tucked his watch back in his pocket.

Madysen smiled. "Thank you so much." More time had passed than she'd realized.

Buddy should be there.

She looked around and saw a woman approach the docks. She looked familiar. Oh, of course. "Excuse me. Aren't you the ballerina who dances with Buddy Merrick's Follies and Frolics?"

The woman stopped and gave a nod. "I am. What can I do for you?" She spoke with an accent Madysen didn't recognize.

"Do you know if Mr. Merrick is on his way?"

She shook her head. "He's already on board the ship. Aren't you the girl he wanted to take along to sing?"

Madysen nodded. "And marry. But I can't marry him, and I was hoping to explain. I thought he'd be here to board the ship with me, but I've changed my mind. I wanted to give him back his expensive ring."

Why was the woman looking at her that way? Like she was sorry for her.

"Mr. Merrick cannot marry *you*. He is already married. His wife awaits him in Seattle."

"What?" Madysen got to her feet. "He's *married*?" That low-lying, two-timing, horrible man!

The ballerina nodded. "I am sorry."

Madysen's heart pumped a steady rhythm. So why would he . . . ? She took a deep breath and almost laughed.

She didn't care! Not that Buddy was married, or that he'd conned her. The man she truly loved was out there. Waiting for her.

Madysen produced the ring and held it out. "Well, would you see that he gets this back? Don't tell him that you told me. Just tell him that I send my regrets."

She leaned in closer over the ring and studied it. "The ring is worthless. Purely costume. You might as well keep it." She shrugged.

"No. Please take it to him. I want him to know that I *refused* him. I came here to tell him that I couldn't leave my family and couldn't marry him because I love another. That's all he needs to know."

The ballerina nodded and took the ring, a slight smile on her lips. "He is not used to being refused."

"Good. Let this be a lesson to him. Hopefully, he won't try it again."

The woman's smile widened.

"Last call for Seattle!"

Madysen looked toward the ship. A man with a megaphone had made the announcement.

"Last call for Seattle!"

She couldn't stop grinning. She was staying here! Staying *home*!

"That's me." The ballerina touched Madysen's arm, then made her way to the steamer.

Madysen sat back down.

"I see that you decided not to go."

That voice.

Her insides did a little flip.

She turned. Daniel stood not ten feet away. She'd never even realized he was there. Goodness, but she was rather blind to her surroundings. "I couldn't go."

He didn't move. "Why not?"

"My family needs me."

There was a hint of a smile on his lips as he came and sat down beside her. "Is that the only reason?"

She gave an insulted sniff. "No, of course not. The sheep need me too."

He was silent for a while. "Is that the only *other* reason?"

She studied his face. It was such a good face. Honest and strong. Small lines that showed how often he laughed. His blond hair fell over his left brow, begging her touch. Madysen reached her fingers to do just that. "No." She smiled and let her touch trail down his cheek. "*You* need me."

"It took you long enough to figure that out."

She nodded. "It did, but it's all right because I figured out that I need you too. Nothing would have been right if I had left Alaska. My music wouldn't have been nearly as important without you in my life."

He cupped her chin and leaned closer. "You are an infuriatingly stubborn woman."

"I am."

"And you always think things have to be your way."

"I do."

He grinned. "But you're in love with me, and I'm in love with you. And I really don't think anything else matters quite as much."

She started to speak, but he covered her mouth with his and kissed her.

Goodness! Thank heaven she was sitting down. She'd have hated to disgrace herself by fainting.

Daniel would never let her forget it.

———

Well. This was an interesting turn of events.

Judas cleared his throat. "I am sorry to bother you two, as you look quite caught up in the moment."

Madysen straightened and stood. Her cheeks flamed pink.

Daniel stood next to her, a protective arm around her waist. Interesting indeed.

Judas smiled as he went on. "I'm wondering if you know where Buddy Merrick has gotten off to." He studied Madysen's bemused expression. "Miss Powell, I thought you were leaving with him. To marry him. And yet I find you here kissing another."

"Yes, well, it seems Mr. Merrick cannot marry me. According to that beautiful ballerina from the show, he already has a wife." Madysen shrugged. "But it doesn't matter, as I had already made up my mind to remain here. My heart has become . . . otherwise engaged."

Ah . . . so the lovely Madysen Powell hadn't been taken in by the con man. Good thing she figured it out. Why would Merrick go to such lengths for his ruse? To even involve *him* to try to convince the girl to go with Merrick?

Daniel pulled Madysen a bit closer, and she leaned against him. She glanced over her shoulder at the steamer heading for the *Corwin*. "I gave Mr. Merrick's ring to the ballerina, and she promised to give it to him once she was on board."

Judas frowned. Had he heard right? "On board? She's not going anywhere. I bought out the contracts for the troupe."

Madysen's face went ashen. "Oh no. I'm sorry, Judas. She just left on the last steamer."

He looked out to where the steamer was disembarking the passengers onto the *Corwin*. A sinking feeling washed over him. "It would seem I've been robbed." The sale of the show and needing Judas's help to convince Madysen to go with him—it was all a scam to get his money.

The ticket master made his way toward them with a lockbox. Judas stopped him. "Ralph, tell me, did you see the performers from the Follies and Frolics board the *Corwin*?"

"Yes, sir, I did. The tenor came through early with Mr. Merrick. Later, the chorus girls arrived with some of the others. That beautiful dancing lady just boarded. I think, sadly, they have all departed from us."

Well played, Merrick.

Judas shrugged, making sure his tone was sorrowful rather than furious. "And stole a great deal of money from me." The steamer was starting to make its way back. Meanwhile, the *Corwin* looked to be already under way. Judas turned and fisted a hand inside his coat.

Ralph pursed his lips. "You could go after him, but the ice is coming in awfully fast, and the smaller boats are having trouble, sir."

"Oh, of course. He no doubt planned it this way." Judas fought the urge to pace. *Nobody* did this to him. This was the kind of thing *he* did to others.

"Mr. Reynolds."

Judas turned back to Daniel.

"You could wire the police in Seattle to take Mr. Merrick in hand when he gets there. You might even be able to get word to the ship and have him placed under arrest."

Of course, why hadn't he thought of that? "Yes. Yes." His anger eased, and he drew a deep breath. "Miss Powell, this young man of yours is quite resourceful."

Madysen smiled. "I like to think so."

He gave her his most beneficent smile. "And that wedding gift I wanted to spoil you with stands. I presume the two of you are engaged?"

"He hasn't exactly asked me yet." Madysen angled a smile at Daniel.

The young man immediately dropped to one knee and smiled up at her. "Madysen Powell, will you be my wife?"

Her expression, her every movement, bespoke adoration. "It took you long enough to ask, but yes. Yes, I will marry you."

Daniel rose, and she was in his arms. Though whether he'd pulled her there or she'd leapt into them, Judas wasn't sure.

Daniel chuckled. "You were the one who was slow to come around, but I forgive you."

She started to argue, but Daniel kissed her instead.

Judas laughed out loud as he turned away. Would that all women could be hushed so easily. "Come along, Ralph. We have a wire to send."

"I'm so happy!" Havyn rushed to Madysen, who laughed as her older sister hugged her tight. They'd all gathered for a late breakfast. "We couldn't believe you were gone this morning. We thought you'd decided to stay, and no one could fathom that you would leave without saying good-bye."

"And I wouldn't." Madysen looked from Havyn to Whitney, her heart overflowing. Amazing how everything was clear now. "I will always tell you two my deepest secrets, which is why I let you know about being engaged to Daniel the second I got back."

Daniel took her hand and squeezed it as he looked to Grand-dad and then Dad. "I apologize for not asking either of you for her hand first. I had to act rather quickly lest I lose her again."

"You're forgiven so long as you promise to always be good to her . . . better to her than I was." Dad's tone was bittersweet.

Chuck wrote something down and handed it to Daniel, who held it up and read, "'I approve and will pray for you.'"

Madysen gave her grandfather a frown. "That sounds like you think he'll need special prayers if he's married to me."

Granddad nodded, and everyone, including Madysen, laughed.

Epilogue

December 1904

The wedding had been beautiful. Madysen watched her new husband greet their guests. He was so tall and strong. So handsome.

She couldn't wait to have him all to herself.

"I see that look."

Havyn came up to her side and wrapped an arm around her waist.

Heat crept up Madysen's neck. "I'm beginning to have a new appreciation for all the looks that you and John share. I can't even begin to tell you how much I love him."

"That's good to hear—I was praying you would come to your senses sooner rather than later."

Madysen laughed. "Well, thank you for praying."

"That's what good sisters are for. To boss you around and pray for you."

Havyn smiled at Whitney as she joined them. "And to get you out of trouble. Don't forget that one."

Their older sister half smiled. She still wasn't herself, but at least she tried to smile more often.

Daniel walked up to Madysen and put his arm around her shoulders. "Maddy in trouble? I can't imagine such a thing. . . ."

"Oh, just wait. We have lots of stories." Whitney winked at her.

"Don't you dare. Turnabout's fair play, if I recall." She raised an eyebrow at her sister.

"Fine. I'll only use them for the direst of circumstances."

As they all laughed together, John wheeled Granddad over. "Well, this looks like fun."

"Apparently, there are some interesting stories about Maddy getting into trouble." Daniel pulled her even closer.

"Just Maddy?" John shook his head. "These ladies have a plethora of tales on each other."

"I look forward to hearing them all." Daniel kissed her forehead, then looked deep into her eyes.

Oh my.

"But first . . ." Havyn began.

Madysen pulled herself from Daniel's spell and turned to her sister.

Havyn took John's hand. "Since you all are here. We have news to share—"

"We're expecting a baby!" John nearly shouted it, a beaming smile on his face.

Hugs and congratulations went all around, and Maddy's heart soared. How could she have ever considered leaving? This was where she belonged. Where they all belonged. Together.

Mama would be so proud.

Daniel hugged Havyn, almost lifting her off her feet.

He was perfect.

A perfect match for her. A perfect helper for her whole family.

How could she ever have doubted that God had brought them together? And look how He did it. Through healing, laughter, love, family . . . manure.

She grinned.

And sheep. She mustn't forget the dear sheep.

Daniel walked back to her. Once she was safely ensconced in his arms again, he whispered in her ear, "I can't wait for us to start our life together."

And then he kissed her. A kiss that made her knees weak.

Cheers sounded around them.

Madysen leaned against Daniel, willing her wobbly knees to steady.

He grinned as if he knew exactly how she was feeling. "Are you ready to go, my love? I'm guessing your family won't mind celebrating on their own."

"I'm ready"—she leaned her head against his chest—"but my knees aren't yet."

"Well then, allow me." His strong arms went around her, and he lifted her, cradling her against his chest.

The cheers sounded again.

And followed them as he carried her out the door.

THE END

A Note from the Authors

There are times in this life when mercy feels easy to give and other times when it seems impossible. The struggle can be overwhelming. This past year, during the global pandemic, it has been eye-opening to see people's reactions to different circumstances. More than ever, we need mercy. And we need to extend it.

We pray that you have had the opportunity to get away to a different time and place through this story, and hopefully, you've had the chance to share the mercy of our Savior with someone else.

We can't wait to share Whitney's story with all of you next January.

Kim and Tracie

Acknowledgments

Tracie and I would like to thank our invaluable team at Bethany House. Dave Horton, Dave Long, Steve Oates, Noelle Chew, Amy Lokkesmoe, Paul Higdon, Kate Deppe, and all the other team members that make this happen. It is a joy to work with all of these phenomenal people.

Huge thanks also goes out to our brilliant editor, Karen Ball. Whew, she makes us work, but the story is so much better because of her.

To my critique group: Kayla Woodhouse Whitham, Becca Whitham, and Darcie Gudger, where would I be without you? Becca, you went above and beyond for this story. Thank you.

To our husbands and families—we love you. Thanks for all you do to help us on this journey.

And to our Lord and Savior—the Giver of true endless mercy. Thank You.

Tracie Peterson is the award-winning author of more than one hundred novels, both historical and contemporary. Her avid research resonates in her many bestselling series. Tracie and her family make their home in Montana. Visit www.traciepeterson. com to learn more.

Kimberley Woodhouse is an award-winning, bestselling author of fiction and nonfiction. A popular speaker and teacher, she has shared the theme of "Joy Through Trials" with hundreds of thousands of people across the country. Kim is a pastor's wife and is passionate about music and Bible study. She lives and writes in the Bitterroot Valley in Montana. Visit www. kimberleywoodhouse.com for more information.

Sign Up for the Authors' Newsletters

Keep up to date with Tracie and Kimberley's news on book releases and events by signing up for their email lists at traciepeterson.com and kimberleywoodhouse.com.

More from Tracie Peterson & Kimberley Woodhouse

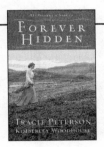

When her grandfather's health begins to decline, Havyn is determined to keep her family together. But everyone has secrets—including John, the hired stranger who recently arrived on their farm. To help out, Havyn starts singing at a local roadhouse—but dangerous eyes grow jealous as she and John grow closer. Will they realize the peril before it is too late?

Forever Hidden • THE TREASURES OF NOME #1

You May Also Like . . .

Accompanied by her best friend, Thomas Lowell, Constance Browning returns from studying in the East to catalog the native peoples of Oregon—and to prove that her missionary parents aren't involved in a secret conspiracy to goad the oppressed tribes to war. As tensions rise amid shocking revelations, Constance may also have a revelation of the heart.

Forever by Your Side by Tracie Peterson
WILLAMETTE BRIDES #3
traciepeterson.com

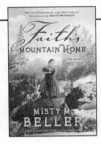

Nate Long has always watched over his twin, even if it's led him to be an outlaw. When his brother is wounded in a shootout, it's their former prisoner, Laura, who ends up nursing his wounds at Settler's Fort. She knows Nate wants a fresh start, but struggles with how his devotion blinds him. Do the futures they seek include love, or is too much in the way?

Faith's Mountain Home by Misty M. Beller
HEARTS OF MONTANA #3
mistymbeller.com

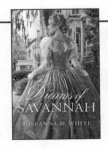

After receiving word that her sweetheart has been lost during a raid on a Yankee vessel, Cordelia Owens clings to hope. But Phineas Dunn finds nothing redemptive in the horrors of war, and when he returns, sure that he is not the hero Cordelia sees, they both must decide where the dreams of a new America will take them, and if they will go there together.

Dreams of Savannah by Roseanna M. White
roseannamwhite.com

BETHANYHOUSE

More from Bethany House

Troubled by painful memories, Olivia Rosetti is singularly focused on running her maternity home for troubled women. Darius Reed is determined to protect his daughter from the prejudice that killed his wife by marrying a society darling. But when he's suddenly drawn to Olivia, they will learn if love can prove stronger than the secrets and hurts of the past.

A Haven for Her Heart by Susan Anne Mason
REDEMPTION'S LIGHT #1
susanannemason.net

In this epistolary novel from the WWII home front, Johanna Berglund is forced to return to her small Midwestern town to become a translator at a German prisoner of war camp. There, amid old secrets and prejudice, she finds that the POWs have hidden depths. When the lines between compassion and treason are blurred, she must decide where her heart truly lies.

Things We Didn't Say by Amy Lynn Green
amygreenbooks.com

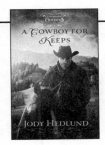

After being robbed on her trip west to save her ailing sister, Greta Nilsson is left homeless and penniless. Struggling to get his new ranch running, Wyatt McQuaid is offered a bargain—the mayor will invest in a herd of cattle if Wyatt agrees to help the town become more respectable by marrying . . . and the mayor has the perfect woman in mind.

A Cowboy for Keeps by Jody Hedlund
COLORADO COWBOYS #1
jodyhedlund.com

BETHANYHOUSE